For Sun.

Chapter 1

'Please, not tonight! I implore you, please, not tonight!'

With another cough and a splutter the engine slowly came to a halt with steam pouring from under the bonnet and the young woman who was driving slumped in her seat as she looked out into the dark night.

It was a dark, dreary, miserable night and the rain was beating down on the road savagely. Not more than two minutes earlier she has passed through a flood under a railway bridge that quickly flooded her old Mini's engine. Unfortunately for her, at this time of night the road was deserted. Surrounded by fields and darkness she slowly felt fear descend upon her, yet she was aware enough to control herself and she tried to think clearly.

Quickly, she grabbed her top of the range mobile phone out of her Gucci handbag, both presents from her father, and as quickly as she had grabbed her phone she flung it into the empty passenger seat when she realised that there was no signal. Panic was now starting to mingle with the fear and she peered through the steaming-up windows into the darkness.

A memory managed to surface through the fear and she remembered that there was an emergency phone back at the railway bridge. Reluctantly, tentatively, she exited the car, her scantily clad body shivering as the rain slammed into her flesh, and she walked back to the bridge.

She did not know that while these events were unfolding a pair of eyes was watching her.

*

'Pardon me? What do you mean you can't help me? I'm a young lady whose car has broken down, and I feel a little scared right now as it is quite late and I'm on my own.' She had successfully reached the phone that was at the railway bridge. The lady on the other end of the line sounded bored, very bored.

'I'm sorry, as I've told you; this phone is solely for the reporting of accidents concerning the bridge. We are not a breakdown service.'

'But, but, could you at least pass a message through to a breakdown service for me, or maybe the police?'

'I'm sorry; I'm not authorized to do that.'

'Look, you are being terribly unreasonable.....'

'I'm not being paid to listen to abusive phone calls.....'

'I'm not being abusive!'

'I have given you a warning. I am now terminating this call. Make no attempt to call back.'

'No, please don't do...'

But she was only talking to a ring tone.

*

Now panicking even more she made her way back to the car and slumped int

Everything to Nothing

A novel by Mark Henthorne.

Sequel coming soon!

Website: www.everythingtonothing.co.uk

Follow on Facebook: http://www.facebook.com/pages/Everything-to-Nothing/290085217675838

Follow on Twitter @Everything2Noth

To Willy and Maria,

Sorry the print is a little off!

Wishing you all the best in your life in BA!

Love,

Mark 'The Author' Henthorne.

25/1/12.

London.

© Mark Henthorne, 2011

All rights reserved. No part of this publication may be reproduced, stored in a retrieval system, or transmitted, in any form or by any means without the prior written permission of the author.

All characters in this publication are fictitious and any resemblance to real persons, living or dead, is purely coincidental.

o the driver's seat. Struggling to think because of the fear and also now because of the cold, she thought that she vaguely remembered that there was a garage about half a mile further on.

She searched through her Gucci bag but this time she pulled out a bright red device about the same size as her mobile phone. It had a switch on one side and circular strap at the end, which was attached to a pin that was plugged into the device. She slipped her hand through the strap and pulled the device sharply away from her wrist disengaging the pin. The device emitted an unbearably loud, high-pitched noise which caused her to screw up her face in distaste and she did not let it ring for more than a few moments before re-inserting the pin which made the noise cease.

After taking the keys out of the ignition, she opened the door, stepped out, shuddered, closed and locked the door and started on her lonely walk to the garage.

*

Simon had long given up waiting for his date. He had called and called her but his calls went straight to her answer phone. It was almost like her phone did not have any signal or it was switched off. So now he was with his friends in a bar in the local town, drowning his sorrows at being stood up by his beautiful date. His friends talked as young men of that age talked; one minute it was football, the next the young women in college, then back to football. Simon though was not really listening. All he could think of was the gorgeous woman who should have been with him at that moment. Her thoughts though were not turned to him any more as her night was just about to get a lot worse.

Chapter 2

The rain showed no sign of abating. If anything, it seemed to her to be getting heavier. Ten minutes had passed since she left the car and she topped a rise in the road. She stopped walking and gazed narrow eyed through the rain. There, only a few hundred meters away was the garage. She let out a sigh of relief

Fields surrounded the garage and directly on her left was a hedge that ran from the railway along the road. On the other side of this hedge there was only darkness, and as she stood peering into the distance, seemingly through the hedge a figure appeared.

'Now you're very young and very sexy to be out all alone at night!'

*

He was on the other side of the hedge, peering through it, listening to the starter motor turning over, trying to get the engine going. He had a rudimentary knowledge of mechanics and he could tell that the Mini was not going anywhere just by listening to the attempts of the engine to start. He rubbed his hands with obvious glee and a grin appeared on his face that could be said to not belong on the face of a sane man.

He always came to this spot when there was heavy rain. The road under the bridge did not drain properly and it always flooded. A number of times he had seen cars break down due to a flooded engine, but up until now the occupants had never been what he desired, a single woman on her own.

This woman was young and no doubt fresh so he thought. She was dressed incredibly sexily. Low cut top, push up bra, which showed her large breasts off to perfection, and a very short skirt that displayed her long, tanned legs. This woman had already been down to the bridge and as he watched her through the hedge making the phone call he masturbated. He heard what she said he was that close to her and he liked her voice. He imagined what her scream would sound like as he parted... The thought was lost.

A grin appeared on his face as he saw her slam the handset down and watched her walk back to the car, muttering and cursing to herself. He continued to peer through the hedge as he walked, continued playing with his penis.

As she reached the car, he thought to himself that he should strike now, but he decided against it as he correctly guessed that she would now walk to the garage.

*

As she saw the figure step out in front of her, her eyes were automatically drawn to his erect penis and for a moment she froze. He was slobbering and drooling as he reached for her, his penis throbbing against his stomach and as his hand closed around her upper arm her survival instinct took a hold of her.

In a split second she pulled the strap on her rape alarm, pressed it against his ear and then drove her knee into his groin area. She saw him wince as the noise blasted and screamed into his ear, heard his breath leave his body in a big rush as her knee connected and then witnessed him falling to the ground, moaning and groaning.

She stood over him for a few moments, trying to get her shocked breath back, the alarm still raging in her hand unnoticed. She gave him another kick in the groin just to make sure, and then ran for the refuge of the garage.

Chapter 3

From a distance, Michelle spotted Simon from across a crowded bar. To say she was surprised to see him would be an understatement. When a young gentleman has arranged a date with a stunningly beautiful young woman it is more traditional for the gentleman to turn up to the date.

Michelle thought about going to speak to him but from what she could see he and his friends looked very drunk even thought the night was still quite early and that was a confrontation she simply did not want to have. Instead she excused herself from her friends and exited the bar to make a phone call.

She dialled Sally's mobile number that she knew from memory but she only got her voice mail. She left a message and then searched her phone's memory for Sally's home number, a number she rarely called.

A cultured, well-spoken voice answered the phone. 'Hello. How may I help you?'

'Hello. Is that you Alfred?'

'Indeed it is. How may I be of assistance?'

'Is Sally available?

'No. She departed at around 8 o'clock in her Mini and has not been home since. Whom is it that is calling?'

'It's Michelle.'

'Ahhh,' his voice noticeably brightened, 'young Michelle! I presumed, as does her father, that she was with you.'

Michelle could have hit herself. Sally's cover story for dates that she did not want her father to know about, which was ninety-nine percent of them, was Michelle, and vice-versa. 'No, she isn't tonight,' Michelle reluctantly had to say. 'When she comes home Alfred, could you please ask her to call me?'

'Of course, my dear. I will instruct a member of the staff to leave a message on her door and I will have one of the maids inform her as soon as she enters the house.'

Michelle laughed to herself as Alfred referred to Sally's residence as a house. 'Thank you Alfred.'

'My pleasure Michelle. Goodbye.'

'Goodbye Alfred.' Michelle closed her phone and said out loud, 'I hope she is okay.'

Now definitely intent on confronting Simon, she returned to where she had spotted him but he had moved on. Cursing, she could not understand why Simon would stand up the gorgeous Sally to go drinking with his drunken friends.

Michelle shook her head in mild bemusement and wished she had the opportunity to have the chance to go on a date with someone as attractive as Simon. Excusing herself again, this time she wandered through the bar to the toilets where her reflection caught her eye in the mirror. She knew she was no Sally, but she was still attractive. She was more voluptuous than Sally, larger chest, bigger thighs and not as pretty, but she was still beautiful. Just no Sally. And didn't she know it.

Most of her life she had been in her best friend's shadow, and she supposed she always would be. Whenever they were out together the boys flocked around Sally, almost totally ignoring Michelle. What Michelle had yet to realize that if she was not with someone as perfect as Sally then the boys would flock around her; she was beautiful in her own way. Being around Sally, seeing how she was treated like a princess by everyone in her life had eventually dented Michelle's confidence. Her confidence had been briefly built up, only to be dashed to the ground by her ex-boyfriend who stayed with until he had sex with her, taking her virginity, and then dumping her shortly afterwards.

She pulled out a small makeup bag out of her handbag, not Gucci but how much did she wish. She rouged her lips a little more and then released the clip that let hair long brown hair cascade onto her shoulders, only to decide to continue to wear it up. Michelle fixed her hair into the style it was before and scrutinized her figure. She was beginning to wish she had dressed a little bit more conservatively, not only because it was cold, but mainly because she did not feel comfortable. Her breasts, which were very noticeable anyway, were struggling to stay inside the top she was wearing and the short skirt was also not leaving much to the imagination. She studied herself some more in the mirror stating that she needed to lose more weight. She was not fat, though, far from it. She just could not see her true self as she was blinded by the competition that is her best friend.

She shrugged her shoulders again and muttered quietly, 'There is nothing I can do about it now.' And then she stated loudly, 'Right, let's go and find Mr. Right young lady!' She turned expertly on her high heels and went back into the bar.

Chapter 4

She reached the forecourt of the garage after running as best she could in her inappropriate Prada footwear. By now, she was sobbing and shaking uncontrollably as the shock and realization of what had just occurred took a hold of her. As she passed into the shelter of the garage she stopped running and noted that there was a shop to the left of her that was closed, and in fact the whole garage seemed deserted.

She did not really believe in God, but all of a sudden she found him as she started to pray that there was someone in the garage. Unsure of how long the man would be incapacitated for, she panicked as she realised that of course he would have seen the way she had ran and could right now be chasing after her. This set off another bout of sobs and then faintly, over the drumming of the rain on the roof of the garage, she heard music. She looked all around her for the source of this most welcoming of sounds but could not see where it was coming from. Guessing that it must be coming from the rear of the complex she quickly realised that she did not want to go round to the back. It was dark along the driveway leading to the music, and the last place she wanted to go to was into the dark. She stood there for a few moments, what felt like to her an eternity, trying to compose herself, which she managed to do a little. She managed to stop the sobbing, but the shudders and shivers would not leave her, partly shock, partly fright, partly coldness. Eventually her courage built up by telling herself that whatever could be in the darkness is probably, hopefully, not going to be worse than what could be running down the road after her.

After a little more hesitation she walked to the left of the building and along the driveway, keeping close to the wall of the shop, away from the fence on the other side of which was just blackness. Time slowed down for her. Eons seemed to pass as she walked along the driveway and then suddenly a courtyard opened in front of her surrounded on three sides by large sheds used by the mechanics. There was faint light in the yard caused by light passing out of the slightly open door of one of the sheds. She made her way quickly across the yard to this light and hopeful sanctuary. She reached the threshold of the door and paused as she heard the voice singing along with the song that was playing.

Despite all that had happened to her in the last hour she could not help a small smile appearing briefly on her face as she heard the terrible noise that was meant to be singing coming through the door. The smile passed quickly as she crossed the threshold and stepped into the brightly lit mechanics' shed. She began to sob again as relief overwhelmed her and then puzzlement as she couldn't locate the body that must accompany the voice. It was after a few seconds of confusion that she saw the feet protruding from under a car. She walked across the few yards and bent down and shook the feet.

'Hello. Could you please help me?'

'What the fuck! Ouch!' The surprising shock of having his feet shaken had so surprised him that he had tried to sit up whilst he was under the car. He had banged his head against the underside of the vehicle after which he slid out quickly from under the car; wrench in hand, ready to defend himself if needed. Instead o f what he expected to see, which was a someone with intentions to rob, mug or murder him, his eyes met the most beautiful eyes he had ever seen. They were emerald green and mesmerizing.

The rest of the face was strikingly beautiful too. Her lips, big and full, her nose perfectly formed and her long black hair. All this was attached to a body which was, in his eyes, perfect. Full, large breasts, flat stomach, slim hips and long, tanned legs. These features he noticed in the couple of seconds it took for him to think of something to say. He placed the wrench by his side and said, 'Who are you? You scared me half to death!'

'Sorry.'

'You okay? What are you doing in this area at this time of the night? Why are you in my garage more to the point?'

'Sorry, I, I, I've broken down up the road there towards the railway bridge. A man just tried to attack me.'

'Let me guess, the flood right? I'm not complaining; it's good business for the garage.' Then what she just said then registered on his tired mind. 'Did you just say that you got attacked?'

'Yes.'

'Shit! Where is he? Did he follow you?'

'I don't know where he is now. I kneed him and ran off.'

'Where did you knee him?'

'Here.' She pointed coyly to her groin area.

'Good girl! That should have put him down good and proper! Don't worry. You're safe now. I've got my wrench! First, let's get you into the office. There is a heater up there and a kettle. Nice cup of tea will fix you up.'

'Yes, that would be nice.'

'Sorry, I don't really know what to say. A cup of tea is probably a stupid thing to offer you.'

'No, it's good. Thank you. Heat is good too right now.'

'Well, let me get my T-shirt on and then we can go to the office. I always work with my T-shirt off when the boss is not around. Gets really stuffy under the cars.'

She managed to get her sobbing under control again as she felt safer in the presence of this mechanic. She watched him stand up and she could get her first proper look at him. He stood about six feet tall, slim and muscular with broad shoulders and the trunk of his body petered down to a slim waist. His stomach was smooth, well not smooth but bumpy with muscle. She guessed his age to be around her own, maybe a little older, but it was hard to tell as his face had little patches of grease and oil on it. He had dark, almost olive skin that covered the most handsome of faces.

He smiled at her as he reached for his T-shirt that was on top of the car and this smile lit up his face and his light blue eyes. His hair was ruffled and unkempt and became even more so after he had pulled his T-shirt onto his body. 'You're lucky I'm here. Usually gone by sevenish, especially on a Friday. Got a lot of work on though and the boss pays good overtime especially on a Friday. Got to work hard to get the car I want. The office is across the courtyard unfortunately. The re's a phone there too. Might be an idea to give the police a call in case this idiot is still out there. Anyway, back out into the rain for you unfortunately.'

'That's okay. I'm soaked anyway.'

'Yeah, good point.' He smiled again, lighting up his blue eyes, and then he led her out into the courtyard and as he was locking the door he said, 'My name is David. Nice to meet you.' He offered his hand, which she accepted.

They shook hands and she said, 'My name is Sally.'

*

They scampered across the courtyard and reached the back wall of the shop. There was flight of steps that led to a door on the first floor of the store. David ran quickly up the slippery metal steps whereas Sally took her time, her heels making the steps ring every time she took a step.

By the time she had reached the top David had the door unlocked, opened and was holding it open for Sally. He closed it behind him, locked it and slid a bolt across that was at the top of the door. Then he switched on the light and they both blinked like startled rabbits caught in a car's headlights as the bright lights affected their vision.

The office was small. It contained a battered desk with a chair and a filing cabinet behind it, a refrigerator and also a small camping stove with a gas bottle attached to it. There were posters on the wall but the first thing that caught Sally's eyes after they had adjusted to the light was a calendar with a picture of a blonde woman. This woman had un-naturally large breasts and was lying on a beach with her legs wide apart. Both the top half and the bottom half of her body were completely naked.

David glanced at Sally and noticed what her eyes were focusing on. She glanced at him and saw him blush, obviously embarrassed. He awkwardly tried to say an apology as he strode across to the wall and tried to take the calendar down. 'Sorry. Erm, we are not used to having, erm, females in the office.'

'It's okay. Nothing I haven't seen before.'

David was fumbling, trying to get the pin out of the wall. He managed to, eventually, and all the time he was fumbling and struggling he was turning redder and redder. She could not help thinking that his embarrassment was quite cute. After all, she was a woman and it was not as if she had never seen those parts of the female anatomy before.

He took down the calendar and hid it in front of his body with his back turned towards her, as he flipped the pages over to the start of the calendar. He looked noticeably more at ease and less red as he turned back towards her, the calendar now successfully turned to the front cover. David walked towards the desk, but in his anxiety he tripped on a rip in the carpet and dropped the calendar at Sally's feet.

As it fell, the pages flipped over to the delightful picture of Miss February bent over a hammock with both the top and bottom of her body exposed, and in her hand was a bizarre looking tropical fruit. Sally shuddered to think what she was going to do, or had been doing, with this fruit. Then she glanced at poor David.

She smiled as she saw him go such bright red that it looked as if his head may explode.

He bent down at her feet, picked up the calendar, quickly turned away and stepped over to the desk flinging the calendar onto the floor behind this piece of furniture. He turned around and sheepishly looked at her. 'Sorry.'

She was trying her hardest not to laugh out loud and make the situation any worse. 'That's okay. Like I said, half the population of the planet looks like that without any clothes on. Nothing new or exciting to me. How about that cup of tea?'

She could almost see him thanking her for the change of subject and for understanding his male dominated work environment. 'No probs. Fingers crossed the kettle has got water in it so I don't have to go out into the rain to the tap.' He picked up the kettle, and took the lid off. 'Superb! Half full.'

He placed the kettle on the little stove, which he lit and then turned and looked at Sally. Their eyes met and she tried to, he did, smile. He could not help admiring in the faint office light, her beauty, admiring how sexy she looked, not only because she was dressed incredibly sexily, but also the fact she was soaking wet stirred an emotion within him. As the microseconds passed while their gaze met, his initial urges as a young, virile male passed and he noticed how scared, how vulnerable she looked. Then his mind would flick back to how perfect her face was, how her perfect young body attracted him.

He had had girlfriends in the past, and due to his good looks, his past romances were usually with attractive young women. Though none of these females had made him feel as if a lightning bolt had just struck his heart. Right at that second, as their eyes locked together, his heart seemed to miss beats, his chest seemed to be constricted, breathing was difficult. He looked away briefly, certain she would be able to read the thought that had just occurred to him. He threw this thought out of his mind quickly, almost disgusted with himself, as he remembered her helpless, scared state.

She was glad when their gaze met again and she was able to drown a little bit more in his eyes. She was surprised at the way she was feeling after all that had taken place in the last hour. She knew she was in shock and she knew she should be more scared than she actually was, but she was not. For some reason, this man in front of her, this handsome man, with his wet T-shirt stuck to his body highlighting his toned muscles, made her feel safe.

All manner of thoughts raced through her mind as their eyes were meeting for those few seconds. One thought entered that surprised her, the one she never expected to come into her mind. Now it was her turn to look, in fact turn away, as she tried to force this image out of her mind. She was surprised with herself for feeling, thinking erotic thoughts. Of course young men interested her, but only a little.

She was well aware from a young age that she was beautiful due to the mirror showing her so and also due to the number of dates she was invited on. Some of these dates she accepted and she had left a behind a long line of broken hearts. She first kissed one of these dates when she was fifteen, but split up with him the next day. She had kissed plenty more dates, even let one of these put his hand up her top, but she split up with him soon after. And then of course there was the summer in Dubai, but she did not want to think about that right now. Sally was well aware that most of her friends were about to or had lost their virginities. Sally mentally wanted to lose hers; she had just never met anyone who physically made her want to do it, except for the previous summer but she didn't want to think about that. She did not think that lack of physical arousal would be a problem with David.

As these thoughts were racing through their minds, there was awkward silence between them, as they both did not know what to say or what to do. He was looking at her back, trying hard not to concentrate his gaze on her buttocks, racking his brain trying to think of something, anything to say. She was pretending to look at posters on the wall showing expensive and exotic super cars. She broke the silence with a question that surprised him because he would never have thought a young lady would be interested in cars. Sally was not that interested right then, but the silence between them seemed to her to be awkward and she just had to say something, anything. 'What kind of car is this?'

He walked over a few of paces and stood next to her. 'It's called a Bugatti Veyron.'

'It's beautiful.'

'Certainly is. My dream car. It costs a million pounds though.'

'Wow! For a car? It looks fantastic.'

'Believe me when I say that it is.'

They contemplated the picture of the car for a few more moments and then the whistling of the kettle interrupted their reverie. The fact that made Sally's question even more surprising was the fact that in one of her father's many garages were two Bugatti Veyrons.

Chapter 5

'God Michelle, I'm feeling horny tonight!'

'Sarah! You can't say that!'

'It is only the truth Michelle! I might have to find myself a good looking boy and take him home tonight!'

'Be careful Sarah.'

'Why?'

'Well, for a few reasons. First, sexually transmitted diseases…'

'Yeah, yeah. Yawn, yawn.'

'Secondly, don't get pregnant. It will ruin your life.'

'Let me introduce you to a new word Michelle, abortion!'

'That's not funny Sarah. Abortion is not a form of contraception. Please! Make sure it is safe.'

'Okay, okay.'

'And, well, you don't want to get a reputation.'

'What do you mean reputation?'

'Well, guess.'

'You mean slag?!'

'Well, kind of, yes. How many guys have you taken home recently?'

'I don't know. Quite a few!' Sarah giggled.

'Exactly. Some of the girls at college are talking.'

'What? Calling me a slag?'

'Basically, yes.'

'They're just jealous because they couldn't get laid if they wanted to.'

'I'm sure they could. You said earlier tonight that boys are only interested in one thing. Therefore, if you think about it, any of those girls who couldn't get laid if they wanted to, actually could because the boy wouldn't be interested in them, just what they can give the guy. It is just that they are not, erm, easy.'

'Oh! Meaning I am?'

'No, I didn't say that.'

'No, but you implied that. You are too prim and proper Michelle for your own good, with your therefores and wherefores'

'I didn't say where…'

'Yeah, I know, but you might as well have. Life isn't the romantic play that you seem to think it is. You only get one life Michelle and I'm going to make sure that I enjoy mine! If that means taking a few boys to my bed then so be it!'

'Okay then. It's your life.'

'Lighten up. Go and find yourself a man tonight, have some fun, receive some oral sex, have sex! I totally intend to!'

'Well just be careful then, okay?'

'I will be careful. I'm on the pill and if the guy looks like he may have a disease I've got a box even though I hate using them.'

'A box of what?'

'God, you really are naïve! Condoms Michelle, condoms. Look, here's one for you.' She reached into her bag, retrieved the box, took out a condom and gave it to Michelle.

'I don't want this,' and she tried to give it back.

'Keep it. You never know.'

'You don't care about your reputation then?'

'To tell you the truth Michelle, if you are as a good friend as I thought are this conversation would never have happened. You should be happy for me that I am enjoying life!'

'I am.'

'You've got a funny way of showing it.' Sarah double-checked her hair and make-up in the mirror then haughtily exited the restroom and walked back into the bar.

Michelle and her friends had left the bar where she had spotted Simon and she had tried to call Sally a few more times but without success. The conversation she just had with Sarah was typical of their conversations nowadays. Sarah had always been diligent in school and college, but ever since her father had left home she had gone off the rails. Michelle had tried reasoning with her but her words fell on deaf ears and Sarah was about to go further off the rails later that night.

While Michelle was leaving the toilets to return to the bar she threw the condom Sarah had forced upon her into a bin.

Chapter 6

David had plugged in a small fan heater and organized a battered chair and a battered stool, and positioned them in front of the heater. They were both sat down now, huddled over hot cups of tea taking occasional sips. Sally at first was in danger of spilling the hot liquid onto her legs as her hands shook, but as she took more sips the chance of her doing this reduced as the level of the drink dropped and her hands slowly stopped shaking.

David had tried to instigate a conversation, but it was hard to talk when the other person involved in the conversation kept on giving one word answers. He had tried open and closed questions and both of these styles of query received yes and no answers even when it did not make sense to answer with this kind of response. As he grew older, David would realise more quickly when someone does not want to talk. He only realised this now, however, when he had asked many questions.

So now they sat in silence, David trying his hardest to think of something, anything, interesting to say, Sally trying her hardest not to think of the animal who had tried to attack her and just wishing she was at home. David then thought of something that did definitely need Sally's attention. 'Sally. Sally?'

She ignored, or just did not hear her name; she was just staring at the heater. He did not know why his arm decided to shake her leg. His brain was firmly set upon the idea of shaking her shoulder to get her attention, but his arm made a beeline for her leg. Before he could get his arm under control, its hand was touching the soft, smooth flesh of her leg, the part just above her knee, her thigh in fact. The touch made her whole body jump in surprise and if the cup had been fuller she would have got burnt.

She looked at him, eyes wide, startled at his touch. He drew his hand away quickly and tried to say an apology. 'Sorry. I didn't mean to startle you.'

'Why did you touch me?'

'Sorry. I tried saying your name. You, erm, didn't answer. You were in a different place I think.' He laughed a small laugh, hesitantly.

'Yeah, I was, I think, somewhere else.'

'I was going to ask you,' David quietly asked, desperate to get her mind off him touching her there, 'whether you wanted to call the police?'

'No,' she strongly, quickly stated. 'It is my fault. Look at me; I'm dressed like a harlot.'

'Harlot?'

'Doesn't matter. I'm not wearing much. It is my fault.'

'It's not!' David was surprised, shocked at Sally's thinking. 'You should be able to dress and do whatever you want to safely. That is what the police are there for, to make sure everybody is safe.'

'No. It is okay. What can they do? They would just think it is my fault for dressing like this.'

'I'm sure they won't.'

'It doesn't matter what you think, it matters what I think. Look, I'll pay you. Can you please take me to my car and see if you can fix it?' Sally's tone had cha s side, him circling round the passenger's side, noting the damage to the car in the lights of the truck. All the windows had been smashed, not just the windscreen. All the panels in the car had dents, not just the bonnet, including the roof.

'The bastard!' Sally strongly stated.

David was examining the roof. 'Whoever did this…'

'I think we know who did this.'

'He has jumped on the roof too. Lots of dents on it!'

Sally seemed more disheartened as she studied the car. 'What now?'

'Put it on the truck and take it to the garage. Then we definitely phone the police.'

'Shouldn't we leave it here? The police will want to check it on site.'

'Yeah, good point.'

David could not help wondering how she did not object to calling the police now when she had found out that her car had been attacked, but didn't want to when it was just herself that got attacked. David was now looking into the interior of the car. 'Ohhhhh, the disgusting bastard! That's sick!'

'What?' Sally made a move to look into the car.

'No. Don't look. It is disgusting, please don't.'

'I'm a big girl… Now don't try and restrain me from looking in my own car. I'll knee *you* in the balls!'

He stood aside. 'Okay. Your choice.'

She looked through the passenger window frame and recoiled back at the sight that greeted her. On the driver's seat was a big pile of excrement and around, hanging on the steering wheel was a liquid substance that looked white and sticky in the light.

'This guy is obviously very sick,' commented Sally.

'Very.'

'What's that on the steering wheel? Looks almost like, like egg white?' She turned to look into his gorgeous blue eyes and saw him blush.

He tried to look into her eyes but could not. 'I'm not sure.'

'Tell me! I know you know. You just blushed!'

'I think, well, I'm not sure. Look, why don't we…'

'Tell me!'

'Okay. Brace yourself.' He paused for a few moments, thinking of the best way to say it. He decided that the direct way, to get it over with, was probably, hopefully, best. 'I think it's sperm.'

'Oh God! I feel sick!'

Suddenly, her strength and strong resolve deserted her and disappeared into the rainy haze. She spun round and vomited onto the grass verge.

Chapter 7

'It's a tragedy! An absolute tragedy!'

Simon was slumped at a bar in a club, sipping what looked like water but was in fact vodka, straight, on the rocks. He was not quite drooling and dribbling but he was not far off. Talking seemingly to someone about a tragedy, it would have only been his vodka that found out about the tragedy he was discussing because there was nobody within listening range to hear his words of wisdom.

Next to Simon was one of his friends. He looked like he was quite happily having a little nap. Theoretically, he was. An alcohol induced nap. He had passed out almost as soon as they had entered the club. The rest of Simon's friends were pretty much in the same state, all except one though, Peter.

He was happily walking around the club on his own, chatting and joking, shaking hands with lots of people who he seemed to know and be friendly with. He was not completely sober though, just pleasantly tipsy. Earlier in the night he only seemed to be very drunk. Claiming a shortage of money he had avoided going in a round with his friends and he purchased his own drinks. At first, he drank with his friends, matching them pint for pint, shot for shot. He drank enough just to get himself drunk, not inebriated, just happily, confidently, tipsy.

His appearing to be drunk was an act, which is surprisingly easy to do when surrounded by people who are really very drunk. When he reached a stage of drunkenness he was happy with, the stage were his confidence is high and his tongue loosened, he practically stopped drinking.

Un-noticed by his friends, the few drinks he did buy usually went unfinished. He acted drunk and as boisterous as the rest of them but as soon as he entered the club he lost his friends and seemingly sobered up in a flash yet he maintained his happy, confidently tipsy state with an occasional vodka and coke. Peter's logic was that one is not going to acquire female company for the night by being like Simon, that is slumped at a bar talking to yourself.

Peter was talking to some people near a bar close to the entrance when he noticed a group of sexily clad females enter the club. He was disappointed to see that Michelle who he had spotted earlier that night had borrowed a cardigan from one of her friends as he enjoyed watching her breasts. That was as far as his attraction towards Michelle went though. He knew he stood as much chance of scoring with his own mother tonight as he did with Michelle. Michelle's last boyfriend, a friend of Peter's, had firmly closed and locked the gate to that tunnel. No, Peter was interested in another one of Michelle's friends, Sarah. She was building up quite a reputation in their college for putting her tunnel about and he had intentions of driving along her tunnel that night.

Peter was not incredibly good looking, he was just average. The traits he did have going for him were that he was a good speaker, gift of the gab so to speak, and he was naturally funny and witty. His strongest personality trait though was his confidence. He was supremely confident. For every knock back he received tonight he would bounce right back and try to pull another woman. He stopped talking to his acquaintances, leaving them laughing, and went to lean on the railing of a balcony that overlooked the dance floor.

'You seem different now. More, well, normal.'

'As opposed to being abnormal usually?'

'You see, I would never have expected you to say a sentence like that. I thought you only knew lewd and childish vocabulary.'

'Then you don't know me then do you?'

'No, I guess I don't.'

They stopped talking and both drunk a little of their drinks. He kept on glancing discreetly at her legs, knowing that he was going to explore what lay in between them later that night. As this thought was racing through his mind he decided to put his eggs in one basket and said, 'I fancy you. Have done for ages.'

It was perfectly timed. She was mid-drink and the surprise of what he said made her splurt out of her mouth the liquid she had partly drunk back into her glass. She started to cough, attracting the solitary security person's attention who thought it was someone being sick, but on seeing it was just someone coughing returned to talking to a member of the bar staff. Peter moved a little closer so he was right next to her and started patting her back.

In between coughs she managed to say, 'You what?!'

'I fancy you. Have done for ages.'

She pushed his arm away and looked into his eyes to see if he was winding her up again. 'Are you serious?'

'I wouldn't joke about something like this.'

'Knowing you, you would.'

'But that's just it Sarah, you don't know me.'

Sarah looked at him more closely, smiled drunkenly at him, and said, 'I suppose I don't. You're a lot nicer when you are not with your friends. What are you going to do about it?'

'About what?'

'Fancying me. If you are so confident that I fancy you then surely you should do something about it?'

'I think I may do just that.'

He leaned closer to her, and she leaned into him. Their mouths touched and his tongue parted her lips and slid deep into her mouth. She pushed his tongue out with her tongue and slid it into his mouth and they sank deeper into a passionate kiss, the kiss that was going to change both their lives.

The thoughts raced through their minds as they kissed. Peter hoping his breath did not smell, Sarah the same. Peter hoping the bulge in his pants would not be too noticeable, Sarah happy she worn a small jacket, happy because it covered her now erect nipples. Peter hoping that he was going to be lying in between her legs that night, Sarah hoping the same. They broke off the kiss and looked deeply into each other's eyes.

'This is an unexpected turn of events. From hating me to kissing me in the space of a few minutes.'

'I've fancied you for ages. I've never tried to kiss you before because I thought you were a tosser. Now I think differently about you after talking properly to you.'

'In that case, I only have one more question to ask. My place or yours?'

'Hotel room?'

'My parents are away.'

'Yours.'

They both simultaneously stood up and Peter said, 'One minute. I need the toilet.'

'Me too.'

There were toilets attached to the room and they parted with a brief kiss as they went into the respective toilets. Peter looked into the mirror that was above the urinal as he relieved himself. 'Now, that was not too difficult. Had no idea she fancied me. That was just a joke. See her reaction though...' he said to himself. 'Glad she is drunk too. Makes it easier.' When he had finished he went over to the condom machine, but it was empty.

With a shrug of his shoulders he exited the toilet and waited a few minutes outside in the room. She eventually came out and linked arms with him. He looked at her and smiled, she returned his smile with a smile of her own. They did not say anything as they left the chill out room and proceeded into the main section of the club. They walked around the dance floor holding hands to the exit and left the club.

*

Michelle saw them leave the club and she said to herself, 'Oh no, Sarah. Any one but him!'

Chapter 8

'I don't believe it! Now my phone is working!'
'I guess it wasn't before?'
'You guessed right David, you guessed right.'

They had returned to the shelter of the truck's cab and they were all set upon returning to the garage to contact the police. Sally then remembered her phone and more optimistically than anything else, she took it from her bag. The signal bar was full. 'Piece of shit crap phone!'

David did not know what to do or say. Sally was obviously very angry, even more so after she had been sick, which she was obviously embarrassed about, as how of weakness that had made her even angrier. She had recovered from the bout of nausea quickly and David saw the determination return to her eyes. She thanked him for holding her hair out of her face while she was vomiting and it was then that David suggested the shelter of the cab.

Sally dialled 999 after a quick enquiry with David as to who would be best to phone. He had replied with the simple answer of 999. When the call connected, at first Sally did not know what to say as the reason she was calling. It took an intervention by David to state the obvious reason, she had been attacked. The operator then professionally asked her whether she was physically fine, did she need an ambulance? Of course, Sally replied negatively and the operator took her details, name, date of birth and where she was now, this location she obtained from David. She did know where she was, just not the proper name of the road. This information she gave to the female operator who re-confirmed it, plus she also stated Sally's mobile number, which surprised Sally at first. She then realized the operator would have technology that would enable her to see the caller's number. Sally confirmed this detail too and the operator concluded the call by stating a police car would be with them in fifteen to twenty minutes. The conversation ended and Sally roughly thrust her phone back into her bag seemingly even angrier than before the call. 'Fifteen to twenty minutes she said! Fifteen to twenty minutes!'

David was a little puzzled. 'Until what?'

She snapped her head round to the right and glared at him. 'Until doomsday! Until pigs fly! Fifteen or twenty minutes until the police arrive!'

'Oh, okay.'

'Just as well I'm not dying, hey?'

'Yes, true.'

'Rhetorical question, David.'

'Oh, sorry.'

David look out of the driver's side window for a few moments feeling a little bewildered as to why Sally was venting her anger at him. He turned his face back towards Sally and said, 'Yes, it is a slow response…'

'Slow?! That's an understatement!' She glared at him again.

David mentally bit his tongue, now getting annoyed with Sally's attitude, released his tongue, bit it again and then managed to calmly continue with what he was initially saying. 'It is a slow response, but, we are quite a way out of town h ere and it is Friday night. They will be busy.'

'Well, like I said, I'm glad I'm not injured.'

'An ambulance would maybe come quicker.'

'Maybe.'

For a few minutes there was silence. Sally was furiously angry, more than she had ever been before and she knew she was taking it out on David. She glanced across at him and saw him looking glum and very soggy, staring out of the window. She could not help smiling to herself as she realized the situation in which she had met the man who for the first time in her life she could feel herself already falling for. She thought how handsome he was and this was indeed true. David was effortlessly handsome and his personality was shining through in his willingness to help her as much as he possibly could do. Sally struggled to compose herself, not let her feelings show and also to control her anger. She felt sorry that she had been angry towards David and obviously upset him. She reached across and placed a hand on his shoulder. 'David?'

He turned and looked at her, his eyes noticeably brighter, enjoying her touch. 'Yes?'

'I'm sorry. You've been so good to me. I'm sorry. I didn't mean to be angry at you. It is just that, well, I am so damn angry! My poor car!'

'It's okay.'

'No, it's not.'

'It is. I understand. I'd be full on mad too.'

'Thank you for understanding.'

'It is not difficult for me to understand why you are angry.'

He smiled at her, his bright blue eyes gazing into her brighter, emerald green eyes. For a few moments they both drowned in each others' eyes then came the distinctive sound of a police siren. They both jumped and they moved away from each other.

At first they could not tell from which direction the car was coming from, but then in the rear view mirror, above the rise, David saw a flashing light heading away from the garage towards them. They both turned to look out of the recovery vehicle's rear window and watched the police car drive quickly along the road.

'Only took them about ten minutes anyway Sally.'

'Yeah. It is alright now.'

'And look at that. The rain has stopped.'

They turned away from the window and looked at each other, deeply into each other's eyes.

'Isn't that the way it always goes?'

*

There were two policemen in the car and after taking one look at the scene they decided to call in a forensic team to take samples and search the car. It took half an hour for these specialists to arrive and in the meantime one of the policemen interviewed Sally while another asked David some questions, Sally in the police car, David outside.

After David had spent five minutes talking to the constable the conversation finished. He then walked around the Mini again, studying the damage, and then returned to the truck. Sally, after another ten minutes came and stood next to him. She had a blanket around her shoulders and joined David in leaning on the front of the truck looking at the car. 'That was pretty painless,' she said.

'Nice guys.'

'Yes. I have to go to the police station sometime next week and look at some pictures.'

'He has attacked other women then? They have an idea who it is or they wouldn't want you to look at pictures right?'

'I don't think they have any idea. The pictures are just a measure they have to go through. They have said that there is no record of any other attacks in this area.'

Sally said all this matter of factly, without a trace of panic or fright in her voice. David was more impressed with her strength with every passing second. He envisioned most women in this situation would be crying and being hysterical. Sally was just cool and calm. He then thought it could be shock, that how lucky she had been had not registered on her yet.

As they were talking a car approached, but this one was unmarked and was driven by a middle-aged man and his partner was a young, pretty woman. They both exited the car, walked round to the rear and each got a silver briefcase out of the trunk. They had a brief word with the two policemen and introduced themselves to Sally and David.

The two police scientists worked quickly and methodically in the lights of the truck and their car, almost too quickly for Sally's liking. The woman took samples of the semen and excretion and Sally thought surely the man should have volunteered to do that gruesome task, and then took photographs while the male dusted for fingerprints. The male quickly came and took Sally's fingerprints to compare with the ones found in the car to Sally's. He found no new fingerprints, which, the male scientist stated was surprising.

'Surprising?' said Sally, as both scientists came over after they had finished with the car. 'Why?'

'Simple really,' said the male forensics expert as he removed his gloves. 'If he's gone to so much trouble to leave as much D.N.A. in the car as possible then I would have expected him not to have bothered wearing gloves.'

'Fair enough.'

'All I can say is that he probably has a criminal record from before we used D.N.A. as evidence and, therefore, we could have his fingerprints on record but not his D.N.A.'

'But you have D.N.A. from other cases don't you?' asked David.

'Yes, that will enable us to match this incident to previous incidents, if he has any previous incidents on file. Doesn't mean we know who he is though. D.N.A. is only useful if you have a human to match it to. We don't. That is why a national D.N.A. database would be good. If we had fingerprints then we would probably be able to trace him. Until the day the government introduces a national D.N.A. database... Anyway, have to go. Jim, Robert,' he said to the two policeme n, 'I'll have the results and report on your desks a.s.a.p. Bye and goodnight.'

With that, the scientists got into their car, this time the woman driving and she executed a quick U-turn and sped away into the night.

'That was quick,' said Sally.

'Yep. Very. They know their job. What now?' In apparent answer to his question one of the policemen came over.

'That is it. The car can stay here until morning.'

'No, I will take it to the garage.'

'Erm, not too sure about leaving you here alone sir. But then again, he'll be long gone. Okay, take it, just be quick. We've finished with it. I feel sorry for the person who has to clean it up.'

'Me too,' said Sally.

David did not say anything.

'Miss, we will give you a ride home.'

'Thank you officer.'

'None of that needed young lady. I'm Jim, he's, well, you already know. Say your goodbyes. We have to go.' The policeman walked to his car and joined his partner inside the vehicle.

Sally turned to look at David. 'Thank you so much David for helping me tonight. I will give you the keys to the car just in case you need them.'

'Thanks, I might need them. My pleasure to help you. I'll take your car to the garage. You can come by whenever next week to collect it.'

'Thanks again David. I don't know how to repay you but I'm sure I'll think of a way. Here is my mobile number.' She took a card from her purse. 'Call me if you need to speak to me before picking up the car.'

He accepted the card and said, 'Thank you. I will call you if I need to. You be careful from now on.'

'I will be. I have to go. They are waiting.'

'Okay. Goodbye Sally.'

'Bye David.'

She turned to go but then turned round and quickly kissed him on his cheek then quickly pulled away and stepped speedily over to the car. Sally smiled at him and gave a little wave as she put one leg into the car and he smiled and waved back.

She knew she had fallen for him. He knew he had fallen for her. After the smiles she put the rest of herself into the car and almost before the door had closed the vehicle turned around and quickly sped away from David.

He briefly touched his cheek where she had kissed him and then went to his truck to start to make the preparations to take the car to the garage. Throughout all the time he was preparing, to when he closed his eyes that night to sleep, he had images of Sally playing through his mind, her beauty, her dazzling, mesmerizing emerald green eyes, her full lips, her long legs and the image of the last smile she had given him as she turned to look at him as the police car drove away.

Chapter 9

Michelle's night dragged on. She wandered round the club, stopping occasionally to talk to her friends who had started the night with her and also to people that she knew. She went occasionally for a dance but dancing on her own turned out to be not much fun. She spotted a few attractive young men but they were so drunk and so lecherous that she soon gave up trying to talk to them. Her friends that she encountered did not seem to mind being molested and groped by these drunks but Michelle could not stand it. All her friends seemed to have their tongues thrust down some guy's throat whenever Michelle encountered them and they did not appreciate being interrupted. Later on in the evening she walked into part of the club where Simon was.

He was still sat at the bar, but at a different place to where he was the last time she had seen him. Michelle was surprised to see him at this bar as it was in a quieter corner of the club and he also seemed a lot more sober than the last time Michelle had seen him. He was actually sat up and did not appear to be drooling anymore.

She nearly approached him to speak last time she saw him, but as she was just about to start a conversation she realized there would not be much point. She saw his mouth moving and she realized that he was talking to himself and also that he definitely was drooling. This time though he was sat up straight and was sipping what looked like water.

Michelle liked Simon. Of course, one of the most attractive guys in college appealed to her physically, but she also liked him liked him. He was funny, intelligent and he always had time for anybody. He was in her English class and he had gone out of his way to help her one day when she was stuck on part of the course. She had never forgotten this and since then she realized that she would never, ever be able to date someone like him. They were playing different sports, never mind in different leagues. As she approached him she had no intention of trying to get with him, she just wanted someone to talk to. 'Still on the vodkas Simon?'

Simon jumped as he felt the breath on his ear and then turned to look to see who was speaking to him. He was pleasantly surprised to see it was Michelle and Michelle was happy to see that his eyes were not too badly glazed over. 'Oh, hey Michelle. No, I'm trying to sober up; I'm on the white wine!'

Michelle could not help laughing at this. 'Okaaay. I don't think that is going to work Simon.'

'Hey, you'd be surprised! Half an hour ago I couldn't see never mind speak, and now I can!'

Michelle laughed again. 'Mind if I join you?'

'Of course not! Always got a few words to say to my favourite Shakespearian!'

'I don't think that is a word Simon.'

'It is now! Pull up a pew and let's talk the night away!'

'Okay then, I will.'

Michelle reached round and tried to pull a bar stool closer to him but it would not budge. She tried again and it still would not move. Simon then jumped do wn from his stool and said, 'Bloody heavy these things. So people can't smash them over each others' heads!'

'Right, okay.'

'Sit down, sit down.'

'You can't move me and the stool! Don't be silly Simon!'

'How dare you! I'm as strong as a bull!'

'I'm sure you are, but not after a gallon of vodka you aren't!'

'I'll prove it to you! Sit down!'

Michelle reluctantly lowered herself onto the stool and Simon promptly tried to move the stool closer to his. He was putting that much effort in that the stool started rocking and so did Michelle on top of it.

'Simon, stop now! I'm going to fall!'

'Nonsense! This is how to do it, gotta get it rocking!'

'I don't think it is the…..'

Her words did not get out. The amount of rocking Simon had achieved, and with Michelle sat on the stool, it was far too top heavy. With a mighty crash and lots of flying limbs the stool toppled over and Simon slipped and fell backwards. Michelle gracefully fell from the stool and landed on top of Simon who luckily broke her fall. She was lay on top of him, their eyes locked together and they both started laughing simultaneously, which soon turned into hilarity. There was one person in the vicinity that did not find it amusing though, a security man, otherwise known as a bouncer.

He approached the collapsed and still giggling couple with the speed of a panther and the grace of a buffalo, barging and shoving and elbowing the few people out of the way who were in this section of the club.

'I think you had better get up now!' Simon said between guffaws of laughter.

'No way! I am quite comfy here thanks!'

'Please! I'm getting squashed!'

'Saying I'm fat are you?!' Instead of standing, Michelle relaxed even more and squashed him some more.

'No, no, I mean, anyone would feel heavy in this position!'

'Think I'll have a little sleep!'

'I don't think you will young lady! Get up now!'

Michelle looked up and saw the stern looking bouncer glaring down at her. 'Whoops!' she whispered into Simon's ear. 'Rhino Bob is here!'

She rolled off him and stood while Simon scraped himself off the floor. 'Sorry, sir. We fell over!' Simon still had a big grin on his face which did not impress Rhino Bob at all.

'I'll show you falling over!' He grabbed Simon's arm and shoved it up his back. Simon let out a gasp but wisely did not try to resist.

Michelle was not impressed. 'Get off him you big brute!'

She leapt onto Bob's back and started to pound his shoulders. It was then that it went from bad to worse for the couple as the cavalry arrived. One of Bob's colleagues plucked Michelle off his back and flipped her over his shoulder in a type of fireman's lift. They walked over to an emergency exit, Simon still wisely not showing any resistance. Michelle though was. All the way down the emergen cy exit stairs she pounded and kicked and screamed.

The bouncer just chuckled and commented to his colleague, 'She's a bit feisty isn't she Graham?!'

'I'll show you feisty you imbecile!'

With this Michelle renewed her thrashings with increased vigour until she felt one of the bouncer's hands slide into her knickers and start to molest her most sensitive parts. This made her freeze in horror. He groped her for the last few steps of the staircase until they reached the exit door when he removed his hand.

With a thrust of his hip Graham opened the door and pushed Simon away with a clip round his ear for good measure. Simon stumbled away and watched as Michelle was flipped back over the bouncer's shoulder, but he carefully made sure she landed feet first.

Michelle was still full of indignation at her rough treatment and turned straight back around and started to pound the bouncer on his chest. 'You beast! How dare you molest me like that!'

The bouncer started to laugh as Michelle's slaps and thumps bounced off his barrel chest. It was only when she started to try and scratch out his eyes did he grab hold of her hands and easily restrain her. 'Now, now young lady! Calm down! Don't mind being punched but I draw the line at having my eyes scratched thank you very much. Can you take her away mate?'

'Yeah, of course. Come on Michelle, let's go.'

Michelle shrugged off Simon's hand and shouted, 'I'm not going anywhere until these men, I use that word loosely, apologise for treating us like this!'

The bouncer rolled his eyes and simply pushed Michelle away. She stumbled back five or so feet and by the time she had recovered her footing the bouncers had slammed the door shut and were making their way back up the stairs.

While sniffing his fingers the bouncer who molested Michelle stated, 'Bloody hell Graham! It is always the flamin' girls that are the flamin' worst!'

'Tell me about it, man,' replied Graham giving a rueful shake of his head, 'tell me about it.'

Chapter 10

Peter and Sarah flagged down a taxi easily as it was still quite early in the night. He told the driver his address and as soon as they set out he started to warm Sarah up some more with lots of deep, passionate kisses and lots of leg stroking and breast fondling.

The taxi driver was happy. He loved watching young couples in his taxi, the way they totally threw away their inhibitions and seemed to forget that there was another person in the car. All throughout the journey he seemed to spend most of his time with his eyes fixed on the rear view mirror and was pleased to see these two really going for it. He saw the young woman part her legs; he saw the young man's hand disappear up her skirt which was near enough hitched right up over her hips. He saw fingers sliding inside her pink, lacy panties and a middle finger disappear inside her. He heard her little grunts of pleasure and noticed the bulge of the young man's pants grow and grow.

This continued for a few minutes and the driver was disappointed when she pulled away from him and looked almost shyly at the rear view mirror. Sarah saw the driver tip her a wink after which she blushed and pulled her skirt back down. Peter tried to carry on but Sarah gently pushed him away and whispered into his ear that they would carry on later.

Peter realized that they had been getting a bit adventurous with somebody watching them and he noticed they were nearly at his house anyway. Instead, he wrapped one of his arms around her and she leant against him. Occasionally he would lean down and kiss the top of her head until they pulled onto his street. He told the driver what house to drop them at and he paid the fare.

They walked up his driveway hand in hand and Peter kissed her on the doorstep. He then unlocked the door and they both almost fell through it in their eagerness. As soon as the door closed behind them Peter reached round Sarah's back and unclipped her bra and unzipped her skirt. Sarah pushed him away and Peter thought he may have made a mistake moving so fast. However, he saw her place her thumbs inside the waist of her skirt and knickers and pulled them down in one movement. Peter was amused and delighted to see a patch of darker pink in the crotch of her panties caused by her wetness. He pulled her to him and she stood in front of him with her feet wide apart giving him ample room to caress her, which he did.

With every stroke and every finger insertion she gave out moans and groans of pleasure and Peter's hand got wetter and wetter. While he was caressing her she fumbled and struggled to undo his belt, and in the end Peter removed his hand and did it himself. He pulled down his jeans and underwear in one action as Sarah had done and immediately he sprang erect, hard and long. Sarah looked down and was very pleased to see his size and she immediately started to stroke him, feeling him throb lively in her hand.

After a few moments of stroking and pleasuring each other Sarah moved away from him, turned her back, dropped onto her knees, and then leaned forward, leaning on her hands, thrusting her buttocks into the air.

Peter was amazed at how forward she was but he did not complain. He dropp ed onto his knees behind her, lined himself up and in one slow movement slid his full length into her hot, tight and dripping wet vagina.

Sarah let out a long groan of complete and utter pleasure and arched her back as she shouted out, 'Now that is the best feeling in the world!'

Her single groan soon turned into loud groans and yelps of more complete and utter pleasure as Peter started to thrust in and out of her, each thrust of his met with a thrust of hers. It did not last long for either of them.

Peter managed to control himself until he felt her stiffen in his hands and she let out a scream of ecstasy. Then he felt her start to shudder and shake as her orgasm ripped through her body. With a few more thrusts Peter emptied himself into her and Sarah let out another long groan of complete and utter pleasure as she felt him pour into her. Peter also shuddered and shook as his orgasm ripped through his body and they stayed in this position for a few moments, both of them panting and occasionally involuntarily shaking as the pleasure subsided. Slowly he then eased himself out of her and flopped himself onto the floor on his back.

Sarah lay down next to him on the hall floor and he put an arm round her and she closed her eyes as she placed her head on his chest. 'Do you think this could be the start of something special, Peter?'

Peter was shocked at her question but he did not show it in his answer. As far as he was concerned this was a one night stand to be enjoyed, talked about with friends and then promptly forgot about. However, he did not think that answer like that would endear him to Sarah so he lied easily. 'Definitely Sarah,' he kissed her shoulder, 'definitely something special.'

*

Simon and Michelle walked down a street in the town, talking and laughing together, getting to know each other even more. They reached a wine bar that was still open and quiet. There were only a few couples inside it and Simon asked Michelle whether she would like to stop for a glass of wine. She nodded and they went in to take a seat at a table in the window. Simon asked her what she wanted and was about to stand up to order at the bar when a waiter came over and took the order. They sat there for hours talking.

They talked about everything and anything. Their lives so far, where they wanted their lives to go, ambitions, hope and fears. It was only when the waiter came over and stated it was four o'clock in the morning and that they were closing did they realize the time. Simon muttered an apology to the waiter and settled the bill, pushing away Michelle's hand when she offered him some money.

They left the bar and started to walk. Michelle was astonished when, as they started to walk, Simon slipped one of his hands into hers. He turned his head to look at her as they walked and said, 'I can't remember a time when I have enjoyed a woman's company as much as I have tonight.' This astonished Michelle even more. 'I mean, how long were we talking for? Two, three hours? I don't know. The time flew by and I really enjoyed myself.'

'I enjoyed myself too.' They stopped walking and for an instant of instance Michelle thought that Simon was going to kiss her. Instead, he looked into her e yes and shook his head and started to walk again.

'You seem puzzled about something?'

'I am. There I am dating all these girls from college, and not from college, and they are all brain dead, and I am sat there on the dates trying to talk to them like I have talked to you tonight, but just as I am talking to them I see no glimmer of life or sparkle in their eyes. Dead eyes.'

'Dead eyes?'

'Yeah, it is hard to explain. You know when you talk to somebody you usually look into their eyes don't you?' She nodded. 'Sometimes you see a spark, a flash in their eyes, a spark and flash of life. Like I see with you. Someone with dead eyes you don't. There is nothing there; no spark or flash, they just seem, well, empty. With you though, with you it's endless sparks and flashes. I enjoyed talking to you tonight for that reason. Because you have that spark and you listen and comment and question. I've read in these bloke magazines that women like to be listened to, they like questions and comments. Well, so do men. They don't want to sit there and listen non-stop to a woman rattle on about nothing like a little chatter-box. Intelligent men like a conversation too. Most of the girls I have dates with have been, and I say this with no exaggeration, are beautiful. I am sat there thinking what the hell are they doing with me? Then I realize that although they are stunningly good looking, they are also stunningly stupid. So that is why I have enjoyed being with you tonight. Because you're clever.'

'Wow! That was one hell of a speech, Simon! You shouldn't only judge someone though on their eyes you know.'

'Why not? Ninety nine percent of the time I am right. Dead eyes.'

'And I also know lots of beautiful, intelligent women.' Thinking instantly of Sally.

'I suppose I can be too judgmental. Anyway, I have enjoyed tonight and I would like to take you out to dinner some time.'

'Pardon me?!'

'Dinner some time. How about it?'

'You want to take me out?'

'Yeah, why not. We have got on so well tonight it would be stupid not to see if we can carry it on wouldn't it?'

'Erm, well, yeah, I suppose it would. What about Sally?'

'Sally who?'

'Sally Gallagher. The girl you were meant to meet for a date tonight?'

'You know Sally?! Why didn't you say that earlier?! She stood me up the bitch!'

'She is a close friend.'

'Oh, right, erm, okay. Erm, I'm sure she is a lovely person and not at all bitchy.'

'Keep on digging Simon; you'll get out of that hole soon!'

'Whoops! Sorry Michelle. Didn't know she was a friend. How do you know her? She goes to that posh school doesn't she?'

'We met when we were very young and have been friends ever since even though we have always gone to different schools. She does go to the Mount, yes.'

'Anyway, she stood me up.'

'Did she? Weird. She was looking forward to it.'

'What happened to her then?'

'I don't know. I tried to phone her before when I saw you earlier. She wasn't at home and her mobile went straight to voice mail so I don't know.' There were a few moments of silence until Michelle realized she didn't know where they where or where they were going.

'Just a few more minutes and then we are there.'

'Where is there?'

'My brother's apartment.'

'Why are we going there?'

'No taxis this late and he is away. I've got a key.'

'I should really go home.'

'We'll see if we can order you a taxi from his place.'

'Okay, sounds good. Nothing is going to happen tonight Simon, so please don't try anything.'

'You know something Michelle, there was a point, before, when I was going to try and kiss you. But I decided not to. I didn't want to spoil what has been a great night by letting physical things get in the way. So I am going to be a gentleman. I am going to give you a coffee, and I do mean a coffee, order you a taxi and then you can go home. Then I am going to text you and make sure you got home okay. Then I am going to call you tomorrow and then at some point, hopefully very soon, I am going to take you out on a proper date. How does that sound?'

'It all sounds good and like a plan!'

'Excellent and here we are!'

*

Peter eased himself away from Sarah and gently lowered her now sleeping head onto the hall floor. He stood up and walked through to the kitchen picking up his jeans as he went. He placed them on the sideboard and reached into one of the pockets and pulled out a small plastic bag which contained pills.

The pills were a light blue and etched into the faces of these pills was the image of a butterfly. He reached into the other pocket of his jeans and removed a big, thick wad of money and also five small plastic bags containing a white powder.

He placed all of these on the sideboard and then went upstairs, carefully stepping over the still sleeping Sarah, entered his bedroom and opened up the bottom drawer in a chest. He removed a ledger and took this downstairs. He stepped over Sarah again and returned to the money and the drugs in the kitchen. He pulled up a kitchen chair and proceeded to carefully count the pills. He then counted the money and made some notations in the ledger.

'Excellent,' he said out loud, 'I balance! Tabs and money match up. Quite a lot of coke sales tonight too!'

'What are you doing?'

Peter jumped what looked like a mile as Sarah crossed the kitchen to where h e was sat. Peter was rapidly trying to hide the drugs but Sarah was too quick for him and she picked up a couple of the tablets and looked at them closely. 'Are these what I think they are?'

'And what do you think they are?'

'E's.'

'No, they are painkillers for my back.'

'Rubbish. Painkiller's you record in a ledger?!'

Quickly she grabbed the thick black book and glanced down at the figures and words next to them. 'Blue Johnson? You've named an ecstasy tablet after yourself? How quaint.'

'Yeah, yeah. So they're E's.'

'Oh, and I suppose that this,' she quickly grabbed one of the clear cellophane bags, 'is washing powder? You're a dealer?!'

'More like a part-time dealer.'

'Still a dealer though. You know, I have sometimes seen you in the club going from person to person, shaking hands with lots of people. I have never thought twice about it, I just thought you were more popular than I imagined.'

'Popular in a way, yes.'

'So you pretend to shake hands with them but really you are exchanging drugs for money?'

'Yep.'

'You've made that much?!'

'Not tonight, no. Some of that is left over from Friday.'

'Still, it looks like a lot for two nights work.'

'I had a couple of good nights. I am getting a good reputation.'

'Right.'

There was a few moments silence as Sarah studied the white powder and prodded and played with it in her fingers. 'I want to try it.'

'You what?'

'I want to try it.'

'You can have an E.'

'No, I have tried it. Didn't like it. I want some of this.'

'The coke?'

'Yep.'

'No chance. Too expensive for free handouts.'

'I'll be straight to the police tomorrow.'

'You wouldn't dare!'

'I would! Give me some.'

Peter shook his head resigned to the fact that she did have him over a barrel. He had been so, so careful over the last few months to keep his actions secret and now he was stunned at his own stupidity. Personally, he did not touch the stuff. He had tried it, out of professional curiosity, but he knew the damage a cocaine habit could do both physically and mentally. 'Okay then. We will use that bag while you have mauled it. It will need extra cutting. I'll be back in a minute.'

He left Sarah still holding the bag and went back upstairs. He returned a few moments later with a razor blade in one hand and a mirror in the other. He was a mused to see that she was still naked and then remembered so was he. For a moment he paused in the kitchen doorway, admiring her as she was bent over the kitchen sideboard. He then approached and took the bag out of her hand.

He ripped open one corner of the bag and carefully tapped the powder onto the mirror. Peter then started to chop the cocaine with the razor blade, removing any lumps and making the powder finer and finer. He cut away a small portion of the coke and then continued to cut this portion, slowly working it into a thin line. When he was satisfied he reached for the wad of money and peeled off a five pound note. He rolled it into a tube and gave it to Sarah.

'Place one end of the note at one end of the line. Place the other end of the note up your nose, not too far though. Then snort it up, just like on the movies.'

Sarah did exactly as she was instructed. She sucked the line up with her nose in one quick movement and was amazed as the feelings hit her near enough straight away. The drowsiness that she felt before taking the coke seemed to fade away into the night. Peter watched as her pupils instantly dilated and Sarah was pleased to note that after a minute or two she seemed to be getting incredibly sexually aroused.

There were beads of moisture where there was none before and she pressed her thighs together. They slid against each other and she could not remember a time when she had felt as aroused as she did right then. 'Wow! Now that feels good! Why don't you take some?'

'I had some just before you came in.'

'Well in that case why is it not having the same effect on you as it is on me?'

At the end of these words she grabbed his hand and placed it in between her legs. He was totally stunned at how aroused she was. The wetness was everywhere; it almost seemed to him that it reached down to her knees. This feeling did have an effect on him and his penis automatically sprang to attention. She lifted her bottom onto the kitchen sideboard and hooked her legs around his waist, pulling him to her. She grabbed the base of him and lined him up and with a thrust of hips he again slid into her.

As he was enveloped in wetness he did not believe was possible he thought to himself that this was a kind of payment he could get used to.

*

Simon still had hold of Michelle's hand which he released as he retrieved the key to the entrance door of his brother's apartment block which allowed entry into the glass fronted hall way. He opened the glass door and let Michelle enter first and he followed her closing the door gently behind him. He lightly took her hand and led her up to the second floor of the block and with another key opened the apartment door.

Simon flicked the light switch next to the door and four spotlights lit the room, all of them directed onto a feature of the room; the first Michelle noticed was focused onto an elaborate rug, the second a huge tropical fish tank, the next a large stereo system and the fourth was trained upon a bar. 'Nice place.'

'Yeah, it is. He is a pilot.'

'A pilot?'

'Yep, he got the brains and I got the nothing!'

'I don't think that is exactly true Simon.'

Simon did not reply but he made his way further into the apartment. He opened another door and flicked another light switch. This light illuminated a large kitchen with a view through the window over the river.

'It gets better! A river view. You'll have to introduce me to your brother!'

Simon almost looked hurt by Michelle's intended joke and she definitely saw a brief cloud pass across his face. 'Materialistic are we?'

'Only joking with you,' and she lightly punched his arm.

'If I end up with a place as half as nice as this I'll be happy.'

'I'm sure you will.'

'You got any brothers or sisters Michelle?'

'One younger brother. He is a nuisance, but quite cute sometimes.'

'Well be thankful he is not older than you, or even worse an older sister. Be thankful you never have to live in their shadow and have your successes continually compared to an older brother or sister.'

Simon was talking as he was walking round the kitchen preparing items for the coffees. He slammed the coffee pot down and turned quickly around to face Michelle. 'Be thankful that your every single fucking move you make, your every decision is not compared to someone else. It seriously pisses you off!'

He turned away again and carried making the coffees. Michelle noticed that his hands were shaking. She moved over to him and placed an arm round his shoulders. Simon did not move but stopped preparing the coffee, he leaned onto the sideboard with his hands and his head slumped down. 'Sorry, I shouldn't have gone off like that. The pressure that I am under sometimes is immense. I mean, I love him to bits, but my parents, my parents; they put so much god damn pressure on me at times.'

Michelle started to stroke and occasionally patted his shoulder doing her best to comfort him. He turned towards her and she was surprised to see that tears were welling up in his eyes. She did not know what to do, whether to move her hands away or to take a step back because their bodies were pressing against each other.

'I've never spoken about this to anyone before. I don't know why I do so now. Guess it's the beer talking a bit.'

'It is okay. You can talk to me about anything. It won't go any further than me.'

'I suppose my mind thought that, subconsciously, and it all just came out in a flood. For the last ten years, ever since I didn't get picked to be captain of the cricket club at the same age as him, I have noticed this pressure, this ongoing comparison. Gets me down some times.'

'It's okay. Talk if you need to.'

'Anyway, coffee.'

Their eyes locked together, their bodies still very close together. He tried to turn round, but she stopped him, tensing the arm that was still around shoulder, and she leaned slowly towards him, offering her lips to his. Simon pulled his head away and Michelle took a step back, obviously annoyed that her offered kiss was refused.

'No, I'm not kissing you Michelle. I'm not going to let the physical side of things destroy what has been a good night. Kisses lead to gropes, gropes lead to removal of clothes etcetera, etcetera.'

She took the step back towards him and placed her arms back around him. 'Trust me when I say that it would not destroy a good night, it would make it more perfecter.'

'Perfecter?'

'Perfecter. And also trust me when I say that it will not lead to gropes and it certainly will not lead to removal of clothes etcetera, etcetera. I want to be kissed, I want to kiss you. Hell hath no fury like a woman scorned Simon.'

'Funny, it is not the first time tonight I have heard those words.'

She looked at him puzzled but this expression soon quickly changed as he leaned towards her with his eyes closed. Their lips touched and the gentle kiss soon turned into one of more passion. The kiss existed for a few more moments, Simon briefly exploring Michelle's mouth with his tongue until she gently pulled away and smiled a beautiful smile at him. He smiled back and slowly turned away from her to continue to make the coffee.

When he had finished making the coffee he handed a cup to Michelle and led her into the apartment's living area. He sat down on a sofa and she sat next to him, curling her feet up underneath her and leaned against Simon's shoulder.

He was slightly surprised at this show of affection but he wrapped an arm around her shoulders and slowly, gently stroked her hair. Her eyes slowly closed as she soaked up his smell and touch, his smell masculine with a faint touch of his aftershave still lingering on his body. As he ran his fingers across her head and through her hair, he could not help noticing how clean and shiny it was, how well looked after. He then could not help himself scrutinizing the rest of her. He liked her face, pretty but not strikingly gorgeous like other women he had dated.

Sometimes when dating such women he got annoyed when other men kept on looking at them and even more annoyed when he caught his date looking at the other men. Simon thought that he would not have the problem with Michelle and even if a man did look at her in that way he did not think she would be rude enough to acknowledge it while in Simon's presence.

His eyes traced downwards to her amazing chest. Large, full breasts and he knew they would also be firm and not bounce around her knees when released from the constraints of her bra. Then his eyes reached the most important part of a woman's body to him; stomach, hips, waist and bum, the true signs of a good figure and whether the woman looks after herself. Her stomach, in this curled up position anyway, bulged a little, but he did not mind that at all. Also, her hips, waist and bum were in nice proportions, not stick thin like some of the girls he had dated, a figure that he had since grown to detest. Michelle was full, voluptuous and womanly. His eyes reached her legs which were also lovely, just what he looked for in a woman nowadays, full, long and smooth.

As his eyes reached the tips of her toes he noticed that she was very lightly snoring, more like purring almost than snoring. Simon was slightly amazed that e ven though she was asleep she was still holding onto the cup of coffee although it was at an angle that suggested it was going to be dropped at any second.

Carefully he removed the cup from her hand and placed onto a table. He then moved away from her and took her head in his hands and slowly lowered her body so she lay down on the sofa and her head rested on a cushion. Simon stood over her for a moment looking at her sleeping form. Her skirt in the process of her being lowered had hitched itself very high and he could not help looking at the dark triangle that lay in between her legs.

His eyes lingered there for a few more moments and then he cursed himself and called himself a filthy pervert. He quickly made his way into one of the bedrooms and removed a duvet off the bed which he then placed over Michelle. He lent down and kissed her on her cheek and then went into another of the bedrooms and undressed down to his underwear. He crawled under the blankets and thought about the night and how much he had enjoyed it. Slowly, sleep descended upon him and he feel into a deep slumber and his dreams were full of Michelle.

Chapter 11

When they were through in the kitchen Peter took Sarah upstairs and they spent the rest of the night together experimenting with each other's bodies. Peter could not believe how good Sarah was in bed and Sarah thought the same about Peter.

When the first line of cocaine started to wear off she asked for another line which he dutifully prepared for her, happy with her style of paying for the drug. After she had taken this in the early hours of the morning they continued with their activities deep into Saturday morning until eventually exhaustion took a hold of them both and they fell into a deep sleep.

When Sarah woke on Saturday afternoon she felt terrible. Peter was still fast asleep and Sarah thought that she had had a bit more to drink last night than she thought, hence why she was feeling so ill. She lay back down hoping to get some more sleep and sleep through the hangover, but for some reason she felt incredibly restless and she kept on tossing and turning unable to sleep. She sat up again and the sudden movement made her feel dizzy and nauseous. The waves of nausea grew until she could contain them no more and she leaped off the bed and dashed out onto the landing frantically throwing open doors until she located the bathroom. She collapsed onto her knees in front of the toilet and hung her head over it.

Eventually the waves of nausea subsided and she slowly stood up. She reached for a glass and filled it with water. As she lifted her head to drink she kept an eye on her face in a mirror and instantly noticed how red the inside of her nose looked. She placed the glass down and leaned closer into the mirror tilting her head so she could look up her nostrils. She slowly placed a finger up her nose and was surprised that when she pulled it out it had blood on it. She shook her head in slight bewilderment, washed her hand and returned to bed. Peter was still asleep, lightly snoring.

She lay back down next to him and closed her eyes, desperately wanting to go to sleep, but her mind was racing and again she felt restless. She was tempted to wake Peter up but did not think that he would appreciate it.

As she was looking over at him her eyes caught the bag of cocaine that was resting on the bedside table. As she noticed it she felt a rush in her body and she was surprised to find a longing in her body that usually only happened when she wanted sex. She shook her head and lay back down but almost instantly the waves of nausea descended upon her again and she could not keep still. She closed her eyes, but all she could see when they were closed was the bag. She quickly opened her eyes again and leaned up onto one elbow and looked at the bag again.

Everything was there that she needed to make herself a line and she remembered how she felt last night after taking some. She carefully stood up and slowly made her way to Peter's side of the bed and picked up the bag. The mirror and the razor blade were also there. She took them all out of the bedroom and into the bathroom and locked the door behind her. She carefully placed the bag on the cistern and scraped some of the coke onto the mirror and prepared herself a line as she had seen Peter do.

However, her small line was in fact a large line as she misjudged how much coke she was scraping onto the mirror. She realized as the line was prepared that she had nothing to snort with so she just shrugged her shoulders and leaned over the cistern and snorted the coke straight up into her nose.

It was more than the delicate blood vessels in her nose could take. She straightened up after taking the drug and she instantly felt a warm trickle of something wet dripping onto her breasts. She looked over at the mirror and pouring out of the nostril, into which she had snorted the line, was blood. She panicked and started to scream and shout Peter's name.

Peter woke from a dream in which he was being chased down a road by a carrot with a gun to the sounds of shouts and screams coming from the bathroom. He instantly rolled over and saw that Sarah was not there and as he quickly sprang to his feet his eyes rested on the bedside table which had nothing on it. 'Oh! The stupid bitch!'

He quickly trotted round the bed and reached the bathroom door. The noise from inside had subsided and he pressed his ear against the door. All he could hear was what sounded like sobs. He took a deep breath and composed himself. He tapped lightly on the door and asked if she was alright.

'Yes, yes, I am fine. There was, erm, a big spider. I hate them.'
'A spider? Sarah, where's the coke?'
'I don't know, you had it last.'
'It was on the bedside table. Is it in there with you?'
'Yes.'
'Can I come in?'
'No! Don't come in.'
'Let me in Sarah. I need to know you are alright.'
'I am alright! Just give me a minute.'

Peter shook his head and looked down at the door handle. He could unlock the door from the outside but he needed something to turn the lock. He quickly returned to the bedroom and got a coin out of his copper jar and then returned to the bathroom door. Using the coin he turned the lock and slowly, quietly opened the door.

Sarah was stood at the sink with her head tilted far back. Peter, in the reflection of the mirror, saw that she has splatters of blood on her chest and that her nose was still bleeding. He watched her for a few more moments until Sarah caught his reflection in the mirror.

'I told you not to come in!'
'Sorry, I had to see that you are okay.'
'I told you I am!'
'Yeah, you look it.'

He took the few steps to her and gently placed his hand on the back of head. He tilted her head forward and instantly the blood started to flow out of her nose, down and into the sink.

'I thought you were meant to tilt your head back for a nosebleed?'
'You'll end up choking yourself. Stay like that and let the blood flow. It will start to stop soon.'

Sure enough, after a few minutes it did, and when it had Sarah started to clean herself up. She pushed Peter away when the bleeding finally stopped and sat down on the lid of the toilet seat. 'What the hell happened to me?'

'Welcome to the world of drug taking. Everything comes at a price, Sarah.'

'I thought I was dying.'

'No, nothing that quite dramatic babe. Your nose isn't used to it. How much did you take?'

Not knowing the difference between large and small she said, 'A small line.'

'On top of the two last night?'

'Yeah.'

'No wonder then.'

'Why didn't you warn me?'

'How could I when I was asleep? There is no way I would have let you take another line.'

'Worried about the impact on profit?'

'No, worried about the impact on your health. Why did you take another?'

'Couldn't sleep, felt sick. I have got the world's worst hangover going on.'

'And how do you feel now?'

'Now that the nosebleed has stopped top of the world actually.'

'See how you feel once that line wears off.'

'I think I need to go home now. What time is it?'

'I think you should. About three.'

'Oh! So late. Where are my clothes?'

'I think they are scattered all round the house. I'll find them while you finish tidying yourself up.'

Peter left the bathroom and walked around the house retrieving Sarah's clothes while she washed. By the time he got back the bathroom door had been closed again so he knocked on the door and Sarah told him to leave the clothes on the landing. He did this and went into his bedroom and got dressed.

Peter then went downstairs and flicked on the television and watched some Premiership football for what seemed like an eternity. Unimpressed with the level of skill on show he stuck it out for a few more minutes until another overpaid sports star missed another easy chance so he turned the television off in disgust. He was waiting only another couple of minutes until he heard Sarah start to make her way downstairs. She took the few paces from the bottom of the stairs and stood in front of him while he was still sat on the sofa.

'I guess I'll be going then. Would you, erm, like to see each other again?'

'Yeah, I don't see why not.' he said. He was thinking that if she was that wild on a one night stand, hell yes he wanted to see her again.

Peter then stood up and gave her a hug and a kiss on the lips. 'Look, about the cocaine, don't tell anyone. Sorry it had that affect on you. You really shouldn't have taken that much though, you need to get used to it.'

'After that nose bleed I don't think I will be touching the stuff ever again.'

'Well, if you ever want to, come round and I will give you some. You will have to pay for it though.'

'I can't see me doing that. But I would like to see you again.'

'Here is my mobile number,' said Peter, giving her a business card, 'so give me a call whenever you want to go out. I am free most evenings apart from, well, Friday and Saturday, for obvious reasons. Do you want a lift home?'

'No, it is okay. It is not far from here. Could do with the walk.'

'Okey dokey then babe. Give me a call and I will take you out.'

'Sounds good. I will definitely call you.'

With that Peter leaned forward and gave her a passionate, deep kiss and took her hand. He led her to the front door and they parted with another kiss and as the door closed behind her Peter said out loud, 'Now that was what I call a wild, wild night!'

Chapter 12

Sally slept fitfully that Friday night. Although what sleep she did have was dreamless, she awoke often and one of two images were always there when she awoke.

The first image she saw was the man, the second was always David. When she tried to get back to sleep she focused all her mind on the image of David and desperately tried to force out the image of the man.

After waking up for what felt like the one hundredth time during the night, Sally gave up with sleep at about six in the morning. It was pitch black outside but she still decided to go for a run, then a swim and hopefully catch her father at breakfast before he went to work.

At first she could not believe that she was going back out into the dark after all that happened to her during the last night. She flicked on the bedroom light and she rummaged in a chest of drawers for her running shoes and sport clothes to wear. She slipped the clothes on, not bothering with underwear, and tied her shoes tight. She heard a noise outside her door and guessed it was one of the maids.

Sally quickly decided that she did not want to see anyone so she walked over to the French windows, thrust them open, and stepped out onto the balcony. She sucked in the crisp, clean night air and she was surprised about how mild it was for the time of year.

Her balcony faced east and she could see the first hint of dawn just touching the horizon, but she knew that full sunrise was still at least an hour away. Sally continued sucking in the fresh air as she did some light stretching of her legs.

She then closed her eyes and purposefully brought the image of the man to the front of her mind and then she said out loud, 'I will not let you affect my life! I will sleep at night, I will not be afraid of the dark!'

With that she sprung over the balcony wall and gracefully fell the ten feet to the lawn below. She landed with her knees bent and instantly started to jog. She jogged for a minute and then sprinted for thirty seconds. As she was running along the lawn she sidestepped bushes and trees, occasionally leaping over the smaller bushes which appeared out of the early morning gloom in a classic hurdlers pose.

After about five minutes running, the lawn ran out and she entered woodland. There was a path through the trees that she followed until it finished against the estate's internal wall after another five minutes of hard running. The path split into two at the estate's furthest wall and Sally took the left hand path.

Here, amongst the trees and firmly against the estate's inner wall it was practically pitch back. However, the darkness did not slow her repetitions of sprints and jogs, nor did it slow her overall pace. Every kink and turn in the path was second nature to her after living on the estate all her life.

When she reached a particularly thick patch of trees she stopped where she would normally have never stopped and closed her eyes. She was not out of breath at all, her breathing was normal, even though she has been running hard and fast for fifteen minutes. As she closed her eyes she again brought the image of the m an to the forefront of her mind. She stood there in the pitch dark with this image in front of her for five minutes.

At first she panicked and her breathing did build up, but then she thought of David and this calmed her. Then she was able to focus all her attention on the image of the man. After a few more minutes she opened her eyes and was comfortable that she had managed to already rid herself of the man's presence over her. She was proud of her own strength of mind and will-power to not let this, what she thought of as a pathetic attack, affect her.

Closing her eyes one more time, and just for fun, she brought the image of David to the front of her mind, only this time he was the image of what she imagined he looked like naked. She chuckled to herself, at her own boldness and then muttered to herself, 'Back to work young lady!' and she resumed her run.

Sally followed the wall right round the estate, noting as she jogged past the front of the mansion that her father's bedroom light was on. She kept on going, round the west side of the mansion until she came back to the original path through the trees that led back to the lawn. She turned left onto it, however, this time she sprinted as hard as she could back along the path, over the lawn, again leaping over some of the bushes, until she reached the landing place below her balcony. This time Sally was out of breath and she bent over with her head between her long legs sucking in mouthfuls of air. She remained in this position for about thirty seconds until her breathing returned to normal and then she lightly jogged around the east side of the mansion to the rear.

As she approached a rear door she caught the aroma of a cooking breakfast, a smell she loved and the memory it brought of a mother hardly known.

She entered the kitchen and quickly but silently made her way through it, desperately hoping that none of the kitchen staff spotted her as she did not want to speak to anyone. Thankfully, they all had their backs turned and she managed to get through unnoticed. Sally exited the kitchen and walked along a long corridor to the end where there was another door and she quietly exited the servants' quarters.

Instantly the décor changed and it became more opulent. Instead of tip-toeing along thin carpet she was now tip-toeing along marble, instead of single burning lights in simple light shades, there were numerous chandeliers burning many lights. Sally, of course used to such opulence, did not even notice this most impressive inner hall.

Instead she continued to tip-toe across it until she reached double glass doors which she quietly opened. As she stepped through them she entered a passageway, on her right side a marble wall, on her left marble columns, beyond which lay a large, deep swimming pool.

She walked next to the columns looking at the crystal clear water and the slight layer of steam that hovered over the pool, until she reached a door with the usual symbol on it that indicates a female changing room. She entered through this door and instantly the sensors detected her. Automatically the lights came on and she made her way over to large, ornately designed wardrobe.

Inside, on a shelf, were a bikini and a large, thick luxurious towel that were always prepared for her. She took the towel out and draped it over a towel heater that she then switched on. Sally changed into her bikini quickly, just dumping her running gear on the floor, and stepped into one of the five shower cubicles where she rinsed off the sweat from her run. She stayed there only for a few moments, and then she went back to the pool and started her swim with an elegant full length dive that made hardly a ripple.

Her front crawl technique had been drilled into her from a young age and it was near enough perfect. She used this technique to quickly do twenty five lengths, after which she switched to breast stroke for another twenty five. After this, she threw technique to the wind and hammered out ten fast, powerful, front crawl lengths, which left her gasping for breath at the end.

Knowing that breakfast would be served in the bright, informal breakfast room promptly at eight o'clock, she had plenty of time for a long hot shower. While she was in the shower, to the casual observer, she appeared to be fondling and stroking her breasts. However, concerned that breast cancer may run in her family, ever since she had developed them, she had been checking them.

Usually she would start by looking in the mirror, but today she changed her routine and did the usual last step while she was in the shower. When she had finished though, she made a point of standing in front of the mirror and examining them with her arms by her side, also with her arms raised. She also checked her nipples by squeezing them, as she had read was the right thing to do, looking for any kind of unusual discharge. There were exquisite carved benches all round the changing room with thick padding on them, so she lowered herself down onto one of them and continued to examine herself while she was lying down.

Sally heaved a huge sigh or relief as she sat up, thankful that she had not found anything worrying in her examination. She had noted that it was best to do a full breast examination at least once a month, so she made a point of doing it on the first of the month after her daily swim. It was not the first of the month, and she cursed herself for not sticking to her routine. Also, she knew she had been a bit naughty doing the steps out of turn, but all she was thankful for was that there was nothing out of the ordinary. It was also coming up to the time of her regular check at the doctors of which her father insisted she partake in.

She had not decided whether to go for a genetic test yet. It was something that she was giving a lot of thought to, but she was worried about how it may change her life if it turned out that she had inherited an abnormal gene from her mother. Her thoughts now lingered on the beautiful lady who she knew so briefly yet desperately wanted to know more. She had left Sally and her father when Sally was young, devastating both of them. Her father became a recluse, not holding an audience with anyone, running his business empire from the end of a phone or through emails. However, without his steadying hand being always present the whole of his empire nearly came crashing down. It took a brave young director to barge his uninvited way into her father's office in the mansion and laid it all down for him in black and white that the company was going down. With her father's strong hand returned to the helm of the company, it went from strength to strength.

Sally loved her father so, so much, but he had never quite filled the void that a lost mother does. He ensured that she was sent to the best schools that money c ould buy, given the best tutorship that money could buy in everything that Sally fancied doing from one week to the next.

When she wanted piano lessons, he employed a world renowned concert pianist to come and teach her. When she announced that she wanted a pony, he invested in a full stable set up for her, with an Olympic gold medallist show jumper to teach her. The gold medallist did not last long with the spoilt little brat as he described her when he told Sally's father that he refused to teach her anymore until she developed some manners.

These words struck home with her father, especially considering that she was eleven at the time. The first time he remembered these words and actually said no to her it created a little bit of commotion. Well, not exactly a little bit, more like a small, yet potent hurricane had hit the mansion.

The sobbing, the tears, the tantrums were a sight to behold and lasted for a week or so. Ever since then she had been expected to work and earn her treats. Her Mini was paid for out of her own money that had she earned when she worked for her father during a summer. He still brought her presents now and then. Most of her attire was straight off the catwalk and he made sure no expense was spared when sending out one of his secretaries to get his daughter a little something during one of his many business trips overseas. The little somethings usually equalled at least a month's pay of the aforementioned secretaries, sometimes two or three months. Sally knew that she had been spoiled as a child, and that she was still treated like a little princess by her daddy. She sometimes wondered if her life would have been any different if her mother had still been alive to see her grow up.

Now she had to confront him about her eventful night and her trashed car, a chore she was not looking forward to. She knew that his reaction would be for personal bodyguards to be assigned to Sally and this worried her because she hated being followed by the guards everywhere she went.

Opening the ornate wardrobe when she was fully dry, Sally took out a silk robe in a Japanese style, draped and fastened it around her amazing body. Not giving another thought to the clothes and towel on the floor, knowing that somebody would tidy up behind her, she left the changing room and quietly and quickly made her way back to her bedroom.

Here she started to change into horse riding gear, and while she was doing so she glanced at the gold carriage clock on the mantelpiece and realized that she had enough time to check her emails before she went to breakfast. Switching on the computer in the corner of her room, she continued to get ready while it was booting up.

The top of the range computer started quickly and it automatically connected to the internet. When she was ready, Sally checked her email account, and also the B.B.C. website to keep in touch with current affairs. Nothing was happening on either website, no interesting emails or interesting stories. She did note, however, that her father's rugby league team that he owned had won last night which should hopefully put him in a good mood. She was meant to have accompanied him to the game last night, but she could not stand going there. She loved the sport, the excitement and thrills and big hits made football look like the most borin g sport in the whole wide world, but she hated the players who were always making hits on her, trying desperately to get her into bed. The football players were even worse. Always flashing their money around, inviting her out for drives in their Ferraris and not seeming to realize that her father paid their wages and that if she wanted to, with a sly word in her father's ear she could end their careers.

Aimlessly she continued to flick through the pages on the B.B.C., noting on the technology pages that one of her father's subsidiary companies was due to release a new MP3 player that was apparently, for the price, the best on the market. She was halfway through the article when the grandfather clock at the end of the hallway outside her room started to chime eight, so quickly Sally flicked off the monitor and made her way back downstairs to the sumptuous breakfast room.

She always briefly stopped and looked out of the window at the view every time she stepped into this room through the double doors. Out of the huge French windows was a large balcony, on which, in one corner, stood a Jacuzzi. Beyond the balcony were the large front lawns and also the driveway which ran along the side of a lake. Past the end of the lake the road disappeared into a coppice of trees towards the imposing wall and enormous gates of the estate.

At this time of the morning, there was still a light mist over the lake giving it an eerie appearance. The island that her mother loved, and where her body rested, was peaking faintly through the mist adding to the eeriness.

Her father was already at the table helping himself to some toast. When he saw that it was his daughter who had come through the doors he leaped to his feet, his face beaming. 'Now then young lady, to what do I owe this pleasure?' he said as he made his way across the thick carpet to greet her. 'Saturday morning and you are up?'

'Not exactly daddy, no.' She leaned forward offering a cheek to accept his offered kiss. 'Couldn't sleep and I haven't seen you all week.'

He took a step back from her, holding her shoulders in his hands, studying her face. 'You haven't slept at all have you? I can tell. Was that you I saw scampering through the trees this morning at some silly hour?'

'Yes, it was.'

'Crikey! Must be serious if you are well and truly up before me, especially on a Saturday! Come, sit down, eat and tell me about it.'

Sally made her away at her father's side to the breakfast table and sat down in a seat next to him.

'Have some toast while it is still hot.' He picked up a little hand bell and rang it. Instantly, from a side door a servant appeared. 'More tea and coffee please, an unexpected guest.'

'Yes Mr. Gallagher.'

'How's the toast?'

'It's good thanks.'

'Now, why don't you tell me what has happened that has made you go for a run before sun-up?'

'Well, you know the road off the B5671? The short cut to town?'

'Yes, of course, goes under the bridge.'

'I was driving along it last night and the car…'

It was only then that Sally noticed the telephone that was resting next to her father's hand as it started ringing. She of course knew that breakfast was the only time in the day that her father refused to be interrupted. You had more chance of phoning and being able to speak to him at three in the morning than at breakfast. If the phone was by his side then she knew that something big was happening.

'So sorry darling, hold that thought.' He picked up the phone and it was only a short conversation. 'This had better be good Andrew, I'm at breakfast.'

Sally of course could not hear what Andrew was saying, but from the look of his face turning to thunder it was not good news. After a few moments the conversation ended with her father saying, 'Right, give me twenty-five minutes,' and with that he slammed the phone down. He instantly picked it back up and pressed two numbers. He had to wait only a split second before it was answered. 'Ray, get the Ferrari out. Get me to the office in twenty-five, no, twenty minutes,' and he slammed the phone down again.

For a moment Sally did not say anything, she let her father have his thinking time. She could tell from the slightly vacant stare that he was probably doing either her complex mental arithmetic or working out how to make himself another billion pounds in ten seconds. She had learned the harsh truth the hard way of what happens when anyone interrupts him during this thinking. After a few more moments she saw her father seem to come back online as he liked to call it and he looked across at her and shot her another beaming smile. 'Needless to say, something has come up.'

'It's okay daddy. We can talk another time.'

'Flamin' solicitors! They cost me a fortune and always make bloody mistakes!'

'The acquisition not going smoothly then?'

'It was until last night. Flamin, bloody solicitors. Anyway,' he leaned forward and gave her another kiss on the cheek, 'have to fly,' and he stood up and started to make his way to the double doors.

'Try and make sure that Ray gets you there in one piece,' Sally called after him.

'He will. He is the best driver in the country.'

'I hope so. Good luck and see you later daddy.'

He turned briefly and shot her another smile. 'You certainly will. We'll finish our talk later, definitely.'

'I hope so.'

He opened one of the double doors and stepped through it and quietly closed it behind him. A few minutes later Sally heard the roar of the Ferrari so she turned to watch it as it raced towards the gates of the estate. Although the office was thirty miles away in the heart of the nearby city, she knew that her father would be there in twenty minutes.

Sally continued to work her way through the breakfast that kept on being put in front of her; cereal, full English breakfast and then fruit to finish. She knew that there was more chance of her flying to the moon today than finishing her conversation with her father. Another problem with having a very successful businessman as a father was that it was extremely difficult to get his attention for more th an a couple of minutes without something interrupting him. In a way she was glad as her father would probably over react to the prior nights occurrences and refuse to let her out without some kind of security being with her.

Eventually she finished the breakfast and stood up. She looked down at how she was dressed and remembered that it was her original intention to go riding. Now she did not feel like it. Instead she picked up the phone and dialled two numbers and instantly Alfred answered. 'Hello?'

'Alfred, it's me.'

'Good morning. How are you today?'

'I'm fine. Can you do me a big favour?'

'Of course, anything at all.'

'Don't tell my father though, promise?'

'Of course.'

'Can you run me into town?'

'Of course, but where is the Mini? Nobody heard or saw you come in last night. We were most worried.'

'Yes, I know. I sneaked in. I didn't want to see anyone. Security knew I was home though; they drove me in from the gates. That is what I don't want you to tell my father, the fact that I wasn't in the Mini.'

Sally had made the police drop her off away from the gates so the security guards did not see the police car. They definitely and would have been obliged to tell her father if they had seen the police.

'Not a problem my dear. I'm sure you have your reasons. Shall we take the Rolls-Royce?'

'Yes, that will be fine.'

'Say, ten minutes outside the main entrance?'

'Better make it twenty, I need to get changed.'

'Not a problem my dear. I will be waiting for you.'

'Thank you, Alfred.'

Sally replaced the phone onto its holder and made her way back to her bedroom and got changed. She had decided that she needed some shopping therapy and while it was early there would be no crowds.

After changing quickly into Armani everything; jeans, shirt and pullover with Nike trainers, she made her way to the main entrance and exited the mansion. As promised, Alfred was there behind the wheel of the quarter of a million pounds car, and Sally entered the rear of the vehicle.

Without a word between them, Alfred proceeded at a statelier pace to the gates of the estate than her father's driver had done, and then turned onto the road that would take them into the town.

During the drive she did not really think of anything, only looked at the familiar countryside as it drifted past her window. As the car made its stately progress it received lots on envious glances from other drivers, and when Alfred stopped at traffic lights people peered into the rear of the car expecting to see someone famous, looking away disappointed when they realized it was not anyone they recognized.

Sally was used to this. All throughout her life people had been staring into th e back of the highly expensive cars her father owned. Once she had asked him why he did not get blacked out windows. His response was that he had worked eighteen to twenty hour days for much of his life; the last thing he was going to do was hide away from his success. Slowly Alfred made his way through the morning traffic and reached their usual drop-off point. 'What time would you like to be picked up dear?'

'I will call you Alfred. I think this is going to be a long one.'

'Oh dear. It must have been a rough night. I'm sure you will tell me what happened in your own time. Take care.'

'I will. Thanks for driving me in.'

'Anytime my dear.'

Sally then shuffled along the seat and exited the car out of the left hand rear door and watched as the Rolls pulled away and moved back into the traffic flow. Most of the people were heading up a street into the main part of town but Sally did not follow them. She took another street which led to the exclusive shopping area which was full of shops like Prada, Gucci and Armani, the kinds of places that the daughter of a billionaire, with one of her bank cards in her purse that magically got paid off at the end of each month, could quite happily spend an unhappy day getting some serious shopping therapy.

What Sally did not realize at that time was the shock she was going to receive in this exclusive part of the town later that same day.

Chapter 13

David also slept fitfully that night, but for a different reason than Sally. Every time he closed his eyes all he could see was her face. That last smile seemed to be imprinted, burned onto his retinas. Whenever he opened his eyes it was as if Sally was stood in front of him the image his mind created of her was so perfect. Eventually he did drift off only to be woken at some time in the early hours by a drunken reveller making their very late way home singing loudly nonsense. David's eyes rested upon one of his many tool boxes and the image of him hurling a wrench through the window and wrapping itself around the singer's neck made him smile and briefly replaced the image of Sally. He resisted the temptation to maim the drunk and instead his brain quickly and annoyingly flicked back to Sally.

'Dum, da, dum, da dum,' he muttered to himself, 'oh when will sleep come?' He contemplated his ramblings for a moment and then said, 'I'm a poet and I don't even know it. Right now I wish I had never met that stupid girl! Who takes their car along that road at that time of the night anyway?!' He closed his eyes but he knew he was wasting his time. 'Ohhh come on now!' again, he spoke out loud, 'I am acting like a twelve year old who has got his first ever crush! She is not that nice!' Again, he contemplated his words and then added, 'Who am I trying to kid?! She is, without question, the most gorgeous woman I have ever laid eyes upon! Right, no point lying here if I am not going to sleep, up you get young man!'

He sprang out of bed and glanced at the clock after which he let out a long groan. 'It is so, so early! What am I going to do?' He thought about his question as he made his way to the toilet and it was while he was there he came up with the idea of going to the garage and making a start on fixing the Mini which he had been intent on doing later that day. David had volunteered to work on Saturday anyway and he would try to make the car better than it was. 'She obviously likes the car,' he stated to himself, 'so what better way to get in her good books than by fixing it?'

Whilst having a quick wash he was thinking about how on earth he was going to fix the car. His thoughts soon stopped though as he remembered the man's bodily fluids and solids that were in the car and he let out a little shudder as he thought about it. Deciding to not come up with any plan until he had arrived at the garage, he returned back to his room and pulled on some overalls along with an old jacket. He then went downstairs into the kitchen and grabbed an apple and a banana, not having anything more substantial for breakfast as his boss always brought the Saturday workers something fatty and filling for their first meal of the day. After putting on his work boots and getting his keys, David exited his house and entered his car. It started with a mighty roar, mainly due to the large muffler attached to the exhaust system rather than having anything to do with the power of his old Ford Fiesta. He expertly reversed the car off the driveway, sped down the street and raced his way to the garage.

While he was driving he had passed the entrance to an estate that he always slowed down to look at when he had time. He could not see anything through the main gate, but after he turned onto a smaller road that wound up and onto the brow of a hill, it gave him a view over the whole of the estate. He pulled over to the side of the road and munched quietly on the fruit while he thought about the lucky people who lived in such a place. He had no idea who lived there, but he imagined they were of course very rich, with garages full of expensive cars. From this position he viewed the house down on an angle so he could see the front and also one side of the expansive mansion. Surprised, he noted that one of the windows was showing a light. 'Didn't think people that rich would have to get up this early!' he commented to himself out loud. Shaking his head in bewilderment as to how anybody could be that rich and still have to get up at six in the morning, he started the car again and continued his drive to the garage.

David arrived at his place of work not too long after his viewing of the estate. He parked round the back, tucking his car out of the way in a corner of the courtyard. Briefly he went up to the office, rearranged the furniture to how it was and washed the cups so no questions would be asked as to who he had had in the office. After flicking a switch that turned on the lights in courtyard he left the office and went down to the truck that was carrying Sally's car. He switched the truck on and then lowered the ramps at the rear of the truck. Pressing some buttons on the side of the truck released the cables that were attached to the car and it slowly rolled back. When the car was fully off the vehicle David unattached the cables and then moved the truck away to its appropriate parking space. He then returned to the car and studied it.

First of all he realized that he would have to face the gross task of cleaning the inside. He returned to the office and rooted around in there until he found some gloves. Also, he filled up a bucket of water adding lots of soap, grabbed some old rags along with a few copies of a newspaper. Going back to the car he pulled on the gloves and laid out one of the newspapers open on the tarmac yard. He then flung open the driver's door and simply scooped up the faeces in his hands and dumped it on one of the papers. He wrapped up the paper and coolly walked over to a skip and threw it all in it. It was only then that he let himself feel a little nauseous but he quickly shoved that aside as he returned to the car to remove the fluid that was around the steering wheel and which had also dripped onto the floor of the car. Taking one of the rags that had been soaking in the soapy water, he wiped away all the 'egg white' and when it was all removed he calmly again walked over to the skip and threw away the rag. Nausea again threatened to overwhelm him but after a few moments he composed himself and started to feel happy now that the gruesome task was out of the way.

Returning to the car he started to scrub the driver's seat trying to get rid of all traces of the excreta. As he worked he pressed the power button on the radio and was happy when it came to life. Humming and sometimes singing along to a popular love song, while the song was reaching its end he thought and thought of the previous night, how beautiful she looked considering the horrendous night she was having, considering how wet and bedraggled she was. He was sure that he would see her again, but he knew that last night they had shared some moments that would hopefully stay with them for a life time.

As the song changed, he resumed his scrubbing and slowly the stain faded.

When he was happy with the interior of the car he sat in the driver's seat, not minding the wetness, and tried to start the car. The key was turned three times until, with a cough and a splutter, the dried out engine caught. 'Yes! They don't make them like they used to! Can't believe it started!'

David closed the door and took the Mini for a quick spin around the yard, loving the wind blowing into his face through the window frame. He did a couple of handbrake turns, enjoying the handling of the Mini, and then he stopped outside one of the doors to the garages, wiping the wind-tears out of the corners of his eyes with a big grin on his face. 'They really don't make them like they used to!' he exclaimed again.

Stepping out of the car he opened the garage and then returned to the vehicle and carefully rolled it in. Inside was everything a person needed for the removal of dents, however, this was definitely not one of his strong points. 'Give me an engine to dismantle any day off the week,' he muttered to himself. However, he got to work, not listening to the radio because he was worried about the power of the battery, and removed the dents as best he could.

David continued working until he heard voices in the yard. He stopped what he was doing and stepped into the enclosure and sucked in the crisp, clean morning air. It was dark when he had entered the garage and now he was glad to see it looked like being a glorious day. Two of his work colleagues came across and he told them how he managed to acquire another broken car since they had left the previous evening. The only thing he did not tell them was a description of Sally. He wanted to keep that image to himself.

Leaving the Mini for the time being, David had to carry on with the garage's work. Around 11am his boss arrived bringing bacon, sausage and fried egg sandwiches with him for his workers. They broke off their respective tasks and sat on chairs in one corner of the yard, ate their sandwiches, and talked man talk. David's two colleagues had been out the night before and they talked about their successes with the women, the copious amount of beer they had consumed and they fight they had been involved in. David listened and laughed along, but when he asked how much money they had spent he inwardly winced. Going out, getting outrageously drunk and fighting was something that had never interested him. He had always thought that instead of drinking all his money away he would save it and spend it on something worthwhile. He was interested in the women side of their stories though.

Knowing he was not academically gifted, David finished his education at the age of sixteen, knowing it was pointless to even try and attempt a college course. Mechanics was something that had always interested him, and he obtained an apprenticeship at this time. Due to him saving and rarely going out, along with his male dominated profession he hardly met any women never mind stunningly beautiful women like Sally. Therefore, all his thoughts, as he feigned interest in his work colleagues' stories, was to make sure that he did all he could to impress Sally and make her want to be with him.

Eventually, long after David was beyond bored with their success stories, his boss came across and shooed them all back to work. With some more overtime under their belts and the work done, his manager dismissed them all, but David sa id that he was going to stay. His boss had noted the Mini in one of the garages but had not commented upon it until now. 'Where did we acquire that Mini from?'

'It is a friend's. She broke down last night. I picked it up. Been doing some work on it.'

'Is she paying?'

'No, I'm doing it for free in my own time.'

'What about the equipment costs?'

'Take them out of my pay.'

'You did say "she" yeah?' David nodded. 'She must be special if you are spending money on her. Tighter than cramp you are!' To this his colleagues laughed and David joined in with a pretend laugh. 'In that case you had better get to it. Are you removing dents?' David nodded again. 'Oh to be a fly on the wall! Not exactly your forte is it?' This gained another laugh from them all, but David did not join in this time. 'Come on then boys, beers on me at The Oak! Let's leave this da Vinci of the mechanical world to his creation, or should that be destruction?!'

With another laugh they left a forlorn looking David stood alone in the courtyard, walked to the boss's car and left him alone to his destructive creation.

He started to feel down as soon as they had left; he always did whenever he was the butt of their jokes, which was quite often. Just because he was different and did not believe in spending vast amounts of cash on nights out, pissing and vomiting out the purchases of the money, he was frequently made fun of by his colleagues. This time though, it did not last for long him being down. This time he was here working, not for the money, for something one hundred, a thousand, a million times more important than money, he was working for the heart of Sally.

*

David worked and worked for the rest of the afternoon on the Mini. He painstakingly removed the dents to the best of his ability, and he was busily finishing a paint touch up when his mobile rang. He looked at the caller identification on the screen and saw it was Simon. He did not really want to speak to him but he thought it would be rude not to. Simon had had a date last night and David supposed he wanted to gloat another success story to him. He pressed the green button on his old, battered Nokia and answered the call.

'Alright Dee. Where are you?'

'Bloody hell Simon! Dee is short for Diane! How many times do I have to tell you?'

'Don't be soft and answer the question!'

'I am at work.'

'At this time on a Saturday? You're usually done by now aren't you?'

'Yeah, I am. Doing some extra work.'

'Some extra, extra, extra work more like. When will you be done?'

'Don't know, hopefully soon. I'm knackered. How was your date?'

'She didn't turn up the bitch!'

'She didn't? Shame, she sounded good.'

'Good? Good?! A sweeping understatement there matie! Stunning more like.'

'Funny, I met a Sally last night.'

'Did you? Where?'

'She brought a car to the garage late on,' said David, slightly twisting the truth. 'Not your Sally though, this Sally had black hair and blue eyes. Yours has blonde and green doesn't she?'

David again twisted the truth a little. Although Sally did have black hair last night, when Simon met her she had blonde, but she definitely had green eyes; he would never forget those eyes. He was inwardly wishing that Simon's Sally was different from his, but he already knew the truth before he started asking the questions.

'Yep, indeed she does, although she changes her hair colour a lot, but my Sally has definitely got green eyes. Coincidence,' stated Simon.

'Must be. What car does your Sally drive?'

'Don't know for sure. Think it is a Mini.'

'Oh, right, my one had a Focus, must be a coincidence.'

'Sounds like it. Hey, I do know something though; I met someone amazing last night. Well, I didn't meet her, I already knew her, just didn't realize how fantastic she is!'

'Oh yeah, who?'

'You won't know her, someone from college.'

'Oh, right. What's her name?'

'Michelle. Really pretty and a good figure, but man, what a personality!'

'Not like you to go for personality.'

'I know! But I think this is the new me! She is wonderful and we are going out on a date next week!'

'Winner. Good on you.'

'Cheers matie. Hey, did you hear about Mike?'

'No, I haven't spoken to any one today. Why, what has happened to him?'

'He only got himself banged up!'

'Banged up? Where?'

'In the police station, where do you think?! He got out late last night. Have a guess what for?'

'I don't know, hitting a police officer with a stick?'

'No, indecent exposure! He was only walking along with his tackle out and walked straight into the arms of two police officers! You should have seen his face!'

'Sounds like a right hoot.'

'Believe me when I say it was! When do you think you will be done then?'

'Don't know.'

'Coming out tonight?'

'Are you going out again? Where to?'

'Probably town again.'

'Nah, I will leave it tonight. I'm broke.'

'Broke? My arse! The amount of work you do!'

'I know, but all that goes to savings.'

'Okey dokey then. See you tomorrow or in the week. Don't work too hard!'

'Defo. Have a good one. I won't. See you.'

'See you Dee!'

David threw the phone away in disgust onto a pile of tarpaulin sheets in the corner of the garage that broke the phone's fall. Lots of things were raging through his mind. The first being that the amazing woman he met last night was the same woman that one of his friends was meant to meet for a date! The second, while David was going along with no-one, Simon moved on from someone as stunning as Sally to another girl in the blink of an eye!

It annoyed him a lot that Simon could move on from one to another without giving a serious consideration to the feelings of someone as lovely as Sally. 'What the hell are you moaning at?! If he has moved on already, and it sounds like he likes this Michelle, then it leaves the road open for you!' This thought, expressed out loud, put a small smile back on his face. 'Excellent! Now that you have thought about it rationally instead of getting angry it turns out that there is probably no reason to get angry in the first place!'

David hummed a happy tune as he walked the few steps to retrieve his old phone. It had switched off but he pressed the on button and it flashed back into life. 'Nokias!' he again exclaimed out loud. 'You can do anything, anything to them and they still work! Now to call in some favours!'

Happy that so far he had got the Mini into the best condition that he could, he sat down on the garage floor, leaning his back against one of the walls, and flicked through the phone book on his mobile until he came to the person he wanted to call. He pressed the green button and listened to the ringing until it was answered.

'Hello?'

'Hello Brian. It is David from Gladstone Garage. How are you?'

'Oh, hello Dave, I'm good. And yourself?'

'Getting by. You still at work?'

'Yep, just finishing off. What can I help you with?'

'Remember that big favour you owe me?'

'You're joking?! On a Saturday?!'

'Sorry, I know, but I really need your help.'

'Go on then. I'm all ears.' David explained the situation to him, again missing out any word about Sally. 'And where, exactly, at this time on a Saturday, do you expect me to land my hands on a full set of windows for a Mini?!'

'Come one Brian, don't give me that, you are the man are you not?'

'Bloody hell Dave, I am good but, ah, bloody hell. Give me an hour. We have got a few Minis in the scrap yard but I have no idea what condition the windows are in. Give me an hour and I will call you back and let you know what I can find.'

'You are the man!'

'Yeah, I am. Bear this in mind though, this cancels out my favour and puts you in debt to me!'

'Not a problem. If you can do this then I will do anything you ask of me for all eternity!'

'I'm sure you will. My wife is going to kill me. Fancy calling me up at this time on a Saturday. Give me an hour.'

'Sounds good Brian, speak soon.'

Brian did not reply but David could hear him cursing him as he hung up the phone. He chuckled to himself for a few moments until he stood up and decided to put the hour to good use by washing and polishing the car while he had all the equipment there to do the job quickly. He worked until the car was practically sparkling and it was then that he looked at the clock on his phone and saw that Brian had now passed his allotted hour. He was reaching for his mobile when he heard a horn blow. He looked towards the entrance of the garage and there, driving a large flatbed truck with a stack of windows strapped to the back of it, was Brian. He saw David and he trundled the truck over to him where he stopped it and jumped down out of the cab.

'You are truly a miracle worker!'

'Tell that to the wife. This is going to result in me getting a call from the solicitors on Monday. She is not a happy camper!'

'Sorry, but a favour is a favour is it not?'

'Tell that to the wife! She thinks I am with some fancy woman! Here you are. Seriously, phone her, you'll find her under "T".' He passed David his mobile. 'Try to resurrect my marriage why I unload the windows.'

David took the phone and pressed the appropriate buttons to find the entry labelled "The wife" in Brian's phone book. He walked away from Brian and the truck, out of ear shot, and for the first time that day, he told the woman he had met only once the full story. By the end of it she totally understood why he needed her husband's help so badly. What woman is not touched by a tale of romance and trying to win a lady's heart?

David swore her to secrecy before he walked back and passed the phone back to Brian. He spoke to her for a few more minutes until he turned to where David waited. 'I don't know what the hell you said to her, she wouldn't tell me, but she was like a little kitten and told me to stay here for as long as I was needed! She's not spoken to me like that for twenty years!'

'Oh well, guess I must have a way with the women! Glad she said you can stay as long as you are needed. How are you at fitting windows?'

'You what?! You want me to help you bloody fit them as well?!'

'Yeah, that would be nice.'

'Nice?! I'll give you bloody nice! This had better be for a good cause!'

'Trust me, it is.'

'Who managed to get all their windows smashed on a Mini?!'

'I can't tell you, but she is worth it.'

'She? Well, why didn't you just say? We'll have these fitted in no time!'

'Excellent! Let's get to it then!'

'Yes boss!'

David laughed at Brian's joke and together they lifted the rear window and fitted it quickly. They fitted the other windows equally quickly, while laughing an d telling each other jokes and amusing stories. Soon they had the windows done and he departed as soon as it was completed back home to his spouse. Later that night, with some pillow talk, Brian got the full story out of his wife about why David so urgently needed the help.

After Brian had gone, David decided that enough was enough and that no matter how hard he tried he could not get the car any better than it was now. He wandered out of the garage into the yard and across to a small flat bed van. Hopping onto the side of it he sat on the edge with his legs hanging over the side and took his phone from his pocket. He flicked through the phone book on his phone until he reached the "Ss". There, at the top was the new addition to his phone book, the new addition to his life. The entry simply read Sally. He took a few deep breaths and pressed the green button. It started ringing.

Chapter 14

Sally spent all morning and afternoon getting some shopping therapy. All the shops recognized her when she entered them and they could tell from her unhappy face that they could make a lot of sales to her that day. She moved up and down the street, going from one exclusive shop to another, trying on shoes, dresses, jeans and every type of clothing that there was.

At lunch time she called Alfred to come and collect her shopping because she could not carry the bags she had accumulated anymore. When she saw the Rolls-Royce depart she got a slight twinge of guilt as she thought about how much money she had just spent. She knew her father could afford it, and she knew that he would happily pay off anything if it made her happy. Sally gave a resigned shrug of the shoulders and for the third time that day she entered a Prada shop to again try on a pair of shoes that had caught her eye.

At around three she decided to have a break so she went to a little coffee shop that she liked and took her usual table in the window. The waiter knew her order and did not ask her. He discreetly got her a cappuccino and a small slice of chocolate cake, leaving the bill on a saucer by her side.

She sat staring at the new apartments across the street that had been erected in the last few months thinking how better it would be if the coffee shop still had a river view. She was lost in her thoughts when she noticed movement at the entrance to the apartment block.

Stood at the door was a young man who she instantly recognized. It was her intention to phone him later that day and she was half out of her seat to go and speak to him until she noticed someone else coming down the flight of stairs. For a moment she froze halfway up while she glared at the young woman leaning affectionately towards the man she was meant to meet for a date last night.

She slumped back into her seat when the man opened his arms and accepted the offered hug, and then she thought that she was going to cry when she saw them engage in a deeply passionate kiss. The kiss lasted to Sally for an eternity and she watched again as her best friend took a step away from him, still holding his hand, and made him laugh with whatever she said to him. He took a step and opened the glass door and again they hugged and kissed while Sally's jaw got more and more clenched, while her knuckles got whiter and whiter as she held the edge of the table top in a fierce grip.

Michelle stepped through the door as Simon held it open and this time it was Simon that had Michelle laughing with some kind of joke. Sally was using all her will power not to run across the street and confront them. Michelle leaned back in and pecked him on the lips and then turned on her toes and walked down the street where she flagged down a taxi. By the time she had stopped watching and glaring at the back of her friend, Simon had returned back upstairs to which ever apartment he had access to.

With a few deep breaths Sally managed to compose herself and relaxed her grip on the table. Leaning back in her chair she could not believe what she had just seen. Her so called best friend kissing her date after obviously spending a night with him! She spent some minutes trying to calm down but she could not. Sally r eached for her hand bag and took out her mobile phone. She phoned her friend.

'Hi Sally. How are you?'

'I'm okay. How are you? Good night?'

'Yeah, it was good.'

'I bet it was.'

'Yeah, it was. What happened to you? I saw Simon out with all his friends. Did he not turn up?'

'No, I'm the one that didn't turn up. My car broke down.'

'Oh, okay. I spoke to him. He was wondering what happened to you. Did you not call him?'

'I couldn't get a signal where I broke down and by the time I did get one it was too late. Where did you end up? Score with some hottie?'

'No, unfortunately not! You know me Sally; I was home and tucked up in bed for one.'

'Were you? Are you sure?'

'Of course I'm sure.'

'Oh, okay then.' Sally paused for a second. 'Bloody hell Michelle! How long have we known each other for? How long have we been best friends?!'

'Erm, a long time. Why?'

'Because I thought that my best friend, someone who I have been friends with all my life would not lie to me!'

'Erm, I am not lying.'

'Michelle, I can't believe you have just said that! The sensible thing to have done was to let me speak and then you would not have had to lie to me about lying.' There was a long silence between the two friends. 'Anything to say?'

'No, I am doing as advised and keeping my mouth shut. Why do you think I am lying to you?'

'For some reason, I don't know why, but Simon has access to one of the new apartments on Church Street, I presume you know the ones?'

'I know the apartments, yes.'

'You know that there is a coffee shop directly opposite the entrance to these apartments?'

'Of course I do. We have been there many times. Just here please. How much is that?'

Faintly Sally heard the taxi driver speak, and then there was a pause while Michelle got the money out of her purse.

'Thank you. Yeah, you too. Bye.' Sally then heard a car door open, close and then the clip-clop of Michelle's heels as she walked presumably to her front door. 'What about that coffee shop then?'

'I am sat at the window table right now.'

Sally heard nothing for a few moments, not even the clip-clop, presumably because Michelle had stopped walking and was trying desperately to think of something to say.

'How long have you been there for?'

'Long enough Michelle, long enough.'

'I am so sorry Sally; I don't know what happened…'

'Michelle how could you?! My date!'

'I know, but after you didn't turn up I didn't think you were interested and he is so nice, and, and…'

'And what?'

'Nothing.'

'So was he good in bed?'

'Now hang on a minute, I didn't sleep with him!'

'Watch that nose Michelle, the end of it will be jabbing the President of China in the eye pretty soon if you tell one more lie!'

'My nose isn't growing this time because I am not lying to you this time. I swear I didn't sleep with him. I woke up this morning on the sofa. He was in bed on his own!'

'Yeah, whatever Michelle, whatever.'

'Oh I give up. I will call you later when you have calmed down and we can talk about it properly.'

'Don't bother!'

Sally pressed the end call button on the phone and slammed it down onto the table. The waiter glanced over at the noise and noticed how angry Sally looked.

Sally was again way past angry. She could not believe what she had just seen and she could not believe the conversation she had just had, the lies that her best friend had told her in such a hard faced way. She stood up out of her seat and ripped a five pound out of her purse and threw it onto the saucer. Picking up her phone she flung it back into her hand bag and collecting her shopping bags she stormed out of the café.

Now that she was so angry she did not even feel like shopping. She could not remember ever feeling so angry, even seeing her car last night had not made her feel like this. There was only one thing that usually got rid of such anger and that one thing was Storm.

She retrieved her phone again from her bag to call Alfred and demanded that he pick her up. Alfred recognized the tone in her voice, one of the few remnants that was left from her spoilt little brat days, and even though he was having a very rare break he did not refuse her request and left the mansion in the Rolls-Royce.

While Sally was waiting she paced up and down in front of the coffee shop trying to control her fury. After what seemed like an eternity she saw the Rolls making its stately progress towards her. While Alfred was still bringing the car to a stop Sally flung open one of the rear doors, threw her shopping onto the rear seat and then flung herself into the car. 'Home Alfred.'

'Yes, ma'am.'

He knew that when his mistress was in this kind of mood it was better to resume all formalities or he could be in for a huge tongue lashing from her, and possibly an audience with Mr. Gallagher himself if Sally thought he had been particularly rude.

'Phone ahead Alfred, have them saddle Storm.'

'Certainly ma'am.'

Alfred pressed a few buttons which switched on the car's inbuilt phone, and when the call was answered at the mansion he told them to do as Sally asked.

As the journey progressed Sally just stared out of the window and occasionally Alfred glanced at her in the rear view mirror. He noticed the frown line and also the slight pout to her lips. He had come to recognize all the signs in all his years as the family's butler as to when Sally was upset. Her haughty attitude, the pout and the clenching of her jaw was a sure sign that if Storm did not make her feel better, Alfred's working life was going to being misery for the next few days.

As they approached the gates of the estate Sally stated, 'I'll go straight to the stables thank you Alfred.'

'Yes, ma'am. However, the road down there is very boggy due to the rain last night, and you know how your father refuses to have it surfaced. Therefore the Land Rover should be waiting to drive you down there if that is okay?'

'Yes, it's fine. Make sure my bags are taken up to my room by somebody. You personally take my hand bag though. Don't let anyone else touch it. I will take my phone should anyone need me.'

'Yes, ma'am.'

Alfred pressed a button on a remote control which made the gates swing open and the car advanced onto the estate. After about half a mile along the road there was a fork. The fork led through a coppice of trees and was nothing more than a dirt track. At the start of this track was a brand new Land Rover Discovery.

The Rolls-Royce came to a halt and as Sally exited the car, without saying anything to Alfred, she saw the driver lean into the cab of the Discovery and use the radio. She presumed that he would be radioing ahead to inform the stable hands of her impending arrival. Stepping up into the rear of the car she again did not say anything to the driver, she just stared out of the window and watched the land roll by as they made their way a mile down the track to the stables complex.

The complex could easily hold ten horses. The stables were organized in a horse shoe around a central paddock that had a small equestrian course within it. Behind the stables, out of view as the Land Rover advanced into the complex, was a full circular track about two miles long. This track was split into two, one side was flat, the other had jumps included along its length. Usually, once or twice a week, Sally would take her beloved Storm around both courses, the flat and the jump, and sometimes around the equestrian course.

A large, powerful mare standing at sixteen hands, Storm was not at home on the tight and little equestrian course. Her reason to be as far as Sally was concerned was to sprint the flat course and jump the bigger fences. Today though she did not think that either of the courses would be enough.

As the Land Rover pulled to a stop, Sally exited the car and walked over to the side of Storm where she stood ready for Sally to ride her. The stable hands went about their work not taking any notice of Sally; they had been forewarned about the mood she was in.

As Sally approached, Storm looked up and let out a little whinny as she saw Sally. She rested her cheek against the side of the horse's head and stroked and muttered some loving words to her. After remaining like this for a few moments she then made her away along the side of the horse checking the saddle and all t he equipment was satisfactorily fastened, in place and looked safe. After this check, Sally put one foot in the left stirrup and swung herself quickly and adeptly onto the saddle.

Not concerned that she was wearing nearly a thousand pounds worth of designer clothes and no safety helmet, Sally dug her heels into the side of Storm. Instantly the horse sprang into a trot and Sally guided the horse across the cobbled yard to the open gate that led out onto the circular track.

As the surface changed from the hard cobbles to the soft grass of the course, she dug her heels in hard into the flank of Storm and the horse surged underneath her. Quickly it accelerated past canter and into a full gallop. Sally's hair flowed out behind her as the wind whistled past and wind-tears appeared at the corner of her eyes.

She did not slacken the pace of the horse though. She did two full circuits of the course, the first along the flat, the second over the jumps which Storm leapt over with ease. Only after two circuits did she ease off the speed and allowed them both to catch their breath. Storm walked along the course for a mile until they reached the top end of the circuit. Here Sally leapt off and walked over to the white fence and lifted up a panel so they now had access to the area outside the course. She mounted Storm again and they went through the gap in the fence. On the other side of the fence, through a wooded area, was a narrow path.

Storm instantly headed to this path, not needing any coaxing from Sally. Slowly she walked the horse along the path and therefore the tears building up in her eyes this time were not wind-tears. Thoughts were raging through her mind, most of them focusing upon the sights that greeted her while she was having a relaxing coffee. As they advanced along the path Sally tried to bring her thoughts together and come up with some kind of plan.

She knew she would forgive Michelle eventually, she had to. They had been through so much together and Michelle had always been by her side through Sally's darkest days, through her mother's darkest days of illness. However, she could still not believe that her best friend would spend a night with the man she was meant to meet for a date that same night. But she knew she would forgive her, eventually.

Simon though was a different story. It had always been an ideology of Sally's never to date someone who had been with one of her friends. Though Michelle said she had not slept with Simon, she could not believe Michelle right now. Even if she did eventually believe her there would always be that question mark hovering over Simon's head. It was something that Sally knew she could not cope with thinking about every time she looked at him. That, therefore, put him off limits, which kind of totally messed up Sally's intended love life.

But then an image entered her mind, an image that had been out of her thoughts until that moment, the image of her modern knight in wet T-shirt and soggy jeans. This put a smile back on her face and her body experienced a rush of blood as she thought about him.

Suddenly, out loud she shouted, 'Don't be so silly young lady! You don't even know him! You shouldn't be having thoughts like that! Come on then my angel, my darling Storm. Let's get rid of our demons and fly with the wind!'

Twice digging her heels into Storm's flank the horse accelerated quickly and burst out of the wood at a full gallop. Sally loved the exhilaration, the feel of the beast in between her legs as Storm thundered along the path. Suddenly in front of them a waist high fence of barbed wire appeared but the horse and Sally did not miss a step. Without decreasing speed they leapt over the fence and for a moment they were flying with the wind. Sally let out a wild cry as they landed and Storm maintained her pace as they exploded out of the landing. They maintained their speed across a field along another path. In the distance was the furthest corner of the estate and the large outer wall wound its way to the corner of the field they bounded across. Built into the wall was a gate and as they approached Sally pulled back lightly on the reins. Storm responded with a reduced speed and they trotted and then walked the last few yards to the gate.

Sally jumped off the horse's back and stepped over to the gate. Attached to the wall was a small metal box containing a small numeric keypad. She tapped in the code, always an easy number to remember: her mother's date of birth. Knowing that as the gate unlocked a light would have gone off in the security centre housed in a room in the mansion, so she paused for a few moments and looked up at the camera that was on the wall next to the gate. Sally gave a little wave as she saw the light on the camera flash three times as the guards acknowledged it was her by flashing the light. They then saw her disappear from view for a moment, and then reappear leading the horse. They then saw her push the gate open and then they disappeared from view as they stepped through the gateway.

Pushing the gate closed behind her, she listened as the electric locks slid back securing the estate once again. There was no way to open the gate from the outside, no numeric keypad, however Sally knew that if she phoned up the security centre later and gave the appropriate password they would unlock the gate for her. She never saw the guard again who had refused her entry into the estate because she forgot the new password. She presumed that he was given his papers after she had spoken to her father about him.

Remounting Storm they proceeded at a more sedate pace along the path that continued on this side of the gate. Sally was not really thinking of anything as they walked. She was trying to remove the image and thoughts of David out of her mind but she was failing, miserably. She knew that he had touched her with his immense good looks, his willingness to help her even though the situation she was putting him into was potentially a dangerous one. As she remembered all that happened last night a sensible voice piped up in her head and it was telling her that she should have informed her father.

She was under strict instructions, and had been from a young age, to report all incidents of this nature to her father just in case the incident was not going to be a one off and in fact the attacker was following her. However, as Sally thought about this, she just knew that her father would insist that she would have to have a bodyguard, or possibly guards, and be escorted everywhere by him, or possibly them. Hate was probably too mild a word to use when she thought of the times that she had to have a personal bodyguard. Her father had frequently stated to her that a girl, now a woman, in her position was a major kidnapping target.

Sometimes, usually two or three times a year, her father would annoy the wr ong person and then he would receive death threats or Sally would receive kidnap threats. It was then that she was followed everywhere by a huge lumbering oaf of a man, or possibly men, usually ex-military with all the personality of a damp rag. Her privacy was invaded, everything was invaded. He would stand outside her room as she got changed, he would jog behind her when she ran, he would st and by the side of the pool when she swam, he would watch with eagle eyes if she shopped for lingerie, everything was invaded. Even after all this, if she thought for one moment that last night was anything more than a one off and not just an unhappy coincidence she would tell her father. It was just not worth taking the risk of upsetting him. If he lost her on top of his wife, Sally knew it would finish him off.

    As Sally thought, she did not seem to realize that she was leading Storm to the top of a hill that looked down onto a certain road that went past a certain garage. They reached the brow of the hill and Sally was surprised when she looked down the hill and there, at the bottom, was the garage where David worked. She looked down onto it and through the fading light she noticed a figure appear out of one the garages and wander over to one of the vans on the yard. This figure hopped onto the rear of the van and for a moment it looked like he was staring at something in one of his hands that was held out in front of him. Then the hand moved to the side of his head and after a few moments she felt her phone vibrate in her pocket followed by the ring tone ringing. Storm shifted under her as the noise startled her a little but she quickly settled. Sally looked at the screen of the phone after she had removed it from her pocket and was surprised to see that it was an unknown number that was calling her. Her thumb automatically went to the red button to reject the call, but then something unknown, a feeling inside her, made her accept the call. She lifted the handset to her ear and simply said, 'Hello.'

    'Hi. Is that Sally?'

    'It is. Who is this?'

    'Erm, hi, it is David. I guess you remember me but I guess you get lots of guys calling you?' David gave a nervous little laugh as he thought his attempted joke crashed and burned. What he did not see was Sally's face visibly brighten, flush and then smile.

    'That's a bit silly isn't it David? Of course I remember you. How could I forget you?'

    'Erm, good. Erm, how are you anyway?'

    'I am okay. Didn't sleep very well.'

    'That isn't surprising. Neither did I.'

    'Well it wasn't a very nice night for either of us.'

    'Erm, no, I suppose it wasn't. Erm, good news about your car, it has been fixed.'

    'Oh! Wow! Did you do it?'

    'Yeah, with a little help.'

    'David you shouldn't have. I would have paid to get it done. You didn't have to spend your day off working on my car!'

    'It's okay. I was working anyway. It didn't take long.'

    'Well, anyway, I'm touched. I will make sure I pay you for it.'

'I must warn you that it is not like it was, I mean, everything is fixed, but the amount of damage… It was impossible to get it like it was.'

'I didn't even expect you to attempt to fix it and I certainly would not expect you to get it as it was so whatever you have done will be fine. How much do I o we you?'

'Well, erm, I don't want money and I would never take money from you any way.'

'No, I insist. How much?'

'No, like I said, no money. You can pay me in another way…'

Sally put on a sultry tone and said, 'Why David, I have only just met you!'

They both laughed at Sally's joke and David went on to say, 'Erm, I didn't, e rm, exactly mean that. You can pay me, by, well, erm, going out with me someti me, I mean, well, you wouldn't have to pay even then, I mean, erm, the payment would be going out for a date with me.' David was shocked as the words came o ut of his mouth. He had an idea that he was going to ask her out but not like this and he then thought that she was going to put the phone down on him. However, her answer surprised him to the point of jaw-dropping.

'I would absolutely love to so long as I you let me pay for everything. That is my only term and is, quite frankly, un-negotiable.'

Sally had been watching the figure on the back of the van as they talked. Not long after the conversation had started she had seen the figure hop back down of f the van and start pacing up and down the yard. After she had given her reply sh e saw the figure leap in the air and start punching the air.

For a few moments there was silence as David tried to regroup his thoughts a nd finish his celebration manoeuvres. Quickly he thought about what she said an d he concluded to just accept even if she wanted to pay for everything. 'Okay th en, if you insist. When would be a good time for you?'

'Anytime. I am free all nights this week.'

'Okay. How about Wednesday?'

'Perfect.'

'What would you like to do?' asked David.

'Surprise me.'

'What time would you like me to pick you up?'

'Well if my car is okay I will drive and pick you up.'

'Are you sure that is okay? I don't mind driving.'

Sally thought that she did not mind driving but she did mind him seeing her house and realising how wealthy she was. 'No honestly, it is okay for me. Let m e know your postcode and house number and I will find directions to your house .'

David gave her these details which Sally easily remembered and then he said , 'When would you like to pick the car up?'

Sally noticed that he had returned to his seat on the back of the van and she was so tempted to inform him that she could come for it right now but she mana ged to bite her tongue. Instead she did say, 'How about tomorrow? Not too early though! Need my beauty sleep if I have a date on Wednesday!'

'I don't think you do. How about eleven tomorrow?'

'Perfect again. Eleven it is then. Give me a call if anything changes.'
'Will do. See you Sally.'
'See you tomorrow.'

Sally pressed the red button on her phone and looked down and saw David jump off the back of the van and do another dance of joy. She felt awful spying on him like this but she was also very impressed about how much a simple date with her obviously meant to him. She looked down at her phone and entered the menu Received Calls and there was David's number. She created a new addition in her phone book and then quietly said to Storm, 'A new addition to my life angel, one that I am immensely looking forward to developing.'

With those words she turned Storm around and made her way through the dusky evening back to the estate.

Chapter 15

Her Saturday went from bad to worse. After leaving his house, she walked home and everything seemed perfect. She felt great and almost skipped her way home. Arriving home she lied easily to her mum about where she had spent the night then went straight upstairs and showered. While she was in the shower the cocaine was still affecting her so she toyed and played with herself, also using the shower head in an imaginative way until she brought herself to orgasm. Thankfully over the noise of the shower her mum could not hear the loud moans and groans as the immense feelings ripped through her daughter's body.

Sarah knew though that even if her mum could hear her she would not be concerned or even notice the ecstasy her daughter was experiencing. Sarah also knew that by this time on a Saturday her mum would have had at least a bottle of vodka and some wine to top it off. As the day carried on she would continue to top this off with probably gin or whiskey depending on what mood she was in. The only way nowadays that Sarah had to judge her mum's mood was by what drink she was consuming at that given moment; gin if she was feeling particularly down, whiskey meant she was hovering around joyous, vodka was the middle of the road drink.

Sarah's mum had not taken notice of anything Sarah did for a long time now. Ever since her dad had run off with a cleaner from his work her mum had been in a downward spiral of ever decreasing spirits, and an upward spiral of ever increasing consumption of spirits. Her parents' history was always something that upset Sarah whenever she thought about it. She knew that her parents were just not meant to be together.

They had spent one night together and her mum had got pregnant after that one night. Fair enough, her dad stood by her mum and married her, but even Sarah could work out that she was a little mistake and indeed her mum had even once kindly put it to her when she was drunk one night, 'Sarah, you are a little mistake'.

Even after hearing this, Sarah, who loved her mum immensely like any daughter does, tried everything to get her off the drink. She tried removing all alcohol out of the house but this just resulted in trips to the local boozers and Sarah had been called out many times to the local drinking establishments to come and collect her highly inebriated mother.

Not wanting to make their problems anymore public than they already were, Sarah tried a different tack and hid all of her mum's bank account cards and savings books so she had no way of purchasing the demon drink. All this resulted in was her mum taking identification down to the bank and withdrawing money without needing her cards or books. So, Sarah again tried a different tack. This involved, during rare moments of sobriety, trying to talk to her mum about her definite problem.

Sarah had done her research and knew that they did have a problem. When she removed all alcohol out of the house and her mum did not have a drink, she noticed that after a short time she started sweating, shaking and she also noticed that she became anxious and agitated. To get over this Sarah allowed her mum s mall amounts of alcohol but this just resulted in a total loss of control. She demanded that Sarah go out and get her more to drink. When Sarah refused she got highly angry and that was when the trips to the local bars started. She definitely knew they had trouble when Sarah came down in the early morning and saw that her mum had not gone to work nor phoned to tell them that she was not going to work, but was instead sat watching television with a large glass of vodka on one side of the table next to her and a large glass of wine on the other side. The sun had not even risen. Needless to say, after a few more mornings like this, she was sacked. Ever since those mornings, Sarah knew that her mum was an alcoholic.

She had tried persuading her mum to seek help by talking to her, but her mum denied that she needed help. "It is just a phase I am going through since your dad left." The phase had been lasting over eighteen months now. Of course, any sentence mentioning the 'd' word led her mum to take another drink.

Sarah had taken to leaving leaflets around the house from local alcohol organizations, but these went unread. Eventually Sarah contacted the organization herself and asked them for help. They told her to try and bring her mum to a meeting. This took around a month of subtle persuasion until her mum agreed to go but she insisted that she went on her own. Sarah knew this was a bad idea and indeed, it turned out to be a very bad idea.

Her mum did attend the meeting; however, she was highly drunk when she did. The meeting organizers did not mind this as much as the fact that during the meeting she pulled out a bottle of whiskey out of her bag and started to drink it. When she then started to offer the bottle around to the other attendees she was asked, in not quite so polite terms, to leave. It was after this disaster that Sarah gave up. She decided that she could not help her mum anymore and left her to her downward and upward spirals of spirits.

Sarah, without the guiding hand of a parent, her father did not help her because Sarah refused to acknowledge that she had a father anymore, became, to say the least, a little wild. She was out partying near enough every night and had built up quite a good reputation for being a party girl. She was also building a reputation for being extremely liberal with whom she took to bed.

Knowing that her mum would be comatose by midnight, there was no problem in taking young men back home and having some fun with them. Over the last twelve months she had tried lots of men in all shapes and sizes, and slowly worked through the book of sexual positions she kept under her bed. One time, when she was on the living room carpet in her favourite position of being taken from behind, her mother had actually walked past them into the kitchen, got a glass of some strong liquor, and returned back upstairs without even noticing her or the black man who had his penis lodged deeply inside her daughter's vagina.

Her promiscuity did come with its problems. She had had an abortion in the last few months and she knew very well that she had Chlamydia, but this did not stop her having copious amounts of unprotected sex with a plethora of partners. The abortion though was one thing that she did not want to experience again, so after the shower she walked naked to her bedroom and took a contraceptive pill. She refused to use condoms as the feeling of a man ejaculating into her, the feelings of desirability that this gave her, was one of the most enjoyable aspects of se x for her. It was after taking this pill that she started to feel nauseous again.

She lay down on her bed and this helped a little, but not enough. She jumped up and returned quickly to the bathroom and knelt down in front of the toilet not for the first time that day. Nothing happened though and she was tempted to stick her fingers down her throat but she resisted. Instead, after a few more minutes knelt there, she returned to her bedroom and started to pace around, feeling again restless as she had in the morning. She was puzzled as to what was making her feel like this and then she remembered Peter's words, "Everything comes at a price Sarah." and then the thought occurred to her that she was addicted.

Although she did not realize it, it was nothing quite so dramatic; however, she was experiencing a severe cocaine comedown. The amount she had taken through the night and the morning was a lot. Being that she was also not used to it resulted in her having all the symptoms of a very heavy comedown. She tried lying down again and relaxing but as soon as she closed her eyes an image flashed in front of her, the same image that she had experienced in the morning, the image of the cocaine bag resting on the bedside table. Her eyes flashed open and this time she said out loud, 'Oh my God, I am addicted!'

Panicking she stood up and walked across and picked up her handbag off the floor where she had flung it before. She removed Peter's business card and her phone and she called him.

'Hello? Who's this?'

'Peter, it's me, Sarah. I'm so glad you picked up. Listen, I am worried. What is happening to me? Am I addicted? All I can keep on thinking about is cocaine! And I feel awful.'

'Oh, hi Sarah. You know something, now is not a good time. I am at my grandma's having something to eat and I pressed the loudspeaker button by accident.'

'Oh shit! I mean, shit, sorry.'

'Look, I will call you back soon. Bye.'

Sarah threw her phone onto her bed and then she flopped down onto it cursing herself. It was only a few minutes later that her phone rang.

'Jesus Christ Sarah! What are you doing?'

'I am so sorry Peter; I don't know what is going on. I don't feel at all good. I feel sick, I can't stay still and now to top it all I've got a headache developing!'

'I'm sorry Sarah but there is not a lot I can do. Remember what I said, everything comes at a price. Look, I can't really talk now; she has only gone to make a cup of tea. You are having a comedown. It is like a hangover after drinking. All you can do is roll with it and it will fade away. You are not addicted, no. What you are feeling is like hair of the dog, you know, when you sometimes might have a drink in the morning and it eases you hangover. It is the same thing you are feeling now. Just because sometimes you might have a drink to ease the hangover doesn't mean you are an alcoholic does it?'

'Tell me about it. I know all about alcohol. Thanks for telling me. I was panicking.'

'No reason to panic babe. It will fade away.'

'Okay. Thanks. Sorry if I got you in trouble with your gran.'

'No, it is okay. Don't think she understood what you were saying. She is coming back. What are you doing Wednesday night?'

'Nothing. Why?'

'Be at my house for eight. We will go out, that is if you still want to?'

'Yeah, of course I do.'

'Sorry, gotta go. See you Wednesday.'

Sarah did try to say goodbye but she was just talking to a silent line. Instead she threw her phone to the other side of her double bed and closed her eyes. 'I just want to not feel like this anymore!' she said out loud.

Slowly the night's activities and lack of sleep caught up with her and she fell asleep, thankfully for her, away from the effects of the comedown. What Peter had decided not to tell her was that the comedown was going to last for quite a few days. She would feel lethargic, unable to concentrate and maybe even depressed.

Thinking that she will feel ill for days, Peter thought, as he sipped his tea and pretended he was listening to his grandma, how he can carry on enjoying her body without having to pretend to like her, to pretend to date her. Then he considered how much she had taken and how long her come down was going to last. Thinking about Wednesday he realised that she would be aching for some more, for some relief from the comedown. So he decided to set an outrageous price when she asked for it and when she said that could not afford it he would say she could pay for it with sex. Peter thought he would get her more and more addicted and the only way she would be able to pay for it would be with sex. He called himself a genius, congratulated himself and then stated why had he not thought of this before?

*

'Don't bother!'

Michelle was stood in her drive-way as she listened to Sally end the conversation. She held her phone out in front of her and for a few moments stared at the screen.

'Shit! Shit, shit, shit!' She stamped her foot as she exclaimed out loud and she spoke another, harsher swear word. She found that a part of her was straining to call Sally back and she had to physically resist the motions her thumb wanted to make. Instead, she stamped her foot again, swore again, and continued along her drive-way to her front door, muttering to herself as she walked, 'I can't believe she saw us! I was going to tell her. Oh shitty, shitty and more shitty! She'll never speak to me again!' By this time she had reached her door and upon opening it she was greeted to a glorious sound.

Her mother's beautiful, operatic voice was drifting through the house and caressed Michelle's ears with its beautiful tones. She stood on the brink of the house waiting for her father's baritone voice to join in the song. When it did not, she knew that he must be out. He always sang when she sang, it was just the way it was, and always had been, ever since Michelle could remember.

Michelle was well aware how her parents had met and even if someone did n ot know the tale they only had to listen to them sing together to be able to guess the tale. They had met when they were both still young, eighteen her mother, twenty her father, both of them performing in a West-End musical. In her mother's own words it was literally love at first sight. This handsome, dashing gentleman sang with her in rehearsals and everybody who watched them that first day knew that they were destined to be together. Their voices softly caressed each other, discovering each other, then as they became bolder they crashed together until they mingled and intertwined and became as one. Michelle knew that after that dramatic meeting of two perfect voices, her father asked her mother out to dinner which of course she accepted. Since then, they had never been apart, both professionally and personally.

Now, for a moment or two longer, she listened to her mother sing in what Michelle could only presume was Italian, and then she advanced into the house to find her. She found her in the kitchen and Michelle was greeted with a sight that was again so typical of life in their house that it would have seemed unusual if her mother was not elbow deep in flour making something delicious no doubt for the dinner party they were hosting that night. Michelle let out a little sigh of contentment and her mother turned as she heard her daughter clip-clop across the tiled kitchen floor.

'Now then young lady, where have you been all night?'

'Sorry I didn't call. Were you worried?'

'A little. I was going to call you if you hadn't turned up soon.'

'Ah, okay, sorry.' Michelle reached past her mother, quickly grabbed a handful of raisins and popped them into her mouth before her mother could stop her.

She did, however, give her a look and say, 'Some things never change. Where were you last night?'

'At Clare's.'

'Deary me Michelle, you are perhaps the worst liar in the world. I can always tell and always have been able to tell. Now, tell me the truth, like you always have been able to.'

Michelle knew her mother was right. They had always had a completely open relationship and Michelle knew how lucky she was to have a parent to whom she could open her heart to.

'If you stayed at a boy's, then tell me you stayed at a boy's. I won't be mad. You are a woman now and you are just following your natural urges.'

'Mother, try not to sound like a presenter on a nature programme! Natural urges?!'

'Don't roll your eyes at me young lady!'

'Sorry. Oh mum, I met the most amazing guy! Well, I didn't meet him, I already knew him, but we have never really talked together properly. He is fantastic! We just talked and talked and talked all night. Then we went back his brother's apartment and he opened his heart to me about some really personal things, and, and he nearly cried which shows a sensitive side, then we kissed and then...'

'I think we can safely say you can stop there! I don't need the gory details thank you very much. I just hope you were safe.'

'Mother!'

'Don't roll your eyes! You look about fourteen when you roll your eyes!'

'Sorry. Anyway, I didn't sleep with him. Don't look at me like that! We didn't. He didn't want to.'

'Pardon? He didn't want to?! That's a first.'

'Yeah, he didn't. Like I said, we just talked and had a coffee. I must have fallen asleep because I woke up on the sofa this morning with a blanket over me and that was it. I left and came home.'

'Wow! He didn't want to? Sounds like a catch to me darling. I am happy for you.'

'He said it would only spoil things.'

'He sounds great. Are you going to see him again?'

'Yeah, I think so. He said he is going to call and we are going to go out.'

'Very good. You go and get a shower now and freshen up. I simply must finish this cake.'

'Dinner party tonight? Who is coming?'

'Who isn't? Everyone from the show. Why don't you come and not go to your granddad's? There will be lots of eligible young men here.'

'I think I am okay now mum. Anyway, you know I hate those young men. They are so pretentious and arrogant. Oh look at me! I'm an actor. I am so handsome and dashing. You want to sleep with me don't you? Erm, no, but I do really need a bucket to throw up into!'

'Michelle!'

'Sorry, but I think I will give it a miss. I am quite happy with Simon, fingers crossed anyway.'

'I hope it works out.'

'Me too.'

'Anyway, out, out, out! Kitchen is off limits for the next hour!'

'Okay. Can I get a cup of tea though?'

'Yes, quickly.'

Michelle made herself a cup of tea and then went upstairs to her bedroom. She placed the cup of tea on a table and flopped onto the bed on her back. Staring at the ceiling, Michelle thought about last night, her conversations with Sally and how on earth she was going to mend things between them. She knew that she should not have gone back to the apartment, but she also knew that she wanted the night to go on and on and that had meant going back there with him. Michelle's thoughts continued to race through her mind and eventually she realized that she was going nowhere. 'I smell!' she said out loud. 'Time for a shower.'

She sprang off her bed and switched on her music system. Although not quite a Bang and Olufsen like Sally's, it was still a good system. It was linked into her home cinema system that her father got her for her eighteenth birthday so she had surround sound when watching movies. It was also linked up to her Sky+ box that her parents had also paid to have installed in her room. Again, although no Sally's father, Michelle's parents were not exactly struggling. A large house in a nice area of the town, two BMWs on the drive and a holiday chalet in Switzerland all told Michelle that her parents could afford to fill her life with these little luxuries.

The music that blared out of the large speakers was a Red Hot Chili Peppers song and Michelle hummed away as she listened, occasionally joining in with the lyrics. She removed the cardigan she had forgotten to give back to her friend, her top and then bra. Even out of the constraints of her bra her breasts did not sag at all. They remained were they were, full, firm and very large. Then removing her skirt and knickers she stood in front of a full length mirror and examined her body.

First of all she started by looking at her breasts, admiring what she classed as her best part of her body, making sure they were in their usual place and not sagging. They were and they were not, so her gaze moved down to her stomach, waist, hips and thighs which all bulged a little. 'Need to lose weight! Get to the gym this week – no excuses!'

Her eyes then focused on the dark triangle in between her legs and she shuddered as she thought about the last man's hand that had explored her most sensitive and intimate parts. She knew that she should really report him, but she also knew that there would no point. 'Who are they going to listen to, a drunk me or a sober doorman?'

Still standing in front of the mirror she parted her legs a little and ran a finger over her pubic area making sure that he had not cut her. She also briefly slid a finger gently into herself and checked the entrance to her vagina for any sore spots and was pleased to discover none. While the tip of her finger was inside her, her thoughts switched unintentionally, but instantly, to Simon, his gorgeous face and fantastic body. Her finger slid just a little bit deeper into her and she found herself involuntary rubbing her clitoris with her thumb. After a couple of seconds she quickly drew her hand away and mentally scolded herself.

Then she spoke out loud, 'No! NO masturbation! No matter how you feel! It is more motivation to go out and find a boyfriend!' She stamped her foot again, a habit that she acquired from Sally and had never quite been able to get rid of, and walked a few steps over to her bedroom door.

Hanging on the back was a towelling dressing gown that she put on and fastened. Opening her door she walked lightly across to the bathroom, halting briefly to listen to her parent's voices, her father's voice now singing along with his wife's, as they both worked together in harmony to prepare for the party. Michelle sighed another sigh of contentment and she stepped into the bathroom, closing and locking the door behind her.

After showering Michelle returned to her room and by now the Chili Peppers album was about half way through. She instantly knew the song and picked up the lyrics. Still humming and singing along, she got dressed in to comfortable, cheap clothes from a local supermarket, no horse riding in Armani for Michelle, and slipped on a pair of trainers.

When she was ready she turned off the music and practically skipped across her room to where she had flung her handbag. She got her mobile and purse out of it and then practically skipped back across her room to the door. Then she made her way downstairs and followed the now talking voices and found her parents sitting in the large conservatory at the rear of the house, both of them drinking what appeared to be sherry.

'Hi dad.'

'Hello my darling. Come and give me a kiss!'

'Oh dad, alright then.' Michelle walked across the conservatory and pecked her father on the cheek. 'I'm going to stay at grandfather's tonight. Can I take the Z4?'

'Cheeky little monkey! You can if you tell me where you spent last night?'

Michelle glanced at her mother but she did not look like she was listening, she had her head buried in the Times, but Michelle knew she was listening. 'Did mum not tell you?'

'Nope.'

'I'm sure she will later! Pleeeaaassseee! Where are the keys?'

'Okaaaaaaayyyyyy then,' her father replied, mimicking his daughter's long drawn out plea. 'In my jacket pocket, in the utility room.'

'Ohhh, thank you! You are a great dad!' She gave him another peck on the cheek.

'Now, now, no need to twist my arm using those little tricks, I have already said yes! Be on your way. Tell dad that I will be there to see him tomorrow about oneish probably. You sure you don't mind staying there on a Saturday night? Not messing up your plans are we?'

'No, of course not. I enjoy it. We'll go for a walk with Jack and we'll stop at the Rose for a meal. We'll play pool and I will try to take his mind off things by being my charming witty self! I know how lonely he gets at this time of the year.'

'Good girl. Go on then before I find out where you spent last night and change my mind!'

'Okey dokey then. Bye. Bye mum.'

'Bye sweetheart. Be careful in that car. Don't be daft!'

'I know. I won't be! Bye.'

Michelle walked out of the conservatory, into the kitchen and then to the utility room. She rooted in her father's pockets for the key and then left the house.

'She seemed in a good mood. Where did she spend last night?'

'I think it best for her to be in the car and away before I tell you!'

Michelle's father simply rolled his eyes and said, 'In that case, I don't think I want to know!'

Chapter 16

'DO I LOOK LIKE A BITCH?!'

'Wh… wh… what?'

'Say what again! Go on, I dare you Tommy, say what again?'

'Wh… wh… what?'

There was a loud explosion right next to Peter's ear and he instantly thought he was going to die. Instead all he saw was a smoking gun move across his range of vision. He then twisted his head upwards and he saw the bullet hole in the ceiling.

'Yeah, look boyo. That's what a bullet hole looks like. Next time that hole will be in the back of your… FUCKING… HEAD if you say what again! Now, think carefully before you attempt to answer this next most simple of questions. Are you ready?' Peter managed to quickly nod his head. 'Do… I… look… like… a… bitch?'

'N… n… no, you don't.'

'Good, I didn't think I did. So, tell me Tommy, why you treating me like a bitch?'

'What?'

Peter did not see the fist. All he could presume once he gathered his senses was that the punch had come from behind him. After he scraped himself off the floor back into the kneeling position he had been told to assume and his vision cleared, he looked directly into the eyes of his questioner. They were blue, ice blue and cold with no trace of emotion. Contrasting the eyes were the flaming red hair and red goatee beard. Peter's eyes glanced down to the gun in the man's big hand and recognized it as a Luger pistol. The history of this pistol was well known to Peter but he really did not want to think about it at that time. All he definitely knew was that he was in big trouble but he did not know the reason why.

'I think the drugs he has been stealing from you have affected his common sense. Shall I hit him again to knock the sense back into him?'

'No, leave him for now. I just trust he won't say what again will you Tommy?'

'Who the fuck is Tommy? Is it any wonder that I am a bit confused?'

'Right now boyo, you is Tommy. I think I can call you whatever I want to can't I Tommy? Considering I am the one pointing the Luger at your right temple right now don't you think that gives me the right to call you whatever I want to Tommy?'

'Ye… ye… yes.'

'Good. Now that we have cleared that little bit of confusion up we go full circle and come back to the original problem that we have here, this problem being why you are insisting, insisting upon treating me like a bitch. So, go on then Tommy, why are you treating me like a bitch?'

'I'm, I'm sorry Reg…' Again Peter's face slammed into the carpet as another punch landed on the back of his head.

'Today, he's Mr. Maxwell. Savvy?'

'Wh… what the fuck is this? Pulp fucking Fiction?!'

'All I want, Tommy, is some respect to be shown to me today. You know what respect means don't you Tommy or you gonna say what again?'

'I… I know what respect means Mr. Maxwell.'

'Good Tommy. I'm pleased about that. Jesus Christ, one day, preferably before I'm drawing my pension, we'll finish this conversation!' This got a laugh from the surrounding people but certainly not one from Peter. 'So, once again I will ask a question and I expect a respectful answer Tommy, which does not involve the words Reg or what. Why are you treating me like a bitch?'

'I'm not Mr. Maxwell.'

'He's not apparently Kevin. He's not. So Tommy, why then does it feel like that I am being FUCKING SCREWED BY YOU?!'

At the end of this question Reg pressed the muzzle of the Luger firmly into Peter's temple. Peter, panicking now, screwed up his eyes knowing that his next few words would seal his fate one way or the other. 'P… p… please Mr. Maxwell. Just, just explain to me why you think that and I'm sure we can sort it out.'

'Mr. Luger here is itching to sort it out Tommy, itching. Not very often that he gets fired in anger, but believe me when I say Tommy he is very close to striking down upon thee with great vengeance and furious anger! You've been screwing me for months now Tommy. Scraping a little bit off the top here, and a little there, thinking to yourself that the thick Scottish bastard won't be any the wiser. But I know, Tommy, I know.'

'I swear I have not been on the take sir, I swear. Everything is straight, I ensure it is. I tell you how much I have sold and give you your cut every Saturday night just like tonight. Why is tonight any different from any other night? Why, tonight, do you think I am on the take? I swear sir, I'm not. Honestly sir, I'm not.'

At this Reg, and the others not in Peter's view, started to laugh quietly, then more loudly until there was general hilarity. Peter just knelt there and looked around and saw everybody in the room laughing. Reg was in fact laughing so hard now that he was wiping tears away from his eyes.

'Did you see his face? Did you? When the Luger went off?!' Everybody laughed.

'We will be talking about this for years!' commented someone else.

One of the men put on a feminine voice and mimicked Peter, '"Please sir, yes sir. Yes Mr. Maxwell! Please don't shoot me Mr. Maxwell. I love you Mr. Maxwell. Bend over Mr. Maxwell while I ram my head further up your arse Mr. Maxwell!"'

Another large bout of laughing followed this and eventually Reg waved them to stop while wiping his own tears away. 'Let this be a lesson to you Peter. I don't like takers and I don't like people with brown noses. You're getting a bit cocky and I don't like it. If you are with us for the long ride you treat me, and everyone else with respect. You're a good little salesman, but that is all you are. You've got a long way to go until you get to play with the big boys. Just you remember your position which for now is nothing, nothing within this organization. You got it boyo?'

'Yeah, I've got it Mr. Maxwell.'

*

He had left his grandma's house in good time to make his appointment with Reg his supplier. On the drive he was thinking about Sarah, about how good she had been last night, how willing she was to do anything he wanted, and how much he was looking forward to more of the same on Wednesday. His parents were away for two weeks and he fully intended to make the most of his time with her. Let her take lots of drugs and have lots of sex with her. Sounds like a perfect night in his eyes.

The drive took about half an hour to reach the out of town house. It was a large house, gated, high walled and secluded. He approached the gate slowly knowing that to drive quickly to these gates was a bad idea. The guard nodded at him as he opened the gates and Peter drove in, leaving his car in the corner of the front courtyard out of the way as he had been instructed to do. He walked down the side of the house to the kitchens where he knew he would be checked for weapons and like usual his knife that he had started to carry ever since he had started dealing was taken away from him.

As soon as Peter walked into the house he knew something was wrong. Nobody acknowledged him or said hello like they usually did. He was unusually searched again before being allowed to enter the room Reg was in which immediately set his alarm bells ringing.

When he did enter and stand in front of the chair where Reg was sitting, he was not acknowledged for a minute and when he opened his mouth to speak somebody behind him hit him across the back of his knees with what he could only presume was a bat of some kind, maybe baseball. Of course, he collapsed to his knees and it was then that Reg first asked Peter whether he thought he was a bitch.

*

'He says he's got it Kevin. Do you believe him?'

'I don't know Mr. Maxwell. Perhaps I should rough him up a bit just to make sure.'

'That's not necessary Kevin. I'm certain I've got it. Can we get down to business now or do you want to humiliate me some more?'

'Believe me when I say that this is nowhere near humiliation Peter. If I wanted to humiliate you I would have one of my Great Danes mount you!' This crudeness gained another laugh from the men.

'Either way, I would like to finish up here so I can into town and start making us both some more money.'

'Stand up, sit down there.'

Peter gingerly stood up, the pain across the back of his legs was severe, and he hobbled over to the indicated chair.

'Business is good for you, yes?'

'Yeah, getting better all the time Mr. Maxwell.'

'Good. Hear you getting quite a good reputation?'

'Yes, I think I am. Regular customers every night in the clubs, more and mor e non-regular and regular contacting me all the time.'

'Good. Anybody contacting you for a large deal?'

'No. Nothing. You told me not to draw attention to myself in that way.'

'Yes, I know I did. And I still want it to remain like that. As soon as someone does, and they will, what you going to do?'

'Exactly what you said Mr. Maxwell. Say I don't have the resources to do that.'

'And the reason why I don't want you to do this?'

'Because I need to remain small time for now. Two reasons. One, I am not ready to start hanging with the big boys yet. Two, I will get noticed and then get heat off the police. And if I get heat, you get heat.'

'Yes, we will. However, I think it is time for you to expand a little. Kevin, go and get Harry.'

'Harry? Who's Harry?'

'You'll see. Been following the football?'

'Yeah, a little bit.'

They chatted for a few minutes about the ongoing football season until Kevin returned. Peter looked over Kevin's shoulder expecting someone to be following him and it was only when Kevin placed a package on the table that something clicked in Peter's mind.

'Expecting a person?'

'Yeah, at first, but I think I know what Harry is now. I'm not too sure about this Reg. I mean, going from small time coke and E dealer to dealing the big-H is a big step as far as I am concerned.'

'It is in some ways, yes. However, I want you to come to the house and pick up a package like this on Saturday as usual.'

'And do what with it?'

'Sell it. It is up to you how, who or where you do it. I am leaving it in your hands.'

'I don't know. I might be standing on people's toes. I thought you didn't want me drawing attention to myself. In my eyes dealing heroin is drawing attention to myself.'

'What if I told you that more than one of your regulars contacts another one of my agents for a stash of heroin more than once a week?'

'It wouldn't surprise me. But I will standing on your, erm, agent's toes if I suddenly steal his customers.'

'I wouldn't worry about him. Turns out he has been treating me like a bitch.'

'Oh, right. And?'

'It is easier for me too. I would only deal with one agent but still be getting the same return.'

'So all I do is put the word out to my regulars and see if they would like to enhance their purchase?'

'You could even do incentives at first, buy one get one free for example. You know as well as I do that once they have that first hit they will be begging you for some more the next time they see you.'

'Right. I suppose it is a good idea. Two things though. First, I know nothing about heroin. I want to be taught about it without needing to experiment with it. Do they smoke it? Inject it? Snort it?'

'Not a problem. That would take two minutes to tell you that. Second?'

'I want more protection. If I am going to be dealing heroin at some point it could turn nasty.'

'You've got your knife.'

'Don't patronize me. You know exactly what I mean.'

'We thought you would say that. Kevin.'

Kevin placed a gun on top of the package and explained, 'This is a Colt Defender. It is a pistol, not a revolver or gun. Small so it is discrete, yet accurate and reliable. It is a stopper too. Damage is high. Be careful if you ever have to use it at close range. It will pass straight through somebody and keep on going.' He picked it back up. 'Load like this.' The ammunition cartridge dropped out of the handle and Kevin showed Peter how to load the cartridge. 'Slide it back in, safety here, pull the slider, point and pull the trigger. Bang, bang.'

'Right. Seems pretty straight forward.'

'It is.' Kevin placed the gun back on the table and picked up the package and opened it. 'This is white heroin…'

'It looks more brown to me?'

'It is really a tan colour but it is classed as white heroin.'

'Right. Okay.'

'There is five hundred grams here…'

'But I can cut it to make more right?'

'Yeah, you can. We leave that up to you. You want to get a good reputation at first so don't cut it too much. I would say two parts heroin, two parts crap.'

'About fifty percent pure then?'

'Yeah. Strong enough to give customers a nice good rush but not too strong so you start getting overdoses. But it will overdose a newbie if they take too much so warn them if you want to, but usually we wouldn't bother with warnings. It is not like we can put a government health warning on H is it?!'

Peter laughed. 'I suppose not. All sounds okay. What should I mix it with?'

'Anything you fucking want. Flour, washing powder, salt, sugar, ant powder, rat poison, anything at all.'

'Tell him how to take it.'

'Yeah, Reg. I was coming to that. If you want to you can keep some of the purer stuff aside and sell it for smoking. You can sell the less pure stuff too for snorting but they won't get as a good hit. Understand?'

'Yeah, all good. What about injecting?'

'Easy. Dilute the powder with water, heat up the mixture, suck it up with a syringe, place needle of syringe in vein and let the good times roll!'

'Come back to smoking. They put the powder into a cigarette or something?'

'I've never seen anyone do that but maybe someone does. No, you chase the dragon matie, chase the dragon.'

'That really doesn't mean much to me?'

'Jeez! How long you been dealing for us now? Six months and you don't know what chasing the dragon is?'

'No, sorry.'

'It is simply heating the powder, usually in foil, and the fumes are inhaled. Of course, not as good a rush as injecting but it's still nice. That is why the purer heroin should be used, so it gives a bigger rush to the chaser.'

'Okay. All sounds good.'

'There is five hundred grams of H there Peter. I'm trusting you. Don't treat me like a bitch or you could end up sleeping with the fishes.'

'I won't screw you Reg. I enjoy working for you and the extra income helps.'

'Good. You working the clubs tonight?'

'Yeah. Go to the usuals in the city. Oh, you had better let the bouncers who are under your control know that I will be armed from now on so they expect it.'

'Will do. You going to try and sell the H then?'

'No. Not tonight. I need to prepare it and myself. I haven't got time. I will still take the gun though, just in case.'

'Good. Make sure it is all okay and you feel okay before you start selling the H.'

'I will.'

'If you make me a good yield on this I will give you more next time and maybe give you a higher cut and or a bonus.'

'Alright Reg. I appreciate you trusting me.'

'No hard feelings about my little prank.'

'No Reg. None at all.'

'Right, be on your way then. See you next week.'

'Yeah, definitely.'

'Bye.'

'Bye.'

*

'No hard feelings! I'll give you no hard fucking feelings!' Peter was fuming as he drove away from the house and he was ranting as he drove. 'Making a fool out of me was the biggest mistake of your soon to be ended life Reg Maxwell. One fine day I am going to take that Luger and blow your fucking brains out! One fine, fine day!'

Chapter 17

After finishing her conversation with David, Sally made her way slowly back through the surrounding land, through the developing dusk, back to the outside wall of the estate. Storm let out a little whinny as she saw the gate knowing that they were nearly home. Sally dismounted and slid her hand into her jeans pocket and extracted her mobile. She quickly flicked to the Ss in her contacts and called the security centre that was based in a room in the mansion. She saw the camera slowly turn towards her and she gave a little wave and then she heard the gate unlock. Again the light on the camera flashed three times and they made their way through the gateway and she closed the gate behind them.

Sally remounted and dug her heels into Storm's flanks who instantly responded into a quick canter. They stuck to the paths this time, there was no leaping over fences, and they quickly made their way back to the stables. Sally said a quick thank you to the groom who led Storm away and then she quickly strode over to the Land Rover that had been sent by security to collect her. While she was being driven back to the mansion one of the cooks called her and asked whether she would be eating at home tonight. Sally answered with a positive and asked the cook to prepare and bring a Chicken Madras to her room in an hour. It only took a few moments to reach the mansion and Sally was greeted formally by Alfred and a maid at the front entrance. 'Did you have a pleasant ride ma'am?'

'Yes Alfred, it was good.'

'Any plans for this evening?'

'No, none. I think I am just going to watch a film in my room and have an early night.'

Sally entered the main entrance hall and walked over the exquisite marble floor passing between pillars of marble. In front of her the hall suddenly expanded into a large circle and curling upwards and round the wall were two elaborate staircases. Directly at the top of the circle there was also an elevator which was installed when Sally's mother's health deteriorated to the point that she could not negotiate stairs anymore. She did not take the elevator and Sally did not think that anyone had ever used the conveyance since the horrible morning when her mother had arrived back from the hospice to die in her own home. At the foot of each staircase there were two immense portraits of a stunningly beautiful woman and as Sally passed the portrait on the left her eyes met the eyes of her mother as usual. She held her gaze for a moment before passing onwards. Alfred and the maid had followed Sally at a polite distance behind her and only when Sally had completed the ritual of gazing at her beautiful mother did Alfred continue the conversation. 'Certainly ma'am. In that case, after your meal has been prepared may I dismiss the staff for the evening? I, of course, will remain on call.'

'Well, my father will need the staff tonight so no.'

'Sorry ma'am, it looks like your father will not make it back to the estate tonight. He managed to call me before and stated that today's business is dragging its heels somewhat and left the decisions of the house to you, ma'am.'

'Okay Alfred. In that case after I have eaten then the staff may be dismissed. I don't need them tonight. Ask one of the maids to fill the Jacuzzi bath in the Go ld Bathroom. I'll be there in ten minutes. Ask her also to place a bottle of champagne in there, a Bollinger, and also a fruit selection.'

'Certainly. Will there be anything else?'

'Yes, my Mini is still at the garage being fixed. I'll need a lift there at ten thirty in the morning.'

'Fine. I will ensure the Rolls-Royce is available.' By now they had finished the ascent of the stairs and were half way along the ornate upper hallway walking towards Sally's bedroom. Sally stopped walking and turned to face Alfred. The maid had subtly left to prepare the bath. 'No! I mean, no, not the Rolls. I'll need you to take me in something a little more subtle, Alfred. Suggest something that states well off, but not daughter of a billionaire well off?'

'Erm, well, in that case how about your father's Mini Cooper?' The Mini was one of her father's toys and he sometimes took it out on a Sunday for a little bit of fun with Ray, a security guard and a doctor should the worst happen, following him.

'He might be using it tomorrow.'

'From the sounds of it Sally I doubt it. I don't think he will be back by tomorrow morning if at all tomorrow.'

'Okay. The Mini will be fine.' Sally started walking again and reached the door to her room. 'I'll be leaving at ten thirty sharp.'

'Will you require breakfast?'

'Yes, of course. In the breakfast room. Maybe my father will put in an appearance.'

'Maybe, but I wouldn't get your hopes up Sally.'

'Yeah, I know.'

'Is everything okay dear? You still seem down?'

'No, I am okay now. The Mini has been fixed and Storm got rid of my worries like usual.'

'Did you crash it?'

'The Mini or Storm?'

Alfred laughed a little. 'The Mini of course.'

'Something like that Alfred. Please don't tell my father. He'll have Ray driving me everywhere and security too. You know how I hate that. Please.'

'I won't dear. Your secret is safe with me.'

'Thank you.'

'I probably won't see you again tonight but don't hesitate to call me if you require anything.'

'I won't hesitate but you should be okay because I don't think I will need you again tonight.'

'That is fine. Enjoy your bath and film Sally. I will retire to my quarters now.'

'Okay Alfred. Sleep well.'

'You too. Good-night.'

Alfred gave a shallow bow, turned and walked quickly yet silently down the hallway towards the servants' quarters. Sally turned, opened her door and entered her room.

On her large double bed were the bags from her shopping trip and there were so many that they overflowed onto the floor. She took her purse and mobile out of her pocket and flung them on top of a bag and then quickly removed all her clothes. Flinging these into a corner of her room, she knew that a maid would come in a remove them while she was bathing, and then she pulled on a silk gown.

Walking over to a set of double doors she slid them open and stepped into the huge walk-in wardrobe, which was the size of a large bedroom in a normal house, and switched the light on. She glanced at her enormous collection of clothes that were all separated into brands and these brands were then separated into different styles of clothes.

There were Dolce and Gabbana casual clothes and striking ball gowns from their most recent collections. Versace was also present, along with Gucci, Prada, Jimmy Choo and sportier, casual brands such as Reebok and adidas. She walked past them, threading through the racks of clothes, until she reached the far wall into which another door was fitted. She opened this and turned on another light that illuminated another smaller, yet still quite large room and each wall was fitted with shelf upon shelf of shoes.

Again, the brands present here were the best and the shoes the most recent, separated again into their individual brands. She knew that she had purchased another five pairs of shoes, three from Prada, one from Gucci and a new pair of trainers from Nike. She knew instantly where these shoes where on the shelves and she randomly selected the equivalent number of shoes from each collection. Two pairs of the Prada she selected had never been worn, the other pair worn once to a ball. The Gucci and Nike had also never been worn. She carried the five pairs of shoes awkwardly to her room and dumped them on the floor. She had planned to give them to Michelle, who knew very well that the best part of her wardrobe were the shoes given to her by her best friend, but now Sally did not know. 'Maybe give them to charity,' she said out loud, but she knew in her heart that they would be going to Michelle eventually.

Sally spotted the bags containing the new shoes and took them out of the bags. She carried them through the racks of clothing and placed them into the recently vacated spaces on the shelves. She took a step back and decided that one of the new pairs of Prada would look better next to another pair so she switched them round. Then she realized that it still did not look right so she spent the next five minutes shifting the Pradas around the shelves until she was satisfied that the footwear was in the best position to be pleasing to the eye.

Absentmindedly forgetting that she was due to take her bath, she walked back into her bedroom and emptied the bags onto her bed. She instantly spotted a Gucci dress that she had bought and she picked it up and held it against her. She walked over to the full length mirror and studied the dress. She did not try it on but instead decided that she did not like it and flung the five hundred pound dress onto the floor with the shoes. Sally repeated this with all her new clothes and eventually she had around five thousand pounds worth of clothes in the rejects pile and about the same amount in the accepted pile.

Quickly scooping up the pile of clothes she had decided to keep she walked back into the wardrobe and hung the clothes in their relevant sections. While she was doing this she rejected another two items and when returning to her bedroom she dropped them onto the reject pile. Absentmindedly again, she left her bedroom and strolled down the hall to the Gold Bathroom. She did not even think that when she got back to her bedroom later that the rejected pile of clothes would be gone and she would not even notice or think about them when she returned to her room. She had no idea where the clothes went to and she did not waste time thinking about it. Did the maid take them for herself or did she take them to a charity shop? Sally did not know nor did she care.

*

In fact her father took control of them. The maid, who looked after the cleaning of Sally's room and therefore her clothes, had once taken a bundle of them to her father as she was bewildered as to what to do with them. She explained to him that ever since she started going on shopping sprees the rejected pile of clothing was a common occurrence. She stated to him that the clothes had never been worn and that they all still had the labelling attached to them. He was equally bewildered as to what to do with them. He took the clothes off her and looked at the labels, some of which had the price written on them. One in particularly caught his eye when he noticed that the label stated it was a two thousand pound dress with real diamond features. He let a whistling sound out of his mouth. 'How often does this happen?'

'Every time she returns from shopping sir. Every time.'

'Right. And she has been going on these shopping sprees now for the last eighteen months or so?'

'Sorry sir, excuse my bluntness, but ever since you have gave her your bank cards.'

'Hmmm, right. So begs the questions, what have you been doing with them for the last eighteen months?'

'They are all stored in numerous wardrobes in the numerous bedrooms sir, because I didn't want to trouble you. But after I noticed the label on that two thousand pound one I thought that it was my responsibility to bring it to your attention.'

'Yes, quite. I'm glad you did. How many clothes are we talking about here?'

'I don't know sir. A lot. Must be at least five hundred individual items. Maybe more.'

'Crikey! I know she spends a lot, and I don't mind, hell the money is just sitting there doing nothing and if it gives her pleasure then so be it, but really, that is a horrendous amount of money to be just throwing away.'

'Yes sir.'

'Right, what I want you to do if go round and collect them all and put them in one place.'

'Okay.'

'Then I will decide what to do.'

'I think charities would appreciate them sir.'

'Yes, that was my first thought. I have charity functions approaching too. I m ay raffle them off. Leave it with me and thank you for bringing it to my attention.'

That is exactly what Mr. Gallagher did. In fact Sally won one of her own dresses back and she obviously had no idea that she once owned the dress. She wore it the next day to a garden party. Mr. Gallagher of course found this very amusing, as did the maid.

*

Sally strode into the bathroom nearly an hour later than the time she stated earlier with Alfred. The bath though was still steaming as the maid had returned to the bathroom every five minutes to apply more hot water knowing that Sally would be late.

The Gold Bathroom was indeed thoroughly gold. The walls were decorated in gold paint; the marble floor was inlaid with strips of twenty-four carat gold. The bath and faucets were gold plated and the chain attached to the plug was a twenty-four carat gold necklace that would have looked fine draped around Sally's neck at a ball. Most people found the room garish and could not stand to be present in it for more than a few moments. Indeed, her father hated the room and was close to stripping it out until Sally asked him not to.

For some reason Sally found the room relaxing. She thought the room was the epitome of opulence and she loved watching people's faces that were shown round the mansion when they were informed that the gold in the bathroom was all real. Sally approached the bath and dipped a finger into it. It was at a perfect temperature for her. Then she placed a hand against the bottle of Bollinger that was placed in an ice bucket that was built into bath. Again, it was at the perfect temperature and Sally made a mental note to congratulate the maid who for once had got it right. On the other side of the bath was a plate of sliced exotic fruits such as guava, papaya and mangoes. She undid her robe and stepped over the side of the bath and slid down into the water. The bath was huge. It could easily accommodate four people in sitting positions and two easily when lying down. Therefore Sally was able to spread herself out and soak all the mental and physical aches of the last twenty-four hours out of her body.

Only after fifteen minutes of soaking did she slide her body up into a sitting position and press a few buttons on a control panel fitted into the rim of the bath. After a few moments and some noise from under the bath, bubbles slowly began to appear from the jets fitted into the bath. Soon these bubbles turned into streams of water and eventually the bath turned into a bubbling cauldron as the jets created a perfect Jacuzzi effect. Sally placed some sections of the fruit onto a smaller plate and then poured herself a large glass of champagne. She reclined so her back was resting on the side of the bath and she wiggled her bottom and body until a powerful jet was firing directly onto her lower back. Placing the glass in a holder that was again built into the rim of the bath, she placed a piece of passion fruit in her mouth and released from her lips a little sigh of contentment. Slowly she made her way through the fruit savouring the delicious tastes, occasionally taking sips of the Bollinger.

After another fifteen minutes there was a discreet knock on the door and Sally told the person to enter. The maid though did not enter fully but instead just placed her head around the door and asked Sally whether everything was okay. Sally answered with an affirmative and told the maid that she would like to eat in ten minutes and for the meal to be taken to her room. The maid answered with another affirmative and quietly closed the door. Sally was glad the maid had interrupted her for she was falling asleep. Probably the maid was aware that this was probable and that was why she had given Sally half an hour before seeing if she was still awake. She reluctantly turned off the Jacuzzi and slowly raised herself to standing. She waded across the bath to one side of it and turned on the gold shower taps that were fitted into the wall. The water came out cold at first so she stood at a distance until it heated up. Then she placed herself under the stream of water and reached for a bottle of shower gel that was discreetly placed. Sally lathered herself thoroughly with the gel and rinsed her perfect body free of the suds. While rinsing she studied her body in the full length gold framed mirror that was opposite the shower.

She turned round at first and studied the back of her legs checking her calves and then thighs, tensing them up making sure they were still muscular. She checked her bottom too, from the side, to make sure it was not sagging and she was pleased to see it was still perfectly round and very firm. Then she turned again and checked her stomach and it was pleased to see that it was still perfectly flat and when she tensed she could see the outline of her stomach muscles. Happy with what she saw, she turned off the shower's taps and stepped out of the bath. She took one of the thick, luxurious towels off the heated rail and dried her body then threw the towel on the floor when done and did not bother emptying the bath: the maid would return to empty and clean the bath and room. With the robe back on she opened the door using the solid gold handle and walked slowly along the marble floor. Bizarrely she noticed that she was drifting along the hallway, not quite walking in a straight line. 'I think I am a little tiddly!' she said out loud and then she caught a glance of her face in a mirror and noticed how flushed her cheeks were. 'I am a little tiddly!'

By now she had reached her bedroom door which she flung open to be greeted with the delightful smell of a chicken Madras that had been placed on her bedroom table. Upon smelling and seeing the food Sally realized how hungry she was so she promptly sat down at the table and quickly started to eat the delicious and spicy curry. With the curry were two types of naan bread, two poppadums and a large portion of pilau rice. Halfway through this mountain of food she started to get full so she had a little break during which she turned on her television and flicked through the channels until she found something remotely watchable.

It was a programme that made a normal person into a manufactured pop star and this seemed to be the preliminary heats. At first Sally, who continued to slowly make her way through the food, could not believe the rubbish she was watching. Some bloke had just taken to the stage with four judges watching and a large audience too and literally screamed at them instead of singing to them, and then had the nerve to change this scream into a rant when he was rejected. Next to see the judges was a young pretty girl who was practically shaking with nerves.

Sally however quickly realized that this pretty girl could sing. One of the judges rejected the girl but the other three, another man and two women, accepted her. The other man sounded Irish and the women seemed nice enough. Then the next person came onto the stage.

The first thing Sally noticed about her was her size. She was a bit on the large side Sally thought, but, as could be evidenced by the previous contestant, first impressions do not count; she might be able to sing. After some initial opening questions one of the lady judges asked her to start. Bizarrely the participant turned her back on the judges and then bent over so all they would be able to see would be an enormously large butt. Poking over the top of her tight spray on jeans was a purple thong and at this sight Sally burst out laughing.

'Can I get a little spanky, spanky!' And on each spanky the girl spanked her own bottom.

Sally stopped laughing and instead just sat there bewildered. She presumed that this was some kind of joke until the camera changed and showed the horrified faces of the judges. One of the female judges was doubled up with laughter and the Irish judge was trying desperately to contain his mirth.

Sally realized that this was in fact meant to be a serious audition and she started laughing too. And it got worse because that was all the poor girl did. She remained bent over spanking her own butt repeating those words for another thirty seconds although to the judges it must have felt like an eternity.

Eventually one of the judges asked her to stop. 'Well, that was a unique performance.'

'Thank you.'

'No, you misunderstand me, unique for totally the wrong reasons. Did you seriously, seriously expect when you woke this morning that if you did a song, sorry, that is disrespectful to songs, a routine like this that we would put you through to the next round?!'

'I was hoping that it was what you were looking for, uniqueness?'

The Irish one took over. 'The problem is you didn't sing. You just spanked your own bottom!'

At those words the woman, who had managed to control herself, burst out laughing again. The other female judge asked the woman whether she wanted to put her through to the next round and between bouts of laughter she managed to state a negative and then all the judges responded in the negative.

For one horrible moment it looked like the girl was going to question their decisions but instead she just said, 'Thank you for seeing me,' and left quietly and quickly.

All through this Sally had been laughing loudly and by the time the commercial break had finished she had eaten her fill and settled herself on her bed still watching the programme. Slowly but surely the previous night and the early morning caught up with her and her eyes got heavier and heavier until they slowly closed.

An hour or so later there was a discreet knock on the door and her father entered the room when there was no answer. He approached the bed and saw her daughter fast asleep, her black hair cascading over the pillow. A lump caught in his throat as he saw the image of his wife present in his beautiful daughter. He walked to the side of the bed so he was directly over her and placed a delicate kiss on her forehead. She was lying on the thick duvet so he pulled each half over her so she was wrapped up in the blanket and then walked over and turned off the television. Quietly he walked back to the side of the bed and kissed her forehead again. He studied her for a few moments and then walked back to the bedroom door and turned off the light. Opening it quietly he left the room casting a glance over to his beautiful daughter's sleeping body and closed the door leaving her to her dreams.

Chapter 18

The Z4's rear end hung out around the sharp left hand bend and for a second, to the casual observer, it looked like the car was on the brink of spinning out of control. Instead, the reactions and skill of the driver snapped the BMW back into line with a touch of corrective steering. The power of the car forced it to over-steer, so even though the car was still turning left, the wheels were briefly pointing to the right. In a split second the driver straightened the car onto a short stretch of road and then reached a sharp right hand bend and the process was repeated.

The rear wheels of the car were smoking and screeching and no doubt if Michelle's parents could have seen what she was doing they would have both collapsed in a heap of severe shock. Now she reached a longer straight stretch of road and she floored the accelerator enjoying the feeling of the g-forces pressing her body into the seat. She knew the country lane like the back of her hand and she knew the braking point for the upcoming hair-pin bend. Pressing the brake pedal she quickly changed down through the gears, leaving the revs high so the engine was screaming every time she changed gear. With a touch of the brakes her left hand left the steering wheel and applied the handbrake. She slid gracefully around the corner, again applying corrective steering when necessary and then floored the accelerator at just the right moment to maintain the optimum level of momentum. The car quickly reached seventy miles an hour and twenty yards before a thirty mile an hour restriction she firmly pressed the brake pedal and dropped the speed of the car to the appropriate speed. After another half a mile she took a right and a quick left turn and then stopped the car after a few hundred yards outside her grandfather's house. She quickly checked her hair and then stepped out of the convertible roadster. Michelle walked up the garden path and rapped on her grandfather's door, leaving the Z4 to cool down after its speedy trip through the country.

*

The fact that Michelle was able to drive in the manner she did was down to having the daughter of a billionaire as a best friend and the billionaire having an ex-professional racing driver as a chauffeur.

Just over a year ago when they had both just acquired their provisional driver's licenses, Mr. Gallagher arranged for Silverstone Racing Circuit to be put at his disposal for a few days. It was his plan to have Ray teach Sally evasive driving tactics for her own security should she ever require them. Sally reluctantly agreed to this, she thought it was such a male thing to be doing, if she could take her best friend along with her. It turned out to be "one of the funnest times of their lives".

For three days, under the direct supervision of Ray, all they did was throw expensive cars around the Silverstone Circuit using both the full Grand Prix circuit and the smaller, tighter inner circuits. First of all they started in brand new Mini Coopers and then they were upgraded to Subaru World Rally cars that were just about road legal. Then to master the art of sliding round corners using vast amou nts of over-steer, Ray introduced them to the perilous TVR Tuscan that was vastly overpowered for the handling capabilities of the car. The girls spent most of that afternoon spinning around in circles after trying to over-steer round some tight hair-pin bends.

However, under the expert tuition of their teacher they mastered the TVRs and were then upgraded the next day to two supercars from Sally's father's collection. The first was a Ferrari Enzo, price approximately four hundred and fifty thousand pounds. The second was the fastest, most expensive road car ever built, the Bugatti Veyron, priced at around a million pounds.

Sally and Michelle spent the rest of the third day flying around Silverstone in these two brand new supercars, honing and mastering their newly developed skills. At the end of the day Ray announced that they were now competent and then told them that Sally's father wanted them to spend a day with him every six months to keep their skills finely tuned.

*

Michelle thought of these three days as she waited for her grandfather to open his door. She knew the next day was approaching fast and it was a highlight of each half year for her. Sally could, although she never did, go to her daddy's garage and use a million pounds sports car whenever she felt like it, whereas Michelle had to wait for the day to come round when the supercars arrived in a truck at a racing circuit somewhere in the country. Sally had told her during a drunken moment a few months ago that she had been sworn to secrecy by her father with the fact that he was in negotiations to let his daughter and her best friend go for a lap each in a sports car around the streets of Monaco on the weekend when the Monaco Grand Prix was due to take place. Obviously the negotiations had failed because it never happened; even Sally's daddy had a limit to what his money could buy. Her reverie was interrupted with a rattle on the other side of the door as her grandfather removed the security chain and opened the door.

'Grandfather! How are you?' Michelle flung herself into the old man's embrace and gave him a big long kiss on his left cheek.

'Well, I was feeling a bit down but now I feel top of the world! How are you precious?'

'I'm fine. Glad to see you.' A small dog approached slowly down the hallway to see who the visitor was. Upon seeing it was Michelle its tail started to vigorously wag and he leaped up on to his back legs and pawed at her legs. 'And here's Jack! Hallo boy!' Michelle scooped up the small King Charles spaniel into her arms and received lots of licks on her face for her troubles. 'Now, now! You are drowning me boy! Here you go, down you go.' She placed the old dog gently onto his feet and linked an arm with her grandfather. 'Now then Arthur, what treats have you got planned for a young lady who is just itching for a good time?'

'You missed out the word beautiful!'

'Oh grandfather, why can't all men be as charming as you?!'

'You'll find someone as good as me one day.'

'I don't think I will!'

'No, neither do I actually. I'm one of a kind!'

Michelle laughed kindly at her grandfather's joke and they made their way along the hall after closing the front door. 'Well, I was hoping we could do what we usually do. Take Jack out for a w-a-l-k to the Rose, have a meal and play some bar games. If I remember rightly I owe you a drubbing at pool!'

Arthur spelled out the word walk because even in his advanced years the word when spoken in full still sent the spaniel crackers. And Michelle let a smile flash across her face at his mention of pool.

She knew he was a pool-shark. However, since they had started playing he had only ever won a handful of games and these usually occurred when Michelle pocketed the black ball out of sequence. For about six months she just simply thought he was not very good. He kept on losing and no matter how hard she tried to throw the game she always ended up winning. Her thoughts about him quickly changed after one night.

*

The Rose and Crown was a quiet local pub, regulars in every night, same people drinking the same drinks. One night though there was a group of rowdy young men present who had obviously mistaken the pub for a noisy high street bar. Her grandfather and she had just started their second game of pool when the men crowded themselves around the table. When they saw how poorly the players were they became even cockier. Every time Michelle bent over to take a shot there was a chorus of wolf-whistles and they gave her grandfather advice every time he approached the table. Halfway through the game one of the men placed money on the table and stated one of them would play the old man for the table. Arthur jokingly accepted the challenge.

The game went badly. Her grandfather missed the easiest of shots and at some points appeared to be shaking. He got badly beaten and then bizarrely asked the young man whether he wanted to make it interesting. Arthur produced a twenty pound note and the young man could not accept the bet quickly enough. He placed a twenty pound note on top of Arthur's and re-racked the balls.

'Grandfather. You don't have to do this. It is okay. Let them play if they want to.'

'Come on now darling. It is not as if he is playing for pride. He lost all his pride during the last game!' Michelle's cheeks flushed and her grandfather looked her straight in the eyes and winked.

The game went almost as badly as the first. Arthur was getting badly beaten and he had seven balls left whereas the young man only had the eight-ball to pot to win. At first Michelle did not notice. It was only when Arthur approached the table after the man had snookered himself on the black and then fouled that Michelle realized something; her grandfather had played the first and much of this frame with his right hand. He now lined up with the cue firmly in his left and Arthur cleared up without moving. Every shot he took the cue ball ended up in exactly the same place it had started from. Michelle stood there gob-smacked as did the young men. She had heard that some professional snooker players sometimes play shots so they do not have to move around the table but not her grandfather!

When the black was sunk by Arthur he reached over and took the two twenties and gave them to Michelle. He then turned to the men and said, 'Let that be a lesson to all of you. First impressions don't count for much and you should always know your opponent before accepting bets. None of you noticed I played with my left hand when playing with my grand-daughter, but with my right during our first game. Oh, and believe me when I say that if I had wanted to I could have beaten you quite as easily with my right hand. I believe that means the table is now ours to continue playing on?' The men sheepishly nodded. 'Good. And, if you don't mind, I would like to play with my grand-daughter without the lewd comments.' The men, humbled, nodded again.

Michelle silently re-racked the balls and the men quickly finished their drinks and left the pub. She broke off and one of the balls ended up hovering over one of the pockets. Somehow her grandfather managed to miss the ball and sink the white ball into the pocket.

'Oh well, thought it was too good to last - back to usual!'

Michelle did not say a word.

*

Her grandfather sat rocking in his rocking chair with Michelle opposite him. Jack was curled up in a ball at his feet staring at Michelle as she told her grandfather what she had been doing that week. She missed out the previous nights antics but let him know that she had a new boyfriend. Michelle knew that he would not like the thought of his precious grand-daughter spending the night at a man's house so she left it there but he would like the thought of her having a boyfriend. He asked his name and she told him Simon, and after he had told her about his trials in getting the garden prepared for winter which she politely listened to, making comments to show her genuine interest.

After this conversation he stood up and announced that it was time to go to the Rose. Michelle nodded in agreement and went and got Jack's lead from the cupboard under the stairs. When Arthur had stood up so had Jack and it looked like he was contemplating leaping onto the rocking chair until he saw the lead in Michelle's hand.

Instead of leaping onto the rocking chair though he leapt up into the air and started yapping and woofing and running in circles throwing in the occasional leap for good measure. This continued until Michelle approached the dog, dropped onto one knee and held out her hand. Arthur had spent a considerable amount of time training his pet and Jack knew that these actions meant calm down, we'll put your lead on then we can go, so he trotted across to Michelle and sat down. She attached his lead to his collar and then stood to leave. Her grandfather meanwhile had been to get a thick coat, scarf and flat-cap and they made their way back down the hall and left with Arthur locking the door behind them.

On the walk to the pub they went a longer way to give Jack a good run. They walked across big open fields, Michelle always linking arms with her grandfather, Jack sprinting off into the distance and then sprinting back to stop at the their f eet for a pat and a stroke and then he was off again. It took them about forty-five minutes to walk to the pub were upon entering Arthur and Michelle were greeted by near enough everyone present. They sat down at a table that was free and instantly people approached asking Arthur and Michelle about their lives. Arthur had quite a reputation for being green-fingered and some of the questions focused on his skills in the gardens. Some of the people who did not come into the Rose very often asked specifically whether he was okay and let them both know that their thoughts were with Arthur and Michelle.

About three months ago Michelle's grandmother had passed away after a sudden illness and she now made a point of spending a lot of time with her grandfather and especially at this time of the year since their emerald wedding anniversary was rapidly approaching. Michelle knew that her parents had planned a huge surprise party and had a booked them a cruise as a present. Now, unknowingly to Arthur, all this had been cancelled and instead Michelle concentrated on making him as happy as possible during their time together. Arthur acknowledged the well wishers with kind words from himself and soon the people stopped approaching the table and they were left to order their food.

They quickly ate their respective meals, hungry after the refreshing walk, both of them occasionally dropping titbits for Jack. After their meal they had drinks and soon Michelle suggested that they move over to the pool table. Their games went as they usually did, Michelle playing her usual game and suspecting that Arthur was not really trying. She had tried a few weekends after the pool incident to bring up his play that night but she did not get anywhere.

He dodged her questions with answers such as, 'Oh, I just got lucky,' or 'Well look at me now, I can't pot anything!' Michelle quickly gave up; however, she did ask her father.

*

'Old Sharky put in an appearance did he?! Not very often he comes out of whatever closet dad keeps him hidden in!'

'Sharky?'

'Yeah, Sharky. You ask old Bill Rogers about him. You know him from the Rose right?'

'Yeah dad, I do. But he is hardly ever there anymore. Can you tell me?'

'I suppose. Why didn't grandfather tell you?'

'I don't know. He wouldn't answer the questions. He kept on saying it was luck.'

'Luck my..!' Her dad did not finish the curse and instead took a deep breath and told Michelle a story. 'You know where your grandfather spent nineteen fifty to nineteen fifty three don't you?'

'Yes, of course. He was a Sergeant in the British Army. He was in Korea during that time.'

'Exactly. Well, he was already good at pool, but as his story goes he met an American woman who took a bit of a fancy to Arthur.'

'But he would have been married to grandmother by then?'

'He insists no hanky-panky went on but apparently they did spend a lot of time together. Even when they were based at different parts of the Korean peninsula they still communicated a lot. He doesn't know it, but I saw letters in the attic one time when I was young. I don't know if he kept them hidden from my mum for all those years or whether she knew. Either way, some of them are quite, well, luvvy-duvvy shall we say.'

'Right, okay, I can understand him wanting company. He was away for three years; I hope he didn't hurt grandmother though.'

'Who knows? Only he and she know the answer to that.'

'What does all this have to do with pool though?'

'Well, it turns out that this lady was the daughter of a famous American pool champion and she taught grandfather to become even better. In the time they spent together all they seemed to have done is play pool! When he was convalescing after his injury, according to the letters written after he returned to duty, the old fox managed to get himself put into a hospital where a certain young woman was stationed very nearby. It seems that once he was back on his feet they spent every passing moment during his six month convalescent period playing pool!'

'Wow! Okay. That explains why he is so good!'

'No, he is better than good. He made a fortune out of it in the sixties and seventies. You know he and mum were stationed all round the world and that I was actually born in Hong Kong of course?' He did not wait for an answer to the rhetorical question. 'All through those decades he used to hustle the Americans who were stationed with or near him. You know what Americans are like; big, boastful, and loud, think they're untouchable and unbeatable at everything they touch? Well grandfather did touch them and did beat them! He hustled his way around the world, from army base to army base, bar to bar in city to city getting him and mum a nice little nest egg!'

'Wow! Great story!'

'Yeah, it is. Bill would be able to tell you better than me. He spent a lot of time with grandfather during those years in the Army. There was a rumour that old Sharky was not beaten, when he was playing seriously that is, and not pretending he was rubbish for the hustle, for something ridiculous like twenty years until he met a certain woman at an army base on Guam.'

'Even bigger wow! He met her again after all those years?!'

'Yep. Apparently they played non-stop for about ten hours and let's just say she put a big hole in his nest egg.'

'Oh dear!'

'Yeah, and ever since that day as far as I know he has never betted on a game until that night with you!'

'Excellent! I love listening to tales like that about our family! That is amazing. What a life he must have led!'

'One thing that can be said about my dad, he has lived life to the full, definitely. One thing though, don't mention this to him. I do believe that there were indiscretions carried out with the American woman and I still think to this day that he feels terrible about it.'

'Okay, I definitely won't.' And Michelle never did.

*

After an hour of playing pool Arthur declared like he usually did that Michelle was now the world champion of pool and that he was giving up for the night. Usually they would sit back down at a table and have another drink before leaving but her grandfather stated that he was tired after spending so long in the garden earlier that day and asked to leave straight away. Michelle of course agreed but not without showing concern. In all the time they had been having these nights together their routine was very rarely broken and only if circumstances were to tally beyond their control, for example, a fire once broke out in one of the toilets. Never before had they ever left early because he was tired.

On the walk home through the streets this time avoiding the dark fields, the conversation was sparse. Her grandfather had been a Sergeant in the army for many years and he had always stood ramrod straight. Michelle could not help noticing as they walked that he now seemed to be stooping a little. With the early departure from the Rose and now this stooping it started to concern her a lot.

Then a little alarm went off in her head and a piece of information forced itself from her subconscious to the conscious part of her mind. She remembered that he is nearly eighty and he had been on the go non-stop today and she thought that she would be stooping a little bit too if she was him.

These thoughts eased her concern a little and Michelle was certain that tomorrow he would be back to usual. The stoop slowly started to straighten as they reached the end of his street and was totally gone by the time they reached his garden gate. Michelle looked down at Jack and even the tireless spaniel's head was drooping with fatigue. She took in a big breath of the crisp cool night air and said, 'One of the reasons I love coming out here into the country, the air is so, so fresh.'

'One of the reasons I am still so fit and healthy the air out here. Better than living in the town definitely.'

'Yeah, it is grandfather. Do you feel okay now? You seemed tired before?'

Arthur was getting his keys out of his pocket as he answered, 'Yes, of course I do. Don't worry about me young lady. Still plenty of time for me to work out how on earth you are managing to beat me at pool so easily!'

The door was unlocked by Arthur and he swung it open and they both stepped into the hall. 'I think we both know that that isn't strictly true. That night with those men. You didn't have to move when you were taking your shots. How did you do that?'

Arthur let out a chuckle as he was removing her outer garments, 'Told you: luck!'

'Rubbish grandfather and you know it!'

'I honestly don't know Michelle.'

'I want you to teach me.'

Arthur led her down the hall into the kitchen where he switched on the kettle and started to prepare some hot-chocolate for them both. 'I've got nothing to teach.'

'Ohhh grandfather!' Michelle stamped her foot. 'Pllleeeaaassseee!'
'Who do you think you are? Sally?'
'Sorry.'
'Hmmmm. You are the daughter of my son and my granddaughter, not the daughter of a billionaire who has more skeletons in his closet than a Russian oil baron who lives in a haunted house!'
'He doesn't have skeletons in his closet! He has just worked hard and sometimes had good luck on his side!'
'Good luck?! Nineteen seventy-eight, he was applying for a military contract. His main rival fell from a ten storey high balcony. Verdict: suicide, but the rival had never shown any signs of depression or suicidal tendencies. Nineteen eighty-four. Sally's father had just lost a court battle over the copyright and patent of a now common household product. You know which I mean?'
'Yes, of course. That is what made him most of his money.'
'He should be a pauper after that court battle. He lost fair and square. Three days after the judgment his rival went missing from his own yacht in perfectly calm seas off the Monaco coast. Verdict: an unfortunate accident resulting in drowning. Utter drivel. Everyone with half a brain knows that, although Mr. Gallagher may not have pushed him off that yacht with his own hand, it was a hand connected to an arm belonging to Mr. Gallagher. Proof of this theory: none.'
'Therefore he is innocent until…'
'Rubbish. He is as guilty as a man holding a smoking gun!'
'Grandfather that is why we have courts, to present evidence to find out if a person is innocent or guilty. You can't say he is guilty just because you think he is! You need proof.'
'My proof is the coincidence that two of his main rivals both died under extremely mysterious circumstances.'
'Only two though. I'm sure to get to a position such as his he would have to push a lot more than two people!'
'Nineteen eighty eight. Aircraft contract with Boeing to make numerous electrical components and the software to run a plane, a contract that would make his company the largest electrical and computer software company in the U.K. and up there with the world's biggest.'
'And?'
'The government stopped him claiming that this contract would give him a monopoly on the industry. The two main people who blocked the signing of this contract were found dead two days after this announcement, one from drowning in his own swimming pool and another was knocked down by a black cab in London.'
'And Mr. Gallagher was the perpetrator?'
'I have no proof and I don't think anybody does unless he bought them off or killed them, but don't you think it is all a little bit too coincidental?'
The kettle had long since boiled but it went unnoticed by both of them.
'I can see what you mean grandfather, yet you can't accuse people without proof. That can't be done in this country.'
'I know we are talking about your best friend's father so try to be neutral abo

ut this and ask one simple question. Does everything I have said to you sound a little suspicious?'

'Okay, as a neutral, yes, it does. However, I know Mr. Gallagher better than anybody apart from Sally and he is not capable of ordering these things!'

'I have to disagree with you. You know his fatherly side. You only know how nice he is to you and Sally. Have you ever been to the office with him?'

'No.'

'Have you ever sat in with him during one of his business meetings?'

'No.'

'I have.'

Michelle could not keep the surprise out of her voice. 'You have? When?'

'Just before I retired from the Army, before you and Sally were born so before I had met him informally. They wanted an experienced soldier's opinion about an electronic component Gallagher and the Army were working on. At that time I was only pushing pens and paper waiting for my pension and some random officer walked into my office and invited me into the meeting. I think he was told to go and find anyone who was experienced in the field and I was the first person he saw.'

'Okay. Then what happened?'

'I was taken to a meeting room and sat down and listened to all they said. I've seen him socially since then, since you got to know Sally we have been together to many of the functions he has thrown for you both, parties etcetera, right?'

'Yeah, we have.'

'Right. Well the difference between him on that day and him on his own grounds hosting a big party was astonishing. He was evil Michelle, pure evil. The electrical component has since been banned by the Geneva Convention as being too, well, evil to be used on any battlefield. But all he saw, Gallagher, were the pound signs flashing before his eyes. He has no idea it was me, and probably does not even remember the insignificant old soldier who so strongly opposed him during that meeting. He had answers for every objection I had. All the military could see was certain success on the battlefield and all he could see was the large contract that was just about to land on his desk followed by an even larger cheque!' Her grandfather took a breather and then continued in a quieter voice. 'Don't say that you know him, you don't. Only when you have looked him in the eye across a table where you are discussing the future of his company and the future of his bank balance and you have seen the evil, determination and pure greed in his eyes can you truly say that you know him.'

There was silence for a moment while they contemplated everything that had been said. Eventually Michelle asked the only question that could be asked, 'What was the component?' For a moment she thought that he was not going to tell her but he did.

'It fitted onto the top of a man's rifle, gun, whatever. It was a small box with some kind of powerful laser in it. I, of course, do not know the exact technical specifications, but I am led to believe that the soldier pressed a button on the gun and the box emitted some kind of powerful laser. How it works is not important. What is important is the result of pressing the button. It blinded, blinded Michell e, the enemy soldiers.'

'Oh my God! That's horrible!'

'Exactly. The laser had a wide field of fire too so it is not as if the soldier had to point it straight into the enemy's eyes, just in the general direction would suffice. Now imagine a whole battalion…'

'How many men is that?'

'It would vary from around 500 to 1000 men. So imagine a whole battalion armed with one of those boxes. If all they have to do is point them in the general direction of the enemy troops they would have been able to blind and therefore kill probably a brigade of enemy troops without even trying.'

'And a brigade is how many men?'

'Around one thousand five hundred to three thousand depending on their roles etcetera.'

'Bloody hell! Three times the number?'

'Yes, easily. Of course, these men would not stare at each other across a battlefield and therefore it is not as if a whole brigade could be wiped out in one engagement, but imagine the power during any engagements that this component would give!'

'I can imagine the effect on the morale of the enemy soldiers too.'

'Exactly. And this is the weapon that your kind and caring father-figure desperately wanted to sell to our military!'

'That is truly horrible.'

'I know. Now what do you think of Mr. Gallagher? Still think he is incapable of ordering murders of anyone standing in his way?'

'It is different, I mean creating a weapon to kill our country's enemies and personally ordering the murder of another man are greatly different things, but from what you have said about his actions during that meeting, well, you never know do you?'

'Indeed. You never know what a man is capable of when his success is being threatened. If you had seen him in action Michelle then you would think he is capable of ordering another man's murder. Trust me, you would.'

For a moment or two they did not say anything then Arthur turned and switched on the kettle again to bring it up to the boil again. He made them both a large mug of hot chocolate and then reached into a cupboard and procured a handful of marshmallows which he dropped into the mugs. He led them both into the living room and Arthur lit the fire. He sat in a rocking chair and draped a blanket over his knees and engaged Michelle in small talk while they drank their steaming chocolate. After fifteen minutes Arthur announced he was going to bed and he came over to where Michelle was stretched out on a sofa and gave her a kiss on her forehead and wished her pleasant dreams.

She listened to him go upstairs and carry out his toilet and then she heard the pitter patter of Jack's feet as he ran upstairs to assume his position at the foot of Arthur's bed. He heard some mumbling as her grandfather said his prayers and then the creaking of the bed as he lay down to sleep. For quite some time Michelle lay there staring into the fire thinking of what her grandfather had said, her best friend's father could be a murderer; he was evil, pure evil.

She wondered if Sally had any indication of what Michelle now knew and she wondered even harder whether it was true. She guessed that there would be witnesses and that somebody somewhere would know the exact truth and not just her grandfather's speculation, yet she also knew that Mr. Gallagher would probably have paid off these people or perhaps had them murdered. The thoughts flew round Michelle's head until they rested on two people: Sally and Simon.

She had meant to phone Sally and try to make up with her but she had decided that it would be better to let her calm down a little first. She would definitely speak to her tomorrow. Then there was Simon. Was he serious? Michelle thought he was or he would have tried to have sex with her surely? Worryingly enough Michelle knew that due to the way she felt right now, if he had tried anything she would have gone to bed with him without a doubt. In a way she was glad she did not as it would have spoiled a great night. He would have to wait. She was not going to be duped again like her ex-boyfriend had duped her. Only when she was certain he was serious about her would he let him into bed with her. As she continued to think she felt her eyes growing heavy and before she stood to go to bed she promised to herself that she would fix things with Sally tomorrow and call…

She felt a vibration in her pocket as her phone started to shake. Out of politeness to her grandfather she had turned off the ring-tone but now she pulled it out of her pocket and it was a number that she did not know. It was approaching eleven o'clock on a Saturday night and she was tired. She was going to reject the call and then she thought it could be Simon so she answered the call.

'Hello? Who is this please?'

'Michelle? It is me, Simon. Can you hear me okay? Pretty noisy here.'

'Hi, yeah, I can hear you. Are you okay?'

'Yeah, I am fine. Just out in town, again.'

He sounded bored Michelle thought. 'Again? You are a dedicated party animal aren't you?'

'Not really. I am pretty bored to tell the truth. I was just checking to see if you are out tonight?'

'No, I am not tonight. I usually spend Saturday night with my grandfather and I am tonight.'

'Oh right. Sorry. I'm disturbing you. Just realized how bad what I said sounded! Only calling you because I am bored! Sorry.'

'It's okay. I didn't notice it in that way.'

'Ah, okay. Nah, I'm not phoning you because I am bored, I am phoning you because I wanted you to brighten my night again like you did last night otherwise I am off home so it looks like I am going home then because you are not here!'

'Yeah, I'm not. Sorry.'

'Ah, okay. No probs. What you doing Wednesday night?'

'Nothing, why?'

'Want to go out?'

'Erm, can I let you know, erm, I mean, yes, of course. Thought I was doing something then this Wednesday but I'm not so definitely.'

'Excellent! I can pick you up at eight if you want? You still live on…' The noise suddenly grew when Simon said the name of her street so Michelle confirm ed it with him and said the time was fine. 'Right, I'm going home now. Don't want to stay out any longer surrounded by idiots who I don't like!'

'Okay Simon, be careful. I will call you tomorrow if you want?'

'Yeah, that sounds great. You take care too.'

'I will' Bye Simon.'

'Bye babe.'

Michelle placed her phone on her lap and thought happy thoughts about Simon and the upcoming date. She reminded herself that she was going to take it nice and slow but then she thought how gorgeous he is and how often in her life she is going to have the opportunity to go to bed with someone as lovely looking as him. She shook her head and tried to clear it of the thoughts racing through it and decided the only way to get rid of them was to go to bed so she stood up from the sofa and made her way up the stairs and into the bathroom.

Quietly she had a quick wash and then made her way to her bedroom and got totally undressed noticing the dampness in her knickers. 'Oh my god,' she mumbled out loud, 'I have only been talking to him and I am turned on! What am I going to be like on Wednesday then?!'

She threw the undergarment onto the pile of clothes and opened a drawer and removed the shorts and t-shirt that she kept there. Quickly she put them on and lifted the thick blankets. She lay down on the bed and drew them over her, pulling them right up to her chin. For a few moments she fought with the feelings being emitted from the horrible thing between her legs that she hated and loved, hated because it made her feel like this when there was no-one with her to make the feelings turn into ones she loved. She tossed and turned for a while until the late hour and the previous night's lack of sleep caught up with her and her eyes slowly closed and she drifted into a deep, dreamless sleep.

Chapter 19

'Bye babe.' Simon closed his phone and thought for a few moments just how foolish he had been. He said out loud to himself, 'You are stupid! How long have you known her for?! And she was there all... the... time...!'

He butted the flimsy cubicle wall in time with the last three words, then unlocked the door and stepped into the toilet. He felt his foot go squelch and slide along the floor until it reached the grip of the tiled floor. Looking down at the floor there was a slip mark present in a large pile of vomit and he noticed that his right shoe was covered in the sick. 'Oh fucking marvellous!' he shouted out loud.

He then reached for some paper hand towels and threw them on the floor and then spent the next few minutes trying to wipe the sick off his shoe without having to touch it which proved to be quite a chore considering he was having to manoeuvre and balance himself on one foot when he was drunk.

After much effort he managed to get the worst of it off his shoe and then he stepped back into the bar. As he walked through the doorway a young spotty kid who could not have been more than 15, and who also looked like he had already obtained ten asbos in his short life, decided that Simon's light coloured shirt was the perfect place to pour his pint of red wine. Bouncing into Simon's shoulder he lost control of the glass and it upended right down the front of Simon's shirt.

All Simon could do was stand there, absolutely gob-smacked, while the kid threw his arms around Simon and shouted down his ear. Simon could not decide what was more annoying, the loud, slurring words that were hammering into his ear drums that he could not understand, or the stench of the teenager's body odour. He managed to prise himself out of his grasp and he pushed the chav so hard that he stumbled and staggered until his feet hit a step then he was catapulted head first straight into a bouncer's face, bursting but not quite breaking the bouncer's nose.

The bouncer, whose nickname was Slasher, was, needless to say, slightly surprised. At first he was even more shocked as the young man threw his arms around him, pressed his mouth to his ear and started to rant something into his ear. This shock was short lived though, and in a truly professional and competent manner he placed his hands on the juvenile's arms and started to squeeze his biceps. The vice like grip tightened and tightened until the bouncer felt him tense up against his body. He forced his arms apart and pushed the youth away from his body still tightening the grip on his arms. Now the whippersnapper was crying out in pain as he felt his biceps being crushed but the bouncer did not stop there.

He forced the lad down onto his knees and then drove his knee squarely into his nose three times. The urchin's nose broke on the second drive and was firmly crushed and splattered across his face after the third. Only when the he was happy that he had inflicted more damage to his attacker than the pubescent had inflicted on him, did he let go of his arms. The spotty lad slumped to floor writhing in agony clutching his nose and then he was clutching his genitals as Slasher drove a steel toe capped boot into his crotch. He then pressed a button on his communication device and one of his colleagues was quickly on the scene. They picked him up between them and carried him to a fire escape door.

Slasher kicked it open and with a count of three they swung him out into an alley then he closed the door leaving the youth to his agonies. Slasher dabbed at the slight trickle of blood trickling from his nose and said to his colleague, 'Little prick!' His colleague nodded in agreement and then they both returned to their normal security stations.

Simon had of course witnessed all of this and at first he felt slightly guilty then he glanced down at his ruined shirt and then quickly the guilt turned to rejoicing as the young man had got his comeuppance. As Simon stood studying his shirt he made the only decision that was possible to him, he decided to go along with the idea that he had stated to Michelle and go home. Making his way past Slasher, who looked at him strangely noticing the wine covering his shirt, he found his friends and told them he was going home. They asked him to stay but of course Simon blamed his shirt for a ruined night and bid them a good night. He exited the bar and made his way down a few busy Saturday night streets towards a taxi rank. As he approached the taxi rank he saw a familiar figure swaggering towards him and he looked for an escape route knowing that if this figure saw him he would be dragged out for even longer. Too late as the figure noticed Simon and hailed him.

'Simon! You slack jawed red necked bastard! You didn't tell me you were out tonight?!'

'Hey Peter. I wasn't but then I got a call and then, well, I felt like a few.'

'You still don't know how to drink do you? Your mamma not teach you how?'

'Piss off! Some idiot chucked his wine on me!'

'Tosser. Want me to have him shot?'

'Wouldn't have minded you doing that, but the bouncer took care of him as only bouncer's can!'

'In a professional manner?'

'Yep, you know it!'

'How many bones did he break?'

'Only one I think. His nose.'

'Ouch! Who you been out with?'

'Couple of lads from college. You don't know them.' Simon noticed the quick hurt look flash across his face.

'No worries. Couldn't have come out tonight anyway, not with you anyway. Got myself a date with a nubile young blonde!'

'What's his name?'

'Very witty! Some chick called Sophie. Met her last night. Good shag so I thought I would come back for some more!'

'Good work! Didn't know you scored last night. Not really spoke to anyone apart from my college mates. Nice one! Is she hot?'

'Well, you know, alright. Good in the sack and after a few J.D.'s and coke that is all that matters isn't it?!'

'Yeah, it is,' Simon replied, rolling his eyes inside his mind.

'Anyway, can't keep a ride waiting for much longer. Better go!'

'Okay matie. Have a top night!'

'I'd wish the same to you but it looks like yours is over!'

'Indeed it is! Going home now to my bed! Speak to you soon. Bye matie!'

'See you!'

Peter continued walking away from Simon and as he rounded a corner out of his view he checked that the gun was still tucked into the back of his jeans and muttered under his breath, 'Gullible arse! Believe anything I say!'

He carried on walking through the streets until he reached a part of the town that contained the main group of bars and clubs. Peter was greeted with a shake of the hand by the bouncer of the first bar he approached and during the hand-shake they exchanged money and drugs. He shook hands with another doorman and the same exchange took place.

Peter spoke into the ear of the second bouncer, knowing he had a tendency to take harder drugs than the cocaine Peter had just given him, making it quite clear that at this time next week he would be able to have a fantastic deal on some quality heroin. The bouncer appreciated Peter's reputation for already supplying a superior level of drug and his eyes lit up when he heard the offered price for a gram. The bouncer then made Peter happy when he told him that he knew other people who would be very interested in such a deal and he would put the word out for him. Peter thanked him and then strode into the bar.

Through the crowded establishment Peter forced his way to the bar while placing the money in his extended jeans' pocket. One of the barmen recognized him and did not ask him what beer he wanted nor did he charge him. The reasons for this occurrence happened a month or so ago.

*

One of the bouncers became suspicious of Peter's actions one night. He noticed that he seemed to know near enough everyone in the bar and the near enough everyone shook hands with him in greeting. This all seemed very strange to the alert security and he was conscious that no-one could know that many people. After witnessing another group of people come over and shake his hand the bouncer decided enough was enough and dragged a surprised Peter into a back room.

'He's been acting weird. Near enough everyone has come up to him and shook hands with him.'

'So what? I'm popular. Not my fault if everyone likes me!'

'Popular my arse. You're up to something. I think he's dealing boss.'

'You dealing in my bar you little scrotum?'

Peter blinked in astonishment and the surprise could not been hidden from his voice. 'Scrotum?! I think you need to check just who it is you're speaking to!'

'Oh yeah, and just who is it that one is speaking to?! All I can see is some little shit standing in front of me who is shitting himself. Max, take him outside and knock him down a peg or two.'

'My pleasure boss.'

'Wait. Before you do that, let me run two words by you and let's see if that changes anything.'

'Two words? You're gonna have to do a lot better than two words to keep yo ur sorry butt out of hospital tonight.'

'Oh yeah. I don't think so.'

'You don't think so? I tell you what Max, this little bastard is gonna be lucky if he keeps his concrete coated feet out of the river tonight. Go on then, enlighten me. What two words are going to keep you, alive?'

'Reg and Maxwell.'

'Oh bollocks.'

'Shit.'

Peter could not keep the smugness off his face.

'You working for him?'

'Yep.'

'Right. Well, erm, why didn't you say?'

'Didn't think I would have to.'

'I'm still not happy with you dealing in my bar even if you have got his backing.'

'Let me see if I can persuade you without needing his backing. How have your takings been in the last couple of weeks?'

'Good. Very good in fact.'

'Did you notice a sudden up-turn about two weeks ago?'

'Yeah, I did actually.'

'You scratch my, sorry our back and we'll scratch yours.'

'What do you mean?'

'Two weeks ago is when I started dealing here.'

'And?'

'And what? Use your brain.'

Peter saw anger on the manager's face and he quickly realized he had gone too far. 'I don't care if you have got the backing of him! You speak to me like that again and I'll take a chance and put a knife in your eye!'

'Sorry. That was rude of me.' Peter paused for a moment and carefully prepared his words. 'What I mean is your takings have gone up because people who want a good, high quality drug know where I am at this time on a Saturday night: in your bar. People who would never normally come in here have started to come in to find me. You scratch our back, we'll scratch yours.'

'And you started here two weeks ago?'

'Yes, a lot quieter than I was tonight. Tonight surprised me and I was just going to bail as things were getting too hot for me. Obviously they did get too hot because I got noticed by your diligent security.'

'Right. Takings have gone up a lot in the last two weeks. Could be coincidence. You really work for Reg? Answer carefully because if I ever find out you are lying to me you can consider yourself drowned.'

'Yes, I do work for him. You want to speak to him? Although he is in Spain now having a holiday and I really don't think he wants to be disturbed by me.'

'No, it is okay. Your word is enough. Let him work Max.'

'Rightio boss.'

'Before you go I want a little something as a good will gesture, something to keep me and the boys entertained after closing.'

'What do you want?'
'A nice big fat bag of charlie please.'
'Consider it done.'

Peter slid his hand down deep into his extended pockets and retrieved a bag of cocaine. He gave it to the owner of the bar who promptly opened it and started to prepare himself a line.

'Take him back now. Let him deal.'
'No probs boss. Follow me.'

Peter followed the bouncer back into the bar and he placed himself in a darker corner and instantly a few people approached him. Since that time the bar was always the first place that he called upon knowing that he would make a lot of easy sales.

*

Peter now sipped his Budweiser on a stool at a high table having small talk with some acquaintances. Every now and then someone would approach and he would make the deal, very simply, very easily with no questions asked by anyone. When one of his customers approached him who Peter thought would be interested in a harder substance to ingest, he made it subtly clear that this substance would be available during the next weekend at a special opening offer price. Some of his regulars showed surprise and stated that they already had a supplier so he then explained that he had it on good authority that that supplier would not be around from now on and to contact him for a steady, high quality supply. Some of his irregular and new customers also showed interest in the heroin and Peter thought how easy it was going to be to make even more money and get his feet more under Reg's table.

After an hour or so more in this bar he felt his jeans start to get heavy on one side and light on the other so he stood from his stool and made his way to the door. Another one of the bouncers stopped him on the way out and asked for some ecstasy tablets but Peter had to explain that he was out of supply so Peter left the bar and made his way back through the streets to the outskirts of town where he had parked his car in one of Reg's secure garages that were dotted around the town. He kept the keys on a chain around his neck, not wanting to drop them when he was rooting in his pockets for supplies or placing the money, and he unlocked and lifted up the garage door, stepped into the garage then closed the door behind him.

After opening the boot of the car he lifted the carpet of the boot out and there, in the hollow where the spare wheel should have been, was a large, metal Samsonite case that was chained to the mounting that usually held the wheel in place. The case needed a combination code to open it and Peter quickly spun the dials and opened it.

The inside of the case was partitioned and in one side were bags of ecstasy tablets and in the other were bags of cocaine. The third was empty and this is where Peter placed the money. Then he took two bags of E's out and five large, medium and small bags of cocaine out of their compartments and placed them in his j eans. In each bag of ecstasy where fifty tabs and that should be enough to see him through the rest of the night. After collecting the drugs he closed and locked everything and left the garage to make his way back into the town centre.

*

His night after this was a pretty standard Saturday night for him. He made lots of sales and generally had a good time. He obtained two young ladies' phone numbers and even managed to persuade one young lady into the toilets of a club for a quick session of sexual intercourse. While he was sat on the toilet she was sat on top of him sliding up and down his penis with her vagina as she snorted cocaine out of the palm of his hand and quickly had an intense orgasm. Peter though was left unsatisfied so he told the girl to stand up and he did too. He lay out a line of coke along the top of the cistern then bent her over the toilet and penetrated her from behind. She sucked up the cocaine like a hoover and then begged for some more. Peter happily obliged and while she hoovered up this line he carried on drilling into her and then had a good, satisfying orgasm. He pulled out of her and then quickly pulled up his underwear and pants and left the girl in the cubicle promptly forgetting about her. He did not even know her name.

After this quickie he left the club, made his way back to his car and then back to his house where he spent fifteen minutes accounting for the drugs sold and the money he now had.

He had had his best night so far, and after the perfect no strings attached sex he decided that there would be no better end to the night than having a glass of Bailey's in bed while watching the episode of the drama he enjoyed which he had recorded using his Sky+.

His parents were still away so he did not have to worry about disturbing them so he poured himself a large Bailey's with lots of ice and made his way upstairs to his bedroom. Turning on the bedside lamp the first thing he noticed were the stains his bed sheets from the previous nights sex with Sarah. He thought about her now as he turned on his television and found the recorded programme in the memory of the Sky+ box.

He was thinking about how much he was looking forward to Wednesday as he settled onto his bed, and all the potential that that night had. He did not really watch the episode of the drama as he thought again about the plans he had for Sarah and as he confirmed them in his mind he gave voice to his plans.

'Give her more coke, get her hooked, set an extortionate price, I reckon she'll even suggest about paying for it with sex – perfect!'

*

After speaking to Peter earlier that night Sarah's condition did not improve. She slept fitfully and eventually a phone call woke her up properly. It was her friend asking where she was and whether she was going to turn up to their agreed meeting. Sarah got up out of bed after saying sorry to her friend for being late and started to quickly get ready, but she still felt dizzy, had a headache and was clo se to being sick. She wanted to go out though because she and her friend were due to meet two guys who they had met the weekend before. Sarah thought about that wild night now as she pulled on tight jeans not bothering with knickers.

They had met the two men at a bar and made it quite clear to them both that if they played their cards right then they were both going to get laid. Sarah's friend, who was just as promiscuous, left first after only talking to the man she had picked for half an hour. Sarah left soon after not knowing that they made their way to the same hotel as Sarah's friend and her new sex partner. It was only after a phone call between the girls that they found out so they all met in one room and there were times that Sarah thought she would never have such good sex in her life again. Both the guys were skilled at lovemaking and there was one point when Sarah had both guys inside her while her friend was sat on one of the guys' face. They continued all night and all morning and the men eventually left the girls completely satisfied when they were usually insatiable.

It was these guys that Sarah was meant to be meeting again on this Saturday night and now as she fastened her bra and pulled on her top, for the first time in as long as she could remember she did not want to go out and have sex that night. Instead she flopped back down on her bed and thought about Peter and how nice he seemed and how much she was looking forward to Wednesday. Then a scary thought entered her head as she considered whether it was Peter she was looking forward to seeing or the cocaine. Unable to decide on this she was sure that she did not want to go out that night so he called her friend back.

'I can't make it tonight darling. I don't feel too well.'

'Oh come on Sarah! I think you are forgetting how good last Saturday night was?!'

'No, I'm not. I feel like rubbish.'

'Why? Pllleeeeeaaassseee!'

'I can't. I wouldn't be able to have sex anyway. I've started my period.'

'Ah, okay. Never stopped you before!'

'It does tonight. I feel horrible.'

'Okay then. Your loss. I will just have to have them to myself aaaaalllll night!'

'Okay honey. Sorry.'

'No sorry required. I will have a great time! Speak to you soon.'

'Yeah, enjoy!'

'I will. Bye.'

'Bye.'

Sarah placed her phone down next to her, pulled off her top and removed her bra and lay there for a while not really thinking about anything. She was just dozing off again when she heard a large crash and a bottle smash somewhere in the house. Sarah closed her eyes again hoping she had dreamt the noises but then she thought she had better go downstairs and check her mum was okay. Reluctantly she stood out of bed grabbing and putting on a T-shirt then made her way reluctantly down the stairs.

She strode into the kitchen and was greeted by a sight that horrified her. Her mother was knelt in, from the smell Sarah presumed vodka, a pool of the alcohol with shards of glass from the broken bottle surrounding her. In her hand was a sponge and she hovered the sponge over her mouth. As Sarah watched she squeezed the sponge and the liquid dripped into her mouth. She had not heard the approach of her daughter so when the sponge was not holding anymore fluid she dipped it back into the pool of vodka and then squeezed it into her mouth.

'Mum, what the hell are you doing?'

'Oh hiya darling! Didn't hear you. Waste not want not!'

'Mum, this is getting serious! You are knelt in broken glass!'

'I'm fine darling. Bit short of money this week. Can't afford another bottle.'

Thoughts rushed into Sarah's mind and were dancing along her tongue ready to explode past her lips but she managed to bite it and keep the words locked away. 'Mum, at least pick up the glass. You might seriously hurt yourself.'

'I'm fine darling. Bit short of money this week.'

Sarah rolled her eyes as her mum repeated the same words without realizing and her mum continued to soak up the alcohol and squirt it into her mouth. 'Mum! Stop that now! Help me pick up the glass.' Then she noticed her mother's shaking hands and quickly changed her mind. 'In fact, just get out of the kitchen for a few moments.'

'Just a few more moments darling. Bit short of money this week.'

'NO! Get out now before you cut yourself!'

Sarah managed to grab the sponge and then took a step back in complete amazement as her mum, her mother, the woman who had carried her in her womb, lowered her head to the floor and started to lick and suck the vodka straight from the floor showing no regard to the slivers of glass that were near her tongue and lips.

'Oh... my... God! MUM! Stop now! You are going to cut yourself! STOP!'

Sarah had never physically restrained her mum from potential harm but now she had to as her mum showed disregard to Sarah's pleas and carried on licking. She grabbed a handful of her mum's hair and pulled her head away from the floor and then continued pulling her out of the kitchen. Her mum struggled a little but quickly gave up as her daughter was too strong for her and she was dumped onto a sofa in the living room.

'For fuck's sake mum! What were you thinking?!'

'I need a drink honey. Ever since your dad left. Blame him not me.'

'Right, okay mum, I will. For now stay out of the kitchen.'

'I need a drink though honey. Ever since your...'

'You just said that mum! Be quiet now. Watch the television while I tidy up.'

'Right, okay. Could you get me some wine please?'

'Where from mum? There is no wine.'

'You'll have to go out darling.'

'No mum. I don't think so. I've told you before I am not buying you anymore drink. Get it yourself.'

'No money darling. Please. For your mum.'

'And where do I get the money from mum? I'm at college remember? I don't work.'

'Get me some wine. Please. Ever since your dad...'

'Oh shut up mum, please shut up! Wait here. I'll tidy up and then see how you feel. Okay?'

'Okay darling. Turn on the television please.'

'Right I will. Don't come into the kitchen though, okay?'

'Okay. Need a drink though. Hurry to shop and get me one.'

Sarah did not bother replying this time. Instead she ignored her, turned on the television and returned to the kitchen closing the door behind her. First of all she got a broom from a cupboard and swept up the glass then got some kitchen roll and wiped up the mess the vodka had made. Sarah then stood in the kitchen for a few moments and contemplated what she was going to do.

She knew that she should not give her mum alcohol yet she also knew that to not to may push her mum over the edge and she would start getting withdrawal symptoms which would lead eventually to violence. She contemplated phoning her friend back up and hiding away from the problem by having herself a very good time. But in this instance she knew that she could not go out and leave her mum in this condition after what she had just witnessed. 'The only thing for it then,' she said out loud, 'is to get her a drink so she isn't violent and eventually she will pass out.' She thought about this for a few moments and realized that if she did she would actually be feeding her mother's addiction which surely would not be a good thing to do. 'I don't have a choice!' was her final conclusion so she reluctantly went back into the living room.

'I've tidied up. Don't ever, ever, do that again mum! You could have done yourself a serious injury!'

'I know dear. Need a drink though. Here. I found this in my purse.' She handed Sarah a five pound note. 'See if you can get me a couple of bottles of wine or a bottle of gin.'

'With a fiver mum?'

'Tell Sid it is for me. He'll understand.'

'Oh, right, so now we're a charity case?! Tell you what mum, why don't you go out and get it?'

'There's a programme on I want to watch. You go, for your mum. I really need a drink.'

'Right. No problem mum. I'll make your alcoholism worse. Not a problem. And when are you going to ask me how seeing you like this makes me feel?!'

'I know darling. I'm not an alcoholic though. It is just a phase I'm going through. Ever since your dad ran off with that bitch...'

'Stop mum. Just please be quiet. Wait here. Do not move from the sofa. I'll be five minutes.'

'Awww, you're a good girl looking after me like this. Hurry up though.'

'I will.'

Sarah quickly made her way back to her bedroom and retrieved her purse. She opened it and cursed out loud as she saw how little money she had. Her next payment from college to help fund her studies was not due for a few days. All she could do though was shrug her shoulders and walk out of the house towards the shop.

A few neighbours greeted her and she could not help notice the sympathy in their eyes and faces. They were all aware the condition that her mum would be in right now and they all probably knew where Sarah was going. She reached the shop and used her mother's five pounds and her own few pounds to purchase a bottle of gin that would hopefully quench her mum's needs and eventually knock her out. Sid at the shop did not say anything to her beyond the needs of courtesy but again Sarah saw that look in his eyes. She could not cope with the prying eyes on the way back home so she took an indirect route which meant her walking down the alleyways. She twisted and turned along them avoiding the rubbish, dumped junk and dog dirt until she reached her back gate. Reaching over the top of it she unbolted it and flung it open closing it behind her. Sarah walked across the back yard, which was full of weeds, then opened the unlocked back door.

She thought at first as the door opened that her mum was with somebody then as she made her way into the living room it turned out that she was having a nice chat to herself. What was even more worrying, no horrifying, for Sarah was that she was asking questions then answering the questions herself and even nodding as she listened to the reply that she must have believed was coming from another person.

This image brought a tear to Sarah's eye and she interrupted her mum's conversation and gave her the bottle of gin. She did not bother with a glass. She simply unscrewed the cap and took a big swig from the bottle. She did not even acknowledge her daughter's presence let alone say thank you. The tears were rolling freely down Sarah's face but these went unnoticed. Instead all that Sarah could do was leave her and go back upstairs away from the horrible sight of her mum drinking herself to death.

Lying on her bed Sarah cried for some time until she got her emotions back under control. She could not avoid the fact of how much her mother had deteriorated over the last couple of months. Sarah, with her wild lifestyle, hardly saw her mum but made a point of at least checking she was alive every day. Sometimes she would go days without returning home and not seeing her but she always phoned to make sure she was okay.

Now, obviously, she has not been okay and as Sarah thought about it even more she realized she could be doing more to help her. These thoughts though started to make Sarah depressed and anxious and worried, but instead of facing up to them she ran away from them again like usual.

She stated out loud that life was too short for feeling miserable and worrying about things that she could not do anything about. So instead of thinking about how she could possibly help her mother, she instead peeled off her tight jeans and mentally and physically hid away from the problems in her life. She turned on her television and pressed play on the D.V.D. player. On the screen the image of a man having sex with a woman appeared and Sarah stood in front of the television soaking up the image for a few moments. 'I wish I was doing that right now,' she said out loud, 'but I've got the next best thing!'

Turning away from the television she pulled a suitcase out from underneath her bed and flipped it open. Inside this case were a lot of sex toys ranging from huge dildos to the famous Rabbit Vibrators, to Pleasure Pearls and even a couple of strap on vibrators for when she was with one of her female friends.

For a young woman who wanted to escape from the many problems in her life the case contained many perfect solutions to the most pressing of problems such as an alcoholic mum. She moved the toys around until she found the two that she wanted to use. The first was a clitoris stimulator that she would use to get her going and the second was a large Rabbit Vibrator that she would use to finish herself off.

For about an hour and a half she watched porn, occasionally changing the disc, and in that time using a wider variety of toys she had five orgasms and successfully managed to forget about every problem and issue in her life. It was only when she was just about satiated and placing the case back under her bed did she remember about her mum. She was tempted to just totally ignore and go straight to bed and concentrate instead on the feelings of pleasure that were still coursing through her body, but instead of the tip of a large vibrator landing at the pit of her stomach, this time a feeling of guilt landed there so she quietly made her way downstairs.

Her mother was now firmly passed out in the chair that Sarah had left her sitting in. She knew that she should at least try to get her to bed but that would mean waking her up and Sarah quickly thought that she would rather not wake her knowing that there would be strong possibility of being sent out for more drink as she spotted the empty gin bottle where it had been flung onto the floor. Instead, she returned back upstairs and took a blanket off her mother's bed and placed it over her sleeping body.

Still naked, she turned off the television and threw the gin bottle into a bin in the kitchen. For a moment or two on her way back to the stairs she studied her mother's sleeping body. She thought that it was hard to believe that by eight o'clock the next morning her mother would be drinking again. All Sarah could do was shake her head and ignore the plight she and her mother faced. She focused instead on the feelings of pleasure still flowing through her body and returned to her bed where she masturbated and then feel into a deep sleep.

When she woke at nine o'clock the next morning she went downstairs for a drink of water. Her mother was awake and watching television. From somewhere she had found a bottle of red wine. It was three quarters empty.

Chapter 20

Sally met David at his garage Sunday morning as planned. The awkwardness was clearly present as David tried cracking small jokes and making small talk, while Sally blushed and laughed at his small jokes. They stood looking at the car, while David pointed out the work he had done.

'Sorry, tell me if you don't want me to know, but I can't work out who the guy was who dropped you off? He looked too old to be your dad, but not old enough to be your grandfather.'

'Why wouldn't I want you to know? He's my uncle. You're right though, he's quite a bit older than my dad.' Alfred was in no way related to Sally, but she had already decided that to tell him that he was her butler would be a bad idea at this time.

'That explains it then. Nice car, the new Mini. YoillwatgooutW'nesday?' The question had been gnawing at the back of David's mind, and before he knew what was going on, the words had tumbled out off his mouth in one quick, incoherent sentence.

Sally had her head in the car admiring David's work so all that he could see were a pair of round, incredibly firm pair of buttocks looking up at him. 'Pardon?'

He took a deep breath and this time the question tumbled out a little better. 'You still wanna g'out Wednesday?'

'Huh? Do I want gout on Wednesday? Erm, no thanks David, I think I'll pass!' She straightened up out of the car and looked at him. He blushed.

'Oh behave! You know what I mean!'

'Well, I think when you ask a lady that question it is better that you ask her and not her buttocks!' He blushed even deeper. 'But in answer to your question, I still stand by my answer I gave to you yesterday. I stand by it even stronger now after I've seen how much work you must have put in yesterday on my car. I feel bad that you won't take any money for it. At least let me pay something?'

'No, we talked about this yesterday and we made our arrangement.'

'Okay, no worries. In that case I'm still paying for everything on Wednesday, and I do mean everything.'

'That's fine.'

'Good.'

There was a moment of more awkwardness between them before David said, 'Why don't you take her for a spin around the yard, make sure she is okay?'

'I'm sure she will be if you've worked on her.'

'I wish I had your confidence. Go on, please.'

'Okay.'

Sally hopped into the seat and closed the door behind her. She started the car first time and drove it sedately around the yard; however, she was itching to start executing some hand-brake turns to see his face! She pulled up alongside him and wound down the window. 'She seems fine. Thank you so much. Want to come for a quick spin?' He blushed again which surprised Sally. It was not like she was asking him to give her a sensuous massage, just go out for a little drive.

'Erm, well, no, I can't. I have to get home. My gran. She, erm, makes us, well, go to church on a Sunday. I mean, I don't want to go, I'm not religious or anything, but I've got no choice. One Sunday I didn't go she, she's got a key to our house, and I went home after work on the Monday after the Sunday and all my clothes were out in the lawn in bin-bags. She'd bolted all the doors so I couldn't use my keys and every time I tried to get in she called me a sinner and Satan's spawn!' Sally laughed out loud. 'My parents couldn't let me in because if they went anywhere near the doors or windows she threatened them with either a knife or being removed from her will! I had to sleep in my car.' She laughed again. 'The only concession she would make was one glass of water. I drank it because I was thirsty. She took great pleasure telling me the next morning that she had got the water from the toilet!'

'You see, water is water. It comes out of the tap. It doesn't matter which tap, it's all the same pipes.'

'I agree with you, but you misunderstand me. When I say toilet water, I mean toilet water. She scooped the water out of the bowl of the toilet!'

'Oh my word! That's hilarious!'

'I'm glad you think so!'

Sally laughed and laughed for a quite a while during which David stood next to her car shuffling his feet and looking awkward. 'I'm sorry, I shouldn't laugh, but she sounds like quite a woman!'

'She is. She's tough as old boots and considering she's nearly eighty her mind is razor sharp, never misses a trick.'

'I'd like to meet her one day.'

'You'll see her on Wednesday.'

'Will I? Meeting the folks already? Next you'll be offering my dad a dowry!'

He blushed again. 'Sorry if it makes you feel awkward, but there is no chance you'll be able to drive away without meeting her, sorry. She'll know I'm going on a date...'

'Don't tell her?'

'No, she will know. You don't understand her; she's got a sixth sense!'

She chuckled again. 'Right, okay, in that case I'll be honoured to meet her.'

'Well, if you don't want to I can pick you up. What's your address?'

'No honestly, it's fine. I don't mind. Pick you up at eight?'

'Yeah, that's cool. I'll look forward to it.'

'Me too David. Look in all seriousness, I really appreciate what you've done for me. Friday night must have been as scary for you as me and as for the work you've done on my car, it is just fantastic!'

'It's fine Sally. I enjoyed it. I love working on cars, especially a classic like yours.'

'Yeah, she's great. Thank you again.'

'No probs.'

'Eight then? Your address is...' At that moment a truck took a wrong turning into the garage and turned round. David leaned closer, into the car as Sally confirmed the address with him. 'Oh, I think I said that you're going to surprise me. As a final condition I'm going to surprise you.'

'Okay. It's clear that if this relationship develops I'm not going to be wearing the trousers!' David replied.

'Sorry, I can be a little bossy. If it's okay with you, put something smart on. I'm talking trousers, shirt, jacket, shoes and no denim, and I'll surprise you. Sound good?'

'Yep, sounds great.'

'See you Wednesday then.'

'Definitely. Bye.'

He was still leaning into the car slightly and Sally moved up to him and gave him a light peck on his lips. 'See you honey,' said Sally.

'Bye.'

David took a step away from the car and she slowly edged away. He watched her drive slowly across the yard and turn onto the road. As she turned and went out of view, he touched his lips where she had kissed him. 'Trousers and a shirt?' He muttered out loud. 'Trousers and a shirt? Looks like I'm going shopping!'

*

As soon as the garage was out of sight, Sally floored the accelerator and sped off back towards her home. She was hoping that she would be able to go out for a ride that afternoon with her father but she did not get her hopes up. What she did not know was that he had solved the problems that had occurred the previous morning with the acquisition and he was in fact waiting for the return of his daughter.

As she sped up the drive she slowed down because she was very pleased to see her father out on the front lawn partaking in one of his hobbies, flying model airplanes, which he rarely got chance to do. There were two planes parked at his feet and as she drove along the drive up to him she heard, but could not see, the whine of the plane he was currently flying. She looked in her rear view mirror just in time to catch sight of the plane as it dipped into a sharp turn then he lined it up directly with the back of her car. Sally heard the pitch of the engine increase and saw the plane spurt forwards and rapidly approach her car.

They had not played this game for many months but she knew that this was a direct challenge for a race, or to be more precise, a game of tag. All she needed to do was avoid the touch of the plane for five minutes and she would get a prize, probably a piece of highly expensive jewellery. It was rare that she won, avoiding the plane took all her driving skills, but when she did win the prize was always very worth the effort. The only rule for her father was to tap the car with the plane without damaging the plane.

She knew her father would have already started timing her, so without warning she slammed on the Mini's brakes and the plane shot like a rocket towards the rear window of the now stationary car. Her father had been expecting a manoeuvre of some kind so he was able to react quickly and put the plane into a steep climb then he looped the plane back towards the rear of Sally's car. In the meantime, Sally had again floored the accelerator of the car and sped along the drive. She flashed past her father and she cheekily waved at him and stuck her tongue o ut to which he gave a little chuckle.

Now the plane was chasing her again and quickly gaining on her as the old Mini was revved hard and fast up through the gears. Sally heard the engine of the plane whine even louder and she knew that she was not going to outstrip it in a drag race, not in this car anyway. With a light touch of the handbrake and a light touch of the steering wheel she spun the car onto the lawn in a perfectly executed U-turn and sped back towards her father.

The plane banked over to resume its chase but instead of coming directly at Sally's car he took it high hoping to approach her car with a little more stealth. As Sally sped towards her father she looked ahead and saw the ground dip in front of her. The land there held the water and she knew that today, after all the rain of recent times, it would be like a marsh. Quickly spinning the wheel away from the dip she sped back towards the driveway, but instead of going back along the drive she intersected it at ninety degrees and carried on sprinting across the lawn. All of a sudden she heard the engine increase in pitch again but she was totally unsighted, not knowing from which direction the plane was coming from. All she could do was listen as the engine noise increased in volume, and when she thought the time was right, she spun the wheel and then quickly the other way aiming to spin the car and lose the plane.

Although this was an action she had performed many times on the race tracks, she totally misjudged the slippyness of the grass. The car spun fine the first time, but she had not planned on the second, third and fourth spins.

The tyres lost all friction with the grass and the car spun round and round until eventually coming to a halt in the middle of the large expanse of grass. Somehow she had managed to keep the engine running by dropping the clutch as the vehicle spun, and she could hear that the plane was very close, yet she hoped that her erratic, unpredictable driving had shaken it off. But just as she was accelerating again she heard a light bump on the roof of her car and the plane shot past her with a dip of its wings. She had lost the game of tag.

She trundled at a more sedate pace back to where he was stood and she watched as he expertly landed the plane. It taxied over to him and he reached down to the roof of the plane, which was at knee height, and switched it off. Just as she was stopping, he collapsed the aerial of the radio controller and then he walked over to her door. He opened it her for her and as she exited he took her hand and then gave her a light kiss on each cheek.

'If I was in the Lotus I would have beaten you!'

'I'm sure you would have angel.'

'I made it too easy for you that time.'

'I disagree. I was expecting some kind of aggressive action but I have to say that the numerous pirouettes caught me unawares and have left an intriguing pattern on the lawn which I'm sure I will be hearing about tomorrow from the Head Gardener!'

Sally chuckled and hugged her father. 'I'm glad to see you enjoying yourself for once. You've had a busy few months.'

'You're right, I have. I'm getting too old for this.'

'Rubbish dad! You'll never retire and you know it.'

'Well, I may take my foot off the gas a little in a year or so.'

'Hmmm, I'm not so sure.'

'Want a ride back?'

'You know something darling, I don't. Leave the Mini here and I'll leave the planes here and we'll send someone out to get them. No, we are going to walk back to the house.'

'It's a mile daddy. Are you sure? When was the last time you walked anywhere? You'll be out of breath after a hundred yards!'

'Cheeky little thing! I'm fit as a fiddle! No, we'll walk. What's more, get your phone out.'

'My phone? Why?'

'Get it out and give it to me.'

'Okay dad.' Sally reached back into her car and retrieved her mobile then placed it into her father's hand. It made a beeping sound as he turned it off.

'Now for mine.' He turned his own phone off and then threw them back into the Mini and closed the door.

'Daddy, what if someone needs you? You can't do that!'

'If someone needs me they are going to have to cope for an hour while I walk with my lovely daughter. I'm thinking of changing my regime a little Sally, which will involve spending more time with you and passing a little bit more responsibility to my subordinates. But, after yesterday's fiasco, I'm wondering whether that is a good idea. Never mind. For now they'll have to cope. Onwards and homeward!'

They started to walk back towards the house, Sally linking her father's arm, but he made them walk in a circular route, spending as much time as possible walking towards the mansion.

'Yesterday, at breakfast, you started to tell me something. I'm really sorry I ran out on you like that. But, well, you know what it's like.'

'It's okay daddy, I understand and what I wanted to talk to you about doesn't matter now. I've fixed it.'

'Ah, okay. Good girl. How's everything else? Not got a new boyfriend to introduce me to?'

'I've had a couple since we last spoke properly. I'm sorry I don't introduce you to them, but you know I don't like them knowing how rich we are.'

'You should be proud of it Sally. I've worked very hard to get us into this situation.'

'Dad, you misunderstand me. I am proud of it. I am the proudest daughter in the whole world. I know how hard you've worked, and what you've sacrificed. It is not that I am ashamed to be this well off, far from it. It is just that, well, you know, money attracts the wrong kind of people. I don't want guys to date me just because of how rich we are. I want them to get to know me and fall for me not my bank balance.'

'But this is you. Your bank balance is you. You can't hide away from it. I've done that, I've told people I am not who I am, hid it from them, but I've never met anyone who has not held it against me afterwards when they find out who I am.'

'I know that, but how am I meant to tell whether a guy likes me or my money?'

He mulled this over for a few moments. 'I suppose you can't.'

'Exactly dad, exactly. So I'd prefer them to like me for what I am not for what my bank balance is. And then, when I feel that the time is right, I will tell them. Then, if they can't handle it, they would obviously not be the right person for me.'

'Risky strategy Sally, risky. I've never met anyone who can handle it.'

'Well, we'll see. This is the way I want to try it for now.'

'Okay. Your choice angel.'

Sally nodded in agreement and they walked in silence for a while, skirting the lake. His wife's, and her mother's island, was visible through the mist that seemed to always hover over the lake. They paused briefly and stared across the still water to the island.

If one was to cross the water in the small boat which was in the boat-house that was a short walk from where they now stood, one would see a small beach. From the top of this small strip of sand there was a narrow path that ran through large, over-hanging trees to the centre of the island. Here there was a clearing in the trees. Within this clearing was a large marble tomb, which was frequently visited by Sally or her father, sometimes other relations and friends, and the small shrine outside the tomb always had fresh flowers. Here, in this shrine, was a small kneeling bench, a cross, and on the back wall a mosaic of small tiles that created a stunning image of Sally's mother that seemed to shine when the sun was at the right angle to cast its rays upon her face.

'Do you miss her daddy?'

'Of course I do angel. Every second of every minute of every day.'

'It has been a while now. Have you, well, have you never considered, well, you know...'

'Finding someone else?'

'Yes.'

'I have thought about it. Some companionship would be good, especially as I get older. I loved her with all my heart, and she loved me more than I could ever possibly love her back. She was an amazing woman Sally. I, we, you and I, would definitely, one hundred percent, not be where we are today if it was not for her unwavering support in the early days of building my business. Yes, I miss her like crazy, and that is why there is no way I could ever love another. I'll be honest with you as I hope you'll be honest with me in the future; there have been other women since she left us. I'm a man Sally, a more mature man but I still get natural urges. I tried to resist them at first but my physical body overcame my weaker mind and I've taken women to my bed, but never once have I ever loved them, never once have I thought I would like to make one of those women my wife. I don't know why I tell you this now, I really don't, but I hope you understand what I've said.'

'Of course I understand daddy,' she hugged his arm tighter, 'but I disagree with you. Your love for each other should be a building block. She'd want you to be happy. She'd want you to have some companionship and she certainly would not ever dream of wanting you to be lonely, never ever would she want that, surely?'

'Yes, I suppose you're right. I've just never met anyone who can come close to her glory, her beauty, her personality, her unwavering support for me.'

'Maybe you'll find her in the future.'

'I doubt it angel, I really do, unless you want to marry me?'

'Dad! Honestly!'

He laughed out loud and quickly picked up his daughter and spun her round, and round. 'Dad! Put me down! Your back! Remember what the doctor said!'

He continued to laugh as he stopped spinning her and linked her arm again. 'Anyway, enough being morbid. It is nice to talk about your mother, but let us continue and talk about happier things. How's college going? There is no way my beautiful daughter is single! Tell me about him!'

'Okay dad, let's carry on walking. I'm hungry and want some soup. Shame we haven't got our phones. We could phone ahead and get them to make us something.'

'It will only take chef a minute to knock us up some broth!'

'Indeed! Onwards then dear father!'

'Indeed young lady, onwards and upwards!'

They turned away from the lake and made their way to the mansion. Suddenly her father stopped and exclaimed out loud. 'My word! How stupid of me! I forgot!'

'You forgot something?!'

'I know, astonishing!' One of the many reasons he had been so successful was his prodigious memory. 'It has been a busy week. Never mind.'

'So what have you forgotten? You're taking your lovely, adoring daughter away to Fiji again with no phones or internet to disturb us?'

'No, but I think you may prefer what I'm just about to tell you.'

'Well please continue then father, please continue!'

'You know of course that I've been sponsoring a Formula 1 team this last season?'

'Yeah, of course.'

'It's good for business. I get a small section of the car to advertise on and a section of the driver's race suits. Expensive, but my marketers insist it pays for itself. Anyway, I mentioned having some corporate tickets to the C.E.O., and he has given me three.'

'Oh, brilliant! Who are you going to take?'

'Well, I was thinking of taking a couple of guys from work.' He paused for a moment, waited for her pout and the I-want-line to appear, but they did not and he thought that maybe his little girl was growing up.

'That's great! They'll really appreciate it!'

'Don't be silly Sally! As if I would want to spend such a precious weekend with two stuffy business men! I was thinking of you and Michelle, that is if you don't mind hanging out with an old man for a weekend?'

David briefly popped into Sally's mind and then an image of her best friend with her tongue down her date's throat, but she had already made up her mind to forgive Michelle, so she replied, 'Of course we won't mind! We'll be honoured to spend it with you! Which Grand Prix? The British?'

'No, he twisted my arm for a little bit more money so I twisted his a little harder!'

'Good! Where then?'

'Monaco.'

'Monaco?! Really?! Wow! That's going to be amazing! Thank you so much dad!' She swung around him and kissed him firmly on both cheeks.

'I haven't finished yet. He twisted again, and so did I!'

'Go on, what next?!'

'Well, I'll tell you later if you're good!'

She stamped her foot, and the pout and the I-want-line appeared and he reversed his earlier thoughts. 'Tell me now or I'll sulk and sulk and sulk!'

'Okay then baby. On the Saturday afternoon, well more like early evening when all the qualifying is done, we get an hour on the track in sports cars!'

'Oh... my... God! Seriously? Seriously? How have you managed to twist his arm that much?!'

'Money talks angel, money talks.'

'Talks?! It must have been shouting! Can we afford it?'

'Don't be ridiculous Sally. It wasn't that much! They got those fines last season, remember? I said I'd help them out a little.'

'A little?! How much?'

'A little.'

Another pout and another line. 'Tell me!'

'Okay. Four million.' He said it casually, like they were discussing the new cost of a first class stamp.

'Four million?! Bloody hell dad, that's a lot!'

'It's not really angel. The money is just sat there so we might as well use it. Anyway, I can probably get some kind of tax break on it; put it through the books as a corporate event.'

'Nice, but still, four million!'

'It's nothing to us and you know it.'

'Yeah, I suppose. Wait until I tell Michelle. She'll start doing back-flips she'll be so happy!'

'I'm glad angel. We can all look forward to it together.'

'We'll be looking forward to it and looking forward to it and looking forward to it!' She pressed her body against his and rubbed against him almost like a cat would that wants feeding. 'Daddy, are we going to take the yacht?'

He looked down on her as she pressed herself against his arm. 'Enough of your female tricks little lady! I've already booked a berth right next to the track. That cost quite a lot too, mainly because I had to buy off the people who were in the queue ahead of us, but it will be worth it!'

'That's brilliant daddy! Thank you so, so much!' She kissed him again firmly on the cheek and skipped along next to him as they approached the mansion.

He was overjoyed to see her so happy, but as they got close to the house a member of the household staff ran out of the front doorway. He muttered under hi s breath, 'Oh, oh. This doesn't look good!'

'Ohhh bugger! Sell-up daddy, let's buy an island where it is quiet and we can chill out, where there are no phones or anything!'

'It doesn't quite work like that darling. I'm sorry, again.' By this time the staff member had reached them.

'Sir, sorry to disturb you. Urgent call. One of your directors. They've been trying your mobile?'

'My mobile is in the Mini which is over there.' He pointed through the mist and the outline of the car could just be seen. 'Send someone to bring the Mini back to the garages along with my planes and then bring our phones back to us. I'll be in my office.'

'Certainly sir.'

He turned to look at his daughter. 'I'm sorry angel. Yet again our time is disturbed. I really must do something about this. Sure you don't want to take over the business after me?'

'Definitely. And what would be the point? If you want to spend more time with me you couldn't because I'd be the one answering the urgent calls instead of you!'

'Good point well made! Right, I must dash. I will try to catch up with you later. Sorry.'

'It's okay. Go. It must be important.'

'I'm on my way. We'll catch up again soon, I promise.'

'Yeah, I know dad. Go on.'

He leant down and kissed her on each cheek and then dashed past Alfred who was now present at the top of the front steps. Sally approached him and walked up the steps to him. 'Good afternoon Alfred.'

'Good afternoon Sally.'

'My car and my father's planes?'

'Of course. I'll send someone straight away.'

'Thank you.'

'Anything for lunch ma'am?'

'A soup, please Alfred, one of the chef's special chicken broths, and some thick, crusty bread. Could you ask someone to stoke the fire in east-wing drawing room and have the soup ready in fifteen minutes.' The sentence started as a question, but definitely finished as an order.

'Of course. Anything else my dear?'

'A box of chocolates.'

'Of course.'

Sally walked past him into the main hallway. 'Oh, and ask someone to look in the library for the sequel to Wilbur Smith's *River God*, I believe it is called *Warlock*, and ask them to bring it to me in the drawing room.'

The library was massive. Shelf upon shelf of books stretching from floor to ceiling, it was one of the biggest rooms in the mansion, second only to the Great Ballroom. It had been created by her mother and was one of her only few vices considering the money she had at her disposal. The shelves were packed with literary classics, modern books and a plethora of first editions. The monetary value o f the collection was immense, but to Sally it was priceless; it was part of her mother.

Usually she would enjoy finding her own books; her mother's spirit seemed to be present in the library, but today all she wanted to do was curl up in the sumptuously decorated and furnished drawing room and read a good book.

'I'll ensure that the book is brought to you in the drawing room with haste.'

'Thank you Alfred.'

'Is that all ma'am.'

'Yes, thank you.'

He gave a slight bow and walked off into the mansion to pass on Sally's requests to the appropriate members of staff. Sally wandered through the mansion to her room where she changed into silk pyjamas. Then she proceeded down to the drawing room and as she entered a maid was laying out the soup and the Wilbur Smith book on the table. Sally did not even acknowledge the maid's presence and instead sat at the table to eat the soup and bread. The maid lit the fire and then tentatively approached Sally. 'Ma'am, sorry to disturb you.'

'Yes, what is it?' She did not raise her eyes from the book.

'Ma'am sorry. We appear to be out of stock of the chocolates you requested.'

'Right, well, send someone out to get them then.'

'Sorry, ma'am.'

Sally flung her book down and turned to stare at the maid. 'What now?'

'The butler asked whether the Belgian chocolates you like would suffice?'

'Yes, yes, whatever. Please. Just go and bring them. Then ensure I'm not disturbed again unless I ring the bell.'

'Of course.'

The maid gave a little curtsey and left the room. The maid thought she had got off lightly as she scampered through the halls back to the kitchen to obtain the chocolates. In the past, when something had not been available, it would have been a full scale tantrum, sulks and quite possibly an audience with Mr. Gallagher and then quite possibly sackings.

As she reached the mammoth kitchen she flung upon one of the walk-in larder doors and from the wide selection of available confectionary she retrieved a box of fine Belgian chocolates. She then scampered quickly back to the drawing room and placed the chocolates next to Sally. She gave a little curtsey and left the room.

Sally had not acknowledged her and had probably not even realised that she had been into the room. When the maid discreetly looked into the room after a few hours it was empty. She presumed correctly that Sally had retired to her bedroom for the evening and she proceeded to tidy up the room. The maid noticed the box of chocolates on table and rolled her eyes. They had not even been opened.

Chapter 21

Michelle slept well at her grandfather's house like she always did. She waited there until the early afternoon and helped him prepare a Sunday lunch for Michelle and her parents. Nothing more eventful happened until she got home and decided to call Sally. Her mobile was off for some reason so she tried Sally's private house phone and after a few rings it was answered.

'Hello?' answered a sleepy sounding voice.

'Sally, it's me. Are you asleep?'

'Well, I was. What time is it?'

'It's only six. You tired?'

'Yeah, long weekend.'

'Tell me about it.' There was a momentary pause until Michelle said, 'Look, we need to talk. Can I come round?'

'Now?'

'Yeah. Is that okay?'

'I suppose. Do you want to have some dinner here? We could watch a movie perhaps?'

'Yeah, if you don't mind.'

'I don't mind, but remember you've got some explaining to do.'

'I know, I know. Hang on. I'll check I can borrow a car again. Dad!' She paused. 'Daaad!'

'What! Don't shout at me from another room, I can't stand it! What?'

'Can I use the BMW again?'

'Again? I'm going to start charging you petrol!' He knocked on her door.

'Come in.'

He opened it and put his head through the gap. 'Where to?'

'Sally's'

'Right. Back at ten. Don't roll your eyes; you look about fourteen when you roll your eyes!'

'Okaaayyy! You sound like mum!'

'In that case your mum has a point! Back at ten.'

'Right, okay dad. Thanks.' He closed the door and Michelle started to speak to Sally again. 'Yeah, no probs.'

'I heard.'

'Cool. Half an hour?' asked Michelle.

'Yep, no probs. Hey, we could make a night of it. Have a proper girlie night. What do you think? We could watch the new Brad Pitt movie. Johnny is in it too!'

'You and Johnny Depp! He's not that nice Sally!'

'Whatever! Just because you fancy Tom Hanks!'

'Look, I never said I fancied him, I just said he was quite cute!'

'Again, whatever. You going to stay then? I went a bit mad yesterday and got a lot of new clothes. You can have a look, oh, and there are some shoes here too for you. Oh, and I've got some amazing news! You'll never, ever believe or guess it!'

'Minor problem, no way he's going to let me stay out all night, especially if I'm driving.'

'Don't worry. I'll send Ray or Alfred.'

'They'll hate you!'

'I don't care. We pay them enough.'

'Fair point.

'Pick you up in fifteen minutes?'

'Perfect.'

'Want me to come in the Rolls! We can pretend we're princesses like we used to!'

'Are you drunk Sally?!'

Sally laughed. 'Come on, it will be fun!'

'Okay, whatever you want. I'll have to clear it with the grump and then all should be good.'

'You've got him wrapped around your little finger so I'll set out now then!'

'True, true. See you soon babe.'

'Definitely! Bye!'

'Bye!'

Michelle put the phone down on her bed and quickly stripped off her clothes and grabbed her favourite jeans and a comfortable top. She quickly ran downstairs and listened for her father and mother. She couldn't hear them so she headed to the rear of the house where there was a door into the garage.

The rear of the garage had been converted into a performance studio, with sound-proofed walls. There were no windows, just a door with a red light above it. The red light was not lit which meant they were not performing so Michelle tapped on the door and it was opened from the inside.

'You're just in time. We were just about to start,' said her mum. This meant the red light would have been turned on and Michelle would not have entered unless the house was on fire or other such disaster was occurring.

'Sally has invited me to her place for the night. Can I go?'

'You can go, but you've got college in the morning. Back for ten.' Her dad turned away from her and started to press buttons on the equipment.

'Huh? I'll get dropped off by Sally in the morning. I don't see what the difference is.'

'Your exams are coming up. Back for ten.'

'Huh? No they're not. They're next year.'

'Your mocks are coming up.'

'They're not important and I'll be fine with them. I've been revising.'

'They are important because universities use them to judge whether they'll give you a provisional place or not. Back for ten.'

'Dad! Let me stay at Sally's!'

'No! Back for ten. You want to be a lawyer; here are some words you need to get used to - case dismissed!'

'Ohhh dad! She's coming for me now!'

'Well she can still come for you and her butler can bring you back for ten!'

Michelle stamped her foot and the argument was about to escalate until her mum beckoned her out of the room. She held up one finger and mouthed one minute to Michelle. She stepped out of the room and her mum closed the door behind her. Michelle pressed her ear to the door to try and hear how the discussion was going but the heavy soundproofing meant she could hear nothing. She lightly kicked the door and muttered, 'Stupid soundproofing!'

After a few moments her mum opened the door. 'Your father has kindly agreed that you can stay at Sally's tonight but there are some conditions. If you do go to a bar you are to be back at Sally's for ten. You then call your dad's mobile from her house phone, not your mobile, with the house number not hidden so your dad can check that you are actually at Sally's. Understand?'

'Yes. No problem. We're not going out anyway; we're going to watch a movie.'

'That's fine sweetie. Thank your dad for letting you stay out.'

'Thanks dad.'

'I'll be waiting for your call.'

'Okay. I'll definitely call. Better go and get my overnight things together. Good luck with the rehearsing.'

'Thank you. You have a good night.'

'You too.'

Michelle stepped out of the studio and walked back through the house and threw some essentials into a bag such as her toothbrush and a change of underwear. She then moved downstairs into the living room and occasionally peered through the curtains to check for the arrival of Sally. She arrived almost exactly when the fifteen minutes were up and Ray flashed the lights of the Rolls-Royce. Michelle picked up her bag and ran out of the house, closing and locking the front door behind her.

A few people were on the street, but they were locals and they were quite used to seeing expensive cars pulling up outside the Walmesley's abode so they did not even give the expensive car a second glance.

Ray had got out of the car and held open one of the rear doors and took Michelle's bag from her. She got into the car and hugged and then kissed her best friend on the cheek. The interior of the car was exquisitely designed as one would expect in a Rolls-Royce. In the rear of the car there were two individual seats as opposed to a lounge seat configuration. Each seat was covered in sumptuous cream leather. Between the two seats was a centre console which housed storage compartments, controls for the rear entertainment system and also a cool box that currently contained an expensive bottle of Krug champagne.

As Ray got back into the car and proceeded at a sedate pace back towards the mansion, Sally opened the champagne and poured the drink into two crystal glasses that were held safely and steadily in one of the storage compartments designed for this purpose. Sally pressed a button on the centre console and a privacy screen rose between the front and rear of the car. It was not a usual feature of this particular model of Rolls-Royce, but her father had it specially fitted at a, for him, small expense.

They clinked their glasses together and said, 'Cheers!' to each other.

Michelle sunk into the thick leather chair and let out a sigh of contentment. '

At moments like this I'm sooooo glad we became friends!'

'Yes, it's good isn't it.'

'It is more than good, it is blissful!'

'Indeed.'

There were a few moments of silence before either of them spoke. 'Hey, I've got the new Red Hot Chili Peppers video set-up to go. He looks so hot! You want to watch it?'

'Lordy, if it's not Johnny it's Kiedis. He can't even sing that well.'

'What?! How dare you?! He is gorgeous and he sounds like an angel!'

'Okay, okay, whatever. Put it on then.'

Sally pressed another button on the centre console and because of the way the privacy screen was designed it left the rear of the two front seats exposed. This design therefore allowed the rear occupants to view the twelve inch monitors that were housed in the back of the two front-seats.

When Sally pressed the button they automatically swung open and when she pressed another button the music Blu-ray started to play. They watched this in silence for five minutes or so and when it had finished Sally pressed another button and the screens swung back into their housing.

'Well, what did you think?'

'It was good. One of their better recent songs.'

'Good? It was brilliant. Didn't he look hot?'

'Not my type.'

'Oh, and I suppose Simon is?!' The words leapt out of Sally's mouth before she could stop them and the words crashed into Michelle's ears before she could call them back.

Michelle looked slightly surprised that the topic had been brought up so early into the evening, and so abruptly. 'Erm, well, you've got to admit that he is kind of hot!' Michelle replied hoping to make a joke out of it.

'Yeah, exactly why I was having a date with him, because he is kind of hot.'

'I'm sorry Sally, but I thought you hadn't turned up and that for some reason you weren't interested anymore.'

'Well, I didn't turn up because my car broke down, my phone signal went, I got drowned in the rain and looked like a rat…'

Michelle let out a little laugh. 'A rat? That would be a first! One of the best looking women in the world looking like a rat!'

'Well, thank you for the compliment, but believe me when I say that Friday night I looked like a drowned rat!'

'Okay, I believe you. Carry on. It sounds like an eventful evening!'

'It was. So, my phone signal went, I got soaked and looked like a rat, I got attacked and then I kneed and kicked him in the balls, I ran in my new Pradas which was highly traumatic…'

'Whoa, whoa, whoa! Back up a little! You got attacked? Who by? Where?'

Sally pressed a button on the centre console. 'Ray?'

'Yes Sally?'

'Can we go back via a slightly indirect route?'

'Of course. Anywhere specific you would like me to head towards?'

'The coast, then go along the coast road and then home. Is that okay?'
'Of course.'
'Thanks Ray.'

Sally then proceeded to tell Michelle about everything that happened, and everything about David.

'So you're meeting him on Wednesday?' asked Michelle.
'Yep.'
'Then what about Simon?'
'Well even though I don't agree with what you did, he's all yours. After everything that David did for me I really want to get to know him better. The way he helped me and the way he took so much of his time out to fix the car…'
'He sounds great. Which is exactly what I think of Simon.'
'So what happened if you didn't sleep with him?'
'Believe me now?'

Sally nodded in the affirmative and looked slightly uncomfortable. So Michelle told Sally all about her night. While they were talking the level of the champagne dropped and Ray continued along the coast road which they had just reached.

'And that's it. We're also going on a date on Wednesday.'
'Are you? Cool. We could double-date?'
'No, not on our first date.' said Michelle.
'Yeah, I suppose it wouldn't be appropriate.'
'And it would be slightly awkward considering you were meant to have a date with my date earlier in the week!' exclaimed Michelle.
'Indeed. Let's forget about that now. It clearly wasn't meant to be. Call it fate or karma, whatever you want to, but let's forget about it.'
'Okay, fine by me.'

They sipped their champagne and looked at the view as the Rolls-Royce majestically made its way along the road that hugged the seashore.

'Crikey!' Sally lifted the bottle out of the cooler. 'We've had most of the bottle!'
'I know. I can tell!' Perfectly timed Michelle gave out a little hiccup.

They giggled, chatted and talked as Ray turned away from the coast and headed back inland towards Sally's estate.

'I've just thought of something! You said it was running in your Pradas that was highly traumatic, not the attack?'

Sally laughed. 'Well they were both highly traumatic experiences, but getting attacked just about beats running in the Pradas as most traumatic by a nose!'

It was Michelle's turn to laugh and by now they had reached the country road that led to the gates of the estate. Just as they were approaching Sally dropped the privacy screen and saw headlights heading towards the Rolls at quite a pace. However, the oncoming car sensibly slowed down when the driver saw the Rolls indicating to turn onto the estate, and as the car went past Michelle leaned forward in her seat to pick up the cork from the champagne from where it had fallen.

*

As David glanced into the interior of the Rolls-Royce he was surprised to see that the car did not have privacy glass and he caught a glimpse of a pretty looking young lady with brown hair. He was on his way back from the garage where again he had been putting in some serious overtime. Behind the brunette, in the other seat, he thought he saw a quick flash of black hair and then he was past. He looked quickly into the rear view mirror hoping to catch another glance of the other person in the car, the one with the black hair, the same colour as Sally's hair. He was concentrating so much on the rear of the Rolls-Royce that he nearly went straight on at a sharp right hand bend. His Fiesta's muffler roared as he quickly downshifted and firmly braked, swinging the car into the corner. As he regained firm control of the car his thoughts flashed back to the flash of black hair he had seen in the back of the Rolls, but he immediately rejected it.

'No way! Just a coincidence,' he stated out loud. He thought about it some more then shook his head and said out loud again, 'No way young man, coincidence! You couldn't be that lucky!'

*

Ray parked the Rolls in front of the main doors and the girls scampered through the chilly night air into the entrance hall. Michelle was used to the opulence in which her friend lived but every time she entered the magnificent room she was always staggered. The hall had more floor space than her whole house and the massive paintings on the wall of Sally's mother still looked bigger than her house even after all these years. For a few months after Sally's mother had passed away, Michelle had had nightmares concerning those pictures and how they came to life and chased her through the mansion. But that was many years ago and now Michelle hardly glanced at the paintings as they made their way up the stairs and along the lengthy corridors to Sally's bedroom.

On entering Sally picked up the phone and ordered some food from the kitchens. They both fancied something junky to soak up the champagne so it was a burger and chips for both of them. As they waited, Sally noticed the pile of clothes and shoes that had not yet been cleared away by one of the maids.

'Just as well the maid who usually tidies my room is off today otherwise the shoes would have gone already.'

'Yeah, but where do they go Sally?'

Sally shrugged her shoulders and muttered, 'I don't know.'

She took Michelle into her wardrobes to show her the new clothes and shoes that she had recently brought. Although used to it, Michelle was always again staggered about the size of Sally's wardrobes and the fact that they were full of dresses and ball gowns valued at thousands and thousands of pounds that Sally would probably never wear or at best wear only once. They then went back into Sally's bedroom and Michelle tried on the numerous shoes that Sally had decided that she did not want anymore.

'I'll have them all if that's okay?'

'Of course it is silly! Shame you're not my size in clothes too.'

'I don't think any other woman is your size in clothes Sally. How the hell is your butt so small but your tits so big?! It pisses me off!'

Sally laughed and looked a little embarrassed. She was of course fully aware of her friend's forever battle with her weight, even though Sally had told her numerous times that she had nothing at all to worry about and that she had a great figure. Sally decided to quickly change subject as they both placed Michelle's new shoes back into their boxes.

'Shall we start the film why we wait for the food?'

'Yeah, why not.'

Sally walked across the room to her Blu-ray player and HD-LCD television. She switched everything on and then wandered back over to the bed where Michelle was already curled up.

As Sally kicked off her shoes Michelle asked her a question. 'So are you going to shag David then or what?'

'What?! Michelle! You can't ask me that!'

'I just did.'

Sally mused over the question for a few moments and then flopped back onto the bed beside Michelle. 'I've wanted to have sex for ages now but never found a guy who, well, you know, turns me on enough, not only physically, but mentally too.'

'You think David will?'

'He will physically. God, Michelle, he is gorgeous. Those eyes, blue like the sky.'

'But an arse the size of Belgium?!'

Sally laughed. 'Are you drunk?'

'A little. You know champagne makes me silly!'

'Yeah, I know. Anyway, he's got a great figure too, slim and muscular. He had his T-shirt off when I first saw him in the garage.'

'Nice. What's Simon's figure like?'

'I don't know. You'll see that before me young lady. You gonna shag Simon?'

'I hope so!'

'On Wednesday?'

'No way! After that tosser?!' Michelle was of course referring to her ex-boyfriend. 'Nice and slow this time, nice and slow.'

'We'll see.'

'No, I mean it. At least six months,' stated Michelle.

'There is no way he is going to wait six months! And there is no way you will either!'

Michelle laughed. 'Okay, maybe a couple…'

'Of dates!' Michelle laughed again.

'Shall we?'

Michelle nodded and Sally pressed play on the remote control and the movie started. After twenty minutes or so the food arrived along with another bottle of champagne.

'Champagne and burgers, an unusual combination for a Sunday!'

'Indeed Michelle, indeed!'

They had moved to the table in Sally's room and stopped the movie while they ate and talked. It was half way through the meal when Sally remembered the conversation with her father earlier in the day.

'Bloody hell!' She slammed down her fork.

Michelle jumped and exclaimed, 'What?!'

'You are never, ever going to guess or believe the conversation daddy and I had before!'

'Well if I'm never, ever going to guess you'd better tell me!'

So Sally told her about the conversation she had earlier with her father and as she progressed Michelle's mouth gaped wider and wider until Sally was sure her chin was going to land on the table.

'He is going to take you and me?!'

'Yep!'

Michelle then pushed herself away from the table and ran across to the bed and dived onto it. She then leapt back onto her feet and started to jump up and down on the bed.

'I can't believe it! Monaco, Monaco, Monaco!' She bounced some more and then jumped off the bed and ran over to her friend and hugged and kissed her on her cheek. 'Thank you so, so much!'

'Thank my dad. Hey, you're choking me'

'Sorry, sorry. Oh my God! Where's your dad?'

'In his office I presume.'

Michelle ran back over to the bed and bounced some more. It was then that the door was flung open and Sally's dad marched in.

'Now then young lady! I thought we were years past me having to come and stop you using my daughter's bed as a trampoline!'

When Michelle turned and saw it was him she jumped off the bed and ran over to him squealing then jumped and flung herself at him, wrapping her legs around his waist and her arms around his neck.

'Michelle! His back!'

She hugged him a couple of moments more and then dropped down and kissed him on both cheeks. 'Sally just told me! Thank you, thank you, and thank you again!

'That's okay Michelle. I'm looking forward to it as much as you!'

'It will be brilliant!' Michelle then ran squealing back over to the bed and started bouncing again. 'I can't believe it!'

Sally had clearly seen enough of her friend enjoying herself so she ran over and dove onto the bed, crashing into Michelle sending them both flying. Then they both sprung to their feet and bounced together.

'The broken bed and mattress will come out of your allowance!'

They both stopped briefly then Sally squealed this time which led to another bout of jumping. He watched them for a few more moments and then shook his head in amusement and left the room laughing to himself.

Eventually they both collapsed in a heap onto the bed, both out of breath. They giggled some more until Sally suggested they finish their food and after this t hey continued with the movie. There was no more talk of the trip to Monaco, it seemed too far away for discussion at the moment, but it was only a few months away and the excitement would build for all of them.

Michelle would sleep in the room adjacent to Sally's and after the movie had finished she quickly called home as instructed and then they talked a little about the impending examinations for both of them, even though they attended different colleges. Sally had been at the highly expensive Mount school since she was seven years old, and Michelle had followed the usual route of education, primary, followed by secondary followed by a sixth form college.

The conversation moved onto their hopes and ambitions. They both wanted to study at university, hopefully one of the best such as Oxford or Cambridge. Sally had always wanted to be a commercial pilot and even though she had enough money to never have to work it was still a profession that she was considering pursuing. Sally asked Michelle whether she still wanted to be a lawyer and it was then that the phrase innocent until proven guilty lit up in Michelle's mind. She knew that she would be walking on very thin ice; however, she carefully broached the subject anyway. 'Sally, do you remember much about the early days of your father's business?'

'What do you mean?'

'I mean, clearly his companies are massive, are highly profitable and have made him a huge amount of money, but I've often wondered how he started, how he got to such a strong position?'

'I don't know. He got most of his early money in the seventies and eighties before I was born. My earliest memories are of this house, but I know I lived briefly in another place; I have no memory of it though. Why?'

'I've just been wondering. Have you ever heard of him doing anything, well, bad?'

Sally looked at her puzzled. 'What do you mean bad?'

'Erm, persuading people about contracts, threatening them perhaps?'

'Threatening them? No, never. That's quite a strange question to ask me Michelle after all these years. Why has it occurred to you now?'

'I don't know. Just been hearing stories about rich men, and skeletons in their closets. I'm not implying that this applies to your dad, but I was wondering whether you had ever heard anything?'

Sally looked even more puzzled. 'No, never. I believe, although I've never asked him directly, that he had a lot of luck, right place, right time kind of luck.'

'Ah, okay. Sorry. Didn't mean to offend you. I was just wondering, that's all.'

'Now that you've brought it up though, it would be quite an interesting question to ask him. I've sometimes wondered myself, but never enough to ask him. Didn't seem to matter when I was younger, so long as I had a pony I wasn't really bothered! We could ask him, maybe in Monaco!'

The mention of Monaco sent the conversation off on a tangent and it never made its way back to Sally's father's history. After chatting more about the exciting trip, Michelle moved into her room, showered in the en-suite and sunk into the luxurious, mammoth four poster bed that could have easily slept a family, never mind a young lady who spent the night dreaming of a certain young man.

In the bedroom next door, Sally also spent the night dreaming of another certain young man.

Chapter 22

The days that followed were pretty much normal for everybody. Sarah did not make it into college on the Monday or the Tuesday but this was not unusual. Given her wild lifestyle she was frequently missing from class early in the week, usually putting in an appearance on the Wednesday. But even this day she missed as she decided to catch up on some much needed rest in preparation for what she hoped would be a wild night with Peter.

She got up in the late morning of Wednesday and when she went downstairs for some breakfast she was not surprised to see her mother sat watching the Jeremy Kyle Show while consuming a bottle of whiskey. Sarah was just in her knickers and bra but this did not concern her as she leant over and pecked her mum on the forehead. Her mum gazed vacantly up at her and muttered a good morning and then turned her attention back to the television.

Sarah stood next to her and watched the program for a few moments. This show was typical of the Kyle show and other similar shows such as Jerry Springer. Basically it consisted of numerous unemployed people embarrassing themselves on national television, talking about their problems and woes which Jeremy would then try to correct. Sarah laughed at the irony that this particular program was about people drinking too much alcohol. She could not help wondering whether her mum would learn anything that would lead her to reducing her vast consumption of alcohol but she very much doubted it.

'Mum, I'm going out tonight.'

'Okay dear. You have a good time, but before you go could you nip to the market for me and get me something nice for tea?'

Sarah thought that maybe she was not too bad today; she never usually asked for food.

'And some beer.'

'Beer mum?' This was a new one.

'Yes deary, beer. I'm trying to cut down on spirits.'

Sarah near enough staggered. 'You're trying to cut down?! Mum, in the last few days and nights you've drank bottles and bottles of spirits ranging from whiskey right through to absinthe! No matter how hard I try you always want to drink. And now you've suddenly decided to cut down?!'

'This program has really made me think. I don't want to end up like them.'

'Jeremy Kyle is going to help you stop drinking?! You won't listen to what I've been trying to tell you for months, but you're listening to Jeremy fucking Kyle?! Bloody hell mum, this I got to see! If you're serious about packing in then let me take this whiskey and pour it down the sink.'

'Take it. I would have done it myself but it was the only drink I could find.'

'Well, if you wanted to pack in you wouldn't have started to drink this, you would have poured it away yourself!'

'I know darling, but like he says,' she nodded towards the television, 'one step at a time.'

'Right, okay.'

'And I'd like you to organise me an appointment with the alcohol organisation.'

'Mum, I organised a meeting with them for you a few months ago which resulted in you getting a national ban from all their meetings!'

'But I've never been to one of their meetings before. You sort it out for your mum.' She patted Sarah's arm and returned to the watching the program, but Sarah was not going to let it go that easily.

'What the hell do you mean you've never been to a meeting before?! You went there, and, and…' Sarah was bordering upon speechless.

'Book me a meeting deary. There's a leaflet over there.'

'You really don't remember do you?' Sarah shook her head in bewilderment. 'You got thrown out. You offered the other members a drink from a bottle of whiskey!'

'I'm sure I didn't.'

'But you did! I had to come and get you, which was the most embarrassing moment of my entire life!'

'Book me a meeting. There's a leaflet over there.' Sarah again shook her head in bewilderment and reached for the bottle of whiskey. 'Leave that for now. Get me some beer and I'll pour it away then.'

'Right, okay then mum.'

'Phone up now for me.'

'Right okay mum.'

Sarah took a few steps over to the phone and picked up the leaflet. She took a deep breath and dialled.

'Hello.'

'Hi, my name is Sarah Jones.'

'Hello Sarah. How can I help you today?'

'I was wondering whether I can ask you to allow my mum to attend one of your meetings?'

'Of course Sarah. But can I ask you one question; it is your mum who you're phoning for, not you?'

'No, genuinely my mum.'

'And has your mum asked you to call or is this something you are doing without her knowledge? Because if she does not want to come herself then her attending a meeting will not be beneficial.'

Sarah contemplated this question for a moment and then with a touch of pride in her voice stated, 'No, it is something she has asked me to do for her.'

'That's good. We're actually meeting tonight. Will she be able to come?'

It would mean cancelling the date but Sarah quickly made the decision that this was more important. 'Yes, definitely.'

'Very good. What was your surname again and also your mum's?'

'Both our surnames are Jones.'

'Okay, fine.' Sarah heard her tapping on a computer. 'Jones, Jones, Jones. And your mum's first name and postcode?'

Sarah told her.

'Ah, here we go. Oh! Oh dear! Erm, let me confirm those details with you.'

Sarah confirmed the details with her.

'Well, it looks like your mother caused a little bit of trouble the last time she attended a meeting. I've never seen anyone given a national ban before Sarah.'

'She's better now. Last time I made her go, she didn't want to, now she does. Can you not give her a chance?'

'I'll have to ask. Can you confirm your telephone number for me?'

Sarah did so.

'I'll call you back very shortly.'

Sarah paced around the living room while her mother continued to watch television. After five minutes the phone rang and Sarah dashed to answer it.

'Hello, is that Sarah?'

'Yes, it is.'

'Hello Sarah. My name is Jim and I was the leader of the meeting that your mother attended. I'm sorry to say that what your mother did that night was the worst I have ever seen in many years of leading meetings. There is no possible way we could offer her a place. I'm very sorry.'

'But, but she is willing to stop! I really believe that with some help and guidance she could stop drinking.'

'I'm sorry, but I can't be persuaded. We have to consider our other members. Some of them were deeply shaken with what your mother did. I'm sorry. Goodbye.'

Sarah started to speak again but he had already hung up. She turned round to face her mother. 'Great mum! Well done! The only meeting for alcoholics in our area and you're banned from it for life! Well fucking done!'

'Never mind. I'll take care of it myself. Could you move out of the way of the television please deary?'

'You'll take care of it yourself?!' Sarah was again left speechless so she stormed out of the living room and back upstairs. 'Sort it out herself!' she ranted as she threw on some clothes and a jacket. 'This I got to see!'

*

Sarah took her time strolling the couple of miles to the supermarket. She would have taken the bus but she needed the money to help towards buying some food and some cosmetics for her date. It was a cold day and she muttered against the government who were trying to reduce the number of cars on the roads, yet the price of public transport was generally more expensive than driving. It made no sense to her.

She strolled around the supermarket too, taking her time, in no rush to get home. In front of the lipsticks she thought about which dress to wear that night and found a lipstick that matched and was not too expensive. Having naturally good skin and being naturally pretty, she did not use much makeup, however, she did need some more foundation so she picked her usual and moved on. When walking through the lingerie section she noticed a gorgeous set of deep red lingerie. She first checked the size which was fine and then the price discovering there was no way she could afford it. She then checked for a security tag and was pleased to see that there was not one fitted. Then she quickly glanced around and up along the walls and the ceilings, looking for people then cameras. She did not see either so she did what she always did when faced with something that she could not buy; she slid it very quickly and discreetly with a practiced hand under her jacket.

She got her mum's beer after this simple act of shoplifting, she opted for eight Carling, nothing too strong, and hoped that it would indeed be a start for her mum. Sarah thought she was helping her mother's addiction by giving her weaker alcohol. She did not realise that she was still fuelling her addiction and still making it worse. This thought did not occur to her though so she brazenly approached the cashier and paid for all the items in her trolley, her jacket easily hiding the stolen lingerie. She strolled out of the supermarket, past the security point, and walked at a faster pace home as the temperature had dropped while she was shopping and shoplifting. On arriving home her mother was asleep, but Sarah noticed that the whiskey had been consumed.

Shaking her head she took the bottle into the kitchen and before throwing it into the bin she peered into it and noticed three empty bottles of spirits already in there. She had emptied the bin about twenty-four hours ago, so presuming that her mother had slept for at least eight of those twenty-four hours, that left sixteen hours and even Sarah, maths not being her strong point, could work out that her mum had consumed at least one bottle of spirits every four hours. Not for the first time that day, Sarah shook her head in bewilderment. She unpacked the shopping and placed the beer in the fridge and then took her new makeup upstairs with her as she started to slowly get ready for her date.

*

Peter's day was spent chilling out and tidying his parent's house in preparation for his visitor that night. His parents were still away and he had no intention of leaving the house with Sarah tonight even though he knew that she was probably expecting to be taken out and wined and dined. At around seven o'clock that evening he got up from the sofa where he had been watching some snooker and started to get ready. When it got to quarter past eight and she still had not arrived he was reaching for his mobile when there was a tapping on his door. He walked down the hallway, checking himself in the mirror before opening the door. Peter was actually surprised about how good she looked.

Sarah had lightly curled her blonde hair into ringlets and applied a little makeup, highlighting her big, brown eyes which were sparkling. She wore a rich blue dress that was low cut and her new bra pushed up her breasts into an inviting cleavage. The dress was also short, and her legs looked toned and tanned after she had applied a subtle tanning lotion to them. He almost felt guilty about what he had planned, the drugs and the sex, but he quickly toughened himself up mentally and told himself that she was just another person to exploit, to take pleasure from and then forget.

'Are you going to invite me in or keep me standing on the doorway?'

'Sorry, come in, come in. I was just considering how beautiful you look tonight!'

'Thank you. Very nice of you to say.'

She pecked him on his lips, then turned and walked into the house. He followed her, admiring the back of her legs and her tight bottom. Taking her arm he led her into the kitchen.

'Wine?'

'Yes please.'

'Red, white or rosé?'

'Rosé please.'

'No problem.' He opened the fridge and took out a bottle of rosé and poured each of them a glass.

'What have you got planned for us tonight?'

'Whatever you want to do Sarah. We could go out for a meal, go for drinks or go for a movie. What do you think?'

'How about all of the above, but without the going out part?'

'Are you sure?'

'Yeah, I'm sure. We can eat here, get a Chinese or something, we can drink here and we can watch a movie here. Plus, if we go out there are no beds are there?' Peter's surprise must have shown in his face. 'I'm not a shy girl Peter. I didn't go to this effort to sit here and play chess.'

'I, I suppose not. Just not used to my dates being, well, so forward.'

Sarah walked towards him, swinging her hips, her heels tapping on the tiled floor. 'Are you complaining? Would you prefer it if I was a demure, naïve girl, someone who you've got to date for months before you get into my knickers?' By the end of this sentence she was pressing herself against his body, rubbing against him.

'I like you just the way you are, and if you want to be forward then that's fine with me. It wasn't a complaint.'

'Good, I'm glad to hear that. So, what are you going to do about it?'

*

Sarah's mind was racing. She had no idea that she was going to be this open with him, this forward. It was her full intention to have a proper date for once, have a meal, watch a movie, some kissing with her knickers staying firmly on her body. But, she really liked him, and after seeing him stood in the doorway looking so handsome and smelling so good, she knew that she wanted him to be her boyfriend, to date her seriously. Unfortunately, the only way she knew to get a man to like her was to offer herself to him, quickly and openly.

*

'What am I going to do about it? For now, nothing.' He kissed her quickly on the cheek.

Sarah did not know what to say. She had never been refused before when offering herself in this manner. 'What do you mean nothing?'

'We've got all night.' It was then that he saw the look in her eyes and realised that he may have actually offended her by slowing the seduction down a little.

'I really like you. I was just trying to show you how much.'

'I know you like me and I like you too as proven the other night. But there are other ways you can show a guy you like them Sarah, without offering to shag them at the opening to a date.'

'Okay, I'm sorry. I just thought you'd like me more if I gave you sex.'

'I do like you, and you look amazing tonight. Don't worry about it. Let's just see how the night unfolds.'

*

Peter's mind was also racing. He could not believe he was knocking back sex, yet there was a method to his madness, or that was what he was quickly trying to convince himself. His thoughts were that he needed to get the drugs involved somewhere tonight and then his plan of getting her hooked and her paying for it with sex would start to happen. There was another question too though that he was thinking about, should he get the heroin involved? He would just see how the night developed.

'Why don't we go and relax in the living room, have some more drinks and see what the night brings? To be perfectly honest, I'll be gutted and regret it if I don't make love to you tonight. Let's build up to it though, be romantic.'

'Okay. That sounds fine and lovely. Sorry. I don't want to put you off. I'm not very good at the whole date thing. Not been on many.'

'I don't know why not. You're lovely.'

He leaned forward and pecked her on the lips to which responded by pressing her body against his again. Peter leaned away though, and then took her hand and guided her into the lounge. They curled up together on the settee, cuddled and hugged together and exchanged a few more kisses, some which lingered and were more exploratory. Eventually, Peter suggested ordering some food and they both agreed on Chinese which was delivered from a local restaurant.

After consuming this they decided together on a film to watch during which they had more kisses and in fact missed the end of the film as their hands were now exploring each other's bodies. Peter had just run the zip down on the back of her dress and she had just unfastened his belt with a touch of eagerness, when Peter's mobile rang. She moaned as he reached to answer and he was just going to busy the call when he noticed that for some reason Reg, his supplier, was calling him. 'Shit! What the hell does he want? Hello Reg. How are you?'

'I'm fine thanks Peter. And you?'

'Top drawer. To what do I owe this pleasure?'

'Spot check. You know the drill. I want to know your inventory and money taken. Then I'll compare to how much you show me on Saturday.'

'Right, okay. Can I get back to you tomorrow? A bit busy at the moment.'

'No. You've got an hour.'

'Okay then. I'll call you then.'

'No, I'll call you in exactly an hour. Make sure you're ready.'

Reg did not wait for a reply and Peter stood up from the settee throwing his mobile onto a chair and he fastened his belt.

'What's wrong?' Sarah sat up looking concerned.

'I've got to do something. Actually, you can help if you want, if you don't mind, then we can get back to our date. This isn't something I can get out of unfortunately.'

'Okay. I'll help. No problem.'

'Thanks. Follow me then.'

He led her by the hand upstairs into his bedroom. The house had been changed since it was originally built. The entrance to the attic was originally above the landing, but since his room had been extended the entrance was in a corner of his bedroom. He stretched up to the attic hatch and pulled it down which clicked a mechanism that lowered the ladder. Quickly climbing up, he grabbed two large suitcases, swung them down and lowered them onto the floor.

Peter climbed back down the ladder and flung open one of the suitcases. Sarah let out a gasp as she saw the contents and let out another gasp when the second suitcase was opened. The first case was full of ecstasy tablets, bags upon bags of them.

'Can you count those bags for me? Each bag should contain fifty tabs. Don't count all the tabs, but spot check every five and see that they contain fifty. Write down on this piece of paper the number of bags in total and the number of bags you spot checked.'

'I didn't know that when I agreed to help you I would be counting drugs Peter!'

'Please, there is no way I can do this without you in an hour. I've got to weigh all this coke!' He indicated towards the second suitcase.

'Okay. I'll do it, but don't get used to my help.'

'No worries, I won't.'

So they both started to count and weigh the drugs. Peter was pleased with the quick progress she made and was confident that her accounting was correct. The time went quickly, too quickly, and Peter was surprised when he glanced at his watch and saw that his hour was nearly up. He left a bag of cocaine in the scales, a bag which had split that Peter was in the process of changing. There was lots of the fine powder loose in the scales and Sarah noticed it.

Before she knew what she was doing, she had dipped her finger and thumb into the powder and pinched some of the cocaine into the palm of her other hand. She was in the process of snorting it when Peter burst back into the room with his phone pressed to his ear.

As he saw Sarah knelt down snorting the coke he involuntarily said, 'What the fuck?!' This of course raised a query from Reg. 'Nothing Reg, nothing. I thought I saw someone outside.'

'Okay, whatever. Have you got your figures?'

'Yep.'

He recited his inventory to his supplier and he stressed that he had been under tight time constraints so he asked for a ten percent error margin which

Reg agreed to.

'I'd like you to bring it all with you Saturday so we can double check it and make sure you're not on the take, okay?'

'Yeah, of course.'

During the conversation Peter had been shooting daggers at Sarah but she ignored him and finished off snorting the cocaine from the palm of her hand. Peter and Reg concluded the call with some basic civilities and then Peter threw his phone across the room and it smashed into the far wall. 'What the hell do you think you're doing?!'

'Enjoying myself while you were on the phone.'

'Enjoying yourself? With my drugs? You're snorting my profits! You'll have to pay for it.'

'I don't. Remember Friday? The police?'

'There is a difference between now and Friday. You've been handling the drugs; you've got it all over you. The police won't believe you're not involved. Plus, you've been counting drugs, there is accounting detail in your handwriting so don't threaten me with the police because it doesn't stand up to scrutiny. So, I'll now refer back to my comment, you'll have to pay for it.'

'Well, I can't for it with money because I'm broke, a common occurrence with an alcoholic mother to look after.'

'Right, well, I'm sorry about your mum, but I need some kind of compensation for snorting my profits. I don't like it, and I don't appreciate it.'

'Okay, okay. Look, I really enjoy taking this,' she stood up and dusted off her hands. 'I want more but can't afford it. So…'

'So what?'

She walked over to him and stopped in front of him. Sarah hooked her thumbs into the shoulder straps of her dress and pulled it down until she was stood in front of him in her sexy lingerie that included stockings and suspenders. She knew that she had never looked better, young, slim, big breasts, flat stomach, and long, luscious legs with a shaved area of luscious female flesh between them. She slowly turned in front of him, pulling her knickers to the side and showing him one of her buttocks when she was facing away from him, then she pushed him backwards towards the bed until he fell onto it after which she straddled his hips and started to give him a lap dance.

'If you give me drugs you can do whatever you want to me, anything at all.' She swung her hips on top of him some more, grinding her shaved crotch into his. 'I'll give you blow jobs whenever you want, vaginal sex, anal sex, anything at all. I'll invite some of my gorgeous, very promiscuous friends and we can have a massive orgy, anything at all. All you have to do is give me some of that glorious white powder whenever I want and I will give you whatever you want, without restriction.'

He leaned up so he was looking into her eyes and gave her a strong, passionate kiss. Then he pulled away from her and simply said, 'Deal.'

*

He did not expect it to unfold like this. He had expected her to be reluctant to take it, that he would have to force it upon her. But now as she slid up and down his penis, moaning and groaning on top of him, his chest still had the remnants of a line of coke on it, with another line ready for her to consume also on his chest. She stopped riding his engorged organ for a moment and leant forward to take in the other line. As she finished sucking it up she licked her finger and ran it over her nose and then licked her finger again to ensure that she had taken in all the drug.

Peter was in his own world of ecstasy. Like any man, he had always enjoyed sex, but he was now realising that he had not known sex before he had it with Sarah. She was insatiable, which suited him perfectly, and her technique and some of the positions she put herself in blew his mind. She took him to heights of ecstasy unknown not only with her vagina, but also with her hand and mouth.

After finishing the drug she sprang off him and twisted quickly round and placed her dripping cleft within reach of his mouth and tongue. He accepted the offering, ran his tongue up and down her labia, consuming her juices while she swallowed his penis deeply down her throat. They stayed in this position for a long time, both of them having an intense orgasm, neither wanting the other to stop. Eventually, she lifted off him chuckling as she noticed that his face was soaking wet. She reached for the bag of cocaine and took some in her hand and snorted a lot of it. 'I just cannot get enough of this! I cannot get enough of this feeling!'

'If you can't get enough of this, I've got something a little stronger you could try?'

'Anything! I want to feel even higher!'

She stretched her arms towards the ceiling as she shouted this so Peter gently lifted her off him with her hips and she rolled across the bed, leaning on arm, her eyes closed and a smile on her face.

Earlier that week Peter had prepared some of the heroin. Not wanting people to overdose on him, he had cut the drug with flour. From a separate suitcase, which he had not included in the accounting because Reg knew that he had not used any yet, he lifted a small bag of prepared heroin already in the syringe. He had decided to prepare the heroin out of professional curiosity and also because he planned to take some syringes with him over the weekend to handout to people who were interested in an instant hit without having the need to cook-up the drug. By using a simple search on a popular internet search engine, he had found how to prepare the H.

He had learned to use a spoon, a lighter and how much water to use. He had learned to use a small cotton ball when sucking the heroin into the syringe to help filter out any impurities. He had learned on the same webpage how to inject it, to place the needle flat to the skin, to inject directly into a vein and how to spot if the point of the needle was not in the vein.

Peter could not believe that he was about to give a woman, someone who had stressed that she really liked him, some heroin, but due to the way he was feeling right now he simply did not care. He wanted more of her, more of her body, and he had to ensure that he got it.

However, he was aware that she had not tried anything like this before so he discreetly opened the bag, took the syringe out and squirted some of the heroin into a pot plant that was on a shelf. He apologised to the plant, and then walked back over to the bed.

She heard him approach and he noticed that her eyes were totally glazed over and that her pupils were hugely dilated. Sarah smiled at him as he lay on the bed next to her and he reached over her to where his jeans had been thrown. He pulled the belt off and reached gently for her arm. 'Sure you want to do this?'

She smiled at him and the trust on her face almost made him stop. But then she swung her body round and wrapped her legs around his waist, resting her still wet crotch against his. That tipped him over the edge. 'Of course I'm sure. What is it?'

'A stronger cocaine that's all, but you have to inject it to get the full affect.'

'Okay.' She chuckled and then asked, 'It's not heroin is it?'

'No, of course not.'

'Okay then. Fill me up!'

She stretched out her arm and he wrapped the belt around her upper arm tightly. He waited a few moments for the blood to build up in her constricted blood vessels until her vein was protruding. He lay the syringe flat against her arm, so the needle was pointing down her vein, and then slid it fully into her arm. She let a sharp gasp as she felt the pinch of the needle, but the cocaine had increased her pain threshold. He pulled the plunger a small amount at first, and he peered into the syringe to check that there was a touch of blood now mingling with the heroin. There was. He looked at her face and her eyes were now closed again and the smile still lingered on her face. He hesitated again, but she tensed her legs and pressed against him some more so he pressed the plunger.

Almost instantly Sarah arched her back and fell away from Peter. His first concern was that she was overdosing because she did not say anything and her breathing had become very deep and heavy. After a few moments she slowly opened her eyes and tried to speak, but nothing came out but more deep breaths. She closed her eyes again and she felt so relaxed, as if all her worries and anxieties about her mum and her life belonged in another life, belonged to another world.

Then she blurted out, 'Oh my God! Oh my God! Now that is the best feeling in the world! Oh my God, Peter!' She closed her eyes again and her breathing was deep again. 'I feel so, so happy. Make love to me and then I want some more of that joyous liquid!'

Peter obliged. He climbed on top of her and made love to her for a long time, driving her time and again to orgasm, which combined with the euphoria given by the heroin made her feel like she was flying in nirvana or heaven. Eventually she asked him for more of the drug and again he obliged, giving her a little less this time not wanting her to overdose. She slumped away from him again, and then she asked him to make love to her again and this was repeated numerous times throughout the night until in the early hours of the morning, after another hit of the powerful drug, she collapsed in exhaustion and fell into a deep sleep.

He looked down on her for a little while, watching her sleep until a smile passed across his face and he spoke out loud, 'Welcome to my web of sex, drugs and deceit babe. I don't think I'm ever, ever going to release you from it.'

Chapter 23

Michelle and Simon's date was a little more civilised than the drug and sex fuelled antics of Sarah and Peter. As promised, Simon picked Michelle up at eight on Wednesday night and the date proceeded as if they had never been apart over the previous few days.

There was no awkwardness between them, and both of them appeared to show little evidence of nerves. Michelle was surprised that she felt so relaxed and she realised that it was Simon who made her feel like this with his easy going personality and witty conversation.

They pulled into the car park of a country pub and had a lovely meal, each of them thoroughly enjoying each other's company. After the meal they relaxed in the bar area in front of an open fire, holding hands and cuddling up against each other while drinking a mulled wine.

Eventually, reluctantly, they decided to leave. Outside the pub Michelle, a little tipsy and therefore bolder after the wine, threw her arms around Simon and planted a kiss on his lips which he quickly responded to and then they were kissing passionately which Michelle reluctantly ended.

'Thank you for a lovely night Simon. It's been great.'

'I've enjoyed myself too babe.'

'What are you doing Saturday night?'

'No plans. Why?'

'Come to mine. My parents are performing so they'll be away Saturday night. We can watch a movie and have a meal or something.'

'Sounds great.'

'Perfect. I'll look forward to it.'

'Me too, very much.' Simon leant forward and kissed her again.

After walking back to the car, hand in hand, Simon drove them back into the town and Michelle's house. 'I'd invite you in but... Oh look at that! The curtains are twitching! Kiss me, quick'

'What? You must be joking? You're parents will kill me!'

Michelle though was clearly not bothered. She leaned over to his side of the car and gave him a long, long kiss which she hoped would have the curtains practically falling off they would be being twitched that hard. Pulling away from Simon she looked deeply into his eyes and giggled.

'Are you drunk Michelle?'

'A little! Red wine always makes me go a little silly!'

'I thought you said earlier it was champagne?'

'I think it could be all alcohol!'

'I think it might just be! Look, on a serious note, I'm sorry if I got you into trouble with Sally, but, I would not change anything that has happened. I really like you Michelle, already, and I'm falling for you. Apologise to Sally for me, but to tell you the truth, I prefer you to her at least a million times!'

Michelle blushed a little. 'Thank you Simon. You don't know how much that means to me.' She leant across again to give him another kiss but he lightly held her back with the flat of his hand.

'What about the curtain twitcher?'

'Fuck 'em!' With that she pulled him closer and kissed him again, longer and even more passionately than last time. 'Right, that kiss will probably mean that both my parents have probably had heart attacks on the spot but it was worth it! Should we make it a bit earlier on Saturday, say seven?'

'Perfect. You'd better go. I think I can faintly hear your dad sharpening some knives!'

Michelle laughed and then gave him another peck on the cheek. 'See you Saturday.'

'Definitely. Wouldn't miss it for the world.'

She smiled at him and then reluctantly got out of the car, gently closing the door behind her. As he pulled off she waved and watched him drive away until he turned at the end of the street. Michelle let out a sigh of contentment and then walked up the garden path to her front door that was unlocked so she quickly entered the house out of the cold night air.

'Hello? Is the front door unlocked for a reason?'

Her mum came out of the living room into the hall. 'I unlocked it for you. He looked very nice.'

'Did you see him?'

'Faintly. Is he a good kisser?'

Michelle blushed. 'I wouldn't know mum, I've never kissed a boy.'

Laughing her mum replied. 'Right, yeah, I forget that what I saw could not be described as a kiss, it could only be described as tonsil tennis!'

Michelle blushed even deeper. 'Mum!'

'Just joking darling. I shouldn't have been watching.' Michelle bit her tongue. 'You had a good night?'

'He's magic mum, truly special.'

'I'm made up for you honey, truly I am. Come into the lounge and tell me all about it.'

'Tomorrow mum. I'm tired.'

'Okay. You look it. Off to bed then. College in the morning.'

'Night mum.' She kissed her mother on the cheek and climbed the stairs carefully in her heels.

Michelle collapsed on her bed and let out another long sigh of contentment before rolling over and grabbing her teddy bear which was then firmly hugged. Slowly her eyes closed and she fell asleep, still clutching the teddy, although in her dreams the teddy was of course replaced by Simon.

*

Earlier in the same night, Sally was cursing one of the maids. She had simply asked for the brown Prada with high heels to be prepared for her, not the black. Also, she had got the wrong skirt, had somehow managed to get Dolce and Gabbana mixed up with Gucci, and because it had not been prepared correctly Sally's whole process was ruined.

When getting ready to go out, Sally followed the same process every time to ensure that she was comfortable, confident and looked her best. Now this process was out of synch and she was starting to get vexed. She stormed into the wardrobe and retrieved the correct skirt, changing her mind on the way back and grabbing another. She tried them both on, opting to go with the second, and pulled on her selected top which the maid had at least managed to get right.

Cursing the maid again, she put her shoes on and stormed out of her bedroom slamming the door behind her. She caught a glance of herself in a mirror in the hallway and paused for a second to check her blonde hair.

*

On the Monday in preparation for her date, she had borrowed her father's helicopter and flew herself down to London. She had been learning to fly for a couple of years and had passed the test a couple of months ago that allowed her to fly solo. Her father hardly used it at the moment because he had moved his personal office from his head office to a regional office and rarely had to commute to London now that people came to see him rather than him going out of his way to meet them. Occasionally though, he would have a meeting with an important client and fly to London because nothing gave a greater impression than landing in your own helicopter on top of your own well appointed head office building while the client watched on.

It was a glorious day when she set off and she could see for miles. The journey was smooth, and because of the route she took she hardly had to worry about other aircraft. This changed as she got over London and her senses were heightened in the crowded airspace. Without incident she landed the helicopter on the landing pad that was situated on top of her father's head office building and it made her chuckle to see numerous men in suits come racing out of the elevator, some of them desperately trying to pull on their jackets or straighten their ties. It was clearly with some relief that they saw it was the daughter of the boss rather than the boss who climbed down out of the helicopter, yet one of the men still came across to her and guided her away from the still spinning rotors towards the elevator.

'Miss Gallagher. What an unexpected surprise,' he stated once he was away from the noise of the rotors. 'Is there anything we can help you with?'

Another man, the company secretary and her father's chief confidant and trouble shooter, got in the elevator with them. The rest of the men waited for the elevator to return.

'If you could organise a limousine for me to be taken to Knightsbridge that would be splendid.'

'Of course, not a problem Miss Gallagher. Anything else?'

'No, that's all.'

The secretary still had not said anything which was typical of the quiet man, quietness that hid a highly intelligent mind and a person who would organise the movement of mountains if it meant that it pleased Mr. Gallagher. Company directors came and went, but James had always remained at her father's side. Sally turned to address him knowing that if she did not he would not instigate a conver sation with her. Perhaps one of the most eligible bachelors in London, Sally knew that not only was he quiet, he also was painfully shy around women in social situations.

'James, how are you?'

'I'm fine thank you Sally.' He leaned forward and hugged her and she offered him her cheek. 'And how is the big boss?' Only James would ever consider referring to her father in such a casual manner.

'He's fine. Busy. Have you not spoken to him today?'

'Yes, this morning. He's here in a couple of days. A meeting with some Japanese clients.'

'I bet he's looking forward to that like a hole in the head!'

'Quite Sally, quite. The elevator had stopped. 'Please, Sally, would you accompany me to my office? Unfortunately, I believe the limousines are out at the moment taking some other clients to Heathrow and other such errands. If I had known I would have kept one aside for you. I'll order one for you from my office.'

The other man in the elevator stayed in it and went further down the building to his office while Sally and James made their way to his corner office that overlooked St. Paul's Cathedral in the City of London. On approaching the office, his secretary rose from her desk upon seeing who the visitor was.

'Cynthia, some tea please, and order a limousine straight away for Miss Gallagher who wishes to be taken to 22 Knightsbridge. Sorry, how presumptuous of me. I presume you'll be going to your hairdressers Sally?'

'Yes, thank you James.'

'22 it is then.'

'Certainly James,' replied his secretary.

He then led Sally into his office and offered her a seat. They chatted for a little while until his secretary brought through the tea and a selection of biscuits. After these were consumed, Cynthia called through to his office that the limousine was ready. James escorted Sally to the enormous marble lobby of the building and wished her well.

'I don't imagine I'll see you until your birthday ball darling, so until then, take care. I'm in a meeting for the rest of the day, but if you require anything, the smallest thing, ensure that you contact Cynthia and she will come and find me.'

'It is okay James, I'll be fine. Thank you for the tea and the transport.'

'Not at all. You take care and see you soon.' She offered her cheek again and then left the building and entered the limousine with the chauffeur closing the door behind her.

They crossed London quite quickly due to the roads not being too congested because of the time of day. The limousine soon pulled up outside 22 Knightsbridge, Sally's hairdressers. The chauffeur opened the door again for her and as she exited the car a few passers-by stopped to see if it was anyone famous and when disappointed they carried on walking.

Sally did not find it necessary to tell the chauffeur to wait knowing he would anyway, so she proceeded into the hairdressers which was actually more beauty salon than hairdressers. While her hair colour was being changed from black to blonde, she also had a pedicure and a manicure. She was in there for about two h ours before she paid. As this salon was one of the best in London it cost Sally over five hundred pounds.

Leaving the salon, not giving the cost of her beauty treatment another thought, she got back into the limousine and was driven quickly back her father's office block. The security guard stood when he saw her coming up the steps and pressed the button to call the lift for her. Sally did not thank him; instead she pressed the button that took her to the roof of the building, back to the helicopter. Such a journey was a common occurrence, once every couple of weeks and frequent hair colour changes, expertly done, were one of her appearance trademarks.

The flight back home went as smoothly as her outward journey, and now later that week as she looked at herself in the mirror, she was impressed with the quality of the colouring. Taking a step back she admired herself in the full length mirror and she just knew that David's jaw would be on the floor when he saw her, but she had to get there first and because of the stupid maid she was now leaving later than expected.

She raced through the house, down the stairs and through the front doors to the waiting Mini that someone had brought round for her from the garages. Sally jumped into the car and sped off along the driveway to her date's house.

*

'Erm, David, you look very nice, but I don't think slippers are in vogue at the moment?'

When she had pulled up outside his house he had come down the driveway to the driver's window and she noticed that on his feet was a pair of slippers.

'You'll have to come in. She's hidden one of my shoes.'

'What do you mean? Who has?'

'My gran. Remember, I told you, she's a nightmare! She won't give it me back until she meets you.'

Sally laughed. 'I told you not to tell her!'

'I didn't! But I'm a mechanic Sally. I'm a man who wears dirty overalls and who is covered in grease and oil all the time. She can therefore quite easily spot when I'm going out with someone.'

'Okay.' Sally turned off the engine and got out of the car. 'Bless her! You should be flattered that she shows interest.'

'I am, in a way. I was hoping she'd be at bingo or something, but she cancelled it with her friends claiming that she was under the weather. Then I noticed that one of my shoes had gone, and well, she insists that she meets you. You look stunning by the way, but I'm pretty sure you had black hair the other day?'

'I change it a lot. Do you like it?'

'I love it. You look fabulous.'

'So do you, very dashing, apart from the slippers of course!'

David laughed. 'Come on then. Let's get this over with!'

Surprising him, Sally took his hand as they walked up the drive and she noticed the face of an elderly lady peering at them through a window. David pushed open the front door and led her into the living room where his gran was stood.

'Hi gran. This is Sally. Sally, this is my gran, Ethel.'

'Nice to meet you Ethel,' Sally said and she held out her hand.

'My word young lady, you should be on the front cover of Vogue.' She accepted Sally's hand and did not leave go of it. 'You are a lovely looking young lady.'

'Thank you, Ethel. You look lovely too.'

'Oh, don't be silly, but thank you anyway. Sally eh?'

'Yes, Sally.'

'So Sally, why are you going out on a date with my sinner of a grandson?'

'Gran! Please!'

'Oh Ethel, I'm sure he's not a sinner. He was very kind to me recently and he does look very dashing tonight doesn't he?'

'He scrubs up okay, but he's still a sinner.'

Ethel still had hold of Sally's hand as they contemplated David who looked like he was wishing for a hole to come and swallow him up.

'Doesn't go to church. Leaves his poor gran stood in the cold because he forgot to pick her up. A sinner he is.'

'Gran! I forgot to pick you up once over a year ago and I've been to church every Sunday since the last one I missed over six months ago. Forgive and forget? Isn't that a church teaching?'

'See how he speaks to me darling? Bring back national service is all I can think of. That would whip sinners like my grandson into shape!'

'Gran, please! Where's my shoe so we can go?'

The elderly lady started to laugh which got louder and louder. 'Your face! Your face! My word, my word!' Her laughing got louder. 'You're here taking this lovely young lady out and I'm here calling you a sinner! Oh dear, where's my inhaler? Your face!'

Sally started to laugh too, and as she did this it sent Ethel off into fresh bouts of laughter. She sat down on a chair, but still kept hold of Sally's hand. She wiped her eyes with her other hand, wiping away the tears of mirth. 'Your face, oh deary me. I damn well nearly wet myself!'

'Grrraaan! Please!'

After a few more moments Ethel managed to get control of herself. 'Oh deary me. Deary me. His face!' She looked up at Sally. 'Sorry darling, just my little joke.'

'That's quite alright. It was very funny!'

'In all seriousness though, he may be a sinner…'

'Gran!'

'But he's a lovely young man, looks after his gran he does.'

'I'm pleased to hear it Ethel. He seems to be a lovely man to me too.'

'Can we go now? Where's my shoe?'

'I'm not quite ready David. Ethel, I'm sure he was a lovely baby?'

'Jeez Sally! Don't add fuel to the fire! Let's go!'

'Funny and beautiful! I'm sure we'll meet again; I have a good feeling about you. Your shoe is in the dog's basket.'

'In the dog's basket?! Gran!' David stormed out of the room and walked into the kitchen to retrieve his shoe.

'I'm sorry Sally, but I couldn't help winding him up. He's been so nervous and edgy all day,' Ethel laughed loudly again, 'I just couldn't resist!'

'Well, I think you've done a grand job Ethel. I look forward to meeting you again.'

'I'm sure you will.'

David stormed back in. 'Can we go now?'

'Yes, I'm ready now. Very nice to meet you. It's okay, don't stand up. See you again soon.'

Ethel now released her hand and said, 'Definitely. I'll look forward to it. And you,' she pointed a crooked finger at David, 'remember how you've been brought up, no sex before marriage!'

'Gran! I don't believe you!' David's patience had clearly snapped and he strode firmly across the room and pulled Sally towards the door. 'Thanks gran, bye gran!'

'Have a good night!'

As David hustled Sally out of the house all he could hear come from the living room were his gran's wild cackles. Sally was desperately trying to keep her face straight.

'Jesus Christ! She was on form tonight!'

'Now, now David, don't blaspheme you little sinner!'

David looked at her horrified and then Sally could no longer contain her mirth and burst out laughing. He looked at her even more horrified and then started to laugh himself. By the time they reached the car they were both suffering big bouts of hysteria and they were still both laughing and talking about his gran's antics as they arrived at the restaurant.

At first David thought that Sally was making a mistake. He knew the restaurant only by reputation and would never contemplate coming here. 'Erm, Sally, you know this place don't you? It's pretty top notch you know, expensive.'

'Yeah, I know it. It's okay. My treat remember?'

'But...'

'No buts. It's fine. I've worked some overtime and I can afford to treat us both as a one off. Forget about the cost and enjoy yourself.'

She stopped the car in front of the restaurant and a parking valet came and opened Sally's door. She got out of the car and then the man ran round and opened David's door. David exited the car looking slightly bewildered and was even more bewildered when the valet got into the driver's seat and drove the car away. 'He's just stolen your car.'

Sally laughed. 'It's okay. He'll park it for me.'

Linking his arm they both walked towards the entrance. The maître d' had his head down reading the guest list and glanced up quickly as Sally and David approached his position. Then he looked again, and showed a face of surprise and then he placed a huge smile on his face. 'Miss Gallagher! What an honoured surprise! I didn't see your name on the guest list for this evening.' David looked even more bewildered and was bordering upon being embarrassed that they had just walked into this most exclusive restaurant without having booked a table. He wa s on the brink of dragging Sally back out of the establishment until the maître d' said, 'But I'm sure we can fit you in.'

He then clapped his hands and a waiter seemed to magically appear by his side. He muttered into the waiter's ear and although David could not be sure, he was semi-certain that he heard the maître d' say, 'Clear table one, now!'

The maître d' smiled at them both and tapped his pen until the waiter quickly returned and whispered something into his ear. 'Miss Gallagher, your table is ready. Please, follow me.'

They followed him through the restaurant and numerous heads turned to see them. As David passed a table he overheard someone arguing with a waiter. 'How dare you ask us to move in the middle of our meal! I booked this table months ago! It's our anniversary! I've never been so insulted and I'll make sure that we never come to this restaurant…'

David quickly moved away from this table and felt rather sorry for the waiter who was being berated. The maître d' took them right to the front of the restaurant, to the table in the middle of the restaurant right in front of the stage, a table that was swiftly being redressed. With a flourish the maître d' pulled out a chair and motioned for Sally to be seated. With an equal flourish he pulled out David's chair. David quickly sat down, embarrassed that the other couple had been moved to make way for them.

'Ma'am, to drink?'

'A glass of white wine please Samuel.'

'White wine Miss Gallagher? Could I tempt you with a bottle of champagne, on the house of course?'

'Thank you Samuel. That would be fine.'

The maître d' signalled to one of the waiters who quickly scuttled off to get the champagne. 'I'll leave you in the capable hands of Lucy, one of my top waitresses, but I insist that if anything is not to your satisfaction then please let me know and I will correct it to the best of my ability.'

'Thank you for your kind attention Samuel.'

'A pleasure ma'am.' Samuel gave a small bow and then quickly walked back to his position at the entrance.

David still looked bewildered. 'Jeez Sally. That poor couple who were at this table. And a free bottle of champagne? How on earth did you pull this off?'

Sally was itching to tell him that her father owned the restaurant, but she resisted. 'My dad used to work here as a manager. They still treat me well, but that maître d' especially likes me.'

'You can tell!'

'Yeah, I suppose you can.'

As Sally contemplated her date across the table, she was thinking that bringing David to this restaurant was perhaps not the best idea, not the best place to bring him if she wanted to be discreet about her wealth. Never mind. They were here now and she had to try and relax him.

The champagne quickly arrived and David noticed that it was a Bollinger, and even he knew that this was an expensive drink. The sommelier showed Sally the bottle and she nodded so he expertly popped the cork and poured a sample int o her glass. She tried the sample and nodded again, so he filled up her and then David's glass.

'Cheers!' Sally offered her glass across the table and David clinked his against it.

'Bloody hell Sally, I feel a little out of my depth, Bollinger champagne!'

'Enjoy, and relax. Imagine we're in McDonalds or somewhere. No difference you see? This restaurant is just like a McDonalds, it's just somewhere to eat.'

'Okay, but excuse me if I don't agree with you!'

Sally laughed and passed him one of the menus. David quickly noticed that the cheapest starter was twenty pounds, and the most expensive main meal was one pound under a three figure cost. He equally quickly decided that he was glad that Sally was paying.

'What do you fancy? I'm going for all three courses, starting with prawn cocktail and then the lobster. Have you ever tried lobster?'

David quickly noted that she had picked the meal that was one pound under one hundred pounds. 'Erm, no, I fancied a steak. Bloody hell Sally, these prices! A steak is fifty pounds, and a fillet steak is sixty!'

'Oh, the steaks are worth it, very good.'

'Does it come with diamonds?!'

Sally laughed and shook her head. 'No, it doesn't. Pick whatever you want, it doesn't matter tonight. It is our first date and after the weekend we had I think we deserve to splash-out a little.'

'Yeah, I suppose we do. In that case I'll have the garlic mushrooms followed with a sirloin steak.'

'That's fine.'

The waiter appeared at Sally's side and she gave the order and then proceeded to try and relax her date. He responded well to her questions and she was surprised with his intelligence and views on the world. She gently savoured her glass of champagne as they talked, but she noticed that David was quaffing his quickly, which she did not mind as it would probably relax him.

Their starters came and went, as did their main courses, and they both declared that they were full and did not want a dessert. Sally asked for the bill and David caught a glance of it and shuddered as he realised it was three figures with the number two being the first figure. They had not been there long when they left and the performer was just starting her first song on the stage as they left the restaurant.

They waited in the lobby of the restaurant while the valet got the Mini from the parking lot. Sally took David's hand while they waited and pressed herself against him, taking him by surprise. 'Did you have a good time?'

'It was a magic, thank you so much Sally. Are you sure you don't want me to contribute? I mean, I imagine it was a lot?'

'No, it's fine, remember our agreement, it is my treat, although don't expect to be brought to a restaurant like this on every date. You might have to make do with a McDonalds every now and then!'

'That will be fine, and I'll bear it in my mind for our next date when I'll be paying!'

Sally laughed, and then surprised him some more by giving him a kiss in his lips. 'I'd invite you back to mine for some coffee, but my dad is there and I guess you don't want to meet the folks just yet?'

'No, that would be a little bit too soon! I'd invite you to mine but my gran is there, and well, you've seen what she's like!'

Sally laughed then led him by the hand out to the Mini which had arrived. 'She's lovely, and you know it.' The valet had opened Sally's door and then he scampered round to open David's.

'Yeah, she is lovely,' David replied as he settled into the car, 'but she can be a pain in the bum as evidenced this evening!'

She drove them sedately through the country lanes, holding his hand when she was not changing gears. He noticed that they were not driving back to his house but appeared to be heading out to the coast, and indeed after a few more miles they pulled onto the coast road.

'I love it along this road at night. It is so peaceful.' After saying this Sally then turned off the road and into a car park that was next to the beach. 'Let's go for a walk.'

'Huh? It's freezing Sally!'

'Nonsense! It's a little fresh, that's all.' As she opened the car door and swung her legs out, the cold wind whistled straight up her skirt raising goose bumps along her legs. 'Hmmm, maybe it is a little chilly. Perhaps we can stay in the car?'

'I think in this instance it would be a good idea.'

So she closed her door and turned to face him. 'You do look very handsome tonight David, very dashing.'

'Erm, thanks. So do you. Not handsome though, very beautiful.'

She smiled at him and leant across the middle of the car to kiss him which he responded to. Sally was very pleased to see that he was a good kisser and was even more pleased that her body responded when his hands started to wander.

All too often in the past, when she had been with a boyfriend, her body did not respond to their touch, she felt nothing. Now, as David caressed her thigh, she started to feel hot and there was definitely something happening in between her legs. Before they got carried away, and not wanting to lose her virginity in a car, she pulled away from him, smiling at him as she did so.

'Shall I get my knight in shining armour home then?'

'I suppose we better had. Work in the morning, and I suppose you've got college?'

'Yep, unfortunately. Exam time.'

'Be worth it when you get good grades.'

'They're only practice exams.'

'Yeah, but if you do want to go to Oxford like you mentioned before then you need to study damn hard.'

'Unfortunately, what you say is true, too true, and I've been slightly lacking lately.'

Sally started the car and made their way back along the coast road towards the town and David's house.

'Hey, I forgot. You didn't tell me which college you go to?'

Sally quickly made a decision about this one and decided to be truthful. 'The Mount.'

'The Mount? Jeez, your dad must be minted!'

'Not really, it's just that he believes in getting a good education and he works hard, long hours in order to give me this chance.' That wasn't a lie, Sally thought, he bloody does!

'That's like one of the best schools in this area.'

'One of the best in the country David.'

'Yeah, true, true. I would have loved to have gone there, to be given a chance like that. Instead I got lumbered with a good old comprehensive. It was so frustrating for me. I wanted to learn, but unfortunately I was strongly in the minority. The rest of my year just fucked around in class so the poor teachers spent more time controlling the class than teaching the class. I tried to study outside class, but with my parents continually arguing from dawn until dusk it was a little hard.'

'I can a imagine David. Sorry you've not had the opportunities I have.' She took his hand and squeezed it.

'But that's life. You get the rich who have everything, and the poor who have nothing. People, politicians mainly, say there is not a class divide in this country anymore. Bullshit. My other gran, my dad's mum, died because of breast cancer because we could not afford the best treatment. And you hear about these celebrities who go to clinics in Geneva or Paris or who knows where, and they pay the price and they get the best treatment and they survive. So, if my parents could have afforded the best treatment she would still be alive. How is that fair?'

Sally had not told him how her mother had died, and she was close to taking great offence to what he was saying. 'It is not fair. Sometimes though David, even relations of billionaires die because of cancer after receiving the so-called best treatment. It is a horrible disease and it does not choose its victims based on social status, wealth, religion or whatever.'

'Yeah, you're right. But does it seem fair to you that people with wealth have better lives, while other people have nothing?'

Sally was now getting a little annoyed. 'Maybe these people have wealth and better lives because they have worked bloody hard to achieve it?'

'In that case those people deserve it. What about sportsmen though, people who get paid millions for kicking a sphere that bounces around a field? And the nurses who save people's lives get paid peanuts? How is that fair?'

'Although I agree with you that the wages modern sportsmen get are totally obscene, you have to remember that it is all about supply and demand. How many teams in the Premier League at the moment?'

'Twenty.'

'Twenty multiplied by eleven?'

No hesitation. 'Two hundred and twenty'

'Good maths!'

'Always been a strong point.'

'Anyway, two hundred and twenty football players start in the games in the Premier League every weekend then, right?'

'Right.'

'How many nurses do you think are in our local hospital?'

'I don't know, but I imagine more than two hundred and twenty. I see the point you're trying to make.'

'Yeah, there are a lot more people capable of becoming nurses than top flight footballers. Therefore, supply and demand. Footballers can demand the ridiculous wages because the clubs know that high quality footballers capable of playing in the Premier League are few and far between. Therefore, the clubs pay their players a high wage to tempt them to play for their club.'

'It's still obscene though.'

'I totally agree with you. It is totally, totally obscene and wrong that anyone be paid that much for kicking a pig skin around a field, but because of the supply and demand factor the players can request and be paid such staggering salaries.'

'Indeed.'

'I'm sorry about your gran. I had someone very close to me die of cancer. It's horrible. I was only young, but I remember watching her waste away...'

'Your mum?'

'Yeah, how did you...'

'You told me earlier in the night that she had died.'

'Well, yeah, my mum. Breast cancer too. I was only young too. I hated watching her die like that. I kept on expecting to see her back in her kitchen, making me cakes, but she just got sicker and sicker. I didn't really understand what was going on.'

'Neither did I.'

The conversation halted as they both became lost in their thoughts and soon Sally pulled into David's street where she pulled up in front of his house and turned to face him.

'I've had a great time David, a really lovely time.'

'Me too. Thank you for the meal.'

'Thank you for fixing my car!'

'No problem. Anytime.'

She leaned across and kissed him. 'Saturday night?'

'Yes, definitely.'

Sally then asked him, 'What do you want to do?'

'Do you like the theatre?' Sally was not expecting this and the surprise must have shown on her face.

'Just because I'm a mechanic doesn't mean I can't appreciate the finer things in life!'

'I know, sorry. I just wasn't expecting the theatre to be offered to me. I'd love to. What are we going to see?'

'I can drive us into the city to watch Les Miserables if you like?'

'Perfect. Which theatre is it on at?' David told her and she was relieved because it was not the theatre owned by her father.

'I think the doors open at seven so shall I pick you up at six?'

'That sounds brilliant!'

'Oh, don't expect executive seats or anything.'

'I won't and I could be sat behind a pillar for all I care so long as I am enjoying myself with you.'

'Oh, thanks Sally. That's a lovely thing to say.'

He leaned forward and kissed her, deeply and passionately until he heard a distant banging on one of the windows in the house. He looked up and saw his gran with her face pressed against a window shaking her finger at him and clearly mouthing the word sinner at him.

'I don't believe her!' David muttered under his breath.

'Now, now David that is the language of Satan! You'll burn in hell!'

'Bloody hell Sally, don't you start!'

They both laughed until David leaned forward again and engaged Sally in another deep kiss. The banging on the window was renewed with increased vigour and carried on even after David ended the kiss.

'Right, better go before the old bat has a seizure or something.'

'David!'

'Sorry, but come on, I'm an adult and I can't kiss you?!'

'She's a lovely lady and she cares about you which you should be grateful. She's just from a different generation, you have to understand that.'

'Oh I understand it alright. I understand that she should be locked in a padded room with a stick between her teeth!'

'David! That's your gran you're talking about!'

'I know, I know. Right, seven, no six on Saturday? Where do you want me to pick you up from?'

'I'll come here and you can drive us to the theatre.'

'Eh? That doesn't make any sense? Why don't I just pick you up from your house?'

'Because I've got to take my uncle to the airport so I'll get ready before and come here after dropping him off.'

'Okay, if that makes you happy.'

'It does. You'd better go. She's going to smash that window if she hits it any harder!'

They both laughed and David gave her another kiss before he got out of the car. He watched as she drove slowly down the street, waving out of the window before she turned and was gone from his view. He walked up the drive and opened his front door to be greeted to the sound of his gran laughing hysterically from the front room.

'Your face! Your face when you saw me banging on the window! I nearly wet myself!'

David stood at the bottom of the stairs shaking his head in amusement at the merriment his gran was giving herself. He did not enter the living room but instead from the foot of the stairs said, 'Goodnight gran.'

Then he went upstairs to bed, the hysterics of his gran eventually dying down.

Chapter 24

'How did it go? Did you get laid?'

'Michelle! Behave yourself!'

It was the day after their respective dates and Michelle had called Sally on her mobile. 'Well, did you?'

'No, I did not! He's a good kisser though and he made me feel very hot in the car!'

'I bet he did! You didn't lose your virginity in the back of a Mini did you?! That's not very romantic. At least that idiot, my so called boyfriend, ex-boyfriend now thankfully, seduced me into a bed, not into the back of a car!'

'Michelle, my virginity is one hundred percent intact thank you very much. Considering how much you're talking about sex all of a sudden I guess this means you got laid?'

'Nope.'

'You didn't?'

'No, I told you, nice and slow with Simon, nice and slow.'

'I'm sure!'

'I mean it. At least six months.'

'No way.'

'Seriously, six months.'

'When are you seeing him again?'

'Saturday.'

'Then I'll give you until Saturday before you're in bed with him.'

'Not going to happen Sally. When are you seeing the gorgeous David again?'

'Saturday. We're going to the theatre?'

'You're not taking him to the theatre your dad owns are you? Fancy taking your new boyfriend, who incidentally doesn't know how rich you are, to the expensive restaurant that your dad owns!'

'I know, not my smartest move. No, all his suggestion and he picked the theatre. Les Miserables. I've seen it, but it's good so I won't mind sitting through it again. And you? Where are you going?'

'My place.'

'Your place? And your parents?'

'Out. They'll be in London performing.'

'Like I said, Saturday!'

'Not going to happen!'

'Hmmm, we'll see. Hey, my dad came to my room before,' Sally rolled over on her bed and put her mobile to her other ear, 'and he told me that he'd been talking to the C.E.O. of the Formula 1 team. He told us what cars we'll be driving around the track. We're going to be driving…'

*

As Sally and Michelle talked about and planned their trip to the Monaco Gra nd Prix, Sarah was having one the worst days of her life.

She had woken up in Peter's bed at about nine the next morning with him snoring next to her and at first felt fine. Looking round the bedroom, Sarah saw the empty syringes but instead of being concerned she shrugged her shoulders and tracked down her handbag. She removed a package from the bag and took a contraceptive pill, after which she went downstairs and made them both cups of tea. When she came back upstairs Peter was awake and thanked her for bringing him the tea.

'That was pretty wild last night Peter. Just what I needed. Been having a lot of trouble with my mum at home and needed a blow out.'

'I thought you had a blow out on Friday?'

'I've got a *lot* of trouble at home and I need a *lot* of blow outs!'

'Fair enough. She bad?'

'Horrendous. She doesn't move from the chair in the living room unless it is to get a fresh bottle of spirits. Dad left, with a cleaner from his work.'

'Ah, okay. Bastard.'

'Yep. What was that you gave me last night? Was it really cocaine?'

He laughed inside at her naivety. 'Yeah, just a stronger version. Want some more?'

'Yeah, I think I do.'

So he got out of bed and got another syringe, but this time he did not squirt some of the liquid into the pot plant. She sat down on the bed and he prepared her arm for her. Then he slid the needle into her arm and again the affect on her was near enough instantaneous. She collapsed backwards onto the bed with her eyes tightly closed and her breathing deep and heavy. Peter left her to her drug ecstasy and wandered downstairs to get some breakfast.

After he had not heard anything for an hour he thought he had better go and check on her. As he walked into his bedroom the first thing he noticed was the smell. It made him feel nauseous and he soon saw the reason why. The heroin had clearly made Sarah feel sick and she had obviously attempted to make a dash to the bathroom. She had not made it because there was a pile of vomit on his bedroom floor. After vomiting she had then returned back to his bed because she was curled up on it fast asleep. He walked over to her and looked at her face to check that she was still breathing. She was, but he noticed that she still had vomit around her mouth and had in fact managed to transfer the vomit onto his pillow and duvet.

Peter managed to catch his temper before he exploded at her, but only just. He did shake her awake though and loudly said, 'Sarah, wake up Sarah. Come on honey, you've been sick.'

Sarah groaned. 'What time is it?'

'About noon.'

'Shit. I was meant to be in an exam an hour ago.'

'Never mind. You've been sick. Go and take a shower why I clean up.'

'Shit, sorry. I felt sick. I don't know why.'

'It might be the drugs. You've taken a lot.'

'Yeah, I think so. Sorry, I'll go for a shower.'

She walked out of the room, stepping around the pile of vomit. When Sarah was out of the room Peter cursed her and started to strip his bed. When this was done, he took the bed linen downstairs and placed them straight into the washing machine which he started. He then returned back upstairs and contemplated the sick. 'How the fuck am I going to clean that up?!'

Deciding on a plan of action he went downstairs, unlocked the back door and retrieved a shovel from the garden that was not too dirty. When he returned back upstairs, Sarah was getting dressed and offered to help as Peter scooped up the vomit onto the shovel. Once it was all on the tool, he poured it carefully down the toilet and then went back down into the kitchen for some cloths and carpet cleaner. Cursing Sarah again, he returned back to his bedroom and cleaned the carpet and once this was done he was quite happy with the result.

'Sorry.'

'It's okay. It's partly my fault. I allowed you to take way too much.'

'I wanted it though, so sorry.' There was a very awkward silence between them. 'I think I'll go home. I need to check on my mum.'

'Okay. Do you want to come back tonight?'

'I'll see. Depends how my mum is. Is it okay if I call you?'

'Yeah, of course.' Peter walked over and kissed her, then took her hand and led downstairs.

'Thanks Peter, I had a good night.'

'Anytime. Be careful going home.'

'I will be. I'll call you later.'

She reached up and kissed him on his cheek. Then she turned, walked down his path and turned towards home. As she walked she felt very light headed and relaxed, but this was to swiftly change on reaching home.

*

'Mum, I thought you were cutting down?'

'I had the beer deary.'

'Yeah, I know mum, but the whole point of having the beer is to not have the spirits after the beer!'

'Oh, but I didn't have the spirits after the beer deary, I had the same at the same time. Look!'

Sarah's mum pointed to what looked like a pint of lager. Upon sniffing the lager though Sarah quickly realised that not only was there lager in the glass, there was also a large amount of spirits. 'What spirit is in this glass mum?'

'Gin. And something else too. Can't remember what.'

'Gin? Where did you get gin from mum?'

'I found some cash in your room. I used that.'

'You're fucking joking me mum?! For fuck's sake! That's my college money, the money I need to get to college every day and to eat too! Thanks mum, thanks a fucking million!'

'You get some more next week don't you deary?'

'Yes, but what about the rest of this week mum? I haven't got a penny!'

'Did you phone up the alcoholics place? Is there a meeting I can go to?'

'I phoned up yesterday mum. You're fucking banned remember, banned for life! And if you weren't banned then perhaps I would not have gone out last night, perhaps I would have taken you to the meeting. Perhaps I would not have had sex with a guy all night and not taken more drugs than a Colombian whore! But no, you had to get yourself banned so that is exactly where I spent last night, hiding from you and the upset you give me, getting screwed in every position I could think of while taking copious amounts of illegal drugs! And then, and then to top it all off nicely, you've spent my fucking money on something you said you were trying to cut down! Thanks a million mum, thanks a fucking million!'

'Did you have a good night? That's lovely. Is there a meeting I can go to? An alcoholics meeting?'

'You're taking the piss?! You've got to be taking the fucking piss?! I just told you NO! There is no meeting in our area, we've got no money because you keep spending it on booze so I can't take you to another meeting in another area and we can't drive because guess what? We haven't got a car! That got sold a few months ago to get us out of debt with the bank because you keep on spending the money on booze! Vicious circle you know mum, vicious fucking circle!'

'That's lovely dear. Where did you go last night?'

'A boy's house mum. I got laid so, so many times and like I said, I took many, many drugs.'

'That's lovely dear. Did you have a good time? Did you manage to phone the alcoholics place for me?'

If looks could kill, Sarah's mother would have disintegrated on the spot. Instead, all Sarah could do was storm upstairs to her room and lie down on her bed. It was only then that she started to feel unwell.

At first it was mild as the final effects of the heroin wore off. Then she started to get mild stomach cramps, similar to discomfort she felt at certain times during her menstrual cycle. But she was surprised when she put the cramps down to this because she had only just had her period. When she raised herself into a sitting position to see if this eased the cramps, she started to feel dizzy and the room started to spin a little. So she lay back down, and this eased the dizziness, but not the cramps. Then, a little later, nausea descended on her so she scampered to the toilet and spent some time with her head hovering over the toilet. Sarah did not vomit though, so she returned back to her bed and closed her eyes.

She was surprised when she woke up a few hours later, and was relieved to see that the cramps and nausea had faded. But now there was something else. For some unknown reason, her skin felt itchy, mainly her arm that the drug had been injected into. To her, this was worse than the cramps and nausea. She scratched her arms with her longs sharp nails, leaving long red marks on her previously young, unblemished skin. But, the more she scratched, the worse the itching seemed to get. Closing her eyes, she tried to think whether she had changed her shampoo or cleansing products recently, but her mind seemed cloudy and she could not think. When she opened her eyes, she glanced at the clock and it was early evening. She then spent some time trying to remember who and where she had to go to that evening. Eventually her mind tracked back to Peter, but she was surprised about how foggy and slow her thinking was. And the itching, the itching. After scratching her arms again so much that she cut herself, she decided to take a shower to see if this eased it.

While taking the shower she discovered that turning the heat up as high as she could stand helped ease the incessant itching. Also, the shower helped clear her head, yet she was surprised again when she tried five times to pick up the bottle of shampoo from the floor of the shower, eventually managing to grab it while overbalancing and she crashed into the tiled wall. Thoroughly she cleansed then returned to her room to call Peter who reluctantly agreed to come and pick her up, so she pulled on some clothes, not bothering with underwear.

After five minutes which she spent lying on her bed, she heard a car horn outside and she unsteadily walked downstairs. She popped her head into the living room and caught her mum swigging from a bottle containing a bright yellow spirit. Without saying anything, Sarah quietly closed the door and went out to Peter.

*

'What did you do this afternoon?' Peter asked her as he slowly made his way through the streets back to his house.

'Nothing. Slept. I've been feeling a little sick and I think I must be allergic to some kind of cleansing product because my skin, my arms especially, are so itchy.'

Peter contemplated this for a moment. During his time searching the internet for information on heroin, he had discovered that this itchy feeling was an effect of taking heroin.

'Might be your shampoo or something. Or might be your washing powder. Have you changed it recently?'

'No, I don't think so. I can't really remember.' Sarah thought this strange that she could not remember, but Peter did not. He knew that heroin decreases mental functioning even after one dose.

'It will come back to you.'

'Hopefully. What are we going to do tonight?'

'I don't know. Watch another movie, or we could go out?'

'No, I don't feel like going out. Movie sounds good.'

'Okay, whatever.'

They completed the rest of the short journey in silence and when Sarah entered the house she went into his living room and collapsed onto the settee. 'I feel rough.'

Peter thought she looked rough too, not as attractive as she looked the previous nights they had been together. She had no makeup on and was very pale, yet her bra-less breasts looked brilliant as she lay on her back and he thought he might as well quickly try his luck. He sat next to her on the settee. 'Roll over.'

'Why?'

'Just roll over.' She obliged, and he pulled off her jacket.

He caught a glance of her arms and was not surprised to see them looking red and inflamed, with clear scratch marks present on them. Pulling up her short sl eeved top, he asked her to lift up her arms, which she did, so he pulled the top over her head leaving her naked from the waist up. He whispered in her ear to wait right there, then he ran upstairs and retrieved some aromatic massage oils from his bedroom. Returning to her, he poured some of the oil onto his hands, dripping some of it onto her back.

Sarah let out a little moan as she felt the liquid land on her back, and she moaned some more as his hands went to work, giving a full back massage. When he worked down to her lower back he reached under her waist and unbuttoned her jeans. Then he slowly pulled them down and was not surprised, but still enjoyed the fact that she was wearing no knickers. He poured some more oil onto her bottom and down the back of her thighs, after which he massaged her bum and her legs. While he massaged her legs, he gently parted them so he could see her pussy, and was pleased to see it shining with moisture. What he did not realize was that this moisture was from his oils, not from her own natural secretions.

Although she was enjoying the massage, Sarah did not feel any sexual arousal at all, which certainly surprised her. After receiving such a sensual massage, her insatiable sexual appetite would be usually crying out for more intimate touches, but now she felt nothing. When he had finished on her calves, she heard him stand up and remove his jeans. She craned her head round and saw him standing there, naked from the waist down, and a large erection pointing at her. 'Peter, thank you, the massage was lovely, but I really don't feel like this tonight.'

He did not say anything at first, but instead knelt in between her legs and leaned forward so he could whisper into her ear. 'Remember how you felt last night? Do you not want to feel like that again?'

'I do, but…'

'I've got plenty more of the drugs for you. Remember how good you felt when they hit your body?'

Sarah's mind was in turmoil. Her body was crying out for some more of the drugs, she knew that the itching and cramps would go if she could have another dose. But she did not want to have sex, not like this, not just for the drug when she was not even turned on. 'No, I really don't feel like it…'

Peter cursed her in his head. 'Wait there.'

Peter walked quickly out of the room again, back to his bedroom where he picked up a bag of cocaine and also some of the syringes of heroin. Sarah had not moved so she rolled over to see him when he re-entered the room.

'How about some of this?' He waved the bag in front of her nose. 'Or perhaps madam would prefer some of this?'

Sarah let out a little moan of longing when she saw the syringes being waved in front of her and she leaned forward to make a grab for one of them. He quickly moved his hand away and made a negative noise.

'No, no. I want something first.'

She moaned again. 'What?'

'You know what.'

Sarah sighed and then leaned back on settee and parted her legs. Quick as a flash, Peter threw himself between her legs, forcing them further apart with his body. He quickly lined up his penis with the entrance to her vagina and without w arning forcefully slid it into her. Sarah dug her nails into her shoulder, not because of pleasure, but because his strong penetration had hurt her. He was very disappointed to find that after the initial moisture caused by the massage oil, her deeper reaches where dry as bone. Pulling out of her he reached for a bottle of the oils and poured some over the length of his erect organ.

'Peter, sorry, I really don't feel…'

But she did not finish the sentence because quickly he pressed himself between her legs and pressed himself down on top of her. He lined up again and slid his oily organ into her. This time the oil made his passage easier, but it was still a discomfort to her. When he started to thrust he enjoyed it, but to her it was misery. With every one of his thrusts he grunted, and she let out a moan which he took to be moans of pleasure.

After a few minutes though he noticed that she was not moving at all, not like the previous times they had sex. Previously she had bucked under him, rotated her hips and met each of his thrusts with one of her own. Now though it was like having sex with a sack of potatoes. He decided to carry on though, because he was still enjoying the feel of her vagina even if she was just lying there.

Eventually for her, she felt him tense, heard him moan and then felt his warm, oily ejaculate pour into her. He then lay on top of her for a few more moments, breathing deeply and squashing her, before he drew his penis out of her and she shuddered as she felt him draw out of her now sore vagina. Standing up, he grabbed his jeans and pulled them back on before turning back to her. Sarah had rolled over and had her face buried in a cushion.

'What was wrong? Why didn't you want to do it?'

She turned away from the cushion and the look she gave him was one of pure venom. 'I told you I didn't want to do it before you forced me!'

'I didn't force you. All you had to do was say no.'

'I did say no, remember?!'

'Not after I got the drugs, I actually don't remember you saying no. Speaking of drugs, here's your reward for having a vagina like a desert and for lying there like a sack of spuds.' He threw a syringe at her which she caught.

'That's what happens when a woman doesn't want to have sex and isn't turned on! She's dry and she just lies there!' Sarah quickly spat back at him.

'Whatever. I'm going for a shower.' With that, Peter stormed out of the living room.

For a few moments Sarah lay, breathing hard, fuming inside. Then she said out loud, 'He near enough fucking raped me the wanker!' A few moments later she felt the syringe in her hand. She held it in front of her face, contemplating the liquid inside. 'Fuck it!' she exclaimed again out loud. 'If he's going to do that to me then I'm going to take some of his precious fucking drugs!'

Spotting her jeans on the other side of the room where Peter had thrown them, she strode across to them and pulled her belt from the loops. She slid down the living room wall so her back was resting against it. Quickly she tightened the belt around her upper arm and slapped the skin on her arm.

Due to Peter doing it for her last night, she was not exactly sure what she was doing, but as she slapped she saw a blue blood vessel slowly protrude from her arm. Guessing this was the correct place, she laid the syringe against her arm as Peter had done the previous night and slid the needle into the vein. Pausing for a moment, she studied the needle sticking out of her arm and she nearly did not press the plunger. Then she got another sharp stomach cramp and felt her skin still itching. So she pressed the plunger down, the liquid shooting into her vein, into her body. Quickly the opiate raced through her blood, crashing into her brain which released the euphoric feeling into her body.

Her skin increased in warmth and her body felt weighed down so it was no surprise when she stopped leaning against the wall and her upper body slumped to the floor. As her breathing deepened, through the euphoric mist, she noticed that the cramps had gone, and marvellously the itching had stopped. She descended into a semi-conscious state and was only half aware when Peter came into the room and shook her shoulder.

'You okay?'

'Oh God Peter, that is the best feeling in the world.' She closed her eyes again and then quickly opened them again. 'You should try some. Have some with me, please.'

'No Sarah, I'm not going to. You enjoy yourself though; have as much as you want.'

'Okay, I will.'

With that she closed her eyes again and Peter returned to the settee and turned on the television, simply ignoring Sarah as she was lost to her drug induced ecstasy. After about half an hour he watched her slowly push herself up into a sitting position. He noticed that her recovery time was already shorter than last night and was astonished about how quickly she had become addicted and how quickly her tolerance seemed to be growing. He also thought that if this was how quickly people became addicted to the drug then he was going to make a lot of money selling it on the streets.

As he considered this, he thought that he was treating Sarah a little like a 'guinea pig'. He was interested in the effects of the drug and while he considered this some more he decided he would carry on giving the drug to Sarah to satisfy his own professional curiosity. Since she was rarely or possibly not all, going to be able to pay for it with sex, then he would use her like a scientist would use a rat: for his own experimentation. His final thought on this issue was that it was a perfect idea.

Slowly he watched her become more aware of her surroundings. While she was coming round he had discreetly placed another syringe in her line of vision and waited expectantly to see her reaction. He was quite disappointed when she came over to him, ignoring the syringe, and sat down next to him on the settee. She placed and arm around him, and her head on one of his shoulders.

'There's some more if you want it.'

'I know. I'll have some later if that's okay?'

'Of course it is. Do you feel up to some sex yet?'

'No, I don't. Not at all.'

When she said this he turned back to the television and was only aware of her when she leant back into the settee. After an hour or so she stood up to use the downstairs toilet and when she returned she slumped against the wall again. Peter watched her as she fastened the belt around her arm again and quickly injected the drug. Again, she slumped to the floor and Peter returned his vision back to the television. This process was repeated until the early hours until he had had enough and went upstairs to his bed, alone. Sarah stayed up throughout the night, regularly taking the heroin, not needing or wanting to sleep.

When Peter returned to the living room in the late morning he found her in exactly the same place, slumped on the floor with a handful of syringes around her. He walked over, checked she was still breathing, which she was, and he noticed that there were no syringes with heroin in them left for her to use in the living room. He presumed that she would be asleep and was surprised that when he gently shook her shoulder her eyes opened instantly.

'Morning. Have a good night?' She nodded. 'I need to go out. Do you want me to drop you off?' She nodded again. 'Have you slept?' She shook her head slowly this time. 'You should.'

'I didn't want to. I wasn't tired. Can I see you tonight?'

'No. I'm busy tonight.'

'When then?'

'I don't know. Can I call you?' She nodded. 'Come on then, I need to go.' He flung one of her arms around his shoulders and helped her to stand. Then he realised she was still naked. 'Can you dress?'

She muttered a yes and the first thing she did was release the belt that was still fastened around her arm. Sarah then tried to pull on her jeans but she ended up falling over twice before Peter intervened and helped dress her.

Leaning heavily on him, he led her out to the car and drove her quickly home. She mumbled a thank you to him, fell out of the car, and then stumbled her way to the door of her house. He watched her fumble for her house keys, which she eventually found, open the door and staggered into the house closing the door behind her.

Peter shook his head and muttered, 'Fucking druggie!' He drove quickly away from her house not giving her another thought.

*

Sarah managed to stagger her way into the living room where her confused mind slowly registered that her mum was actually eating food which was a highly rare occurrence. She struggled to think of what could have happened that would allow her mum to be able to afford food instead of alcohol and slowly her mind remembered that it must be benefits day.

Even though she had not eaten for over twenty-four hours, she did not feel hungry nor did she feel tired. So she slumped down into an armchair, without her mum even acknowledging her, and watched some television. Slowly her mind noticed that the red light, which meant there was a message waiting, was flashing on the phone situated on the table next to the chair. She leaned forward to play the message but it was a few moments before she could remember the correct button to press. Again, slowly it came back to her and she pressed play.

"Hello. This is a message for Sarah. It is Claire Wood from college, your English tutor. I'm rather concerned that you have not been present in your two examinations that have occurred in the last two days. I was wondering whether you could give me a call as a matter of urgency so we can discuss the situation. Thank you."

Sarah leaned back and sunk into the armchair again, not giving the message another thought and she was certainly not contemplating calling her tutor. For a few hours she sat without moving watching the television until she got a sharp cramp in her stomach that made her double up in pain. The cramps came and went for the rest of the afternoon, and then, slowly but surely, the itching started again.

Chapter 25

After she had spent a couple of hours watching television, Sarah had gone to bed in the vain hope that sleep would help her hide away from the cramps and the incessant itching. But the sleep never came. Instead, she lay on her bed staring at the ceiling, desperately trying to ignore the feeling of her skin, but occasionally, subconsciously, she vigorously scratched her arm with her long nails. She scratched so hard that at one point she drew blood, and at other times she broke a couple of her perfectly manicured nails. As she contemplated the broken nails, she bit them off and spat them out onto her bed.

She remained like this for a few hours, closing her eyes now and then; desperate for sleep to descend upon her, but again it did not. Once or twice during these hours she made a dash for the toilet and spent some time knelt before it until the waves of nausea abated, although she never actually vomited. After one more run to the toilet she stayed off her bed and rooted through her handbag for her mobile. The battery was dead and she cursed because she was hoping that Peter would have called her.

So Sarah plugged the charger into the phone and, after a few moments wait, turned on the phone. As it switched on she stared expectantly at the screen and was disappointed that no missed calls messages appeared and no text messages either. So she decided to call Peter and see if she could see him that night.

*

After Peter had dropped Sarah off at her house he had made his way back home and had a relaxing day and afternoon watching television and playing some computer games. Early in the evening he had started to prepare for his night's trade and he was looking forward to earning some good cash by dealing his usual supply of Ecstasy and Cocaine, but also hopefully selling some of the Heroin. He loaded one of the suitcases with the drugs and carried this out to his car where he placed the suitcase securely in the boot. It was earlier than he usually set out, but he was eager and excited to start that night so he drove into town to start dealing, going via the garage to park his car.

As he walked from the garage into the town centre, his mobile rang and he looked at the screen. On seeing it was Sarah he rejected her call and went into the first of many bars he would attend that night. At first he was disappointed. His usual clientele did not seem interested in the Heroin; they all just stuck with their usual orders. Yet in another bar, one customer bought a prepared syringe from him and disappeared into the toilets and staggered out some time later and gave a thumbs-up to his friends who promptly approached Peter to purchase some of the H.

Very quickly he had sold all the prepared syringes, so he rooted through the specially extended pockets of his pants and started to sell the Heroin loose. So desperate were some of the people for a hit, they used the syringes that had been used by their friends, clearly oblivious, or they just simply did not care, about the chance of passing diseases to each other.

All the time he was in this bar, Peter was trying to be discrete, but his customers were far from being discrete. They were openly passing the syringes around right in front of the bar staff and some of them were even cutting down the heroin on a table. When one of the drug users went to a nearby store and came back into the bar with a roll of tin foil presumably so he could chasing the dragon, Peter quickly realised that it was getting far too hot for him in the bar so he quickly left.

As he walked down to the other side of town, as far as possible from the bar, he could not believe how brazen and uncaring the users were, openly sharing syringes and cutting the drug up on the tables. As he walked he felt his phone vibrate and he got it from his inside jacket pocket. On noticing it was Sarah, he again rejected her call and carried on walking to the next bar again not giving her another thought.

*

It was the fifth time that she had tried to call him and it was the fifth time her call got through to his answer phone. She had left a message and hoped that he would call her back but he never did. As it approached midnight the cramps, nausea and the itching were the worst they had ever been. Sarah could barely think straight, all her thoughts were consumed by the nausea, cramps and worst of all the incessant, never ending itching. She scratched and scratched and scratched but the itches did not fade away. Her arms were red, bright red and bleeding where the skin had been broken.

Slumping onto her bed, she tried to gather her thoughts and her thoughts all led to the same conclusion – she had to see Peter, she had to have some more drugs. Slowly deciding on a course of action, Sarah quickly threw some clothes on and grabbed a jacket for the walk to Peter's house. After descending the stairs, she somehow remembered to look in on her mum who was still sat in the chair, passed out with a bottle of something in her hand.

She spotted her mum's purse on the table and with optimism rooted through it hoping to find some cash so she could perhaps order a taxi to Peter's house. All she could find though was about fifty pence in change which she quickly placed into the pocket of her jeans. While cursing her mum for not having any money, she fastened up her jacket then left her house and started the long walk to Peter's house.

*

While Sarah was beginning her long walk, Peter was also walking back to his car to place his earnings in his suitcase. He had sold up. All the drugs he had brought with him from his house had been sold so quickly he was shocked. He was tempted to return home and get some more, but he looked at the pile of cash that he accumulated and decided to instead peel some notes off the pile and go and have a good time and see if he could get lucky with a lady.

As he walked into a bar he was quickly approached by people wanting a dru g but Peter stated he was sold out for tonight. He noted the look of disappointment on their faces and he made a mental note to bring more drugs out with him next time so he could of course make more money. When he approached the bar he noticed a blonde on the other side of the bar and he was happy when she turned around and he recognised her. Just like Sarah, she was getting quite a good reputation recently for being easy and Peter was also pleased to note that she seemed to be quite drunk already. So he ordered himself a beer and then walked round to her and whispered a joke into her ear. She burst out laughing and as confidently and as easy as that he had her attention.

They chatted for a little while until her friends came over and told her that they were leaving. While they waited for her decision whether she was going to come with them, Peter whispered into her ear again and she burst out laughing again. Peter was happy when she told her friends that she would catch them up. Shrugging their shoulders, they left her alone with him.

*

Sarah, meanwhile, had reached Peter's street and was quickly walking through the cold to his house. As she approached his abode, she was disappointed to see no lights were on. She knew that his parents were not due back until Sunday so she banged on his door and waited for a response. When none came, she banged again and again and again. When there was still no response she picked up stones from his garden and threw them at his bedroom window. Giving up when there was still no response, she sat on his cold doorstep, wrapping her coat around her knees and waited.

*

Meanwhile Peter had his tongue firmly thrust down the blonde's throat and was openly cupping one of her breasts in the bar. As she pressed her body firmly against his, he whispered again into her ear and to whatever he had said she nodded then took his hand and led him out of the bar. Peter directed her away from the nearby taxi rank and when she looked at him quizzically he told her that his car was nearby.

When they were walking along they frequently stopped and kissed, until they reached his garage. Again she looked at him quizzically until he opened the garage and she saw his car. Quickly she clambered in and so did he. He drove quickly through the streets of the town eager to get this cute blonde into his bed. Parking his car outside his house, they got out of the car and at the foot of his garden path they kissed deeply and passionately.

Sarah had stood when she saw his car approach, and was about to call his name as he got out of the car until she saw the blonde girl approach him from the other side of the vehicle and shove her tongue down his throat. At first she was shocked, but this quickly changed to anger. 'Who the fuck is she?!'

Peter quickly turned round and saw Sarah quickly approaching them with anger etched on her face. 'Bloody hell Sarah! You scared the shit out of me!'

'Like I give a fuck about scaring you!' She had now reached them and she was screeching, clearly bordering upon hysteria. 'Who the fuck is this slut?!'

'Slut?! I'm no slut. You're the one outside a guy's house waiting for him!'

'He's my boyfriend. I think I'm entitled to wait for him you little slag!'

The blonde turned to Peter. 'I thought you said you were single?!'

'I am honey, honestly I am.' Peter turned to Sarah. 'I am not your boyfriend. Just because we spent a couple of nights together does not mean I am your boyfriend.'

'I thought you liked me?'

'Yeah, liked. I thought I did; now I don't. Get over it.'

'You bastard!'

Sarah lunged at Peter with her remaining nails bared and ready to scratch his eyes out if she could reach. But Peter easily sidestepped her wild lunge, pulling the blonde with him. Sarah could not stop her momentum as she crashed into the car, the tips of her fingers smashing into a window, her remaining nails snapping and breaking. Sarah let out an ear piercing scream and she lunged again, and again Peter moved them both out of the way.

This time Sarah tripped on paving at the edge of the garden and landed sprawled on the wet, cold grass of the garden. It was a hard landing and knocked the wind out of her. She tried to lift herself up but collapsed back onto the grass. Peter and the blonde both looked at her in disgust as she started to sob as she lay face down on the grass.

'Can we go somewhere else please Peter, away from her?'

'Yeah, of course honey. Where though?'

'I don't know. A hotel or something?'

'Okay, sounds good. Let's get back in the car.'

'What about her?'

'Leave her.'

'She might damage something?'

'I doubt it. The only thing she is capable of damaging is herself.'

Chapter 26

Sarah heard the car pull away as the cold wetness seeped through her jeans. Eventually she managed to regain some composure and stopped sobbing. She rolled over and pushed herself into a sitting position. Here she sat for a while, ripping out the grass, muttering and mumbling to herself until, unknowingly, her hands slowly made their way up and down her arms and with the remaining stubs of her nails she vigorously scratched her arms.

Still muttering and mumbling to herself and still scratching her arms, she stood up and walked back to the house, specifically to the gate next to the side of the house. She tried to open the gate but it was locked so she simply scrambled over it, catching her jeans on a nail and ripping them but she did not seem to notice. Sarah walked round the house until she reached the back door which she tried to open, but again it was locked.

The back door had a big window, easily big enough for someone to climb through should the glass not be present. Sarah quickly realised this so she hunted round the garden until she found a rock which she simply threw at the glass. On contact with the rock, the glass shattered and fell out of the door with a loud smash which made Sarah jump. Quickly she moved into the shadow of a bush, hiding, waiting to see if any the houses she could see had lights turned on by their occupants or whether any of the occupants looked out of windows to see what had caused the noise.

Sarah waited for five long minutes under that bush until she slowly approached the back door and, with the rock, gently tapped out the remaining glass. When the frame was clear of the sharp shards, she clambered through the window frame into the kitchen. Without any hesitation, she proceeded quickly upstairs into Peter's bedroom.

Even when standing on the tip of her toes she could not reach the hatch to the attic. She stopped and looked round the room, scratching and mumbling, until her eyes lay upon a chair. The chair was dragged to underneath the attic hatch and then she scrambled onto the chair and flicked the lock of the hatch. Sarah was not prepared for the quickness of the hatch as it swung down quickly towards her head.

She managed to duck away from it, but in his haste earlier in the night Peter had not put the ladder away properly so it was not locked into place. So, when Sarah released the lock of the hatch, the heavy ladder slammed down into Sarah as she was ducking away from the hatch. It slammed into her back and sent her flying off the chair. The ladder continued its journey and smashed into the top of the chair, breaking the chair into pieces.

Sarah lay on the floor where she had landed, breathing heavily, a look of shock on her face. She managed to roll onto her back where she lay on the floor for some time, sucking air into her winded lungs until she gently pushed herself up into a sitting position. Up and down her back where the ladder had crashed into her she ran her hand and then gingerly got to her feet still breathing heavily.

For a moment she stood at the foot of the ladder and seemed to be contemplating what she was about to do. It was not as if Peter was not going to be able to g uess who had burgled him; he certainly would not need a degree in nuclear physics to work that one out. But then she got another thought which was that she had come this far so she might as well go through with it. Plus, she was stealing drugs; it was not as if he could go running to the police. With this thought she climbed the ladder.

It was her initial intention to simply lift the suitcase that contained the drug, the red one if she remembered rightly, and carry it home. But, on trying to lift it she discovered it was too heavy for her to lift down from the attic without doing herself an injury. So instead she dropped down off the ladder and rooted through his room for a bag which she eventually found.

In all eagerness she scrambled back up the ladder with the bag and opened the suitcase. She grabbed as many as the syringes as she could see and then grabbed as many of the packages of the powder that she could fit into the bag, but when she tried to lift the bag she realised she could not, so she had to remove some until she could comfortably lift it down from the attic. She did not bother returning anything to their original positions, but instead made her way downstairs and brazenly out of the front door which she pulled closed behind her. Sarah slung the bag over her shoulder and started the long walk home.

*

Peter left the hotel in the early hours of the morning, sneaking off, leaving the blonde to face in the morning the bill of an expensive hotel and two bottles of expensive champagne. He had enjoyed her body, but she was just another person to be used for his pleasure and promptly forgotten. Driving quickly home he was looking forward to a long shower and good sleep to refresh him for tonight's business.

Upon opening his front door he felt a draft blow from the kitchen but it did not really register with him that this was strange. Instead, he made his way upstairs taking his shirt off as he went. He turned the light on in his bedroom, threw his shirt onto his bed and turned away, not registering the sight before him. However, he quickly turned back around and looked again into his room.

The broken chair, the open attic hatch and the ladder was down where he had definitely not left it. For now though, he did not panic. It was quite feasible for the hatch to drop and the ladder to drop too. Hell, how many times had he not put the ladder up properly and then have it nearly knock him out as it dropped towards him? Lots of times. What was puzzling though was how the chair had managed to walk itself over from his desk to underneath the ladder? Still, he did not panic and decided to check the house for any signs of a break-in.

Peter scampered downstairs and felt the draft again and this time it did register. He threw open the kitchen door and turned on the light. There was glass scattered all over the kitchen floor and now the panic did set in. He ran back upstairs into his bedroom and quick as a flash scaled the ladder. Throwing open the red suitcase he looked inside it, looked away and then looked in again as if he expected the missing drugs to reappear between the moments he looked. He slid back down the ladder and for a few moments he paced around his bedroom trying to re gain his temper. He failed, miserably. He kicked the ladder and then screamed at the top of his voice. 'You fucking BITCH!'

*

Sarah had reached home and had taken a couple of hits of heroin and was just falling into a drug fuelled state of ecstasy when distantly, seemingly from another planet, she heard a loud banging. With her belt still fastened around her arm, she stumbled over to the window and noticed a car parked askew across the street. The banging happened again and from outside she heard someone shout, a male voice.

'Open this fucking door or I'll knock it down!' There was no response so the battering commenced again. It must have been loud and violent because after this attack on the door and another threatening verbal comment, Sarah heard the door open.

'Can I help you deary?'

'Yes you fucking can you alcoholic bitch. Where the fuck is your druggie daughter?'

'She's out I think. Do you want to come in and have a cup of tea and wait for her?'

'A cup of tea?! A cup of fucking tea?! Go and get her or I'll come in there and get her myself!'

Sarah peered across the street and noticed that some of the neighbours were either stood at their windows or stood at their front doors. In her lingerie and with the belt still tied around her arm, Sarah stumbled downstairs.

Peter spotted her appear at the foot of the stairs. 'You know what I'm here for Sarah. Get them and then I'll go and leave you to your pathetic life!'

'Mum, go and sit down.'

'Okay deary.'

Her mum went back into the living room and Sarah turned to confront Peter. 'I don't know what you mean.'

'Yes you damn well fucking do! Go and get them and then I'll leave!'

By now both of Sarah's neighbours were stood in their respective gardens watching the scene unfold, one of them clearly staring at Sarah's lacy lingerie clad large breasts. 'Oh right, do you mean the drugs that you've been dealing? I don't know where they are.'

'Considering you've got a fucking BELT tied round your arm Sarah, I think you do know what I mean! You've got ten seconds to go and get them otherwise I am going to come in there and beat the shit out of you and your mum you little fucking druggie! Go and get MY FUCKING DRUGS!'

Sarah turned to one of her neighbours, a huge man, ex-marine and hard as iron girders. 'See Bob, he is a drug dealer. Didn't your youngest die because of a drug overdose?'

Bob nodded in the affirmative. 'I'll tell you what sunshine, why don't you get back in your car and stop disturbing the peace otherwise I'll step over this fence and rip you apart!'

'Fuck you old man! Sarah, be sensible and go and get me what I want, there's a good girl.'

Peter did not see or hear Bob step over the low fence and he did not realise that he was behind him until he felt a large arm wrap around his neck and drag him down into a headlock.

'I don't like dirty drug dealing scumbags coming into my neighbourhood, threatening my good neighbours, breaching our peace and waking me up! Now, we're going to walk over to your car and you're going to get into your car and go back to whatever drain you crawled out of okay?'

There was no reply so Bob squeezed Peter's neck a little harder. 'Okay?'

'Yes!' Peter replied in a raspy, breathless voice.

Dragging him by the neck he walked Peter over to his car and pushed him against it, twisting his arm up his back, applying a lot of pressure that made Peter wince in pain.

'You ever, ever come to this area again and I will rip you limb from limb. Savvy?' Peter nodded. 'Good. Now get in your car and fuck off!' Bob quickly released Peter and slammed his head into the roof of his car then quickly stepped away from him and folded his huge arms across his huge chest.

Peter turned to face him. 'This isn't the last you'll hear about this old man. And as for you little drug taking slag, you'll get yours!' With that Peter got in his car and screeched and sped away. After he had gone, without saying a word to anyone, Sarah quietly closed her front door and returned back to her bedroom.

Afterwards, when the events were discussed by Sarah's neighbours, she was oblivious to them. She stayed hidden away in her bedroom, taking the heroin, becoming more and more dependent on it, more and more addicted. As for Peter he had to explain to his supplier how he had managed to lose a few hundred pounds worth of heroin.

Chapter 27

'You did what?!'

'Reg, I didn't do anything. I was burgled and some of the heroin, not all of it, was stolen.'

'Did you just leave it round the house so any fuckwit could break in and steal it?!'

'No, of course not. It was hidden away but they found it.'

'Well it was clearly not hidden well enough!'

'Yes, I know that now. Look, Reg, I've had the best night I've ever had. I'm making you more and more money and I believe it is only going to get better. Fair enough, this is a blip, a mistake, but a blip on an otherwise unblemished record. I'm going to learn from it and make you even more money, I promise.'

'You promise? You fucking promise? He fucking promises Kevin. Ickle Peter promises!'

Reg took a deep breath and was clearly trying to regain his composure. 'It is just as well you've been good so far otherwise you'd be in the river sleeping with the fishes. I don't usually give people chances, usually it's one mistake and…' Reg ran his fist across his throat. 'But, you're right, you have sold a lot and I am pleased about that. How much do you reckon was stolen?'

'About three to four hundred pounds worth.'

'Let's call it five. That okay with you Ickle Peter?' Peter nodded. 'Good. Hundred pounds a month for five months off your cut. Okay?'

'That's fine. I promise it won't happen again.'

'Right, be on your way. You working tonight?'

'Think I better had. Make some money to cover the losses.'

'Good. Keep up the good work, but preferably without leaving the drugs out in the open where any idiot can steal them!'

'Roger that.'

Peter quickly turned and left. He was very tempted to have his revenge against Sarah and her neighbour, tempted to drive round to their respective houses and put a bullet in each of their heads. But he knew that would not be a good idea. He had already drawn enough attention to himself and it would not be the smartest move considering the number of witnesses present in the street last night. He decided to take his punishment for mixing business with pleasure and to draw a line under the whole affair and put it quickly behind him.

*

Sarah though, could not put the drugs behind her, nor did she want to. She quickly made her way through the few prepared syringes during the rest of Friday night and Saturday morning, and then was left with packages of powder that she did not know what to do with. She was hoping that she had taken enough to overcome the withdrawal symptoms but a few hours after using the last syringe, like a vicious circle, the cravings started again, along with the cramps, nausea and itching.

Studying the packets of powder, she wondered how to turn the powder into the glorious liquid that gave her so much pleasure and allowed her to hide away from all the pain and misery in her life. Sarah looked over at her computer and wondered if she could summon enough intelligence from somewhere to operate it. Deciding she would have to try, she stumbled over to the computer and sat down in front of it.

She was still dressed only in her lingerie and if one was to study her previously unblemished skin, one would see that it was now very blotchy and her arms, she had varied which arm she injected into, were showing signs of heroin use. They were very red and bruised around the injection points and, faintly, heroin track marks were beginning to show. On top of this, her skin was red and cut due to her constant scratching whenever the heroin was not flowing through her body.

While she waited for the computer to load, she scratched her arms again and again until the computer finished its loading cycle. The computer had a broadband connection so she was quickly able to load up the internet and start searching for drugs that were in a powder form with a light brown, tan colour.

'Bastard. He told me it wasn't heroin!' she exclaimed. 'Never mind. How do I prepare it?' With another simple search using a popular internet search engine she quickly found the answer.

'Simple enough. Spoon. Piece of cotton wool. Some kind of heat source, matches? A lighter! All in the kitchen! Now, I don't want to kill myself here. How much?' Again, another simple search told her the answer.

So Sarah went down the stairs into the kitchen, stumbling as she went down. From somewhere a couple of brain cells collided and reminded her to check on her mum. She quietly pushed open the living room door and her mother was in her usual position. As long as she was still breathing, Sarah did not really care, so she quietly closed the door behind her and completed the few short steps into the kitchen. Quickly she collected the items she needed and returned to her room to prepare another hit of the powerful drug.

Consulting the web pages she had found, she learned how much heroin to use and then halved the recommended amount to ensure that she did not overdose. Following the same method that Peter had, she placed the heroin and water into the spoon and heated it up until the drug had dissolved. Then she drew the solution into the syringe through a piece of cotton wool. She checked the syringe for air bubbles as the article on the internet advised her to do and the solution appeared to be clear. So she fastened the belt around her arm, making a fist to pump up the veins in her arm. When the blood vessel was clearly visible, she slid the needle into her arm and depressed the plunger, pumping the mixture into her body. Quickly she drew out the syringe and waited for the rush to hit her.

She waited and waited. She felt a small rush but it was nothing in comparison to what she was used to. Cursing, and feeling frustrated, she prepared another hit, this time using slightly more heroin. In total, over the course of a few hours, she had five hits of varying strength until she created the right mixture that gave a good, solid rush. She stood up from the crouching position she had been in while she was using the drug, removed the belt and slumped onto her bed.

Sarah had not slept for a couple of days, nor had she eaten anything. As she l ay, if one was to look down on her and compare her body to a week ago before she had taken the first drug, one would certainly notice the weight loss her body had gone through already. She looked gaunt, pale and had very dark circles around her eyes.

The drug rush slowly subsided and she rolled onto her side, curling up into a ball. Heroin causes insomnia, hence why she had not wanted or needed to sleep for a few days, but heroin can also cause period of oversleeping. Sarah fell asleep early that morning and did not wake until a vicious stomach cramp ripped through her body in the afternoon of the next day.

She did not know or care what day it was. All she cared about was getting rid of the cramps, itching skin and the thoughts of her mother drinking herself into an early grave, and the thoughts of Peter with that blonde. So she simply got up out of bed to simply cook herself another hit to hide away from the misery that was her life.

Chapter 28

While Sarah was sleeping through Saturday in drug induced unconsciousness, late afternoon Saturday Michelle was starting to prepare for her date with Simon. Michelle's parents had already left for their performance so she had the house to herself.

In every room in Michelle's musically orientated house, she had the radio on the same channel so as she moved around the house she danced and sang while she slowly got ready. While bathing she shaved all potentially hairy parts of her body and enjoyed the Jacuzzi feature of her bath.

After bathing she showered and thoroughly washed her newly cut hair. Unfortunately she could not quite afford the helicopter to London so she had had to make do with a cut from a local salon. When she felt comfortable and felt ready, she settled down in her bathrobe to watch a re-run of the Formula 1 qualifying for the Melbourne Grand Prix. Just as she had turned on the television, her mobile rang.

'Michelle, it's me. You ready for your night of hot sex?!'
'Sally! I've told you! Nothing is going to happen tonight!'
'Hmmm, I'm sure.'
'Anyway, what about you?!'
'Oh yeah, I can't really see me losing it in the theatre!'
'Fair point!'
'What are you doing?'
'Well, believe it or not, I'm watching the qualifying for the Formula 1.'
'Huh? Why? Thought you'd be prepping yourself?'
'I'm all prepped. All I need to do is put my clothes on and I'm done.'
'So why are you watching the cars?'
'Well, I was thinking that this is going to be a once in a lifetime trip, so I want to know something about it.'
'Right, okay. We're not going to watch the cars you know.'
'Huh?'
'We're going to get some sun, get very drunk, go to the casino and blow a million on black!'
'Sounds good, but I still want to know something about it.'
'I'll stick to the champagne and blowing it all on black thanks! So what's going on?'
'I don't exactly know. Some cars appear to be going round and round Melbourne in a circle making a lot of noise!'
'Sounds like fun!'
'Hmmm, yeah, well, there's a clock ticking down on the top of the screen. I wonder if that means the
cars all have a certain amount of time to complete the laps before they all explode into a ball of fire!'
'Erm, to be honest Michelle, I doubt it!'
'It would be more interesting than this if they did! What was that about blowing a million on black?! Which car does your dad sponsor?'

'They're a team with British drivers I think, kind of silvery cars. I think the name of his company will be on it somewhere.'

'Oh, right! Spotted one, and there's the name of your dad's company! That makes it a little bit more interesting, but only a little bit. What was that about getting very drunk?!'

'That's more like it Michelle! I think we can leave the cars to my dad and we'll concentrate on champagne and royal princes!'

'Ohhh, do you think we'll meet any royalty? That would be so cool!'

'Almost definitely!'

'I hope so! When is it? When do we go? How are we getting there? Where are we staying?'

'Slow down there! When is it? I don't know, but I'm at my computer so I'll google it. Hang on… Formula 1, that makes sense, Formula1.com. Erm, races perhaps, yeah, here we go, calendar. Monaco… twenty-second to the twenty fifth of May!'

'May! That's ages away!'

'Not really Michelle, a few months.'

'I'll have to go shopping!'

'We'll go shopping and it will be my treat!'

'Really?! Wow! Thanks Sally!'

'My pleasure. You're next question was when do we go. I imagine the Thursday or Friday. How do we get there? In my dad's jet of course!'

'Oh my! This is going to be amazing!'

'And we'll be staying on his yacht right next to the track!'

'Wow, wow, wow! I wish it was May already!'

'Well, so do I, but don't wish your life away honey,' said Sally, remembering something her mother had once said to her.

'I know, but it is going to drag and drag and drag! Oh no, what about our exams?!'

'I've checked already. The dates for our exams don't clash with this weekend so we'll be fine. We'll just have to study extra hard before and after and we'll be fine!

'Perfecter and perfecter!'

'Perfecter?'

'Never mind.'

'What time is it?'

'Nearly five.'

'Nearly five?! Shit! I was out on Storm for ages! I'd better go. Not even showered or anything!' Michelle faintly heard a bell ring which was Sally summoning a member of her staff. 'Right, I've really got to go. You have a good night!'

'You too!'

'I'll call you in the morning, but not too early because I think you're going to be having a late night!'

'No way! In bed for ten, on my own!'

'I think you'll be in bed for nine not on your own!'

'Nope. Not going to happen!'

'We'll see. I have to go. The maid is here. Speak tomorrow! Enjoy!'

'You too. Bye!'

But Sally had already gone and Michelle faintly heard her berating the unfortunate maid before the line went dead. Michelle changed the channel to MTV, bored with the Formula 1 qualifying, and watched some music videos for a while until she stood up and went upstairs to dress and apply a little make-up.

At exactly seven there was a knock at her door and she went to open it. It was Simon, and Michelle almost gasped at handsome he looked. His shirt was open at the top, showing his muscular chest and as he smiled at her and leant towards her to kiss her on a cheek, Michelle received a waft of his masculine cologne.

Simon, when Michelle had opened the door, also had almost gasped at how lovely Michelle looked. She was dressed in a short, blue dress and it looked like she had applied a light tan to her slim, slender legs. He noted that she had had her hair cut and the wonders of a push-up bra gave her a large cleavage that Simon just managed to rip his eyes from as he leant towards her and kissed her politely and gentlemanly on her cheek.

She took him by the hand and led him into the house to the kitchen. 'You find the house okay?'

'Yeah, no problem. Nice house. Nice area. What do your parents do?'

'They're both singers, opera.'

'Really? Cool.'

As they entered the kitchen Michelle asked Simon, 'Do you want a drink? I've got some lager, bitter, whiskey, dark rum, Bacardi, vodka, wine etcetera!'

'Erm, a glass of wine please.'

'They're performing tonight in London. They're usually away most weekends somewhere in the country, but this is a series of shows so every weekend for the next couple of months they'll be in London.'

'Sounds good.'

'Red or white or rosé?'

'Erm, white please.'

Michelle poured both of them a glass of white, then took him by the hand and led him into the living room where music was quietly playing and scented candles were lit and they sat down next to each other on the settee.

'I haven't cooked anything, because, well, to be honest, I couldn't be bothered!' Simon laughed. 'So I thought we could order in something. What do you fancy?'

'I'm easy. How about a curry?'

'Sounds like a plan. There's a good takeaway just down the road. The menu is here.'

Michelle reached across and got the menu off the coffee table. For the next few minutes they discussed what to order and then Michelle placed the order with the takeaway.

While they waited, they small talked until after about half an hour their food arrived. Michelle took Simon into the dining room that she had prepared earlier with some more candles and some romantic music playing softly in the background. She sat him down and then went into the kitchen to dish out the food which she then brought back into the dining room with a bottle of red wine.

Slowly they ate together, sometimes drinking the wine, sometimes holding hands, until they had got through the mountain of food and also some dessert. After this, Michelle suggested they retire back to the living room. Here she lit the fire and they lay down together on the settee and cuddled together. It was only a matter of time until their lips found each other and quickly they were kissing deeply and passionately.

Straight away Michelle felt a hard bulge press against her leg and she could not help herself when she pressed her leg into his crotch to feel his hardness some more. The feel of his body next to her, his manly smell and the hardness pressing against her legs made Michelle short of breath and she felt her intimate parts start to become wet.

He either sensed the effect he was having on her or guessed, because his hand slowly slid up the back of her thigh to the base of her bottom and then it was gone again, back down her silky smooth thigh to the back of her knee. His hand lingered here, stoking the back of her knee, and Michelle involuntarily let out a gasp as she had never been touched there before in such a sensual manner. For a few more moments his hand stroked the back of her knee, then it slid up the back of her thigh and then was gone leaving Michelle feeling quite breathless.

With a strong hand he twisted her body round so she was on her back and he manoeuvred himself down her body until he was at her feet. He lifted up one of her legs and lightly kissed her foot, nibbling and gently sucking her toes.

This was all new territory for Michelle and she was starting to get unbearably aroused. From her feet, next he started kissing up the inside of her legs, lifting up each leg so he could kiss and lick her calves. He did this lightly, without leaving a slobbering mess, further up her calves until he reached the back of her knees. By now, Michelle was breathing very heavily, and when she felt his tongue lightly flick the back of her knee she let out a moan and another moan when he transferred his attention to her other leg.

Leaving her legs for a moment, he came back up her body, pressing himself against her, so he was looking down into her eyes. He kissed her passionately and then he was gone again, back down her body to her legs. Gently he wrapped his strong arms around her waist and rolled her over so she was lying on her front. He returned to the back of her knees kissing them again and then slowly he pushed up her dress as he ran his tongue up and down the back of her thighs. He stopped at the base of her knickers and made his way back up her body and moved her hair aside to kiss her on the back of her neck.

All this time, Michelle had been wrestling with what he was doing to her body. She wanted him to stop, she wanted to take things slowly, but she was finding it very difficult to stop nature taking its course. When she felt him slide the zip down on the back of her dress and felt his tongue slide down the length of her spine she let out another moan and she realised she was in no position to stop him.

As he reached the base of her spine his tongue lingered here, circling her lower back. With one hand he reached for her bra strap and unfastened it, and then his tongue was back up her spine to her neck. Here he reached for the shoulder straps of her dress and bra, sliding them down each arm until all the straps came fr ee of her arms. He left the bra straps where they had fallen and returned to her dress. He pulled it up over her bottom and down from her shoulders until it was wrapped round her waist. Again, he slid his tongue down her spine and in the same motion started to pull her lacy knickers down. She helped him by lifting her hips off the settee and with a couple of shakes of her legs and a kick her knickers were off. Simon then grabbed her dress and repeated the process and again Michelle helped him.

Now all that Michelle was wearing was the bra which was still trapped under body, but Simon ignored this. Instead, he returned his tongue to her bottom where he licked and nibbled each cheek, Michelle moaning underneath him. With another strong arm he turned her round so she was on her back and he threw her bra away. Now, completely naked, Simon looked deeply into her eyes then kissed her passionately while a hand slid up her body and started to gently massage one of her large breasts.

Groaning and moaning as she felt his thumbs run across his nipples, Simon's mouth left her lips, went to her neck and then to her breasts. At first he pushed them apart and buried his head in them, kissing and licking her chest between them. Then his tongue slid up the side of one of them until it nearly touched a nipple. But instead, his tongue made circles around her nipple, right round the areola without ever touching the nipple. He repeated this on the other breast, and again on the first. After a few moments of this Michelle started to move her chest trying to coax him into placing the nipple into his mouth. But he kept on making these little circles, frustrating Michelle until she grabbed his head and forced his mouth down onto one of her nipples. Once it was in his mouth, he sucked and licked it before transferring his attention to her other one. By now Michelle was writhing underneath him, moaning and groaning, thinking it would be impossible for her to feel anymore aroused.

She was wrong. Quickly he slid down her body again so his mouth was kissing, licking and nibbling the inside of her thighs. He gently eased her legs apart, running his tongue up to the top of each leg before licking her groin muscles. Michelle was close to stopping him. She had never received oral sex before and she did not think she was ready for it. Just as she was reaching for his head to pull him back up she felt his tongue flick the lips of her vagina. She let out a long moan, and instead of reaching for his head, she pressed her crotch against his face forcing him to lick her.

At first he concentrated on her vaginal lips, licking and flicking them with his tongue. Then, very gently, he eased his tongue into her vagina causing Michelle to let out the longest, loudest moan of the night so far. He concentrated his attentions here for a moment or two before tilting his head up to give Michelle the best sexual experience of her life so far. His tongue rested for a moment on her clitoris, and then slowly he licked it causing the whole of Michelle's body to involuntarily twitch. He licked the hard nub of flesh again and Michelle screamed.

Simon jumped and was going to stop until Michelle forced his head back into her crotch again so he carried driving her to sexual ecstasy. While he was paying her clitoris attention, he slowly slid a finger into her vagina, not too deep, until he found the spongy flesh which indicated her g-spot. He rested his finger tip on this before making gentle circular motions with it, pressing and stroking her g-spot.

Michelle was now moaning and groaning and occasionally screaming as she felt pleasure fly through her body that she had never dreamt possible. The pathetic night that she had shared with her ex-boyfriend had been nothing like this. As Simon carried on, she knew she was close to orgasm when everything stopped. She quickly opened her eyes, not believing that it had stopped and she was just about to berate him when she felt him push away from her. He stood over her and stripped, his penis springing to attention as he dropped his underwear.

This was only the second penis she had ever seen and she was surprised about how different it was. It was longer, wider and just bigger than the other one. Michelle took his hand and pulled him back on top of her so he was between her legs. He lay lightly on top of her, staring deeply into her eyes before he was gone again, his body sliding down her body, and he resumed the oral foreplay. Quickly Michelle's body reacted to his touches and again she lay there moaning and groaning until again she was close to orgasm when he stopped. He came back up her body, staring into her eyes again, between her legs, their hips together.

With a slight movement of her hips Simon found his penis being lined up with her vagina. Very gently he probed until he found the entrance to her vagina and even more gently the large head of his penis parted her wet vaginal lips. Michelle let out a little moan of pleasure and pain, pain because she had never had anything so large part her like this.

The lips enveloped his penis tightly and he slid it into her soft wetness another half an inch and slowly rotated his hips and then pulled out of her again. He repeated this three times until Michelle grabbed his hip and tried to force his penis into her. She wriggled her hips, desperately trying to coax him into her but he resisted against her strongly. Instead, he rested and pressed the tip of his penis against her clitoris and then eased the head into her again before pulling out again.

'Please… Please Simon, please!' And at her begging he slid into her fully.

The pleasure coursed through her body as her vagina was filled up with his long, wide, hard penis and she lifted her hips to force a deeper penetration. Simon had had sex with a number of women, but nothing had ever felt like this, nothing had ever been this wet, hot and tight. He nearly lost control as she lifted her hips but he managed to control his body. With his first thrust she dropped her hips back onto the settee and just lay there, focusing on the intense pleasure that was coursing through her body while he thrusted his penis quickly and firmly in and out of her.

After a few minutes, Simon readjusted his body by moving upward along her body. Almost immediately Michelle noticed the difference. Instead of just her vagina being stimulated it seemed that his penis was now pressing against her clitoris. Quickly she wrapped her legs around his hips and for every one of his thrusts she met it with one of her own. Simon knew that this position was called the coital alignment technique and was a guaranteed orgasm for the woman.

The pleasure and heat grew inexorably from between her legs and spread all round her body. As the pleasure reached its peak she dug her nails into his shoulder which he took to mean faster and harder. He upped the tempo and force of hi s strokes, and then Michelle let out a scream and a long, loud moan that went on and on as an orgasm ripped through her body. Her whole body started to shake, and with the feeling of her underneath him it tipped him over the edge. Michelle let out another long moan as she felt his hot fluid pour into her, his body shaking above her.

As their breathing subsided they stayed locked together, Simon staring deeply down into her eyes. He kissed her passionately and then eased away from her. As he lay next to her he noticed that the cushion where her hips had lay was soaking wet but he did not mention it.

Instead, he took her in his arms, kissed her forehead and ran his fingers through her hair. They stayed like this, cuddling together, neither of them speaking, until Michelle told him that she wanted to shower. He gave her another lingering kiss and then they separated. 'My room is the door that faces you as you come up the stairs. Come up when you're ready.'

'Will do.'

They kissed again and Simon watched her walk out of the living room. He lay back on the settee, relaxing and thinking how lucky he had been to find someone like Michelle. After a short while he heard her call him to come upstairs to which he sprung up off the settee and made his way upstairs to Michelle's bedroom. She was already in bed, under the duvet and she lifted the blanket up for him inviting him into her bed. It was an offer that he accepted and for the rest of that night they made love into the early hours of the morning.

Chapter 29

Sally left her mansion later than she wanted to because one of the maids had put the iron on the wrong setting and burnt her top. She had spoken to Alfred about her and Sally did not expect to see her at the mansion again. However, the top matched everything, the accessories, makeup, including nail polish, so her strict regime of preparing herself when getting ready to attend any kind of function was thrown out of order.

She ranted and raved at the maids as they fluttered around her desperately trying to get their mistress ready on time. It was only when one of them dropped a bottle of nail polish remover on the floor that Sally totally lost her temper and, in no uncertain terms, dismissed them all, throwing shoes and whatever came to hand at them as they scampered out of her bedroom.

Still cursing, muttering and mumbling to herself, she decided she did not have enough time to apply fresh makeup or nail polish so she decided to go for a natural look with no makeup and no accessories. Before storming out of her bedroom she told Alfred to bring her Mini around from the garages, if a member of staff was able to do this simple task without crashing it. On her way out to the car she texted David and told him she would be about fifteen minutes late to which he promptly replied and stated that was fine. As she reached the car she had not seen any staff. Sally guessed, correctly, that Alfred had told them all to stay out of her way. The Mini was parked with the engine running and Sally clambered in and quickly drove along the long driveway to the distant gates.

After a quick drive she arrived at David's house to be greeted with the sight of David scampering out of his house with his gran stood in the doorway berating him. Sally saw a shoe leave his gran's hand and fly gracefully towards David just missing his head. He did not even stop to open the garden gate, instead taking the low wall at pace with a graceful leap. With a few quick paces he was at the passenger's door and he quickly climbed in. 'Drive! Quick!'

'What's up?'

'I'll tell you in a bit. Just drive!'

Sally smiled and waved to Ethel and she received a smile, a wave and a wink in return.

'Don't bloody smile and wave at her! Drive!'

Sally waved again and slowly drove away from David's house. 'What was all that about?!'

'I forgot. I didn't remember. I thought she was going to cut me up!'

Sally laughed. 'What? What happened?'

'It's her birthday in a couple of weeks and I promised at some point last month that I'd take her to the theatre to watch, well, to watch Les Miserables. She saw the tickets I got for tonight.'

'Whoops!'

'Yeah, whoops indeed! She was not happy. She was cutting vegetables when she noticed them. I forgot I'd said I'd go with her.'

'So she found this out when she had a knife in her hand?!'

'Yeah.'

'Double whoops!'

'I know she's only joking, but when she threatens to cut all my clothes up while brandishing a large kitchen knife it does make you think twice about whether she's serious!'

Sally laughed again. 'I'm sure she's not serious. Obviously she was looking forward to spending some time with you and now she thinks that is not going to happen.'

'Maybe. Or maybe she's just evil!'

'David! That's your gran. You can't call her evil!'

'We'll have to agree to disagree. Are you looking forward to the show?'

'I'm looking forward to the show and spending time with you.'

'Oh, right, erm, me too. It's a long show you know, near enough three hours.'

'Yeah, it's meant to be good though.'

'Yep, looking forward to it. Did your uncle get off okay?'

'Huh? Which… Oh yes, no dramas. The traffic was a bit heavy hence why I'm a bit late.'

'No worries.'

They spent most of the rest of the drive making small talk until they reached the theatre which was just a few doors down from the large theatre that Sally's father owns. They entered the building, Sally thankfully not seeing anyone she knew, and she was surprised as they went upstairs. More used to sitting in the best seats in the house or in private boxes, she was disappointed to see that they were in the upper circle, to the side with a slightly restricted view.

'Here we are! Best seats in the house!'

Sally smiled politely. 'Yes, they are. Thank you.' She pecked his cheek and enjoyed watching him blush.

'Sally, we're having a sophisticated night. Control yourself!'

She laughed and sat down next to him, taking his hand and holding it, leaning her body against him.

The show started promptly on time and Sally enjoyed it. She enjoyed sitting where she would never normally sit as it gave her a view of the stage that she would not normally have. The scenes and acts rolled by, and the glances she gave David showed her that he was enthralled with the show and Hugo's story of Jean Valjean, Javert, Fantine and Cosette. She was sure that at the end of the show he applauded louder than anyone else in the theatre and he even threw in a few bravos too.

Impressed with this show of a cultural side to him, she wrapped her arm around him as they left the theatre. Suggesting a walk along the river to which she agreed, they walked and talked, stopping occasionally to exchange kisses which increased in passion the further they walked. They crossed a bridge and walked back through the streets, through the business area of the city. Sally was amused to note that this area would take her past her father's head office. As they approached the office she noticed a limousine parked outside.

She was going to cross the street but David would think this strange as they would have to cross back again in not more than a hundred yards to continue the ir walk in the right direction. She decided that the chance of the limousine being for her father was remote; there were always clients coming and going from the office in the company's limousines, so they continued to walk past the office.

As they reached the bottom of the steps up to the doors of the buildings there was a commotion and two security guards indicated for them to stop walking so there was a clear path from the bottom of the steps to the now open door of the limousine. Sally's heart skipped a beat as she glanced up towards the doors of the office and saw her father approach with James, both of them dressed in tuxedos. She had nowhere to go. She could not go forwards and she could not go backwards as this would confuse David.

Just as she was about to turn away and pretend her mobile had rung James noticed her. With a look of surprise he gently touched her father's elbow and discreetly nodded towards her. With a look of bigger surprise and a big smile, her father started to walk towards her. Panicking now, Sally took half a step back out of David's line of sight and started to vigorously shake her head and mouth the word no. They carried on walking towards her, her father and James looking confused at her actions, until at the last moment something clicked in her father's head and he quickly veered away from them and disappeared into the back of the limousine. James gave a quick confused glance over his shoulder to Sally and then he too got in the large vehicle. The guards waited until the car had moved away until they allowed the pedestrians to walk past. Fifty yards past the building Sally's heart skipped another beat.

'What was that all about? Those two rich guys walking towards us at that building with big idiotic grins on their faces like they knew one of us?!'

Sally could not help laughing as she heard her father, one of the richest, most successful business men in the country, described as having an idiotic grin. 'I don't know. Mistaken identity. It was quite gloomy there.'

'It wasn't that gloomy. Their teeth were giving off more light than a power station! I'd like have their cosmetic dentist I know that much! They hurt my eyes!'

In between laughs Sally was able to say, 'Well, they must have both worked very hard in order to be able to afford, erm, such nice teeth!'

'Hey, I'm not criticizing, just a bit bright at this time of night!'

'Fair enough!' Sally laughed again. 'I love being with you David. You make me laugh so much!'

'Well, I try my best!'

'Keep on trying, doing and succeeding and I think me and you may go far.'

David looked surprised. 'Do you mean that? I mean, are we going to start seeing each other, well, you know, properly?'

'And tonight hasn't been properly?'

'Well, you know what I mean.'

'Definitely.'

'Boyfriend and girlfriend?'

'Definitely.'

'Woo hoo!'

Again she laughed as she watched him skip down the exclusive city street, d oing a passable impression of Morecambe and Wise's end of show dance, as he skipped down the street putting alternate hands behind his head. He received plenty of funny looks as he skipped back towards Sally, took her in his arms and planted a firm, lingering passionate kiss on her lips. Sally gently moved away from him, remembering that she was still in view of her father's office. 'David, someone might see us.'

'So what? Let them see.'

He tried to kiss her again but she moved gently away from him and she was disappointed to see a flash of confusion pass across his face.

'Hey David,' she said gently, 'let's go to my relation's apartment. It's just down the road and we can spend some more time together.'

'Your relation has an apartment here? They must be rich!'

'Yeah, the rich side of the family, not my side unfortunately.'

'How come you've got a key?'

'She works overseas a lot and I go in and water her plants and stuff, check her mail. I've got the key with me.'

Sally always had the key with her. It was her apartment. Her father had bought it for her a year or so ago to give her more independence. She hardly ever used it, preferring instead to stay near her father and offer him some company when he was home.

'Okay, that sounds good. Do you want to eat somewhere first?'

'We can order in.'

'Sounds even better.'

'David,' she said his name gently again as she took his hand and led him to the nearby apartment, 'you can stay if you want, there are two bedrooms, well four, but you know what I mean...' Sally left it hanging for him to draw his own conclusions.

'Yeah, of course Sally. Separate bedrooms. One step at a time hey?'

'Sorry, I know what you men are like!'

'Some men Sally, some men. I like to think, well I work at being different. A few more kisses would be nice though!'

'Not that different then!'

It was David's turn to laugh as Sally led them down a small side street to a block of modern apartments. Sally opened the door and they entered the elevator. David could not keep his surprise off his face as Sally placed her entry card onto a scanner and then pressed the elevator button marked PH.

The lift took them up quickly to the thirtieth floor and the duplex penthouse apartment. The elevator stopped in the apartment and when the doors opened David was greeted to sight of a large apartment spread out before him, with stairs leading to the upper floor and floor to ceiling windows looking onto a huge balcony. From the balcony one could look down onto the river and over the city.

It was a truly impressive place to live and David jumped a little when Sally stepped out of the elevator and said loudly, 'Lights!'

On her voice command the lights turned on brightly and Sally said, 'Three!' and instantly the lights dimmed.

David looked around him looking slightly bewildered. 'That's a neat trick. Li ghts!' And the lights turned off. 'Lights! Ten!' And all the lights turned on, dazzling David. 'Crikey! Like those guys' teeth! Three!' And they dimmed again. 'I'm very impressed. What does your relation do?'

'Banker for a Swiss bank. She's good at her job and gets the pay to reflect that. But, to balance that out she's never home. In fact, I couldn't tell you the last time she was here!'

'Not much good having the money if she can't enjoy it.'

'Yeah, but she'll be retired by forty!'

'Looking at this place she could retire now!'

'Maybe. Come on. It's a nice night. Let's go out on the balcony and chill out there.'

'Sounds like a plan.'

He followed her across the apartment and could not help admiring her tight bottom in the tight jeans as she meandered through the furniture to the glass balcony door. She opened it and they both settled down onto the comfortable chairs. They made small talk until Sally suggested ordering some food and by then the temperature outside had dropped so they made their way into the lounge and cuddled together on the large settee.

'Music. Volume five. Track ten.' She looked at David and said, 'This doesn't always work.'

'It's still impressive that it could work!' After a slight pause the music started. 'It has worked! This is all very impressive.'

'Costs a fortune.'

'Yeah, I don't doubt it for a second!'

'Lights. One.' Some of the lights turned off, the rest dimmed giving a romantic air to the room.

The food quickly arrived and they ate together at the dining table and then they retired back to the lounge and the settee. As soon as they had settled down, Sally quickly turned to David and kissed him deeply and passionately. Not only did she find this fine young man attractive physically, more and more he was attracting her mentally, so she was not surprised when she felt her body react instantly in a manner it had never done before.

The top of her thighs became slick and she pressed them together enjoying the feeling. She was also enjoying feeling the affect she was having on him. Clearly she could feel his hardness growing and growing as his hips pressed against her.

As quickly as she had started to kiss him she finished, knowing that if they carried on both of them would not be able to stop. They talked for a while, and later that night, after many more kisses had been exchanged, they each retired to their separate bedrooms. She wanted it all to carry on, to not stop at just kisses, but she forced herself to stop because she was simply not ready, nowhere near ready yet, but she would be in the not too distant future.

Chapter 30

Winter rolled on for everyone and quickly turned to spring. Michelle and Simon's love for each other grew and grew over these months spending as much time together as they possibly could. After the Saturday night when they had made love into the early hours of Sunday morning, they dated and made love whenever they met, their relationship growing and growing, blossoming like the flowers of the new spring.

Sally had received a couple of calls from the police which basically stated their investigations were ongoing, but she did not expect them to catch anyone. Almost forgetting the frightening circumstances in which she had met him, Sally and David's relationship also blossomed, but physically a lot slower than their friends. They had plenty of dates together, enjoying the cinema, theatre, meals out and they loved each other's company. Yet, Sally sensed that David was getting frustrated at their lack of a stronger physical relationship but she wanted the night that she lost her virginity to be perfect. She thought she knew when that night would occur but it was still a few months away.

Sally had managed, just about, to keep her real status in life secret from David but she knew that she could not keep the pretence up for much longer. Indeed, she had recently made the decision to inform David, take him to the mansion and introduce him to her father, a day that she was not looking forward to. The day she had chosen was the Saturday after her holiday in Monaco. Mr. Gallagher would, well should still be off work and he had, after seeing them that Saturday night, been eager to meet David.

Whenever the girls were together they talked incessantly about two subjects, their relationships and their upcoming trip to Monaco. Sally had not been surprised that Michelle had enjoyed a night of glorious sex with Simon and Michelle was eager for her friend to start a sexual relationship with her new partner so they could talk properly about their experiences, which for now were very one-sided conversations.

They frequently went shopping together, when each of them could be persuaded to leave the side of their respective partners, preparing for their vacation. Michelle insisted on paying her own way, but occasionally a pair of shoes or other such item would be out of her price range so unhesitatingly her friend would buy them for her.

Over the last few months, their four lives had changed immeasurably, but the life that had changed the most was Sarah's. If one was to walk into her bedroom now and compare it to a few months ago, one would see some differences. Her music system was gone. Her bed was gone and only a saggy mattress remained. Her television was gone. All her C.D.s and D.V.D.s were gone. Bizarrely, the only item that she had kept which was worth any money was her computer. In a rare moment of clarity she had decided to keep it as it helped her discover more about the drugs that helped her escape from the misery in her life.

It had not taken her long to use the drugs she had stolen from Peter. In a moment of desperation when the withdrawal symptoms were unbearable, she had called him and begged him for some more. To this request she received a torrent of abuse which concluded in him stating to her that if she ever crossed his path again she would be killed along with her mother.

So Sarah, still showing her naivety about drugs, searched on the internet to find out how she could acquire more of the drugs. She discovered it was easy enough. Go to any red light area of the town or city and there will be dealers there. So she did exactly that.

It was a chilly, early spring night when she walked the three miles from her house into the small red light area of the town. She walked along some of the streets, walking past a handful of prostitutes who stared venomously at her thinking she was going to try and steal their strip of street. When Sarah stopped to speak to one of them she was treated with hostility.

'Excuse me.'

'Excuse me what darling?'

'I'm after some drugs.'

'Drugs? This is my patch so fuck off or I'll cut off your face.'

'You'd cut off my face for asking you a simple question?'

'Look, this is my patch so fuck off or I'll cut off your face.'

From seemingly fresh air a knife appeared in the prostitute's hand and she slashed at Sarah's arm. Sarah somehow managed to react quickly enough and dodged out of the way of the worst of the slash, but the tip of the knife caught her arm and blood sprang from the cut.

'Ow! Jesus! What the fuck is wrong with you?!'

'The fuck that is wrong with me is little girls who can't understand simple English. So, for the last time, this is my patch so fuck off or I'll cut off your face.'

With this last warning Sarah backed away, clutching her bleeding her arm, and then ran off down the street. She reached the corner of the street and stopped running, now shaking and out of breath. Turning the corner she noticed two men stood leaning against a wall. Sarah quickly approached them. 'Excuse me. Excuse me! I've just been attacked!'

'What? Who by?'

'A woman around the corner. She tried to stab me.'

One of the men stepped into the light and looked at her closely, instantly recognizing her for what she was; a drug addicted teenager desperate for a hit. Her gaunt expression, the dark circles and skinny body told him this in one quick glance. 'Welcome to the area honey. That's Crystal. She's mad. You're lucky to walk away with only a scratch. I'd stay away from her if I was you. Why are you in this area? Pretty lady like you could get themselves raped and murdered in a nasty place like this.'

The other man had stayed in the dark. Sarah could not see his face, but his silhouette seemed somehow familiar to her. 'I was after some drugs.'

'Drugs? What kind?'

'Heroin.'

'Heroin. Well, you've come to the right guys. Fifty pounds for three hits worth.'

'Fifty? I haven't got that much.'

'How much have you got honey? You could always get more. Pretty young t hing like you could make a killing in this area.'

'I'm not a whore. I'm in college, studying. I want to become a nurse.'

'A nurse? You'd better stay off the heroin then darling.'

'No, I can do both.'

'You can do both? I've heard that before.' He turned and laughed with the other man who still stayed in the dark.

Sarah thought she recognised that laugh but her drug addled mind could not make the connection. 'I've got thirty pounds.'

'Thirty pounds? Let me guess. Your college money right?' Sarah nodded. 'Tell you what I'd do darling. Go home. Lock yourself in your bedroom with a bucket for vomit, lots of water and plenty of vitamins and minerals. Stay in your room for a week and get yourself off this drug before it ruins your life. If you are only ever going to listen to one piece of advice for the rest of your life, I'd make it the advice I just gave you.'

She appeared to contemplate this man's advice for a moment or two. She almost appeared to be contemplating walking away and getting her life back on the right track. But then a cramp hit her gut like the knife that had just sliced her arm. She winced and subconsciously scratched at her arm. Her decision had been made. 'How much can I get for thirty pounds?'

'Okay. Whatever darling. This much.' He reached into his pocket and pulled out a small packet of the drug and held it out to her.

'Is that it?!'

'Yep. It's an expensive drug. If you want more then bring more money.'

'I'll just take that.' Sarah handed over her cash and took the drug out of the man's hand. 'Are you here every night?

'Most nights.

'Okay. Thanks.'

'No worries. Good luck in college.'

'Thanks.' Sarah turned away and walked quickly away.

Under his breath the man said, 'You're going to need all the luck you can get.'

As Sarah reached the end of the street she turned and looked back. The face of the man who had remained in the shadows lit up as his lighter flared for the briefest of moments. As his shadowy face was shown to Sarah, she let out a gasp as she realised it was Peter. She wanted to return and confront him, but then she remembered his threats and how she had been lucky that he had let her buy the drugs without him attacking her as he had promised. Instead she swore under her breath, swearing her revenge, and then started the long and lonely cold walk back to her home.

*

For the next few weeks Sarah repeated her journey into this dangerous area of the town but as the time went on the thirty pounds she was spending was not getting her enough of the drug, nowhere near enough. And then, as she failed to register for the summer term of college after the Easter holidays, her college pay ments stopped.

In a panic she contacted the college and asked why the payments had ceased. The college informed her that due to her lack of attendance, her lack of submission of vital pieces of coursework and her lack of presence at key examinations, she had been removed from her courses and would have to re-sit the year. Therefore, given all these circumstances, the college had no option but to suspend her payments.

Sarah begged them to allow her back on the courses and to continue sending her payments but they refused stating it would not be fair on the other students who had attended to allow her back onto the courses. With a foul torrent of abuse Sarah slammed the phone down.

'Is anything the matter dear?'

'Is anything the matter dear? Is anything the fucking matter?! Are you on this planet mum? Are you?! If you supported me more, if you were more of a mother to me then perhaps I would not be in this fucking mess. If you had been more of a wife to dad, perhaps he would have stayed! Instead, because of you, I've been kicked off my college courses.'

'Never mind dear. I've done well without no college courses.'

'I think mum that our ideas of doing well may differ ever so fucKING SLIGHTLY!' Sarah's voice increased in volume and hysteria.

She slumped into an armchair, muttering to herself, scratching her arms as she struggled to think of a way to fund her addiction. Earlier that month she had already sold anything she could sell. The only item in the house that was worth anything was her computer but she was not going to sell that until she truly had no other option. She still occasionally used her computer when she was sold a type of heroin she did not know so she could investigate it on the internet and find out how much of the drug she should take.

No-one would buy the old furniture or the even older fridge and washing machine; she had already tried. She stared with venom at her mother as she took a swig from a bottle of dark rum, staring into the space where the television used to be. Sarah had got thirty pounds for it. Looking around the room desperate for eyes to land on something she could sell, her eyes rested on her mother's purse. Without hesitating she asked her mum a question. 'Mum, when's your next social payment due?'

'Today dear. But I've not had chance to get it.'

'Do you want me to get it for you?'

'If you don't mind dear. You know my pin number don't you?'

'Yes mum. Just as well I do because you don't know what it is do you?'

'You're a good girl. Will you get me some vodka on your way back? And some gin? And some whiskey? And some food? I haven't eaten for a while. I can't remember the last time I ate anything.'

'Of course mum. I'll go right now.' Sarah stood and took her mum's bank card from her purse. Turning to look at her mum she leaned over her and kissed her lightly on her forehead. 'Sorry I was nasty before mum. It's hard for us both.'

'It's okay dear. I'm sure your dad will come back one day. It's just a phase he's going through.'

'I'm sure too mum. I'll be back soon.' She lightly kissed her mum again and left the house.

Sarah walked the streets, slept in a pipe underneath a railway line for two nights because she did not want to return home and give the money to her mother. She was hoping that by the time she got back her mum would have forgotten. Sarah did not return home until dark had fallen at the end of the third day.

*

Sarah's mother waited all that day and evening for her daughter to return with the alcohol that she desperately needed. Late that night she had still not returned so she wandered through the house looking in all the places she had stashed alcohol in the past. All were dry.

As she continued to wander through the house she appeared to get more and more confused, checking places that she had already checked and doing this numerous times. After a few hours of this aimless wandering she returned to the living room and slumped into a chair.

Sarah's mother, for the last year, had consumed vast amounts of strong alcohol and had not been without a drink to hand throughout this year. It had now been eight hours since her last drink and she had started to get withdrawal symptoms.

After settling into the chair she fell into a deep sleep that persisted throughout the night and into the morning. When she did awake it was early morning and the sun was casting its light through a gap in the curtains and was shining on the wall. As she focused on the light it seemed to shake in front of her. She noticed that she had a strong headache and looking at the light did not help. Unable to help herself though, she glanced at the light again and it shook again. Now she stared at it, confused and disorientated, and the light seemed to leap out towards her. She threw herself backwards as the light turned into a ball and raced towards her face, turning into a bat as it landed on her face. Springing out of the chair she ran off into the kitchen screaming, scratching at her face and drawing blood with her nails down her cheeks. Then, as if nothing had happened, she returned to the chair and stared into the space where the television used to be.

As soon as she had settled down she shouted, 'Bat!' in a loud voice and ran back to the kitchen door and slammed it shut. She then proceeded to lift every cushion up in the living room and as she lifted each one she screamed, 'Bat!'

When every cushion had been lifted she again returned to the chair, but her whole body was now trembling so badly as she lowered herself into the chair she misjudged her descent and she landed on the arm of the chair which overbalanced sending her sprawling on the floor.

Lying on the floor she stared at the ceiling focusing again on another ray of light which hurt her eyes as she looked at it. So she closed her eyes, yet when she opened them the light had broken into numerous bright objects and these were crawling around on the ceiling. One by one she watched as they dropped and landed on her face. She could feel her heart beating, hammering away in her chest as she experienced palpitations. Screaming and screaming she spent the next five m inutes beating her body as she felt the creatures crawling on her skin, her heart beating rapidly. Soon she was sure she had managed to squash the creatures made out of light and she could not feel anymore on her body but the exertion of beating them off her had left her sweating and her heart was racing then suddenly she started to experience pain in her stomach and chest.

Sarah's mother managed to push herself into a sitting position and drag her alcohol ravaged body to the chair. As she sat there her body started to shake and she started to experience body tremors and these incessant tremors made her feel nauseous. At one point she was sure she was going to be sick so she ran for the bathroom but she could not remember where it was. She ran around the house throwing open doors until she managed to find it where she knelt at the toilet and started to violently retch. Having not eaten anything for days, all she did do was retch and she did this so violently her body was placed under immense strain that it could not deal with and it triggered a seizure.

One moment she was knelt on the floor, the next moment her whole body was lay on the floor and was violently shaking. Her head thrashed some side to side as did her arms and legs. Then as quickly as it had started her whole body went rigid for a few moments and from the corner of her mouth a trickle of blood appeared. Then, as quickly as it had stopped, is started again, going quickly from periods of muscle contraction to periods of rigidity. After a few more moments of this her whole body relaxed and she lay on the floor breathing heavily, eventually sinking into a restless sleep.

She awoke a few hours later and the first thing she noticed was that her tongue appeared to be in some pain, and on further analysis she discovered her whole body was aching. She had no recollection as to why or how she was on the bathroom floor or why her whole body appeared to be aching, but she decided that being on the bathroom floor was not the best place to be so she tried to stand. Using the toilet she managed to drag herself into a sitting position but even this simple manoeuvre was difficult.

Her whole body felt very weak and it was some time before she could regain her breath to achieve a kneeling position. Then, with the help of the cistern and sink she pulled herself up onto her feet where she steadied herself before walking to the top of the stairs. Even though she had checked the cupboard numerous times, she still thought that she had a small bottle of something or other in the cupboard under the stairs so she decided she would investigate it.

Resting for few moments at the top of the stairs, she then took a step down and instantly her weakened leg collapsed from underneath her. As her body started to fall she desperately clawed at the hand rail, her fingers scrambling for purchase but missing every time. Gravity then took hold and she fell head first towards the middle of the stairway. Her foot got trapped in the balustrade as she fell and her leg twisted, dislocating her ankle and as the pressure on her leg increased, her lower leg, to be precise her tibia, cleanly snapped in two.

The pain hit her instantly and she screamed but then her screams were snuffed out as she landed head first on a step knocking her unconscious. Her neck could not support the weight of her body and it also snapped cleanly in two killing her instantly. She bounced down the rest of the stairs coming to rest at the bottom of them, her twisted head hanging loosely against her shoulder, her eyes staring sightlessly into the space where the television used to be. It was in this twisted, macabre position where Sarah found her the next day.

Chapter 31

Sarah crawled out of the pipe early that morning leaving behind the empty syringes. She had hardly slept due to the scurrying of the rats further along the pipes, and she looked and smelled terrible. The previous day she had emptied her mother's bank account taking it to its overdraft limit. The same night she had gone into the red light district and spent most of the money on heroin. Now, with her clothes dirty and body filthy, she casually strolled into the shopping area of the town hoping to steal some toiletries so she could go home and clean up.

When she entered a department store a security guard looked at her with total disdain. He was going to stop her entering the store but as he approached her he noticed that she stank and he did not want to get any closer than he had to. She walked past him and smiled at him showing that she had lost one of her canine teeth. This had fallen out only yesterday due to severe decaying of the tooth and gum. Instead, the security guard spoke into his radio and informed the security centre of his concerns about this customer to which they replied they would keep an eye on the thieving bitch.

Sarah headed straight for the Estee Lauder counter and waited until their representative was deeply involved with another customer. When this occurred, Sarah quickly grabbed a handful of cleaning products and stuffed them into her coat pockets. Unknowing to her, there was a camera watching her. The security centre quickly sent a message to the same guard and he thundered across the store towards the Lauder counter. 'You! Stop! Thief!'

'Shit!'

She ran off in opposite direction from the charging guard, daring a quick glance over her shoulder. This quick glance cost her as she was tackled to the floor by a burly guard.

'Get your hands off me! How dare you treat me like this!' Sarah was thrashing around on the floor, kicking and punching the guard. 'Get the fuck off me!'

'I am! I am! Bloody hell you stink!' He helped her to her feet to which she responded by kicking him in the knee.

'Bastard!'

She tried to run past him as his knee collapsed from under him but by now the original guard had arrived and he wrapped his arms around her.

'Get off me! Get the fuck off me!' And to this plea she added an ear piercing scream. By now a crowd was gathering and the guard received a message in his ear.

'Get the products and get her out of here before she scares off all the customers!' He reached into her pockets and threw the products to the other guard who had recovered sufficiently to hobble over to his colleague.

'Help me get her to the exit.'

'Are we not getting her arrested?'

'Apparently not. They want her out and quick about it.'

'Okay. Whatever. Their choice'

Once the products were recovered they each took an arm and pulled the still kicking and screaming Sarah to the exit. The automatic doors slid open and they threw Sarah into the street.

'You're barred, for life!'

'I'm going to sue the arse off you two for treating me like this!' Sarah then made a move to enter the store again but was firmly pushed away by the guards. 'You fucking bastards, I'm going to take you to court!'

She tried one more time to burst into the store but again she was repelled by the guards. This time though she lost her footing and she was sent sprawling onto the floor. By the time she stood up the guards had entered the store again and were beckoning her to move away. Sarah raised her middle finger to them and then spun away to be greeted by Michelle looking at her with a look of surprise and shock on her face. Michelle also appeared to be holding hands with a gorgeous guy who she knew from college but could not quite put a name to the face.

'Oh, hi Michelle! Been a while!'

'Yes, it has Sarah. You okay? What on Earth was all that about?'

'Slight misunderstanding, but needless to say I was right and they were so in the wrong!' She flashed a smile at Simon who noticed the missing tooth and the blackness of her other decaying teeth. 'Are you not going to introduce me to this hottie?'

'Well, you know him from college. Well you should anyway. This is Simon.' Simon nodded and seemed to be about to offer his hand but then quickly decided against it.

'I've seen him about. I was planning to try and shag him, but I guess that is out of the question now?' She finished the sentence, which was definitely a question, and gave a quick wink at Simon.

Michelle decided to tactfully ignore Sarah's suggestive attitude. 'Where have you been? You've not been in college; you've not been in work. I tried to call you a few times but there was no answer. I tried you at work but they said they had not heard from you in months and had in fact fired you!'

'Must have missed the letter telling me about that. Well, let's just say my life is a little different now.'

'Well clearly. You look terrible.'

'That's what I've always like about you Michelle, your tact.'

'Do you want to go for a coffee and talk about it? The last time I saw you,' Michelle had to pause for a moment while she thought about it, 'was the night me and Simon, well, I saw you leave with Peter Johnson.'

'Yeah, don't I remember that all too well. I think I'll pass on the coffee Michelle, but thanks for the offer. I don't suppose you could lend me some money could you? Fifty pounds would see me through for a few days. I'll be able to buy some stuff and maybe stop myself looking so terrible.'

'Well, I suppose I could lend you something.' Michelle was starting to get her purse out of her bag when Simon grabbed her arm and pulled her away.

'Are you out of your mind?! You're going to give fifty pounds to that druggie?'

'Druggie? How do you know that? Look, she's probably just going through a rough patch…'

'Michelle, she's always been going through a rough patch. She's had more g uys in this town than I care to think about. I know at least two guys who caught an S.T.D. off her…..'

'Well more fool them for not using protection. Look, it's my money.' She shrugged off his hand and walked the few steps back to Sarah. 'Here you go. Not quite fifty but I hope it helps.'

'It all helps. I should be able to get some good H, I mean soap with this.' She laughed and took hold of the money but Michelle retained her grip of it.

She looked into Sarah's eyes, staring into them. 'H? I presume means heroin?'

'Michelle, really, this is a bad…'
'Stay out of this Simon. H is?'
'Is a new kind of soap powder.'
'I'm sure. Please Sarah, don't use this on drugs.'

'Okay, I won't.' She snatched the cash out of Michelle's hand. 'Well Michelle, guess I'll be seeing you. You're lucky Michelle, always have been. Rich, supportive parents; you've never wanted for anything. You should try growing up in a council house with an alcoholic mother and a father who beats his wife and his daughter, who raped his wife and his daughter. I lost my virginity at the ripe old age of eight years old and was raped and sodomised near enough every night until I was ten, until he grew bored of me because I was too old for him. But now look at you! You're practically glowing you're so in love with your handsome boyfriend. I think you've even lost weight off your porky thighs and bum.'

'Now look here. She's been very kind to you giving you some money…'
'It's okay Simon, let her speak.'

'Yeah, you have lost some weight, and you've actually found a bra that fits. From the little porker that used to waddle around school, you've turned into a beautiful woman Michelle, happy and content. And it is with these words I'd like to leave you with today. I hope you both die a painful death in total and utter misery. If you're lucky enough to have children, I hope they die too, also in total and utter misery. I wish you both a long life full of trauma, heartbreak and misery so then you can understand what it's like to be me, to have lived my life and the misery I have suffered. I don't know if it is possible to curse people, but I call upon all the gods in the world to curse you two now to a life full of pain, suffering and misery!'

Sarah did not see the palm of Michelle's hand but she certainly felt it as it slammed into her cheek. She managed to stagger out of range before Michelle could land a second blow and Simon grabbed her wrist as she made to swing again.

In a frighteningly cool voice Michelle spoke. 'How dare you speak to us like that. I've just helped you, been kind to you and you try to curse us. You're pathetic. You look and smell like a rat, so why don't you crawl back down into the sewer where you belong? If our paths ever, ever cross again Sarah you won't find me to be so charitable. There will only be one person who dies a painful death, who leads a miserable life, and that's you as you die a typical drug user's death in a foul bedsit with a needle hanging out of your arm. You are truly pathetic Sarah and I hope I never, ever see you again.'

Michelle shook off Simon's hand and stormed into the department store. He stared at Sarah, trying to control himself, to which she responded by raising her middle finger at him. He took a step towards her and then shook his head, mouthed the word pathetic at her and then followed Michelle into the store.

Sarah raised her middle finger again and jabbed it into the air behind him. Then with a wild cackle she strolled off along the street towards her home.

*

Sarah took a long time to walk home that day wanting to make sure her mother was totally drunk before going home. Eventually though she entered her house at dusk and the first thing Sarah noticed was the smell. During her seizure, her mother had lost control of her bodily functions and soiled herself with faeces. It was this smell that struck Sarah as she opened the door to the house.

Coughing a little as she walked into the lounge area, she was surprised to see her mother's chair unoccupied. Presuming she was on the toilet she turned to go upstairs. It was then she saw her mother's twisted body. Sarah let out an ear piercing scream and she was still screaming as she ran out of the house and she was still screaming as she banged on her neighbour's door.

'Bob! Oh my God! Bob help me!' She pounded the door, pounded and pounded it, while she continued to scream. 'Bob! Please Bob!'

Sarah noticed a light being turned on and the curtains were opened so she pounded the door harder, screaming louder. She saw Bob's face press against the window and a look of surprise as he registered it was Sarah. He moved the couple of steps to the door and flung it open. Sarah did not appear to have noticed the door was open or perhaps did not care. Her pounding fists now landed on Bob's chest and it was some moments before he could grab her wrists and restrain her. 'Sarah! Sarah! What the hell is wrong?!'

She did not stop screaming though so Bob in one huge hand held both her wrists and gently, well for him it was gently but for Sarah it definitely did not feel gentle, twice slapped her across the face. This action shocked Sarah into silence.

'Sarah, are you with me? Nod your head if you can hear me.' She hesitated and then nodded. 'Good. Now, what the hell is wrong? You've got me scared senseless and it takes a hell of a lot to scare me honey.'

Out of breath she managed to mutter, 'My mum.'

'Your mum? Margaret? What's wrong with Margaret?'

'She's fallen downstairs. Her head. I think she's…' With this Sarah burst into tears and collapsed against Bob.

He wrapped his arms around her and called upstairs. 'Clare! Clare! Come down and help me with Sarah.' Bob's wife came down the stairs still clutching the baseball bat that she had grabbed when she heard the commotion downstairs. 'Put the f'ing bat down and take her into the lounge while I go next door and look.'

Placing the bat behind the front door, she put her arm around Sarah's shoulders and gently led her into their living room. Bob picked up the bat and went into Sarah's house.

Like Sarah he first noticed the smell and he flicked on a light switch. Cursing as it did not work; he tried the switch a few more times and then gave up. He took the same route that Sarah had taken a few minutes earlier, and it was only when peering through the gloom did he see the twisted body. He took a few strides and stood over her, looking at the un-natural angle of her head.

During his time in the Marines and Special Forces, he had used his almighty strength to snap many an enemy combatant's neck so he knew instantly that this was a mortal injury. In more hope than expectation, he checked for a pulse in her neck. He did not expect to find a beat and was therefore not disappointed when he did not. He reached up to her eyes and closed them.

Chapter 32

The funeral of Sarah's mother was a sombre affair with only a few attendees who were mostly neighbours. No family attended the funeral, including the deceased's own daughter.

Once the body was removed by the authorities, she returned to the house closing all the curtains. In the week leading up to the funeral she was not seen by anyone, neighbours or the authorities except very late at night when she would sneak out of her house and scamper through the alleys to the red light area to spend the last of her mother's money.

When the police came to question her she did not answer the door. They returned numerous times and on all occasions she did not answer. They left cards asking her to call but the police were not persistent. They learned from neighbours that the deceased was a severe alcoholic and from the post-mortem they had learned that she had suffered a seizure before the fall. They presumed, incorrectly but close enough to close the file, that the seizure struck when the victim was at the top of the stairs, sending her to her death.

On the morning of the funeral, Bob pounded every door and window he could reach to get Sarah to attend the funeral. But Sarah knew when the funeral was taking place and she had not returned home that day. Instead she had spent the day taking the last of drugs she had been able to buy with the last of the money in the pipe under the railway.

Later that day she slowly walked home, still slightly high from her last hit, quietly humming to herself. As she reached the bottom of her street she approached her house from the other side of the road, checking that Bob was not waiting for her. Noting that he did not seem to be around, she skipped and hummed across the street to her front door scrabbling in her pockets for her keys. Eventually finding them she placed the key in the lock only to hear a couple of loud steps behind her. She turned around and gasped as Bob approached her along the garden path. He had been attending the wake in another neighbour's house and had been looking out for Sarah. 'Where've you been Sarah?' She did not reply. 'Sarah, it was your mother's funeral today. You know that don't you?' She shook her head but Bob was of course not convinced. 'Your mother's funeral Sarah and you didn't come. Why didn't you come?' Sarah dropped her eyes so she was staring at her feet. 'Look at me Sarah, please look at me.' Slowly, reluctantly, she raised her head. 'I know you've been going through a bad time, but please, I'm here to help. Please, what can I do to help you?'

Sarah appeared to contemplate the question for a few moments before responding. 'Nothing.'

'You need to go and see the solicitors tomorrow and sort out your mum's estate. I can run you down in the morning.'

'What estate Bob? She, we, have nothing.'

'There are some formalities you need to organise.'

'No, there isn't. She had no money, no insurances. The house is council. There is nothing she could have left me.'

'Please Sarah. Come with me tomorrow. I want to help you.'

'Bob, I don't want your help. I just want to be left alone, totally alone.'

'That's fine Sarah, for now. Grief drives us away from people, but remember where I am when you're ready.'

'I won't ever be ready. Please, leave me alone.'

With that Sarah turned away from him and entered the cold empty house. Slowly she made her way through it and climbed the stairs into her bedroom. She collapsed onto the mattress and suddenly tears started to run down her face. Quickly she wiped them away and reached into pocket and pulled out a small, folded up piece of tin foil which she proceeded to unwrap. Inside was a small portion of white powder. The tears continued to drop from her eyes as she contemplated the powder until she reached across to the other side of the mattress and retrieved a small tray with a teaspoon, matches, a syringe and other items she would need to cook up a hit. And that's exactly what she did, cooked up a hit with her last portion of heroin.

*

The next day Sarah searched through her bedroom trying to find anymore heroin that she could take. Quickly though the usual withdrawal symptoms descended upon her and by evening had become unbearable. Now hardly able to think with the cravings driving her to the brink of insanity, she searched through the house opening every drawer and cupboard, lifting and moving every chair and table, hunting for any money that might still be in the house. All she was able to find were a few coppers under the cushions of a chair in the living room.

Cursing she went back upstairs and rooted around in her drawers until she found some lingerie that fitted her perfectly a few months ago, but now hung off her body like old rags. Her breasts that used to fill the bra and be pushed up into an attractive cleavage now sagged against its cups. From the back of her wardrobe she took a very short skirt and slid this on. Again, the skirt used to fit her exactly, showing her hour glass figure off and her long sexy legs. Now it sat on her skinny hips merely accentuating the thinness of her body. For a top she chose a simple white blouse and then made her way into the bathroom where she still had a few cosmetics left over.

To hide her pale, gaunt, yellowy skin and the dark circle around her eyes, she thickly plastered the make up onto her face, finishing it off with a bright red lipstick. Looking deeply into her once sparkling brown eyes in the cracked mirror, she laughed and said out loud that she looked sexy. Not bothering with a jacket, she left the house hiding her key under a pot in the garden. From here she walked quickly into a specific area of the town.

It was dark when she reached the area of town and she stood on a corner waiting expectantly. Shortly she was joined by a few other women who stared at her until one of them approached.

'You new honey? Never seen you before.'

'Fuck off or I'll chop off your face!'

'What?! I'm only trying to be friendly honey.'

'Fuck off and leave me alone!'

'Well fuck you bitch!'

It was not long before Sarah noticed some of the women being approached by men in cars. Some of them got in and were driven away to return usually about half an hour later. One of the women Sarah noticed was very popular and she kept on being picked up and dropped off throughout the night.

After an hour of standing on the street Sarah was about to give in when she noticed a car approach so she decided to wait and see what happened. Slowly the car crept along the kerb until surprisingly it stopped next to Sarah. The window slid down and Sarah did what all the other girls had done and leaned through the window, smiling her best smile.

'You're new.'

'Yes, I am. New and fresh and ready for you.'

'How much?'

'For what?'

'What do you mean for what? For sex. How much?'

'Fifty pounds and I'll blow your mind!'

'Fifty pounds?! I could drive into the city and get myself a quality whore in a brothel for that much, not some drug addicted dirty whore!' He started to drive off.

Sarah did not give up that easily though. 'Wait, wait! What do you usually pay?'

'I won't go no higher than twenty-five for half an hour with a street walker.'

'Okay. Twenty-five it is then.'

With that Sarah flung open the passenger door and flopped herself down into the passenger seat. 'Where do you want to go?

'Well I'm not going to my place. I don't think my wife would like a threesome with a dirty whore. I presume you've got a room somewhere like all the other women?'

'I've got a house. Will that do?'

'Fine. Where is it?'

Sarah gave him directions and quickly they arrived at her house. Taking his hand, she led him into the garden picking up the key as they made their way past. As soon as they entered the house Sarah removed her clothes and stood in front of her customer in just her lingerie, then she took him by the hand and led him upstairs.

After they had finished he dropped her off back at the place he picked her up from and for the rest of that night she was picked up by another two men. These two men came back the next night and soon Sarah had a regular clientele who came to her near enough every night. She worked every night for a month, usually being used for sex three times a night. Sometimes she was busier, other times she was quieter. All of her earnings, bar buying a little food, were spent on heroin.

Chapter 33

While Sarah was spending her thirtieth night in a row sexually pleasuring another random stranger, Michelle was at Sally's mansion the night before they were due to fly to Nice on Sally's father's jet. It was a gloriously perfect early summer's evening and they were sat on a balcony overlooking the gardens, sipping champagne, chatting idly about anything and everything. 'Just remind me Sally, where are we going?'

This was the fifth time one of them had asked this question to the other in the last hour but neither of them was tiring of answering it. 'We're flying to Nice in my dad's jet. From there we are going to get a helicopter to Saint-Tropez where my dad's yacht is moored.'

'Bliss.'

'I haven't finished yet! We're spending two nights cruising around the Med before returning to Saint-Tropez to pick up my dad. Then we're making our way to our berth right next to the track in Monaco harbour just in time for practice on Friday!'

'Bliss!'

'I haven't finished yet! Friday we have access to the garage so we'll meet the drivers. Friday night we have numerous parties to attend. Then on Saturday we have access to the garage again and then Saturday day, after qualifying, we get to drive sports cars around the track! Saturday night, yes, you've guessed it, more parties and then a private function in the Casino where I'm going to persuade my daddy to let me blow a million pounds on black!'

'Bliss!'

'I haven't finished yet! On the Sunday we have track access to the grid and then before the race we will whisked back to the yacht and we'll watch the race from the comfort of my luxurious yacht! Sunday night we'll attend the after race party and be surrounded by the drivers and all the teams!'

'Bliss! Put your father's jet on standby and let's go now!'

'Minor problem. The jet is still in Madrid where my father is and only gets back early tomorrow morning! Sorry honey!'

'Damn! I can't wait, I can't wait, I can't wait! Let's buy another jet and we can go now!'

'My dad does allow me some leniency with my bank account, but even he would draw the line at me buying a jet!'

'Damn again! Remind me, where do our respective boyfriends think we're going?'

'Your aunt's hen party in Benidorm!'

'Suckers! I almost feel guilty about lying to them. Almost!'

'Me too. More champagne darling?'

'Oh go on then darling, you've persuaded me!'

Sally topped up both their glasses and as they relaxed back into their loungers they both let out a sigh of contentment while they watched the sun slowly sink below the distant horizon. The night descended so they both reclined even further and in the clear evening sky they watched for shooting stars and passing satellit es while sipping their champagne and dipping fresh strawberries into fresh whipped cream.

Soon though the temperature dropped and even the cashmere wool blankets that a maid brought them could no longer keep them warm, so they retired to one of the rooms in the mansion where they finished the bottle of champagne, both of them feeling tipsy when they had finished it. Stumbling and giggling their way through the house, they reached their respective bedrooms and called their boyfriends before eventually they both fell into a restless, excited sleep.

Early the next morning a maid woke them both who helped them finish packing and preparing for their journey. Exactly on time Alfred summoned them down to the Rolls-Royce which took them on the short drive to the private airfield where the jet had just arrived back from Madrid.

It was being refuelled and from a window of the car Sally saw her father walking towards the waiting helicopter. As he saw the Rolls approach he stopped and started to walk towards them. Before the car had stopped moving Sally and Michelle both leapt out and ran the short distance to where he was stood. 'Daddy!' shouted Sally and she leapt into his arms. He swung her round a few times as she kissed his cheeks. When he put her down Michelle threw her arms round him and planted a few kisses on him too.

'Thank you so much for allowing us to go with you Mr. Gallagher!'

'Nonsense. I couldn't think of two people I'd rather spend my time with!'

'Thank you anyway daddy. We can't wait to see you in Saint-Tropez!'

'Me too angel, but I need to go now and close this deal or I won't be able to come at all!'

'Sod the business and come now!' Sally stamped her foot and for a fleeting moment the I-want-line appeared on her forehead.

'If I sodded the business there would be no trips to Monaco because we'd be bankrupt!'

'Good point! Well hurry up and fly out soon Mr. Gallagher!'

'I will ladies. You enjoy the yacht and the cruise. It will be beautiful out there. I'll see you soon!'

'Bye daddy!' Sally placed a few more kisses on his cheeks.

With that he walked quickly away to the waiting helicopter and the girls watched his pilot take smoothly off. Sally and Michelle waved as he flew away from the airfield and then they turned and walked towards the jet as their luggage was being transferred from the car to the aircraft. Soon after that they heard the engines being turned on, and the pilot instructed them to their seats as they began the taxi.

With a rush and a roar of engines the jet thundered down the runway and with a whoop of delight the girls watched the land disappear away from them. Quickly the jet banked over as the pilot turned the plane towards the south-east and the French coastline.

*

During the flight the young ladies were treated to a gourmet breakfast prepar ed for them on the flight by one of Mr. Gallagher's chefs. While eating the meal they also drank freshly squeezed orange juice and watched a movie on the plasma television. After a couple of hours they began their descent into Nice airport and they were treated to a glorious view of the city and the deep blue of the Mediterranean as the plane dropped down to Aeroport de Nice-Cote d'Azur.

Quickly their luggage was offloaded and they were whisked across the Aeroport to the helicopter terminal where they transferred onto a Bell-Ranger. The aircraft lifted off and headed south-west along the French Riviera. Sally and Michelle could not take their eyes off the passing beautiful coastline as they were flown over Antibes, Cannes and soon, almost too soon for them, they descended into the heliport. As soon as they stepped off the helicopter a man was waiting for them and he led them to a large Mercedes that drove them through the streets of Saint-Tropez to the Nouveau Port. Here the Mercedes pulled up alongside a boat that surprised Michelle with its size. 'Oh, it's quite big isn't it?'

'This is just the tender sweetheart.'

'The tender?'

'Yeah, it floats under the main yacht in its own storage compartment.'

'Huh? It floats under the yacht?' asked Michelle.

'You'll see when we get there.'

'When we get where?'

'Out to Samurai, the yacht.'

'So this isn't the yacht?'

'No, of course not.'

'But it's a big boat'

'No, trust me, it's a small boat.'

As they walked from the car to the tender two crew members leapt from the boat to help them onto the deck. When they were settled into the comfortable seats a man approached them from the bridge. 'Miss Gallagher, so lovely to have you onboard again.'

'Thank you Roger. It is good to be here. Roger, this is my friend Michelle. Michelle, this is Roger, the captain.'

'Hi Roger. Nice to meet you.'

'You too Michelle. Are you ready to leave straight away Miss Gallagher?'

'Yes.'

'Perfect. It will take five minutes for us to approach Samurai. Please relax and of course please instruct the crew should you require anything to drink or eat but lunch will be ready for you fifteen minutes after we arrive.'

'That's fine Roger. Please depart when you are ready.'

With a smile he left them and returned to the bridge. The crew cast off the lines and smoothly the boat left Saint-Tropez harbour on the approach to the yacht. As they rounded the breakwater they could both see a yacht moored a short distance away. 'There she is. Samurai!' exclaimed Sally.

'I stand corrected! This is a small boat!'

'Told you.'

'My word. It's huge!'

'One of the biggest in the world!' exclaimed Sally again.

'Wow! It looks it! How big is it?!'

'One hundred and twenty meters long and all ours for two days!'

'It would take two days to see it all!'

'I don't think I've seen it all and we've had it for two years now! It is usually in the Caribbean but my dad had it brought over.'

The yacht was indeed huge. It was in fact one hundred and twenty one meters long, with a beam of twenty meters and a draught of five meters. The superstructure of the vessel was white, but the hull was a deep, royal blue. Its maximum speed was twenty knots and had another four smaller tenders held in various berths on each side of the vessel. Usually the yacht housed a helicopter in a hangar in the rear, but this was away for essential repairs.

Along with the helicopter and tenders, there were numerous jet skis and other watercraft held at various point in the yacht. On one of the decks of the yacht there was a large pool and spa area, surrounded by a large bar. There were also two others bars and spas, one located on the port side, one located on the starboard side. These were hidden behind large watertight hatches when the yacht was moving, yet when they were needed the hatches dropped down giving another access point to the sea. In order for the yacht to function smoothly when it was full of passengers, it needed a crew of sixty, but while it was only Sally and Michelle who would be using the yacht for the next couple of days, the crew was merely thirty.

The tender approached and it drew alongside the yacht. All that Michelle could see was the deep, royal blue of the hull, and as she looked up the side of the vessel she could see one of the two massive radar beacons that she was sure were bigger than her house. Reducing its speed, the tender turned wide around the rear of the craft and was held here while a massive section of the aft of the yacht was lifted up to reveal the docking station for the tender.

Expertly Roger guided the tender; its name was Katana, into the storage berth underneath the main superstructure, between the port and starboard bulkheads of the hull. Slowly it came to a stop, and as the ladies stepped from Katana onto the teak deck that ran around the tender's berth, they were greeted by the Chief Steward. 'Miss Gallagher. Miss Walmesley, welcome aboard! Please, allow me to guide you to your cabins.'

They followed him through Samurai, up two levels until they reached the sumptuously decorated residential area of the yacht. With a flourish the steward opened one of the cabin doors and Michelle could not help gasping as she looked into the cabin.

'Miss Walmesley. This is the Princess Suite. I hope you will find it satisfactory for your needs.'

'It's perfect! Thank you.'

'Please, feel free to settle in. We have lunch ready for you in fifteen minutes which will be served in the pool area.'

'I don't know...'

'I'll come and get you in ten minutes honey. Freshen up. Oh, and change into your bikini, but underneath something less revealing while we eat.'

'Right, will do. See you soon.'

Sally left her and Michelle turned to study the room. The first thing she noticed was the bed. It was huge, it was similar in size to two king size beds next to each other. She kicked off her sandals and her feet sunk into the thick carpet which she ran across and dove onto the bed with a squeal.

Bouncing off the bed she ran across to the windows and opened the curtains which gave her a view of the sea across to Saint-Tropez. With another squeal of delight she found the refrigerator which was full of bottles of expensive champagne and snacks such as caviar and truffles. Turning around she looked into the bathroom and a sigh of contentment left her lips as she saw the large marble Jacuzzi bath then quietly she heard a discreet knock on the door and one of the crew called her name. 'Miss Walmesley. Your luggage.' Michelle opened the door and one of the crew members carried her bags into the room. 'While you are at lunch I can unpack them for you. Is there anything you need now?'

'Erm, yes. My bikini and cotton shawl. They are in that bag.'

'Please feel free to freshen up why I find them for you.'

'Thank you.'

She went into the bathroom and had a quick rinse in the shower until she heard another discreet knock on the bathroom door and the member of the crew stated that Miss Gallagher was here to take her to lunch. Quickly Michelle threw a towel round her and skipped into the bedroom to find her bikini and shawls out on the bed. The crew member was making good work unpacking the rest of her clothes and Sally was lounging in one of the chairs looking out of the window. 'Are you ready?'

'Two seconds honey.' Michelle grabbed her bikini and shawls and skipped back into the bathroom to put them on. A short time later she was ready and Sally stood up from her chair.

'You look good Michelle.'

'So do you.'

'Thank you.'

Michelle watched as Sally left the cabin and all she could do was dream of ever looking as good as her friend. Sally had been to London recently and dyed her hair a deep copper red. It cascaded down her back to just under the strap of her bikini top. Sally must have felt that Michelle was not following her and she turned in the doorway to beckon her friend to follow. The bikini top fitted snugly around Sally's large breasts, slightly smaller though than Michelle's. But it was the stomach, hips and legs where Michelle really lost out. Sally's were toned with no fat on them at all. Faintly you could make out her stomach muscles under the translucent shawl, and her hips and legs also slender but with toned muscle on them too. No matter how long Michelle spent in the gym, no matter how hard she tried she could never look as good as her friend did. She looked into Michelle's eyes and smiled which lit up her emerald green eyes. 'Are you coming?'

'Yeah, sorry. Thank you Sally so much for letting me come with you.'

'Nonsense! It is my pleasure, well our pleasure. We'll both enjoy your company. Now come on and stop being silly! Lunch is ready. I've heard a rumour that it's one of the chef's specialities; a delicious seafood salad!'

'Sounds even more perfect!'

Sally held out her hand which Michelle took and she led them through the yacht, along the corridors that looked like they had been lifted straight out of the Gallagher's mansion, to the large pool area.

*

After the seafood salad lunch the yacht began its journey. It turned away from Saint-Tropez and made its way out into the Mediterranean heading east towards the north shore of Corsica. While they were sailing, Sally and Michelle relaxed around the pool area, swimming or enjoying the Jacuzzi. During this time they were served with delicious exotic fruits and a limitless supply of ice-cold fruit juices to help keep the Mediterranean heat away.

It took five hours to reach the north coast of Corsica and they moored two miles off the island. When Sally told Michelle that they could take the jet skis across to a secretive cove that could only be accessed from the sea, Michelle let out a scream of excitement and they both ran through the yacht down to the starboard hatch that had been lowered for them. While they waited for the jet skis to be brought round from the rear hangar, they relaxed in sun loungers and drank more juice that was served to them from the starboard bar.

Soon enough the skis were ready to go and they were moored next to the starboard hatch. Both the women had used this exciting medium of transport before, so they were quickly away, blasting across the perfectly calm Mediterranean Sea towards the cove. Quickly they arrived at the beach and they both dragged their skis onto it and took their prepared towels and sunshade from the storage compartments on the skis.

The rest of the day was spent swimming and relaxing, with no one around them. The sheer cliffs of the cove stopped anybody seeing them from above and the yacht was far away, so the young ladies were comfortable enough in each other's presence to bathe and swim topless. Within one of the compartments were light refreshments so at one point during the day they lounged in the sand to eat the sandwiches and fruit.

All too soon though the day was over and reluctantly they both loaded the skis back up and made their way back to Samurai. As they disembarked from the jet skis at the starboard hatch the Chief Steward met them and informed them that dinner would be served around the pool area at eight o'clock. When they walked towards their respective cabins Sally could not help notice a sense of heightened activity on the yacht so she approached one of the crew. 'What's going on? You all seem very busy?'

'Oh, nothing Miss Gallagher. Just cleaning and preparing.'

'Preparing for what?'

'Your father's arrival.'

'But he doesn't arrive until the day after tomorrow?'

'Yes, we know ma'am, but we have a lot to do.'

'Okay. Whatever. I'm going to have a rest now so please keep the noise to a minimum around my cabin.'

'Of course Miss Gallagher.'

As they left the steward Sally expressed her thoughts with Michelle. 'Strange. They always start to run around like headless chickens only on the day my dad is due to arrive.'

'I wouldn't think about it. They've obviously started early.'

'Yeah, maybe. Never mind. Right, here we are. I'm going to go to the bridge and call David off the satellite phone. Do you want to come with me and you can call Simon?'

'Yeah, good idea. I wanted to call him but I guess our mobiles won't get a signal out here?'

'Yep, they won't work out here. We'll go up now.'

'Can we change into something a bit less revealing first?'

Sally turned and looked at her friend. She noticed how her breasts seemed to be defying any known laws of physics by somehow remaining in her bikini top. Catching a glimpse of herself in a nearby mirror she also concluded that it would probably not be a good idea for her, the daughter and heiress of a billionaire, to be surrounded by sailors dressed the way they were. 'Probably a very good idea honey,' stated Sally. 'Meet you here in five?'

'Perfect.'

Ten minutes later, both dressed in shorts and t-shirt, they stepped onto the bridge where in a fluster they were approached by the Captain. 'Miss Gallagher. A pleasure. Can I be of assistance?'

'Can we use the satellite phone to call England?'

'Of course, of course.'

'What's going on? Everyone seems very busy?'

'Nothing, nothing at all. Just keeping busy running some safety drills.'

'Oh. Do you want us to come back later?'

'No, no. Now is fine. Please, you know where it is.'

Sally nodded and wandered through the banks of computer screens and aviation style chairs to where the satellite phone was housed. They both phoned their respective partners, both expressing how much they were missing them and how Benidorm was rubbish without them. Claiming the expense of the call, neither of them talked for long so they both made their way back through the yacht back towards their cabins. 'Right, I'm going to have a sleep I think so I'll see you here at eight and we can both go up to dinner,' said Sally.

'What should I wear?'

'Just one of your cotton summery dresses will be fine. Nothing too revealing, nothing that's going to make you hot either because it's going to be a balmy night.'

'Sounds great!'

'Yeah, it does.'

'Are you okay? You seem distracted?' Michelle asked.

'There's something going on.'

'Do you think he's coming early?'

'I doubt it. He sounded like he was very busy to get everything in a fit state to leave it for a few days.'

'He doesn't like to leave it does he?'

'No, because whenever he does someone messes up. He doesn't have anyone he trusts implicitly to control things when he's away, hence why he's always trying to persuade me to join him.'

'And are you going to?'

'I doubt it. I don't want to live like he has done, never seeing my future husband or children, working every hour and every day. There's more to life than that isn't there?'

'Of course there is. But remember, I'm sure he didn't enjoy being away from you or your mum, but he made the sacrifice. Without that sacrifice we wouldn't be stood on a hundred million dollar yacht.'

'Two hundred million.'

'You know what I mean.'

'I suppose you're right. I'm still thinking about it. Anyway, I'm tired after all the travel and swimming so I'm going for a rest. See you later.'

'Okay. See you later.'

*

At seven o'clock that evening Sally's alarm woke her. After a few more moments of resting her eyes, she leapt out of bed and did some light pilates exercises. Once these were complete, she felt more awake and started to prepare herself for dinner. It was while she was applying a little makeup that she heard the distant noise of a helicopter.

Used to hearing helicopters come and go through her life, she did not pay it much attention. Then she thought about where she was. The north coast of Corsica is not renowned for its plethora of heliports. She also noticed it was getting closer and when she listened harder she thought she recognised the tone and beat of the engine. 'Oh my! That's the Flying Star!'

With a shout of delight, she threw her mascara onto the dressing table and raced out of her room, banging on Michelle's door as she passed. Michelle jumped as she heard her door being hit so vigorously and she flung it open without thinking that she was dressed only in her lingerie.

'Get some clothes on quick! He's here, he's here!'

'Calm down! Who is?'

'My dad, my dad! Hurry up!'

Quickly Michelle flung on her dress and followed the now sprinting Sally through the yacht. As they reached the rear of the vessel they were just in time to see the yacht's helicopter touch down on the helipad. They both tried to approach, but the beat of the rotors beat them back, but it was not long before the passenger door was opened and Mr. Gallagher exited the helicopter. 'Daddy!' Sally screamed, but he could not possibly hear her over the roar of the settling engine and rotors.

Instead he waved at them both, and ducking low he walked over to where they were stood, to be greeted by big hugs and kisses on the cheek. Pointing down, back into the body of the yacht, he took both their hands and led them down into one of the lounge areas of the yacht. Once they were away from the noise of the aircraft, Sally flung her arms around his neck again. 'I can't believe you've com e early! I can't believe it! I'm so happy to see you!'

'Me too Mr. Gallagher!'

'And I'm happy to see you both. Hot damn it's good to be back on my yacht!'

'Why? Why have you been able to finish early?'

'I pulled out.'

'What?! I thought this was the deal of the year for you?!'

'It was. But they annoyed me. We're making a deal with the more expensive company instead. I'll pay a little bit more to be treated the way I should be treated.'

'Fair enough. We're glad you decided to do that!'

'Left it with the lawyers and a couple of directors to sort out so no doubt when I get back I'll have to sort out the mess!'

'Well it's about time you gave them a bit more responsibility. I thought the helicopter, the Flying Star, was broken?'

'Amazing how quickly something can get fixed when you threaten to cancel the contract!'

'Indeed! It's so good to see you!'

'It's good to see you too darling, and you of course Michelle. Now, where can an old man get a drink around here?'

'Which old man?' retorted Sally, looking over his shoulder. 'Come on. Let's go up to the pool area. Dinner should be ready now. And you're not old!'

'Hmmm, perhaps you're right. I'd still give you a run out on the squash court I think.'

'I know you would. Come on! Let's go and relax by the pool and we can talk about anything and everything so long as the anything and everything does not concern the company!'

'Sounds good to me!'

Taking both their hands he led them up a level. When they arrived he gave a quick glance down onto the helipad to make sure the crew were storing the helicopter away straight away. Sally pulled him away. 'Come away and relax. They know what to do.'

'I doubt it. That's the reason it broke you know?' he replied, turning to face her. 'They left it out overnight in a storm!'

'Yes, I know daddy, you told me. You also told me that you don't think that they will ever do it again after the roasting you gave them! Trust them to do their job.'

'That's one of my biggest problems Sally. I don't trust anyone apart from you.'

'I'm glad you do trust me, but let's forget about everything and relax!'

'Okey dokey boss. Lead me to the bar!'

'Come on!'

Sally dragged him to the bar where she dismissed the offers of the attendant and made her father his favourite cocktail, a mojito. For the rest of the evening and into the night, they talked and talked about anything and everything; from the hopes and aspirations of the Sally and Michelle to how much they all missed Sal ly's mother. Eventually though, after many freshly made cocktails, a few yawns were exchanged and both the women announced that they were going to bed. They both gave him a goodnight hug and kiss, after which they both retired to their respective cabins.

Mr. Gallagher though was not tired. After all the years of creating his fortune, he only slept for a few hours each night and he was quite comfortable to go for a number of days without sleep. He quickly called James from the satellite phone on the bridge to make sure that nothing had gone wrong in the short time he had been away. James politely informed him to not call again until he returned to England and that everything would be handled while he was away.

Not believing him for a moment, still he made a mental note though to try and resist the temptation to call again, so he returned to the pool area where he dismissed the bar attendant, who he noted looked shattered, and made himself another cocktail. He then remembered that he had forgot to tell James about a small matter and before he realised what he was doing he was half way back to the bridge.

When he did realise he cursed himself, spinning back round and returned to the bar area where he slammed his cocktail glass onto the bar then stripped off his clothes down to his underwear. He let out a quiet shout as he ran to the pool, leapt into the air and tucked his knees into his chest which allowed him to bomb into the water with an almighty splash. Spluttering and coughing he returned to the surface chuckling to himself and then with a kick he rolled onto his back and spent some time floating effortlessly in the pool watching the stars that hung in the clear Mediterranean sky.

After floating for fifteen minutes he swam a few lengths of the pool before leaving it. Not bothering to dry, he padded through the yacht to his cabin where he flung open the door to his balcony and sat in one of the loungers allowing the cool night breeze to dry his body. Eventually, with a relaxed sigh of happiness he left the balcony closing the door behind him. Giving a glance to the clock he muttered that this would be the earliest he had been to bed for thirty years so he decided to read some financial papers on his computer that had been emailed to him earlier that day. He became so engrossed in them that it was only when he felt the need for the toilet that he looked around him and noticed it was dawn. 'Bloody hell!' he muttered out loud. 'So much for relaxing!'

When he had visited the bathroom he lowered himself onto his bed and slept for two hours before being woken by the distant shouts and screams of his daughter and her friend. With a smile he leapt out of bed, put on his swimming shorts, and raced through the yacht to the port hatch where he dived into the refreshing sea and promptly dragged both young ladies deep under the water. With a cough and splutter they all surfaced, Mr. Gallagher laughing.

'Daddy! You nearly drowned us!'

'Rubbish! Right, last one to the rear of Samurai is a rotten egg!'

With a couple of strong strokes he swam away from Sally and Michelle, who both laughed at his antics and quickly followed him towards the rear of the yacht, to the lavish breakfast that awaited them.

*

Back in England, Sarah had just bought some fresh drugs off an acquaintance of Peter's. Her breakfast that morning was a full syringe of heroin. The veins in her arms had long since collapsed so she simply injected the breakfast into her leg.

Chapter 34

To the sound of the yacht's horn, Samurai docked at Monaco harbour two days after Mr. Gallagher had arrived. The previous day had been spent relaxing on the yacht as they cruised towards the state of Monaco, arriving just in time to watch the start of the practice session for the Grand Prix.

After the yacht was docked they made their way around the circuit in a car supplied by the team he sponsored until they reached the pit lane and the team's garage. Here they were met by the Team Principle who introduced them to the drivers.

Michelle could not help notice and chuckle to herself how both of these multi-millionaire drivers' eyes nearly popped out of their heads as they saw Sally for the first time. From that moment, they both never left their side, showing the young women around the garage while Mr. Gallagher had a meeting with the Team Principle in the hospitality section behind the garage.

Michelle was sure that the distraction of Sally was the reason why both of the drivers underperformed during the practice session, both of them coming ninth and tenth respectively. One of the drivers seemed especially smitten with Sally.

As soon as he arrived back at the garage he was back by her side, showing and explaining to her the telemetry of his laps on a computer screen. Without realising that Sally could pay his wages from her own personal bank account, he invited her to the after race party as his personal guest. With a smile she stated that considering her father was one of the main sponsors of the team, that she also had a boyfriend and that she personally knew his girlfriend, she did not think it would be a good idea. Obviously not used to being rejected, with a blushed face of thunder he stated that he hoped they both enjoyed the race and he stormed out of the garage.

'He didn't seem very happy,' chuckled Michelle

'Well, honestly. They think that just because they're well paid and slightly good looking that they can ease their way into any woman's knickers. Really annoys me. Same with those flamin' footballers from my dad's team who always hassle me.' She rolled her eyes. 'They don't seem to realise that in a blink of an eye I could pay their wages and buy their houses and cars which they are always so eager to flaunt!'

Michelle laughed. 'Well forget about him for now and let's go and find your dad.'

'Good idea.'

Linking arms they strode out of the garage, the passes around their necks allowing them access straight away into the hospitality suites behind the garage.
'There he is. Oh and bugger. Look who he's talking too!'

'Never mind Sally. Let's go over anyway and make him feel really awkward.'

Smiling, they both strolled over to where Mr. Gallagher was sat talking to the driver, and Sally casually draped an arm around her father's shoulder. With another deep blush he muttered an excuse of having to speak to his engineer and he quickly walked away.

'Now, how are my two favourite ladies?'

'We're fine.'

'Did you enjoy looking round the garage?'

'Yes, it was good.'

'It will be a bit more exciting tomorrow when the qualifying starts and of course you've got your special treat as well!'

'Oh yes! We've been having such a fantastic time we'd both almost forgot about it!'

'Tomorrow, after the qualifying is finished, they're going to let us drive round in a new Mercedes sports car!'

'Sounds brilliant daddy!'

'Yes, I'm sure we'll enjoy it! Right, I'm done here. I've cleared up sponsorship issues so we can go back to the yacht and relax. Tonight we have a function we have to attend.'

'Oh, I thought we were going to parties?'

'We were. But an invite has come through that we can't say no to.'

'Fair enough. Well let's go back to the yacht and we can relax there for a while.'

'Okay. I'll get someone to bring us transport back to the yacht.'

They waited in the suite for a short time while a car was prepared for them which took them back to the harbour and Samurai. They all spent the rest of the warm day lounging around the pool. Mr. Gallagher's phone never stopped ringing, and for the first time that Sally could ever remember he directed all the callers to a member of his executive board.

Eventually though, after a mutter and a curse, Sally heard him record a message for the phone's answer phone and in what was an absolute definite first he turned the phone off. A little while later he was approached by a member of the crew who informed him that there was a man waiting in one of the lounges to speak to him. Mr. Gallagher strode into the yacht and came back quickly holding three pieces of paper.

'Right ladies. We've been invited to a function tonight. It's black tie for the men, ball gowns for the women.'

A look of panic flashed across each of their faces and Sally informed him, 'Daddy, we didn't bring anything that formal.'

'Did you not? Why not?'

'We thought we would just be attending parties, not events that require ball gowns.'

'Sally, you're the daughter of one of the richest men in the world and you're in Monaco with your father during a Grand Prix weekend. The first things that should be packed are ball gowns!'

'Sorry daddy. I didn't think.'

'Right, not to worry. Rob,' he said, calling to one of the crew, 'get me Boutique Adrienne. Make sure that they know it is me who is calling.'

'Yes Mr. Gallagher.'

They only had to wait a few moments for Rob to return holding a phone which he passed to Mr. Gallagher.

'Hello.'

'Mr. Gallagher. It has been too long!'

'Adrienne. So lovely to speak to you.'

'You too Mr. Gallagher. How can I assist you today?' Adrienne spoke with a sultry French accent.

'We have a bit of a ball gown catastrophe. Can you help?'

'I am very busy today but I will take care of this personally myself. Who are the gowns for?'

'My daughter and her friend.'

'Your daughter? But Mr. Gallagher, I am confused. As you know, we don't stock gowns for children?'

'I think it has been longer than you realise Adrienne. My daughter is seventeen now.'

'No, she cannot be! I remember her with your mother. She was no taller than my waist!'

'Well, she is now. Can you help?'

'Of course. Which hotel are you at?'

'I'm on my yacht in the harbour.'

'Ah, perfect! I will come now.'

'You're coming yourself?'

'Of course. I need to measure the ladies.'

'Excellent. How long will you be?'

'Five minutes, if that. You know my Boutique is only a short walk from the harbour.'

'We'll be waiting for you.'

Just under the stated five minutes, a member of the crew led a woman out to the pool area. She was dressed simply in dark jeans with a simple white top. Her long dark hair cascaded down her back and as she saw Mr. Gallagher she smiled and removed her sunglasses showing her shining brown eyes. 'Adrienne! So lovely to see you!'

'And you Mr. Gallagher.'

'Thank you for fitting us in at such short notice.'

'My pleasure. Now, we must hurry if the gowns are to be ready for this evening. I presume you're attending the ball with Pr...'

He quickly interrupted her. 'Yes, yes. Quite true.' With a look of confusion on her face, Mr. Gallagher then whispered quietly into her ear that their destination this evening was a surprise for the girls.

'I'm sure you will all have a lovely time. Now, where are my two subjects?'

Sally and Michelle walked up from their cabins where they had been to quickly change. Adrienne looked at Sally and gasped. 'Sally! So lovely to see you!'

'Thank you for seeing us at such short notice.'

'My pleasure. Your mother was one of my favourite and most loyal customers. You must miss her greatly, yet you are her image.'

'Thank you. We do miss her, but she would be happy to see us still holding together as a family and enjoying life. This is my friend Michelle.'

'My darlings,' and she kissed both of the young ladies twice on the cheek. 'Now, we must be quick. Just glancing at you I know we have two beautiful gowns that will suit and fit you, but we must measure you and get them to suit and fit you perfectly! Now, where can we go, and keep in my mind I only measure my subjects naked!' Adrienne noted their surprise. 'How can I find you a gown that fits when your clothes get in the way? I must see and measure your bodies so I can have the gowns fit you perfectly!'

'That's fine,' replied Sally. 'My cabin will be best.'

Sally quickly led them to her cabin where they both took it in turns to strip in the bathroom and be measured by Adrienne. As Sally entered and took off her shorts and bikini top Adrienne gasped again. 'If you ever want to model for me let me know. You have the most amazing figure and you have your mother's looks.' She fluttered round Sally with a tape measure, recording the figures on a notebook. 'Did you know that before she married your father, your mother modelled for all the leading fashion houses?'

'My dad might have mentioned it.'

'She was a stunning woman, just like you.'

'Thank you.'

'Right, we're done. Please send in Michelle.

After Michelle had been measured they all made their way to the pool where he was waiting for them.

'Mr. Gallagher, you are all in luck! I have two perfect gowns for tonight that would nearly fit without alterations, but I want all my clients to look perfect so I will have them changed slightly and have them back to you, well, when do you leave?'

'The limousine is coming at six.'

'Then give me two hours and I will have them here for five.'

'Thank you so much Adrienne. Sorry about the short notice.'

'Not a problem. Just remember though ladies, next time you need a gown you know who to call!'

'We'll always be grateful,' replied Sally. 'Thank you so much.'

'I will send the bill to your office in London as usual Mr. Gallagher.'

'Please. I will see you off the yacht.'

With that he took the designer by the arm and led her off the yacht. The rest of the afternoon the girls spent getting ready. Mr. Gallagher acquired the services of two top hairdressers to attend to them on the yacht, paying a large amount of money for them to come at such short notice. Also, he arranged for some makeup specialists to come to help perfect the women's look for the night.

At exactly five that afternoon each of the women received their gowns at their cabins. Almost as soon as Sally had closed the door Michelle knocked loudly on it and Sally told her to enter.

'Have you seen yours?! Have you seen yours?!'

'No, it's only just come. Hang on.' Sally unzipped the protective case and I was her turn to let out a gasp. 'Oh my, it's beautiful!'

'Mine is too. Mine is red though, a really deep red!' Michelle replied.

'No wonder my dad asked her for the gowns. We're both going to look amazing!'

'You'll look amazing, I'll look okay.'

'You'll look amazing too silly!'

'I hope so.'

'Well, I'm going to finish getting ready. I'll see you upstairs at five to six.'

'Sounds good! This is going to be a great night. Do you know where we are going to yet?'

'No. He won't tell me.'

'Well if we need gowns like this I'm sure it is going to be amazing!'

Michelle skipped out of Sally's cabin into her own cabin and when she entered she could not help stopping to stare at the ball gown. She thought to herself that she had never, and would never again, wear anything so perfect. Picking up the gown, she slid into it and then turned to contemplate herself in the mirror.

Her hair had been left to fall naturally, however it had been lightly curled into ringlets. The beautician had only applied the lightest of makeup to her face. Her most striking feature was her lips which had been coated in a deep red gloss that matched her dress to perfection. The gown curved over her large chest which was being pushed up to form a delightful large cleavage and cascaded down her body, flowing out to cover the bulges on her stomach and hips. To finish off her appearance she wore a pair of new black Prada shoes that had been supplied with the gown which added a few inches to her height. She was very happy with the way she looked, but she also knew that as soon as she was stood beside Sally she would feel inadequate and plain next to her perfect friend.

*

A short time later, Mr. Gallagher stepped off his yacht and held out his hand to help the young women step off the gangway. With a woman on each side of him linking an arm each, they walked the short distance to where the limousine was parked. While they walked a few people stopped to look at the three people, each of them laughing and joking as they walked along. A few passing tourists took photographs and as their cameras zoomed in to focus on their faces they were disappointed to see that they were not anyone famous.

When they neared the limousine, the chauffeur opened the rear door for them and they entered the vehicle. Sinking down into the luxurious leather seats, Mr. Gallagher reached to the cool box and poured them all a glass of champagne from the cold bottle of Krug.

Sedately the limousine cruised through the streets of the Principality until the large car came to a brief stop. Through the window Sally could see police and guards checking the limousine and the underside of the vehicle for any kind of explosive device. Quickly they were waved through and shortly after they stopped again where the chauffeur exited the car and opened one of the passenger doors.

Michelle was sat next to this door so she exited first. As soon as she placed a leg out of the car she was instantly dazzled by the flashes from cameras. Blinking, she stepped onto the red carpet and stood up. Instantly the cameras stopped as the journalists realised it was not anyone famous, and then they started again as Mr. Gallagher stepped out of the car. Once again most of the cameras stopped, but a few of them recognised him and carried on taking pictures. With a wave to the crowd he reached back into the limousine and took the hand of his daughter.

As she stepped out of the car the cameras clicked and stopped. Then the photographers, upon realising how beautiful this unknown woman was, like a ripple through them the cameras started again. Flash after flash dazzled the three of them, and then one of the photographers who had recognised Mr. Gallagher realised that this stunning young woman must be his elusive only daughter. 'Miss Gallagher!'

Surprised, Sally turned towards the man who had called her name, and was instantly dazzled as the flash went off. Taking up the cry of her name, more of the photographers struggled to catch her attention for that special photograph where she was looking directly into their lens.

'Miss Gallagher!'

'Please Miss Gallagher!'

'This way Miss Gallagher!'

With plenty of smiles, they stayed there for a few more moments, Sally responding to as many of the cries of her name as possible by turning this way and that way. Slowly her father started to edge them away from the front line of camera men, towards the gap between the two phalanxes of photographers. Still they called her name as they walked along the red carpet, but now she ignored them, eager to get away from the limelight that she did not wish for. She speeded up, and both of them took the hint, quickly following her to clear the group of photographers.

After clearing the gathering of journalists they were able to view for the first time their intended destination. Michelle let out a small whistle through her teeth. 'Is that what I think it is? That's the Prince's Palace. Oh my Sally, we're going into a Palace!'

Which is where they headed to, passing the security guards who waved them under an archway into the courtyard at the front of the Palace. Upon entering the haven of the courtyard Mr. Gallagher turned and studied them both. 'You both okay? That was a bit intense. Sorry, I thought there may be a bit of paparazzi, but nothing like that!'

'It's okay dad, don't worry. You okay Michelle?'

'Yeah, I might get my sight back in a minute!' They all laughed at Michelle's joke as they continued to walk across the courtyard towards the entrance.

'Right, ladies, stop walking for a moment. In a moment, as you can see, we are going to enter the Palace. We are here as guests of Prince Albert the Second of Monaco himself. In a moment you are going to meet him. He knows me, so he'll address me by my first name. I've met him before, so I will refer to him as Sir. You must refer to him on introduction as Your Serene Highness. If he likes you, he'll say you can address him as Sir. If he really likes you he'll allow you to address him as Albert, although I've only ever heard him say that once and that was to your mum Sally. Shake his hand, give a slight curtsey and simply say "It is an honour to meet you Your Serene Highness"'

'Oh goody, a prince!' exclaimed Michelle.

'Don't get too excited, he's round about my age! Do everything as I say and you'll be fine. He's quite relaxed when you get to know him, but he cannot stand not having the proper respect shown to him in public.'

'Okay dad, we've got it. Can we go in?'

'Of course. Shall we?' He offered an arm to each lady which they took, and he led them to the entrance of the Palace.

*

'Ladies and gentlemen, Mr.,' the microphone crackled as the announcer stated his first name, 'Gallagher accompanied by Miss Sally Gallagher and Miss Michelle Walmesley.' And then they were introduced to the Prince. 'Please may I introduce you to His Serene Highness Albert the Second, Prince of Monaco.'

'Mr. Gallagher. So good to see you again.'

Taking the Prince's hand in a firm handshake he replied, 'Sir, it is a real honour to be invited into your Palace.'

'It is my pleasure.'

'May I introduce my daughter Sally, and her friend Michelle?'

Michelle stepped forward first and gave a small curtsey. 'Your Serene Highness. It is an honour to meet you.' He nodded and smiled at her and the smile turned into a positive beam when his eyes met Sally's sparkling emerald eyes.

'You Serene Highness. It is a pleasure to meet you,' and she also gave a small curtsey.

'I thought for a moment that an apparition of your mother approached me. Please, I insist, call me Albert.'

'Of course, erm, Albert. Thank you for inviting us into your home.'

He gave a light laugh. 'It is more of a tourist destination and government building than home now Sally, but it is a pleasure to have you here. I must attend to my other guests, but I insist you save a dance for me later this evening.'

'Again, it would be an honour Albert.' Sally gave him his best smile, which unknowing to her made his heart skip a beat. With another pair of curtseys and a shallow bow, they walked away from the Prince through the throng of fellow guests.

'Well, you both made an impression on him to say the least!'

'I think you could marry a Prince if you wanted to Sally!'

'Don't be silly. He only liked me because I reminded him of my mother. I'm sure he won't even remember my name by ten tonight.'

'I doubt that very much.'

Mr. Gallagher distracted them by placing a glass of champagne into their hands, and then he led them through the guests, stopping every now and then to speak to people he recognised. All the men, even if they were stood next to their own stunning wife, could not take their eyes off Sally. Some of them tried to take her away from her father's side, asking her whether they wanted to come onto the balcony and look at the view, or if she wanted a tour through the State Apartments which they had exclusive access to. To each and every offer, Sally politely declined and stayed close to her father's side.

After mingling and networking their way through the crowd, Mr. Gallagher spent quite some time chatting to another man who was trying to persuade him to invest in their new computer system. Quickly the ladies grew bored with the conversation so they wandered away from him and took up position next to a large ornate stained glass window. Almost instantly they were approached by two men who were old enough to be their fathers. Politely Sally and Michelle chatted to them until Sally asked Michelle did she know where their boyfriends were. Thankfully the two men took the hint. They chatted amongst themselves for a few moments until mid-sentence Sally stopped speaking.

'What's up?' Michelle asked.

'Oh my word.'

'What's up honey?'

'I suppose I should have guessed he would be here.'

'Who?' asked Michelle again, looking around.

'The guy. Behind you. Over your left shoulder. Tall. Dark.'

Michelle slowly turned and looked across the room to where two men were stood, both of them were indeed tall, dark and very handsome. 'Crikey! They both look gorgeous from here! Who are they?'

'The one on the right as you look is his friend. The one on the left is Mo.'

'Mo? I've never heard you talk about a Mo before. Who is he?'

'Crown Prince Sheikh Mohammed.'

'He's a prince? You know a prince?'

'I know lots of princes.'

'Is he rich?'

'He makes daddy look like a pauper.'

'Crikey! You don't seem too happy to see him?'

'I'm not. Let's just say we didn't depart from each other on the best of terms.'

'Why? What happened?'

'Shit! He's noticed me. Double shit. He's coming over.

For the next few moments Sally and Michelle watched the two men walk over to them, watched as the women they walked past turned to look at them.

'Miss Gallagher. It is a pleasure to see you again.' The Prince held out his hand which Sally accepted.

'Prince Mohammed. An honour to meet you again. May I introduce my friend, Michelle Walmesley.'

He took her hand and lightly shook it. 'Miss Walmesley, a pleasure.'

'The pleasure is all mine Your Highness.'

'Please, Mo is fine. Miss Gallagher, I believe you'll remember my friend

Ashraf.' Sally smiled politely but neither of them offered a hand to shake. 'Okay, this is slightly awkward. As an icebreaker, can I offer you both some champagne?'

'No we're fine thanks Mo. How's your partner?' With a flush of his cheeks the Prince stated she was fine. 'Well shame you weren't single last year then maybe this meeting wouldn't be so... awkward.' For a moment there was some feet shuffling and more awkwardness. 'Come Michelle, I need to powder my nose. Nice to see you again Your Highness.' Without waiting for a reply, Sally brushed past the Crown Prince and walked quickly towards the toilets, throwing open the door.

'Sally! You can't speak, and treat, a Prince like that!'

'Well he shouldn't have treated me like he did last year. And as for the sleazeball Ashraf...' Sally placed her fingers in her mouth and made a retching noise.

'What on Earth happened?'

'Ohhh, last year. We were at his palace in his country, sorry, one of his many palaces. I was single, and he told me he was. He's quite a few years older than me, than us, and me being the naïve daughter of a billionaire I fell for him, big time. He swept me off my feet. I was due to leave with daddy, but I begged the Prince to let me stay at the palace with him. I stayed there for a month. Every day we went sailing in his yachts, swimming in private coves, staying on his private islands out in the Gulf. He treated me, well, he treated me like a princess.'

'Last year? Last summer?'

'Yes.'

'You told me you were away with your dad on business, keeping him company?!'

'Sorry, that was a lie.'

'I'd say! I thought you told me everything?!'

'Usually I do honey, but not about last summer. He's the first and only guy to see me naked and I was very content on the last night we were together for him to take my virginity. On the penultimate night though, I heard a commotion coming from along the corridor, towards the Prince's room. It sounded very heated, and apart from staff, I didn't think there was anyone else staying in the palace apart from us. So I put my gown on and walked quietly towards his room. His door was open and I stood in the doorway watching another woman throw ornaments, books, anything that came to hand, at the Prince, to which he casually batted them away with a pillow.'

'His girlfriend?'

Sally nodded. 'If it had been any other circumstance it would have been quite funny, watching the Prince naked using his pillow as a bat. Of course, I quickly put two and two together and came up with three, and we all know that three doesn't go too well in a relationship. Apparently she had been studying overseas and had just got back and heard about the woman the Prince had been seen with so many times.'

'What a bastard.'

'To say the least. I was heartbroken Michelle, fucking heartbroken. He saw me in the doorway and she noticed that he was looking at something else so she turned and saw me. She walked towards me; I can only presume swearing at me in Arabic. I panicked and ran off to my bedroom, locking the door behind me. For ten minutes she battered the door, screaming. I sat on my bed and prayed that the door held. I swear that if she had got through that door she would have killed me; she wasn't rational. Eventually, a few members of staff pulled her away and I can only presume locked her in another room somewhere in the palace.'

'So he didn't even come to stop her?'

'No. He had to rely on his staff. He didn't have the balls to confront her himself, which I suppose says a lot really. That night I didn't sleep, and I didn't sleep for a week. The next morning, early, I snuck out of my bedroom and begged one of the staff to take me to the airport. I had nothing but my passport, some cash and my bank card. I got on the first flight out of there. Turned out it was a flight to Bangkok. I spent a month on my own in a hut on an island, crying my eyes out.'

'Oh Sally, I'm so sorry. I had no idea. I thought you were with your dad, jet setting around the globe.' She put her arms around Sally and hugged her while Sally wiped away the tears that were now rolling down her face.

'He totally broke my heart and as a man who is older than me, a Prince no less, he should have known better than trying to take advantage of a young woman, innocent in her naivety.'

'Yes, he should have. You should have told me, I could have come and supported you.'

'Thank you honey, but it was something I had to get through on my own. Anyway,' she turned away from Michelle, 'I'd better fix my makeup before we go back out there.' As Sally was fixing her smudged makeup, Michelle asked about Ashraf. 'Well, one night the Prince had to attend a function, men only, no way I could go, so he asked Ashraf to look after me. He was quite nice at first, then as the night went on he started to get really sleazy, saying that the Prince and him shared everything. They had slept with the same women lots of times and they weren't bothered about it and other such things. When we were in the limo coming back from a party we had been to, he tried to hit on me and he tried to hit on me strongly. I swear if I hadn't kneed him in the bollocks he would have raped me!'

'You kneed him?!'

'Yeah, he was pissing me off. It was quite amusing watching him roll about on the floor of the limo in the foetal position!'

'I bet it was!'

'I didn't see him again after I had told the Prince. He was not amused.'

'So you had no idea he had a girlfriend?'

'She wasn't his girlfriend. She was his betrothed.'

'Oh my God! What an absolute bastard!'

'Yep. Right, how do I look.'

'As usual, sickeningly perfect!'

Sally laughed and took her friend by the hand, exiting the toilet and leading her across the room in the Palace. As they walked towards the bar both of the girls noticed that the Prince was now dancing quite erotically with a woman who might as well not been wearing any clothes for she was not leaving much to the imagination.

When they were served at the bar, Michelle was surprised when Sally ordered a glass of red wine, cheap red wine at that. 'Red wine? We're in a palace in Monaco and you're drinking red wine, cheap red wine?!'

'I have no intention of drinking it Michelle. Order us two glasses of the best champagne and I'll be back in a moment,' stated Sally who picked up a glass of the wine.

As Sally tried to walk away, Michelle grabbed her arm. 'Sally, where are you going?'

'Stay here darling; you don't need to be a part of this.'

'No, Sally don't, think about where we are, who is watching!'

With a smile and a wicked glint in her eyes, Sally shrugged off Michelle's hand and walked towards the edge of the dance floor where she stood waiting for the music to stop. The blood was racing through her body, fuelled by adrenaline and she struggled to stop her hand from shaking. As the music stopped, she stormed onto the dance floor, speaking just below a shout. 'Hi Mo. How's your fiancée?'

With a flash of anger across her face, the woman he had been dancing with turned to confront him. 'You're engaged?!' He did not reply.

'Yes, he is. This is for breaking my heart, and for all the other women you've taken advantage of!'

With those words, Sally threw the red wine into his face and watched with pleasure as it drained down over his white jacket and shirt. She jumped as the woman delivered a slap to his face and smiled as she watched him wipe the wine out of his eyes.

With a flourish she turned on her heels, and looked straight into her father's eyes who was stood next to Prince Albert. Her father did not look shocked, he did not look surprised; his face was totally impassive. With another smile, she winked at her father, did a quick curtsey for the Prince, and walked off the dance floor towards where Michelle was waiting. 'And on that bombshell darling,' she spoke into Michelle's ear as she linked arms with her and walked towards the door, 'I think it would be a good idea to leave!'

'I think that would indeed be a very good idea!'

*

The next morning Sally was up early, just after dawn. She had not slept well, not because she was upset, but because she could not get the glorious image of a wine soaked Prince out of her mind. From her bed, she watched the sun rise and with another smile she leapt out of bed, put on her bikini and headed to the pool for a refreshing swim.

Discreetly he watched her from the bar as he sipped a fresh orange juice. He was impressed with her technique and speed, and thought that she could have made a good swimmer but persuading his daughter to get up at five in the morning for swimming training would have been a futile exercise.

Eventually she stopped at the far end of the pool and spent some time looking out to sea. As she turned a look of surprise flashed across her face as she noticed her father sat at the bar. With a few powerful strokes she powered to the other end of the pool and lifted herself out of it, her shoulder and arm muscles flexing as she effortlessly left the pool. With a couple of steps she was by his side and kissed him lightly on his cheek. She then took the towel and wrapped it round her body then sat next to him at the bar. For a few moments neither of them said anything until he broke the silence. 'Do you want to talk about last night?'

She smiled at him, and the early sun caught her red hair and lit up her green eyes. For a moment, he thought he was speaking to his wife again, young and beautiful, full of life. 'Not really daddy, no.'

'I suppose you remember the status of the person whose face you threw wine into last night?'

'Of course I do. We were in his country with him last year.'

'And you begged me to let you stay there for some retail therapy and an extended holiday? You stayed in the Burj Al Arab hotel. I know you did because I saw the bill. You stayed in a suite, for a month, at about, if I remember rightly, three thousand five hundred pounds a night.'

'Before we go on, ask yourself after what you saw last night whether you want to know the real story?'

'I don't, but I'm intrigued as to the reason why you threw red wine into the face of a Prince, a Prince who is in control of numerous contracts that we are bidding on and numerous contracts that are currently ongoing which I'm now expecting to be cancelled.'

'I stayed with him at the palace for a month.'

'He's engaged.'

'Yeah, you could have told me that before I stayed with him for a month!'

'Well, if you had told me the truth I would have told you!'

'You probably would have, and I would have been on the first flight back to London.'

'True. So what happened? In fact, I take the question back. I can imagine what happened. She found out?'

'Yes.'

'But you were only in Dubai for a month. So where did you go afterwards? You told me you were doing some volunteer work in Africa?'

'Not exactly. I was in Thailand on my own crying my eyes out.'

'Oh Sally. I'm sorry. I had no idea. What a slimeball taking advantage of my daughter like that!'

'We didn't sleep together daddy.'

'I didn't need to know that, nor would I have asked. What an absolute… Well, I'm not going to give him the chance to cancel the contracts. I'll cancel them all this very day!'

'No daddy, don't. They're worth a fortune to you!'

'And you think in a situation like this I care about the money?! To be perfectly honest, I'm absolutely furious! He should know better than to have done that!'

'It is your choice, but don't think you have to do this for me.'

'I'm doing it because he is clearly an unethical idiot!'

'Well, I can confirm he's an idiot.'

'I'm going to call James now to set the ball rolling. How dare he treat a member of my family like that!'

Without saying anything else, he stormed off into the yacht and Sally resigned herself to the fact that she had probably just cost her father about five hundred million pounds. With a sigh she walked over to the Jacuzzi, picking up a copy of Vogue to read while she soaked in the hot, bubbly bath. Soon Michelle joined her and they spent the rest of the day relaxing by the pool until Mr. Gallagher told them that the qualifying was about to start.

They watched this from the comfort of the yacht, all of them cheering as they saw one of the cars from the team he was sponsoring go flashing by while sipping from a seemingly endless supply of fresh fruit juices. After about an hour and a half Mr. Gallagher let out a loud shout of joy as he saw on the big screen opposite the yacht that both of the cars were on the front row of the grid.

'Yes! Now that makes the sponsorship worthwhile! Lots of television coverage, lots of media coverage as a whole! I wish I had a bigger section of the car now!'

'Well done daddy!' Sally shouted, planting a kiss on his cheek.

For a few moments they watched the replays on the screen and they all celebrated again. Soon after this Mr. Gallagher was approached by a member of the crew. 'They're ready for us on the track!'

'That was quick!'

'Well, it's not just us who have this honour. Quickly! You've got five minutes before the car leaves to takes us round!'

The young women ran off to their cabins, both of them quickly getting ready. Within the allotted five minutes they were back by his side and they all scampered off the yacht to the waiting car. It took them slowly around the track to the pits where they were greeted by a professional driver who explained the plan for the next hour.

Mr. Gallagher went first. The driver took him around the track three times before pulling back into the pits and they switched places. With a roar and a squeal of tyres the powerful Mercedes SLR supercar powered down the pit lane. The girls stood on the pit wall screaming every time there was a flash of silver whizzing past them and a roar of the engine. After five laps he pulled back into the pit lane. The girls ran over to the car and helped him out of the car. 'Wow! That was an experience!'

'If I can have Michelle next please,' asked the driver.

'Oh Sally, you go next.'

'No, it's okay darling. You go. Enjoy yourself.'

'Are you sure?'

'Yes! I'll enjoy watching you. Go on!'

'Okay!'

Michelle climbed into the passenger seat of the car and again after a few laps she swapped with the driver and she thoroughly enjoyed her drive as she blasted round and one lap was even completed in a faster time than Sally's father. 'Younger reactions is the only reason you were quicker!' Mr. Gallagher joked as Michelle learned of her times.

'I can't believe I went that quickly!'

'You know,' said the driver, 'that's actually a quite impressive time considering that was done on only your fourth lap around here.'

'Impressive or lucky?!' jokingly replied Michelle.

The driver laughed and asked Sally whether she was ready. Sally nodded and clambered into the car. Her three demonstration laps were quickly over and she took the wheel of the six hundred horsepower, two hundred and eight miles per hour supercar.

Sally safely navigated the infamous Sainte Devote corner and blasted along uphill through the kinks of the 'straight line', and round the famous Casino corner. She quickly negotiated the Mirabeau Haute and blasted round a few more corners to the slowest corner on the circuit, the Grand Hotel Hairpin. After a couple more turns she entered the tunnel section of the circuit and she loved the sound and roar of the engine as it reverberated around the enclosed track. Her speed increased rapidly as she accelerated ferociously through the tunnel and then without warning the steering wheel started to judder. As they exited the tunnel Sally was dazzled by the sunlight and without warning the car broke right, clipping the wall as it approached the Nouvelle Chicane.

With all her skill that she had honed on the tracks driving her father's supercars, she caught the car before it ploughed into the wall on the left, but as she corrected the car it unnaturally broke right again. Realising she was in deep trouble she slammed on the brakes, but this time the car broke hard right and hit the right wall with enough force to set off the car's airbags. With a screech of tyres and brakes the car careered across the chicane, all four wheels lifting off the track as they flew over the kerbs and with a force that drove the air out of Sally's lungs, rammed into a wall and came to a smoking, shuddering halt.

*

With smiles on their faces Michelle and Sally's father looked down the track waiting to cheer Sally as she flashed past at high speed. Slowly though when the car did not appear the smiles slowly slid off their faces as they realised that something had gone wrong. 'She should have been here by now Mr. Gallagher.'

'I know Michelle, I know.'

With a look of concern etched on his face, he jumped down from the pit wall and jogged over to the garage with Michelle following close behind. As soon as they entered the garage they knew something had gone wrong. 'What's happened? Where's my daughter?!'

'Mr. Gallagher, I'm sorry. There's been an accident further down the track. It looks like the car has crashed although the reports we are getting from the marshals are sketchy at the moment.'

'If anything has happened to her I'll, I'll…'

'Mr. Gallagher, may I suggest we drive round. We'll get some more news as it gets radioed in.'

'Right, let's go, now please.'

They both climbed into a Mercedes saloon and with no-one saying a word they proceeded slowly around the track, through the tunnel. As they exited the tunnel and their eyes adjusted Michelle gasped. 'Oh my God! Mr. Gallagher, the car!' The right hand side of the car was crushed and crumpled against the wall, but Michelle quickly noticed that there was no-one in the smashed vehicle.

Before the car had stopped, Mr. Gallagher leapt out of the vehicle and jogged over to the battered Mercedes supercar with Michelle following. He looked around for any evidence of his daughter and then he saw her, sat on the floor leaning against a section of the wall, her crash helmet on the floor next to her. He ran over to her. 'Sally! Are you okay? Please tell me you are okay?'

At first she did not reply, and as they approached her they could see she was clutching her ribs and tears were coursing down her face.

'Oh my! Are you okay?' With obvious difficulty she took his hand and managed to nod. 'Where's the driver?' As he spoke they both noticed each other, and the driver ran over to them. 'What the hell happened? Is she okay? She can't speak!'

'We're both a bit shook up, sir. I'm more used to it, but it's really took the wind out of Sally.'

'Is that it? Is she winded?' He looked down on her and she nodded. 'Well, thank God for that!' He leaned over and said to her to breathe to which she nodded again. Slowly, with effort, her breathing returned more to normal and she accepted some water from one of the marshals. 'Can you speak now?' asked her father.

Hoarsely, she managed to say, 'Yes.'

'What happened? Can you remember?'

'Yes,' she paused, and took in some more air, 'but not sure what happened. Car broke right, clipped the wall, I caught it, braked, it broke right even more and I couldn't catch it. Hit wall and slid to here. Don't… don't make me... speak anymore.'

'Okay darling, breathe, breathe deeply.' He turned and confronted the driver. 'And how the hell did you let this happen?!'

'Sir, I'm sorry, it happened in a flash. And if I'd reached over to grab the wheel it would have made things worse, a lot worse.'

'Well what the hell happened?'

'I agree with what she said. The car broke right, she managed to catch it like a pro after it clipped the wall, but then when she braked it broke right even more. From my experience, I think we got a right front puncture which made us move right the first time, and when she braked hard the tyre shredded forcing us hard into the right hand wall. I'm sorry, but it was over in a flash. There was nothing I, or either of us, could have done.'

Turning back to Sally he took her hand again and he asked her a few times whether there was anything he could do. Michelle hovered around them looking very concerned.

'Daddy, can you help me up now?'

'Of course sweetheart. Come on, up you get.'

Slowly and gently he pulled her to her feet and for a few moments she leaned against the wall, catching her breath again. From along the tunnel there was a roar of another engine and they all turned to look. Being driven quickly a car approached them, with orange lights flashing. As soon as it stopped the Team Principle leapt out of the car, quickly followed by another man. 'Mr. Gallagher! I'm so sorry! What on Earth happened?!'

The driver answered. 'Blow out. Nothing either of us could do.'

'This is the race doctor. He needs to examine Sally.'

The doctor approached Sally and led her away from the rest of them towards the car.

'Where's he taking her?' demanded Mr. Gallagher. 'Michelle, go with them.'

'They'll go to the medical facility where she'll be examined.'

'Michelle, go now please. Stay with her. I need to speak to the Team Principle about this.'

*

Gingerly Sally lowered herself into a rear seat of the Mercedes with the doctor sat next to her and Michelle took the front seat next to the driver. Very sedately they proceeded around the track until they exited the track near a building which they entered with Sally being supported by the doctor and Michelle.

Michelle was told to wait outside the examination room and Sally was gone for half an hour and in this time Mr. Gallagher had joined her. Anxiously they sat in silence, until after what seemed like hours the doctor came out of the examination room. Mr. Gallagher leapt to his feet. 'How is she? Is she going to be okay?'

'Yes, she's fine. She's shaken up, a bit beaten up and in slight shock. We've x-rayed her chest and I've given her a thorough examination and she's fine apart from some bruising. It can be quite frightening when you get the wind knocked out of you like that and you feel like you are unable to breathe, but she's fine now. I'd still like her to stay in overnight so we can keep an eye on her and examine her again in the morning.'

'That's fine. Thank you doctor. Can we see her?'

'Of course. Please.'

The doctor stepped aside and let them pass into the room. Sally lay on a bed, now wearing a hospital gown, looking very pale, and she was clearly still shaken from the crash.

'Darling. How are you?'

'I'm okay. Just, well, you know, a bit beaten up, but fine.'

'You will be sweetheart, you will be.'

'Is anywhere hurting? Do you want some painkillers?'

'No, honestly, I'm fine. Just a bit sore. I'm just thankful we were in a Mercedes with good safety features.'

'Me too. Nothing I can get you?'

'No, not for now. What happened? I don't really remember. Was it my fault? That expensive car...'

'Now stop that straight away! Don't you dare think that the car is more important than your health! It wasn't your fault. In fact, the driver said that you handled it like a pro, until the tyre shredded and then there was nothing any driver in the world could have done.'

'Oh, is that what it was, a blow out?'

'Yes, definitely. There was nothing you or anyone could have done in a situation like that. I spoke to the driver and he said that you hit the wall at quite a speed so it's no wonder you're shaken up a bit.'

'Right, okay. No wonder then. Can we go back to the yacht now?'

'No, we most certainly can't! The doctor wants you to stay in overnight and I agree with him.'

'But, but, we're going to the Casino tonight.'

'Don't be ridiculous Sally. You've just been in a serious car accident. You're staying here tonight, and that is quite frankly non-negotiable!'

Mr. Gallagher was expecting more of a fight from her and he was surprised when she said, 'I was looking forward to that, but I suppose you're right.'

'Good. Glad to see you see sense. Is there anything you need from us or the doctors?'

'No, nothing, I'm fine. To be honest, I just want to have a rest for a while.'

'Of course darling, of course. Let me help you.'

Mr. Gallagher reached for the electronic device that controlled the bed and lowered Sally to a horizontal position. He plumped up her pillows and tucked the blankets around her, muttering that she needs to rest and that she will feel better in the morning. When he was done, she smiled up at him and thanked him for looking after her.

'Sleep now sweetheart. Michelle and I will return to the yacht, get some of your things and come and see you this evening. Michelle, can you look in Sally's bag and make sure her mobile is there. Put it somewhere she can reach it.'

Michelle followed his instructions and said to Sally, 'Hey you,' she leaned forward and placed a light kiss on Sally's forehead, 'your phone is there. Call either of us straight away if you need anything, right, and we'll be here straight away. We'll be back later.'

'Thank you both for caring so much. I'll see you later.'

With that, Sally closed her eyes and they both sat down in chairs to watch her for half an hour before they quietly left the room.

*

On the drive back to the yacht, neither of them said anything but Michelle could tell he was furious. 'You okay Mr. Gallagher?'

'Not really Michelle, no. To be honest, I'm far from okay.'

'Sorry Mr. Gallagher, at least she's going to be okay. Could have been a lot worse?'

She took his hand and stroked it and this simple act seemed to soothe and calm him a little. 'Yes, I suppose you're right. Thank you for being here Michelle, and I don't just mean here in Monaco, but here in our lives as a whole. Although you may not realise it, you're an inspiration to Sally. I could not believe before we met you at that performance what I had bred, how I had let her get so damned spoiled. After she met you and you became close friends, something changed. All Sally's friends had been like her up to that point, daughters and sons of other well off families. You seemed to offer her a balance, a realisation that not everyone in the world is wealthy. Sorry, that sounds terrible. I know your parents have done well for themselves, but you know what I mean don't you?'

'Of course I do, it's fine.'

'It is like when she met you, and she went to your house for the first time, the first time by the way that she had been in a house with less than ten bedrooms!' Michelle laughed. 'When she met you it was like she had walked out of a cave and had her eyes opened a little bit to what the rest of the world is really like, a touch of realism in her life. I know, and I know bloody damned well that the fact that she was like that was entirely my fault. I know the affect you have on her, and that is why I allowed you both to become such good friends with each other. Note I did say allowed. If I didn't think you were right for her to be her friend then you would not have gotten close to each other. You helped balance her out, and for that I'm eternally grateful to you.'

'I'm grateful to you for allowing me into your lives. It is like I have second family, another caring loving family and I care and love you both as if you were family.'

'That means a lot to me, thank you Michelle. I'm just so relieved that she is okay. The drive round the circuit to her was the longest couple of minutes of my life.'

'Mine too Mr. Gallagher, mine too.'

She stroked his hand for a few more moments until they stopped as they had reached the entrance to the harbour. With a flourish of security passes they entered the harbour and Michelle did not see him again until a few hours later when he knocked on her cabin door holding a large bag. 'I'm returning to the hospital to take some things for her. I presumed you'd want to come?'

'Of course. Give me two seconds, I'll just get changed.'

Michelle picked up some clothes and went into the bathroom to get out of her bikini and into jeans and T-shirt. While she was running a comb quickly through her hair she heard him speak to her. 'You know something Michelle; I don't think I've ever been in this cabin before. Well, I came in here on the viewing after it was finished being built, but I've never been in here since.'

Michelle came out of the bathroom. 'Really? But I suppose why would you when you've got your own suite?'

'But what's the point of having a yacht this size when I don't enter the rooms from one year to the next?'

'For when you've got guests?'

'I rarely have guests. Two, three times a year maybe?'

'Maybe, but the same thing could be said for the mansion. When was the last time you saw some of the rooms at home?'

'Michelle, there are rooms in that house that I've *never* been in!'

Michelle laughed. 'In that case sell it, give the proceeds to charity and live in a smaller house!'

He laughed this time and said, 'I think I'll stick with the mansion thanks, even if I only see or use ten percent of the rooms! Ready?'

'Yep, let's go.'

Another car was waiting for them which took them back to the medical facility. As they entered it the doctor was just leaving Sally's room.

'Doctor, how is she?'

'She's fine Mr. Gallagher. She's young, fit and tough. She'll be fine to leave tomorrow morning.

'Good. Thank you for tending to her. Is she awake?'

'Is she awake? She's watching television!'

'Really? Sounds like she's doing fine then?'

'Yes, she is. I will assess her in the morning presuming nothing happens tonight. We'll speak tomorrow morning.'

'Thank you again doctor. We'll speak tomorrow.'

The doctor stepped round them with a smile and Michelle knocked gently on the door.

'Come in.'

Michelle opened the door and Sally's face lit up as she saw Michelle and Mr. Gallagher behind her. 'Come in, come in, please come in. I'm so bored!' They both walked over to her bedside and gave her a hug and a peck on the cheek. 'Trust me to end up in hospital on our special weekend away! Sorry dad, and sorry to you as well Michelle.'

'Now, now. No need to apologise. What is most important is that you're healthy and recovering well.'

'I still can't remember what happened. I remember coming out of the tunnel and being a bit dazzled, and then the next thing I can really remember is leaning on the wall really struggling to breathe. I don't know who got me out of the car or anything. Have you heard anything daddy?'

'The driver said you got yourself out of the car and then walked unsteadily over to the wall. He didn't call the doctor at first because he thought you were okay. It was only when the Team Principle found out that he summoned the doctor to come and tend to you.'

'Right, okay. I still don't remember. Ah well, never mind. I'm sure it will come back to me.'

'How are your ribs? Anywhere hurting that wasn't before?'

'No, honestly, I'm fine. A bit sore, but fine. I'm just happy I can breathe now. I never, ever want to feel like that again.'

'Well, unless you decide to crash on the Nouvelle Chicane again you never will!'

'Oh stop! Don't make me laugh!'

They small talked their way through the next couple of hours until they were interrupted by a nurse who was surprised that they were still there and demanded they leave. With kisses and hugs goodbye, they both left and spent the night on their own in their respective cabins, both of them contemplating how lucky they had been that the accident had not been more serious and that they had both not lost someone they cared about greatly.

Chapter 35

The day of the Grand Prix dawned bright and sunny. To say Mr. Gallagher was surprised when he got to the pool for a refreshing swim and he saw Sally lounging by the pool would be an understatement. 'And what the hell do you think you're doing here?!'

'And good morning to you too darling father!'

'If you've checked yourself out of that hospital without the doctor giving you the all clear you'll be in more trouble than you've ever, ever been in!' He stood next to her, hands on hips, staring into her green eyes.

'Dad, relax.' She took one of his hands in hers and started to stroke it. 'I saw him earlier this morning. He examined me thoroughly and gave me the all clear. He said to tell you to call him or you can go and see him. He will be at the medical centre all day now.'

'Right, well, I think I'll make that call.'

'Why? Don't you believe me?'

A quick look of surprise flashed on his face, but it was gone before it had really arrived. 'Well, I suppose you're sensible enough not to leave the centre after an accident like that without the doctor's consent.'

'You know I wouldn't do that. I'm fine.'

'Well your ribs don't look fine.' Sally was dressed in only her bikini and the bruising on the trunk of her body was clear to see.

'Dad, thank you for being so caring, but honestly I'm fine. What time does the Grand Prix start?'

'One o'clock. You sure you're okay?'

'Yes! Honestly I am. Thank you.'

'Right, okay, well I'm going for a swim. Let me know if you need anything though.'

'I will.'

He dove into the pool and spent the next hour or so doing lengths and in the meantime a surprised Michelle had joined Sally on the loungers which is where they stayed throughout that morning. At around ten they both left the pool area and went to freshen up before a car picked them up to take them round to the team's garage where they would watch the build-up to the race.

For an hour or so they watched with interest from a discreet distance in the garage, watching the drivers receive their last minute briefings and watching the cars receive last minute tuning. The cars were ready to go out onto the grid forty-five minutes before the start of the race and in the confines of the garage the young women could not believe the noise of the engines as they were started and driven carefully out of the garage to form up on the grid.

At the suggestion of the Team Principle, he led them onto the crowded grid and talked them through the preparations that were happening to the cars at this time. After a short while he left them to return to the garage and they were free to wander amongst the cars.

Sally estimated that about eighty percent of the people on the grid that day had nothing to do with the racing teams; therefore she always considered what happened that day to be remote odds to say the least. That she would be picked out of all those people for an impromptu interview with the British broadcasters of the race.

'Hello, may I have a quick word? We're live going straight back to millions of people in England!' With a look of surprise, and before Sally could dodge past him, he had her boxed in between the cameraman and a group of people. 'Who are you and who are you here with?'

'Hi. My name is Sally and I'm with my father, who appears to have wandered off, and my friend Michelle.'

'Great! And what team are you supporting today?'

'It had better be the British team because my dad sponsors them!'

'Really? Excellent! And have you ever thought of doing some modelling?'

'Erm no, not really.'

'You should. By far you are the most beautiful woman here today, and there are plenty of Hollywood stars on the grid today!'

'Thank you for saying that, but no, I haven't.'

'Thank you for taking the time to speak to us.'

Sally managed to quickly dodge past the cameraman and rejoined Michelle who had a look of surprise on her face. 'Crikey Sally! You were just on television in England!'

'Yes, I know. And I know one person who will be definitely watching the race who will be very, very surprised to see me pop-up on television...'

*

David had just taken mouthful of his orange juice as the commentator introduced the random person he had stopped to speak to. His orange juice was sprayed all over him and the sofa as he realised that his girlfriend was being interviewed on the grid of the Monaco Grand Prix.

*

Sally felt her phone vibrating in her pocket so she took it out and saw David's name flashing on the screen. 'Michelle, it's him. What am I going to say?' They had both returned back to the team's garage after the interview, Sally's face etched with worry and concern. 'What the hell am I going to say to him?'

'The truth.'

'Right. Great help.'

'I'll leave you to it.' Michelle wandered back into garage and started to chat to one of the engineers.

'Hello David. You shouldn't be calling me, it costs a fortune!'

'Considering your dad has got enough money to sponsor a Formula One team you can pay me back!'

'And here I was hoping that right at that moment you'd be making a cup of tea...'

'Unfortunately not. You have mere moments to explain yourself before I hang up this phone and you'll never hear from me again.'

Sally felt like a lead weight had landed in the bottom of her stomach when David said those words. She did not want to lose him. 'David, I'm so sorry I lied to you, but this is neither the place nor the time for this conversation. Can we please, I beg you, speak tomorrow about this? I'll come and see you as soon as I get back.'

'If there's one thing I cannot stand it's being lied to and being made to look foolish.'

'I lied to you yes, but I never intended to make you look foolish.'

'Who *are* you?' David's voice was beseeching, straining for Sally to give him an honest answer.

'You've got a computer right?'

'Yes, of course I have.'

'Google my dad.'

'Your dad?'

'Yes, you know his name, google him.'

'There'll be millions of Gallaghers with his name. Don't be ridiculous.'

'Trust me. Google his name and he'll be the first one out, right at the top. You might even find my name near his.'

'This is nuts! Right, I'm going to call you back in five.'

'I won't be able to answer.'

'Why not?'

'I'll be with my dad, erm, watching the race.'

'Right, of course you will. I'll call you after the race. To say I'm disappointed is an understatement.' Without waiting for a reply, David hung up the phone and ran upstairs for his laptop. He brought it back down with him and as instructed he googled Sally's father.

The first link that he selected took him to a site he had never heard of before called Forbes. From what he could tell, it seemed to be a website of lists, the best this, the richest that. When he clicked the link it took him to a page entitled World's Billionaires, and there, just off the top ten was her father's name. 'Holy... shit!' David muttered to himself. He spent the next few moments reading the summary about his girlfriend's father:-

"Born in 1952 in England, Gallagher made his fortune in electronic components and telecommunications. Son of a coal miner, Gallagher obtained his first patent for an electronic component in 1970 and that component went on to become an essential part of any circuitry. From then on he has not looked back, obtaining lucrative military contracts with governments around the globe. Often referred to as frighteningly ruthless in the boardroom, Gallagher contributes to many charitable organisations. If the ongoing increases in his companies share prices continue, it won't be long before Gallagher breaks into the top ten of the World's Billionaires."

David had to read this twice more before it sunk in, after which he returned to Google and looked through other sites and his surprise and shock grew as these sites also placed Sally's father firmly in the top twenty of the wealthiest men on the planet.

With his attention totally distracted, he missed the start of the Grand Prix and did not watch any of the race. He continued to plough through the websites and even started to google Sally's name. Sites that mentioned her were scarcer, but they were there, stating her as the sole heiress to the Gallagher fortune. Noticing some pictures he clicked on images and pictures of his beautiful girlfriend appeared and even a few of her with her father.

As he looked at the images, from somewhere a memory scrambled to his conscious mind and he remembered where he had seen her father before, it was on one of their first dates, the night when the two men with their manic grins dressed in tuxedos approached them in the city.

He flicked through the images and some were clearly taken a few years ago, but one looked like it was recent, very recent. In the background of the photograph was a limousine, and Sally and her father were standing next to Michelle. Both of the young women looked stunning, and Sally was looking straight into the camera. To say she looked gorgeous was an understatement, and not for the first time since they had started dating David slowly shook his head and asked himself the question what on earth was she doing with him? He clicked the link which led him to a journalist's blog and David read about the many attendees to the Prince of Monaco's party. Half way down the page he found Sally's picture, and he read about how the reclusive daughter of the billionaire shunned the limelight, how she was far removed from the typical young females from wealthy families, the so called 'it-girls', who embarrass themselves on a sometimes seemingly daily basis.

By the time he had exhausted all links and images about Sally and her father, the race had finished and indeed the program had changed. He looked on the BBC website to find out who had won and was happy to discover that the British driver had won in a pretty uneventful sounding race. For a few moments he paced around the living room trying to collect his thoughts before calling Sally.

*

While David was contemplating what to say to his girlfriend who he had just found was incredibly wealthy, Sarah was lying in a semi-comatose state in her bedroom, her head resting on the filthy mattress that was riddled with fleas and bed bugs. A needle was hanging out of her foot.

Chapter 36

'Where are you?'

'In my, erm, cabin.'

'Cabin? Are you on a cruise now?'

'Not exactly, but kind of.'

'Not exactly but kind of? Please Sally, if you like me and respect me as much as you say you do then please, I beg you, start giving me straight answers!'

'Right, okay. I came here after the race because I didn't want to attend the after race party because I was in a car crash yesterday and I'm still feeling a bit tender.'

'You were in a car crash?! What on Earth is going on?! Are you okay?'

'It's okay, I'm fine. Just a bit bruised and battered.'

'Well, erm well, I'm glad to hear it. How did you crash and where is here?'

'I had a blow out just before the Nouvelle Chicane and here is on my daddy's yacht.'

'Your daddy's yacht?!'

'Yes.'

'The Nouvelle Chicane?! Now, I'm not that much of a geek that I know the name of every corner in Formula One, but I do know that the Nouvelle Chicane is on the Monaco Grand Prix circuit so now begs the question what the hell were you doing driving on the circuit?!'

'My dad organised it for us through the team he sponsors.'

'Right, okay. I'm really struggling to come to terms with this. I did as you asked, I googled your dad and you, and I can clearly see that your father is wealthy, and you being the sole heiress makes you, well, wealthy.'

'Yes, it does. Look, David, it would be much better if we talked about this face to face.'

'I'd like to talk about it now. So the old Mini you drive, is that just for show for me?'

'No, that's mine. I did some work for my father last summer, just admin work, and he gave me a salary. I bought the Mini out of that money.'

'Right, but you could afford a, for example, Ferrari?'

'Yes. I could buy a Ferrari on one of dad's credit cards and I doubt he would notice, but I never would without his permission because I would feel like I'm cheating and stealing from him. It would be like you going into your mum's purse and taking ten pounds out without telling her. You just wouldn't do it would you?'

'No, I wouldn't, you're right. So how big is the yacht?'

'Very. Google it. It's called Samurai.'

'I will, later. Can we go for a cruise on it one day?'

'Of course. What are you doing next weekend?'

'Well to be honest, I've got us tickets for the theatre.'

'We'll fly out to wherever the yacht will be instead on Friday and spend a couple of days on it. How does that sound?'

'I don't know Sally. This is all a bit too much for me to take in at the moment.'

'I really, really like you David. We've had a fantastic time together and I don't want it to end…'

'Me too Sally, me too.'

'So, why don't we both sleep on it? We can both get used to the idea and talk about it tomorrow. How does that sound?'

'It sounds good, apart from you've got nothing to get used to, I have.'

'I have to get used to the fact that I've lied terribly to you when I should I have told you the truth. And I have to get used to the feeling of how I feel now when I have the horrible feeling in the pit of my stomach that I might lose you.'

'You're not going to lose me, but you'd better have some good explanations. Where and when do you want to meet?'

'Say seven at my apartment?'

'Where's your apartment?'

'The apartment we always go to.'

'That's your relation's apartment?!'

'In a way, yes. My dad bought it for me.'

'Right, okay. So that duplex penthouse apartment on the thirtieth floor in one of the richest areas of the city is your apartment?'

'Yes.'

'This is bewildering. I'll be there at seven.'

'Okay. I'm sorry David. I never, ever would have wanted you to find out like this.'

'Yeah, I bet. See you tomorrow.'

Sally tried to reply but he had already gone before she could get the words out. In a fit of anger she flung her phone against one of the cabin walls, quickly followed by a lamp and a china cup. With a loud curse she threw herself onto the bed and had what could only be described as a tantrum.

Lying on her front, her legs and arms pounded into the mattress and pillows, all the while she was cursing and getting herself into such a state that by the time she had exhausted herself there were tears rolling down her cheeks.

Furious with herself, she jumped up off the bed and threw the saucer that belonged with the cup against another wall. She then opened the wardrobe door with such force that it shook, and grabbed a small bag into which she started to place a few items of clothing. With another curse, and this time a vase was thrown but it did not break which made her even madder, she walked quickly to her father's cabin, took a deep breath and tapped quietly on the door.

'Erm, yes, who is it? Please wait a moment.' Sally listened and she could hear some scurrying going on in the cabin and then from inside the cabin he started to say as he opened the door, 'I thought I told you I did not want disturbing… Oh! Sally, it's you. Sorry. Please, come in.' He could tell by the look on her face she was clearly not happy about something. 'What's wrong? Who has upset you?'

'Me. I've upset me.'

'Oh. Okay. What's happened?'

'David, my boyfriend. You were right. I should have told him the truth from the outset!'

'What? Why? Has he found out? How?'

'He saw me on the television before, in England…'

'On the television? How?'

'On the grid. We'd lost you. You weren't there.' Sally then proceeded to tell her father what had happened, how she had lied about where she was supposed to be this weekend, and how rightly upset David was. 'So, I want to go back to England now and see him.'

'Do you not think it would be better to let him sleep on it and get used to the idea before you see him tomorrow?'

'I don't know dad, I don't know what is best to do.'

There was a moments silence and it was then that Sally noticed a distinct smell of perfume on the air. For a few more moments she tried to remember where she had smelled that perfume before and then it came to her, Adrienne. 'Daddy, is Adrienne here?'

'What? What on Earth makes you think that?

'That's a pretty distinctive perfume she wears.' Inside the cabin's luxurious bathroom Adrienne winced.

'Yes, she is.'

'Right, well, I'll leave you to it. Sorry for disturbing you.' Standing up Sally asked, 'Can I take the helicopter? Where's the jet?'

He could clearly see the look of hurt in her eyes. 'Sally, I'm sorry. Your mother has been gone from me, from us, for a long time now. I mourn her and I miss her and I always will, but she would not want to see me alone.'

'Yes, I know. I told you that once, not so long ago in fact. It's fine. Can I take the helicopter and jet?'

It was obvious to him that it was far from fine. He decided to leave it for now though. 'Yes, take whatever you need. Go. Now. Go and see him and make this better if you like him as much as I think you do. I'll phone ahead and make sure everyone is ready for you.'

'Thank you daddy.'

She kissed him lightly on the cheek and left the cabin, walking with her head down to the rear of the yacht. Waiting while the helicopter was prepared she realised she had not told Michelle. Just at the moment when she was going to return to the living area of the yacht the pilot informed her that he was ready to depart so she decided to call her later.

Quickly the helicopter lifted off from the yacht and headed south-west along the coast for the short journey to Nice. They landed next to the jet and Sally transferred across. Due to the short time frame, it was not quite ready to take off which annoyed Sally even more. Cursing again, she stared out of the window and considered how someone so wealthy could have so many dramas. She then thought that even with an endless supply of money life was far from perfect.

Soon the pilot announced from the cockpit that they were ready to depart and for the rest of the flight Sally stared out of the window, staring at the clouds below the plane and the occasional flash of land below them.

From where they had taken off all excited a few days ago, Sally now departed the plane in a thoroughly fed up state, and was surprised when both her Mini and the Rolls-Royce were waiting for her. Beside the Rolls stood Alfred who walked over to greet her. 'Miss Gallagher. I trust you had a good flight?'

'Yes, it was fine thank you.'

'Your father called and gave me a short synopsis of the situation. Considering that your boyfriend now knows the truth I was in a quandary as to which transport you would wish to use to go and see him.'

'I think me rolling up in a Rolls would be a bit too much for him to handle. I'll take the Mini. Thank you for thinking of me Alfred.'

'It's a pleasure ma'am. I'll take the Rolls-Royce back to the house then. Please let me know if there is anything I can help you with. Here's the key.'

'I will. Thank you.'

*

From the private airfield it was not a long drive to David's house, but Sally still took her time. She tried to gather her thoughts but all too soon she was pulling onto his street and arriving outside his house. For a few moments she composed herself and then walked along the short garden path to knock on the front door. His mother answered. 'Sally! I thought you were away this weekend? This is a lovely surprise.'

'Yeah, I wasn't really enjoying myself much so I came home early.'

'Ahhh, young love! He's in his room. He's been moping about all day like a grumpy young teenager. Please, come in.' Sally stepped into the house and his mum called up the stairs. 'David? David! You've got a surprise visitor!'

'I've got flu. I don't want to see anyone,' he shouted back.

'No you've not got flu! Don't be rude and come down this instance!'

Distantly Sally heard him swear to which his mum rolled her eyes. Sally then heard his door being loudly opened. 'Gorrrddd mum! This had better be impor...' He had reached the top of the stairs and as he looked down his jaw opened, closed and then opened again. 'You'd better come up.'

His mum rolled his eyes again and apologised for his attitude to Sally. She stepped away from the bottom of the stairs and beckoned Sally up. Seemingly reluctantly Sally proceeded up the stairs into David's room. He was slumped on his bed watching the television which was showing a re-run of the Grand Prix, but he wasn't watching it. Instead he was staring out of the window looking quite glum.

'You okay?' Sally asked.

'To be honest Sally, no, not really. Why didn't you tell me the truth?'

Hesitantly she approached his bed and sat on it when he did not protest. He did protest though when she tried to take his hand by pulling his away and folding his arms. 'You have to understand it from my point of view. I've had dates with guys before where I've told them about my real status in life and it is heartbreaking for me when I see their faces light up as they think they could be on for an easy ride through life courtesy of my father's damned hard work. As I look at them I can see the cogs whirling and spinning in their heads. I knew from that moment on that they would only be interested in my money, not interested in me. Do you understand?'

'Yeah, of course I do. But it wouldn't have been like that with me. I don't care about money so long as we're happy.'

'That's a good thing to say, but I don't think for one minute we would be as close as we are now if you'd known about this.'

'Does your dad know about me?'

'He knows I have a boyfriend.'

'Does he not think it strange that we haven't been introduced?'

'No. He knew the approach I was taking and I'll just add he was heartily against the idea.'

'And Michelle and Simon? Have they been laughing behind my back on the dates we've had together? Are they in on this?'

'Of course Michelle knows, I've known her for years. I don't know if Simon knows. Depends if Michelle told him but I asked her not to tell him.'

'And how the hell did you get back here so quick?!'

'I was wondering how long it would take you to ask that question. My dad's jet was at Nice so I used the yacht's helicopter to fly to Nice…'

'The yacht has a helicopter?!'

'Yep.'

'And your dad has a jet that you can use whenever you want to?!'

'Within reason, yes. He wouldn't, as an example, be very happy if I decided to take it for a shopping spree to New York, he'd expect me to fly commercial.'

'First class commercial though I bet?'

Nodding in agreement, with a smile on her lips, Sally decided to try a different tack. 'David, look at me.' She made an attempt to take his hand again and this time it was accepted. Reluctantly his blue eyes met her green. 'I love you…'

'Pardon?!'

'I love you, and I don't want this to destroy the great relationship we have.'

'You love me?'

'Yes. A lot.'

'Well, well, I've wanted to say that to you for a long time, I just didn't know how.'

'Try it. It's quite easy. First I. Then love. Then you.'

Playfully he punched her arm. 'I love you Sally and I have done for ages.'

'See? Wasn't difficult was it?'

'No, I suppose not. And I suppose having the daughter of a billionaire in love with you does have its advantages!'

'David!' She started to beat his arm. 'You're not meant to think about it in that way!'

Quick as a flash he caught her hand and with a show of strength he flipped her on her back and straddled her across her waist, firmly holding her wrists. They stared into each other's eyes, Sally struggling under him. Slowly he leaned forward and kissed her lips, gently running his tongue across her full, luscious lips. 'You're not meant to think about it in that way.'

'Sally, I'll love you whether you are rich or pauper, peasant or Queen.'

'Good...'

And he did not let her finish. He kissed her again, this one lingering, his tongue flicking against hers. Slowly he pulled away and rolled off to lie down next to her where he wrapped his arms around her, running his fingers through her long copper hair. 'What is your natural hair colour?'

'You'll find out, one day very soon…'

There they lay on David's bed until later that evening, talking, with David learning more truth about his girlfriend, the young woman he loved.

Chapter 37

Michelle was surprised when she discovered that Sally had flown back to England without her, but after speaking to Mr. Gallagher she totally understood why she had wanted to. After relaxing on the yacht, she flew back to England on her own the next day to a reunion with Simon after which she settled back down into the routine of her life, predominantly preparing for her exams, but also spending as much time as she could spare with Simon.

Peter had been surprised over the last few months about how well his drugs career was blossoming under the tutelage of Reg. He had quickly moved his way more into the inner-sanctum of Reg's business taking less responsibility for the selling of the drugs and more responsibility for supplying the drugs.

In a show of trust, Reg had offered him the opportunity to accompany him to Colombia to meet one of Reg's suppliers of the drugs, a trip which showed Peter the dangers of the industry he was becoming more involved in, but also the benefits.

Reg had numerous fronts dotted all over the country, legitimate businesses that he used to launder the drug money. It was a risky business and he had come close to being jailed numerous times during the years, but all the times this had occurred the prosecutors' cases collapsed as evidence was destroyed or witnesses suddenly lost either the will to testify in court or were involved in unfortunate accidents.

He lived in a large detached house out in the countryside that was fortified and had some of the most up-to-date security devices. In order for the police to raid his house they would need a full-scale assault team and with Reg's contacts in the police and courts this would allow him ample time to ensure that any evidence was destroyed before they arrived. He had Porsches, he had Ferraris, he had a summer villa in Spain, and a winter chalet in the Alps of northern Italy and he was a powerful man.

With a word to one of his loyal followers people in his way would disappear, judges would suddenly find pearl necklaces being delivered to their wives and sergeants in the police force would suddenly find that they can afford to send their children to that expensive private school.

It was this kind of power and wealth that Peter craved and he made it quite clear to Reg that he was the man to take over the business when Reg decided it was time to retire to his villa in Spain. This approach appealed to Reg too. With no son and his two daughters too precious to him to get involved in such a dangerous way of life, Reg was now thinking about succession, who could take over the business after he had stepped down.

He did not want the business to be closed down, he had worked all his life setting it up, so that is why Peter found himself being introduced to drug cartels in Colombia, drug lords in Mexico. With knowing nods between them, the drug barons quickly realised that Peter was going to be the man over the next few years who they would be dealing with so they treated him like a king.

They respected his sensible stance when he refused their offer of as much cocaine and heroin as he could consume, but they did quickly realise he was a man for the ladies. On one visit, for two weeks Peter had sex with some of the most beautiful South American women he had ever seen. He sampled everything they could offer him. From pubescent virgins who they had stolen off the streets of Bogota for their client's pleasure, to fifty-five year old women who taught and showed him sexual activities that he would not have thought possible even in his wildest sexual fantasies.

And Peter lapped it all up. He loved it. He loved dealing with these people, negotiating the deals and ensuring that a steady supply of the drugs was being sent to England and between them they created more and more elaborate ploys to evade detection by customs and the police forces.

All the time that this was happening, Reg watched and analysed his apprentice, correcting and intervening when appropriate but usually being impressed with the way Peter conducted himself during these key meetings. Quickly Peter was too busy to go out on the streets and as his value to Reg increased so did his monetary value to Reg so he compensated Peter accordingly.

This enabled Peter to buy a luxurious apartment in the city, a new car and he was never short of attractive women to take to bed. The humiliation he had suffered at the hands of Reg had long been forgotten and as the months rolled by Peter's influence over the business increased.

It was his idea to expand the business into selling Crystal Meth, but over the years Reg had become stuck in his ways and refused to digress into such an unknown quantity, preferring instead to stick with the drugs he knew, cocaine and heroin. It took Peter over a year of persuasion. He showed Reg statistics of how it was more addictive than heroin and cocaine, how the rush lasted a lot longer than either of these drugs, how the courts were seeing more crystal meth addicts through them than heroin users recently.

The winning argument though was the fact that they would lose all the expenses of importing the drug into the country because crystal meth could be manufactured so easily and cheaply. Eventually he obtained permission from Reg to use some money to set-up a small lab in a room in an abandoned warehouse on an industrial estate on the outskirts of the city.

With a simple search on a popular internet search engine he found the ingredients and how to make it. After quite a few failed batches he thought he had the correct compound but in order to make sure he would have to inject it into a human. There was no way he was injecting the vile substance into his body so he simply got a van and took two homeless people off the streets, a male and a female, and restrained and blindfolded them in a cage in the warehouse. Over a few days he injected the drug into them analysing the affects and making slight amendments to the compound until his analysis showed that their bodies were responding to the drug in the expected manner.

After he had finished with them he dumped them back onto the streets and made a call to one of the company's trusted sellers. Peter gave him a supply of the drug and told him to sell it and to use his experience to judge whether the addiction rate was high.

Two weeks later his seller reported back to Peter clamouring for more of the crystal meth. He was selling a large amount to the same people day in, day out, which indicated a high addiction rate and those people were informing their friends of the new powerful drug with the intense high that lasted for at least double the length of a heroin high. With this news Peter got some more resources to work in the lab to up the production. Once Peter had a month's worth of strong sales recorded in his ledger he reported back to Reg.

'The uptake has been, well, phenomenal Reg. The addictive nature, the long high it gives to the user. The dealers I've been using have reported the same buyers buying more and more. I took the sellers off the street one night to experiment, and when they returned there were damn well near enough riots! You know those scenes you see in Africa of the starving people fighting over the food? It was like that!'

'And these figures are right, one hundred percent accurate?'

'You know I don't fuck around with my accounting. They are accurate.'

'So including set-up costs you made a profit in the third week?!'

'Yes! I'll be honest with you, after salaries have gone out at the end of the fourth the profit was smaller, and after I gave the lads a small loyalty bonus for keeping this quiet I made a slight loss over the whole month, but next month with no set-up costs and no bonuses, well, you can see my sales predictions for the quarter, half-yearly and full year over the next few pages.'

'Wait outside why I read it.'

This was a big decision and Peter was used to being dismissed so Reg could think in private. He paced outside Reg's office for what seemed like an eternity while Reg was considering Peter's figures and looking for any flaws in his accounting.

As usual, Reg quickly realised he was wasting his time trying to fault Peter's maths. Once he had all the information and had digested it Reg made his decisions quickly and it was not too long before he called Peter back in. 'I think your sales are optimistic.'

'Pardon me?'

'You heard.'

'I think they are realistic.'

'Justify them.'

'I've seen it. I've watched the druggies come out of whatever holes they live in and buy so much of the fucking drug that in an hour my sellers have to go home! Believe me, they are not ambitious predictions, if anything they are understated predictions!'

'So you think that if you doubled the size of production it would be sold?'

'I think if we tripled production it could be sold, but one step at a time.'

'Yeah, one step at a time. Is the place you're using now big enough?'

'Yes. And I was going to tell you that I've got it in plan to rent out other warehouses in different areas of the city. I'll set up a moving production line. One month we are in warehouse A, in the third and fourth weeks we set-up warehouse B. At the end of the week four we move to warehouse B, close down warehouse A, and in the third and fourth week of production at B we start to set-up warehouse C, etcetera.'

'Good plan, but we'll go through some warehouses.'

'Well, after a six month break there is no reason why can't move back to warehouse A. If it was under surveillance it wouldn't be after six months of no activity being seen there.'

'Right. Double production. Whatever resources you need you can have. Report back to me in a month. Make sure this does not detrimentally affect our sales of H and C. Keep those going in case all this explodes in our faces.'

'It won't, but of course I will. I'll set the balls rolling straight away.'

With a shake of their hands, Peter left Reg and made some phone calls to start more production of the drug with the full intention of doubling their output and income. It was not long before the city, towns and cities nearby were awash with the drug.

*

With a now practiced hand and a quiet click the lock was opened and the door was silently pushed open. The burglar could not believe the number of houses out there that still did not have burglar alarms or had inadequate security, so with a quiet chuckle she crossed the threshold of the house and took the stairs up to the bedrooms.

Upon entering the master bedroom she carefully opened drawers until she found one full of jewellery which she sifted through, placing the more expensive looking items into the bag that hung at her hip. With equal care she closed that drawer and opened more, a big, toothless smile flashing across her face as she found a stash of cash which she again placed in the bag. Crossing the bedroom she opened the wardrobes, standing on tip-toes to look for anything else that could be easily sold. Another smile lit up her once glowing eyes for a moment, before the eyes dimmed down into the dark soulless pits they had become. She had spotted a shoebox, but was disappointed when she opened it and just found some papers, one of which was a marriage certificate.

After she had taken the lighter out of her pocket, simply out of spite she burned the certificate, watching the ashes cascade like grey snow into the shoebox. Placing the shoebox exactly where she had found it, near enough to the millimetre, she proceeded to look in the rest of the drawers and wardrobes in the master bedroom and all other rooms, taking as much care in these rooms as she had in the master bedroom.

By the time she was ready to leave, she had found more jewellery and more cash. Some of the jewellery had belonged to the owner's great-grandmother and due to Sarah's care it would be two days later, when the owner went to get a pair of earrings, that they realised they had been burgled. With a frantic search of the house in case her husband had for some reason moved them, the family heirlooms could not be found and it was only when she found the burnt marriage certificate did she tearfully call the police.

But Sarah had been careful by wearing gloves and any evidence that may have been left had long been walked on or vacuumed up in the intervening days. When the police came, the owners could not even tell them the day they were burgled, only the day of discovery. Of course, by then Sarah had sold the jewellery to a pawn shop and had blown the cash on a new drug that she had just discovered.

*

Sarah still funded her drug addictions by prostituting herself which was still her main source of income, but she had taught herself how to pick locks and this subsidised quite nicely the money she got from whoring. With a now rare flash of intelligence, she had thought about burgling and had used an internet café to access certain pages on the World Wide Web that explained the method. With a little bit of practice on her locks at home, she had managed to keep hold of the council house she had lived in with her mother, she was soon able to open standard door locks and it was not long before she was opening other people's door.

The first three times she had burgled she had done it quickly, noisily and left one hell of a mess, even defecating on the bed of one of her victims, using their pillows cases to clean herself with. But after the third time the victims had returned sooner than she had expected and Sarah had to drop out of the bedroom window, spraining her ankle in the process. As soon as the owners entered the bedroom they knew they had been burgled so they of course instantly called the police and Sarah only just managed to hobble far enough away to avoid detection.

As she waited the next day for one of her regulars, she contemplated how it had gone so badly wrong. She decided there was not much she could have done about them returning home earlier than expected, but if they had not known they had been burgled it would have bought her more time. She contemplated this some more while she grunted and yelped her fake pleasure as the regular was taking her from behind in his marital bed on top of a layer of his wife's lingerie.

It was a long time since she could last remember enjoying sex, the activity that only a year ago was second to only oxygen in a need for a body. Now it was just a way to earn thirty or so pounds a session, and this guy always tipped if Sarah allowed him to dress her in his wife's lingerie. If it meant an extra ten pounds he could have dressed her in a Minnie Mouse costume never mind his wife's expensive silk lingerie.

With a loud groan he sprayed his seed into her to which Sarah responded with a loud moan of her own and while she was moaning along with rotating hips coaxing more groans out of her client, Sarah hit on the idea of creating the scenario that the victims did not know they had been burgled. If she was clever and careful about it, it could be days before they realised they had been turned over. Perfect!

As he cleaned up Sarah took off the lingerie and put on her own clothes not bothering with underwear as it took more time for clients to take off. On average, wearing underwear took up an extra five minutes per session, multiply that by six and it worked out as an extra session a night.

She accepted the money and the tip and they left the lawyer's five bedroom detached house, taking his expensive Lexus back to the red-light area. After pecking his cheek and muttering her thanks, she got out of his car and checked how much money she had in her small, cheap, shiny plastic handbag. She could feel that she was getting irritable and was starting to sweat. Really she wanted one more session so she could get a little food tomorrow, but she knew that if she bought what she really wanted now she would not feel hungry anyway so she walked a couple of streets until she found the guy she was looking for.

'Hey Sarah. How are you?'

'Not bad. And you?'

'Getting by, getting by. What you after tonight? Got some H on cheap, or two for one on big bags of Charlie. Got some crack and some new crack pipes. How does that sound?'

'You always try to sell me what I don't want. Give me ninety pounds worth of your finest mind blowing crystal meth.'

'Roger that. Good shit this Sarah. Very good batch. For a shag I'll chuck in an extra bag?'

Irritated Sarah said, 'Fuck you,' and flicked her middle finger at him. 'Give me it. I want to go home.'

'Okay, okay. Only trying to have a joke honey.' Her hands were shaking as she reached into the bag and he noticed that there was a layer of sweat on her brow despite the chilly night. 'Looks like you could do with a shot straight away never mind waiting until you get home.'

'No, I don't. I'm fine. Here.' She handed over the ninety pounds and she got a couple of small bags in return. 'Is that it?!'

'Times are hard Sarah. Costs are rising with this flamin' credit crunch. More buys less now for all of us unfortunately.'

'Right. Fine.'

She snatched the drugs out of his hand and decided to get one more client so at least she would not have to walk home. It did not take long for her to be picked up and she serviced the client quickly, eager to take the drug. Sarah in the recent months since she had discovered this drug had tried taking it in numerous ways, from snorting and smoking it to swallowing it or placing it in her anus. Tonight she decided to smoke it so she got her short pipe and placed some of the drug in the cup. Using her lighter she lit the meth and inhaled deeply, loving the feeling of the euphoria as it quickly washed over her.

Recently though she had found it necessary to take more and more of the drug to reach the same level of high and the affects of taking a drug that produces about five pounds of toxic waste for every pound of meth produced was showing its hold on her already heroin ravaged body. She was already malnourished after taking the heroin, but now the only word that could be used to describe her face was gaunt and her breasts were now nothing more than empty sacks of skin. But it was the hidden damage she was doing to her body that was slowly killing her.

Currently she had not slept for five days, yet she had had sex fifty times, thirty of those unprotected. Unknowingly and luckily for her two of the men she had used protection with had the AIDS virus, but someone had given her

Hepatitis B. Right now after taking a large amount of the drug she was experiencing a form of toxic psychosis and was hallucinating, muttering and mumbling to herself. Her heart was struggling to deal with the intense chemicals rushing through her blood, and her lungs were rasping and crackling as she took quick shallow breaths. It was a combination of all these symptoms of intense drug use that would lead to Sarah's death.

Chapter 38

'Look, don't be so nervous. I'm sure he'll be fine.'

'You're the first boy I've ever introduced to him.'

'Look, he let us take the jet, he let us take the yacht for a week and he hasn't even met me so surely that is a good sign?!'

'Oh, I meant to mention that to you. Don't speak to him about that. I told him I was with Michelle.'

'What?!'

'I asked him because I had ruined the weekend could we relax on the yacht while studying. He was reluctant at first, but it would have been a firm no if I'd told him I wanted to go with you.'

'Sally, I really wish you hadn't done that. Not exactly the best start is it?!'

'I suppose not, but it was all I could think of at the time.'

'Great. So if he finds out he'll think I'm a liar too.'

'If he does find out, which he won't, I'll tell him you knew nothing about it.'

'Yeah, and I'm sure that'll go down like chilled champagne.'

'Speaking of champagne, do you want some more?'

'Great first impression Sally. "Hi daddy. This is my boyfriend, David. Don't mind him though, he's pissed!" '

'You're funny David! Have some more. Dutch courage and all that.'

'Okay, okay. Go on then.'

Sally reached for the bottle of champagne and lifted it from the cooling cabinet of the Rolls-Royce. 'We're nearly there.'

It was a glorious summer's evening and David looked out of the window. 'I know where we are. My garage is not far from here. In fact, I drive along this road sometimes when I feel like a fast drive. Good road this. You don't live… Nah, you couldn't, could you?'

'Could I what?'

'Live… Oh my, you do! The number of times I've driven past this mansion and wondered who lives here!'

'Well, now you know!'

Majestically the massive gates opened and the Rolls sedately drove through them onto the long driveway. In the distance, over the folds of the land, David could see the mansion and his heart missed a beat as he realised it was the place he had looked down upon many times from the hill he could now see in the further distance.

As they drove along the drive, Sally indicated a track leading off through a coppice of trees. 'We've got stables down there. I'll introduce you to Storm later and I'll trust her judgment implicitly so if she doesn't like you you'll be dumped!'

'Gee, thanks Sally! That lake looks lovely, as does the island. Do you ever have picnics out there? I bet it's lovely on a night like tonight.' David looked across at Sally and he could tell that something he had said had upset her.

'Erm no, not exactly. My mum is buried on that island.'

'Oh bugger, sorry Sally. Trust me.'

'It's okay. You're right though, it is a lovely island. My mum loved it out there, boating on the lake. A part of me wishes my dad hadn't buried her there because it has, of course, never been the same since, but she is resting where she was happiest so I suppose that is for the best.'

'Yeah, I suppose. How long is this drive? And how big is that house? It already looks huge from here but we don't appear to be getting any closer!'

'The drive is just over two miles long. Oh goody, he's here! Well his helicopter is here so that's probably a good sign! You never know if he's going to turn up or not because he's so busy.'

'No getting out of it then.'

'No, you'll be fine.'

'Are you sure because I'm not.'

Sally did not reply. Instead she took his hand and grasped it, stroking it tenderly. Shortly the car pulled up in front of the mansion and David saw the man he had seen in the pictures on the internet at the top of the steps up to the huge doors. Almost before Sally could stop him, David was opening the door to get out of the car.

'No. Wait for the driver to open for you.'

Surprised, David did as instructed and only got out of the car when the door was opened for him, and he stood up out of the car. Sally then got out and stood next to him and they made a striking couple.

Sally had paid for a tailored suit for David, along with tailored shirt, brand new Prada shoes and his black hair was cut in a trendy yet smart manner. His deep blue eyes were shining, his olive skin was glowing. Sally was dressed simply in a flowery summer dress, sandals and her freshly coloured black hair was tied up with a scarf. With no makeup except a touch of red lipstick that made her full lips look even fuller, she looked simply stunning and with the handsome David stood beside her looks were even more enhanced. With a deep sigh of nerves, Sally took his hand and walked over to the steps which her father started to come down. 'Daddy! Lovely to see you.'

'And you.' He pecked her on each cheek. 'You're looking good darling. How are your ribs?'

'I'm all better. A week lay on a lounger doing nothing but studying in the sun has that affect!'

'Great.'

'Well daddy, as you may have guessed, this is David.'

'It's a pleasure to meet you Mr. Gallagher.' He offered his hand which was accepted and Mr. Gallagher was impressed with his firm handshake.

'And it's a pleasure to meet you too David. I have of course heard a lot about you.'

'And I have about you, sir.'

'Sir? Not quite! Maybe Her Majesty will give me the honour next year, but for now Mr. Gallagher is fine. Shall we go to the rear gardens? I thought we could eat outside while it is such a glorious evening.'

For the next five minutes David managed to somehow stop his jaw dragging on the floor as they made their way through the opulent mansion. As they steppe d out of a room, David had lost count of the number they had been in, through the French windows, David managed to somehow not gasp as he saw the expansive gardens with the numerous fountains laid out across the grounds. Mr. Gallagher led them down a path to a table that had been laid out for three, next to one of the smaller fountains which gave an ambience that was present but not overbearing.

They settled into small talk, David making sure he did not say anything that might embarrass him or his host. As they talked, the waiters delivered the four courses and David could not remember a time that he had eaten such luxurious food, yet it was clearly nothing new to Sally or her father and in fact, Mr. Gallagher said to Sally that one of the items of food was not correctly cooked to which Sally agreed.

Soon the conversation changed to Sally's upcoming exams and David shuffled a little uncomfortably in his seat as Sally explained how her applications to Oxford and Cambridge were proceeding.

'What college do you attend David?'

'Erm, well, I don't.'

'Oh really, nothing wrong with that. I haven't got a G.C.S.E or O-level or A-level or degree to my name. What business are you in?'

Mr. Gallagher's seemingly disregard of academic qualifications seemed to relax David. 'I'm a mechanic at a local garage.'

'Really? Well you would have loved where we were a couple of weeks ago!'

'Yeah, he knows dad. Still a touchy subject dad.'

'Oh yes, sorry. I forgot, which is one of the reasons you shouldn't lie Sally, because it takes a good memory to remember the lies that have been told.'

'Yeah, I know dad. Thanks for reminding us about it dad.'

'I don't care for your attitude young lady.'

'Well honestly!' Sally stood up and quickly walked off towards the mansion.

'Now where's she going? I tell you what David, sometimes I wish I'd brought her up a little differently.'

'I think you've done fine Mr. Gallagher. She's a diamond.'

'Yes, I suppose she is as a whole. Just sometimes though… Ah, well. So, do you have any qualifications?'

'No, not really. I've got a few G.C.S.Es, that's all.'

'Some people are not destined for academic greatness. Look at me. I can barely turn on a computer, if I don't have a secretary to type my emails and letters I shudder to think of the kind of tat I'd be sending out. Thankfully my wife was there in the early days to vet everything I was sending otherwise I don't think I'd be anywhere near where I am now!'

'It's good to hear you can still, well, become what you are with limited academic work.'

'Don't get me wrong, if you were sitting here telling me you were just about to enter Oxford to read medicine I'd be happier, but so long as you make my daughter happy then that is all it should really be about. I think it would drive me insane if she dated one of those pompous, polo playing buffoons who are always surrounding her like flies round shit!' David laughed. 'I think I may have just des cribed my daughter as shit, but never mind. It is good that she is dating someone who is more, well, salt of the earth.'

'Thank you Mr. Gallagher. That means a lot to me.'

'Good. Oh, as an aside, you can both stop this little charade about who was on the yacht with her last week. Don't look so worried. I know you had nothing to do with her little scam, however, she should have known better to think I wouldn't find out. I know about everything that goes on in my world and considering what she did in Monaco it would be rather foolish of her to think that the paparazzi wouldn't be keeping an eye on her.' Mr. Gallagher took pictures out of his pocket and threw them on the table. 'Look at them.'

David picked them up and flicked through them. They had been taken with a powerful lens from quite a distance but clearly Sally could be seen in various positions with David, one with her leg draped over him, the next he was applying suntan lotion to her naked back. 'Shit...'

'Indeed. I paid a lot of money to obtain those photos and keep them out of some rag with a signed contract to state they will never be published.'

'Shit. Sorry.'

'You've got nothing to say sorry about. You didn't lie to me. She did.'

They both looked up as they heard the gravel on the path crunch as Sally made her way back to the table. On arriving she gave her dad a hug and apologised for snapping at him. The apology was accepted and then Mr. Gallagher said, 'Just been showing David some interesting photos.'

'Oh daddy! You best not have dragged out the baby photos already! Let me look!'

Before he could offer any resistance the photographs were snatched out of David's hand and as she flicked through them at first she went red and then slowly the blood drained from her face. 'How dare you!' She threw the pictures at her father to which he did not flinch. 'How dare you spy on me!'

'Sally. Stop. He didn't spy on you. Please, don't say anything else.'

'I'd listen to David if I was you because I have had just enough of your attitude today young lady and you are heading towards a full withdrawal of all privileges!'

Sally took a deep breath and it was clear she struggling to control herself. 'Well explain these pictures to me then.'

'I will. I obtained these pictures from a member of the paparazzi who was working for some sleazeball rag that likes to publish pictures of so called celebrities. It seems that your antics in Monaco towards a certain Prince did not go un-noticed. So, for a short time, you're flavour of the month. If I'd known for one second that you were going to that yacht with David I would have stopped you with all my power.' Sally made to interrupt him. 'Let... me... finish,' he growled at her. 'With all my power because I knew what would happen. I have worked very hard to keep you safe and secure Sally, very hard. You make things easier yourself by not putting yourself on the front cover of these rags, but if you did that then I would not interfere. But you don't, so I work hard on protecting you from these idiots with their long distance lenses. This is not the first time I've intercepted photos like this. Hell, when you were gallivanting around the Gulf with that idio tic Prince I don't think I've ever been busier with my phone pressed to my ear offering ridiculous amounts of money for pictures of you with him. Don't look surprised. I've known about you and the Prince before you told me about it in Monaco, but not the full story, not how much he upset you hence why I cancelled the contracts. So, what do I do when I receive a phone call from my security stating that there are photographers taking pictures of you and the man you are with.'

'But… But… There was no security there?!'

'Sally, my poor naïve Sally. There is always, always, always security near you at all times.' He paused and rubbed his eyes. Obviously this conversation was causing him some discomfort. David wanted to be anywhere else in the whole world right now.

'But where are they? I didn't see them.'

'You wouldn't. I know how you hate them so they are told to keep a discreet distance away. You're a kidnap risk Sally, you always have been and you always will be. I do not want my most prized asset stolen from me by some psychotic madman so I keep you safe, but discreetly. A few months ago, I told them to stay away for some foolish reason, but then something happened to you and the Mini? I don't want to know the details, but they were put back on you straight away.'

'But…'

'Sally,' he reached into this pocket and took out his Blackberry which took couple of moments to access, 'last Saturday night you went to the cinema. You watched that rubbish new Bond movie. How do I know it was rubbish? You said it was rubbish when you left. I quote from my security, "Sally did not appear to enjoy the movie. Clearly heard to state it was rubbish." Now, a few years ago I would have put the whole house on alert because whenever something happened you didn't like you got in a mood that shook the whole house! Thankfully you've grown out of that now, but how you are and what you're feeling is still important for me to know because I rarely see you because I'm so busy. After the movie you went to Pizza Hut. You ordered a large meat feast and a coke with a side order of wedges. Sunday, you went shopping and spent over a thousand pounds, including, I quote again, "some sexy lingerie", which as usual my accountants will ensure is paid off.'

'Oh my God.'

'Now, fair enough, I need to train them a little and inform them that I don't need to know when you buy sexy lingerie or any kind of lingerie for that matter, but they are there Sally, they are always there. I've had David and his family thoroughly checked out and if my checks had come up with any kind of skeleton in the closet he would have received a visit.'

'A visit?! A visit daddy?' Sally voice was strained and shocked.

'A visit. He would have been warned off.'

'Warned off?!'

'Yes. So when I go to so much effort to protect you yet allow you to live your life it breaks my heart when you lie to me and force me to confront you like this.'

For a few moments nobody said anything until David spoke. 'I think we both owe your father an apology Sally.' By now though Sally had tears rolling down her face and was unable to speak. 'Well I'll apologise for us then. I'm really sorry we tried to deceive you Mr. Gallagher, and thank you for protecting us, protecting our dignity from these paparazzi idiots.'

Sally though had clearly had enough. With another sob she stood from the table and ran towards the house.

David stood to follow her, but Mr. Gallagher said, 'No. Don't. Leave her be. She needs to think. Also, you need to think. I was going to speak to Sally about this after you'd gone, but I decided I wanted you here. I understand that you've only just learned about Sally's true status in life, yes?' David nodded. 'You need to think whether this is the life you want to become involved in. I know you like Sally a lot, and she likes you a lot, and going off first impressions, which have never let me down in the past, I like you too. But this is a big, a huge, an enormous change from what you're used to. Can you cope with knowing that your every move is being watched? As Sally becomes more popular and more known to the media, I think even I will struggle to keep all stories out of these rags. So can you cope with having intimate pictures plastered in these rags? This is another question you need to consider. I apologise that our first meeting has not gone as planned and that you're probably feeling a little overwhelmed right now, but I give you my blessing to continue to date my daughter. However, if you ever, ever, ever step out of line with her I will know about it and my blessing will be swiftly revoked. Now, I doubt that she'll want to see anyone tonight so would you like me to organise for a car to take you home?'

'Yes please.'

They walked together in silence, this time around the house, to the front of the mansion were a large Mercedes was waiting. Before he entered the car, David turned to speak to Mr. Gallagher.

'I'll consider everything you've said, but I think you know already what my decision will be.'

'Good. I hope you do continue to see her. I think you're good for each other. You add more balance to her life, a balance that I think she needs.'

'Thank you for dinner.'

'My pleasure. I hope we'll meet again soon and our meeting will have a better outcome.'

'Me too. Take care.'

David offered his hand first which was accepted and then he got into the car and was taken home.

*

With a long sigh he watched the car drive away and then turned to enter his mansion. It was at moments like this that he wished that he did not live in such a place that was so difficult to make it feel like it had any soul in. Right now, Sally would be in her room, Alfred would be in his room or in one of the reception rooms; one or two of the staff would be in the staff quarters which left about forty rooms not being used. Add to that the numerous ensuites, gyms and swimming area and it probably meant that around ninety-five percent of the house was not being used at this moment. With another long sigh he looked up at the large image of his departed wife hanging on the wall of the huge hallway of the mansion and shook his head, wondering to himself how he could be so rich, so successful, and live in such a house, yet at moments like this feel so sad and lonely.

He knew he would have to confront Sally before the day was done, but he knew that now was too soon so he went into one of the many receptions rooms and poured himself a large glass of port, and then in a change of mind he poured this into a bigger glass and topped it up some more. For a few moments he sat in front of the cold, unlit fireplace trying to relax but staring into an empty cold hearth was making him feel far from relaxed. So he walked over to the wall to ceiling windows and watched the sunset for a few minutes until he grew bored with that . When he slipped a hand into his pocket he felt his Blackberry and realised he had not checked his emails for a couple of hours, a record for him in the last twenty-five years. But he forced his hand out of his pocket leaving the device where it was, thinking to himself that they need to learn to cope without him for one evening. But he was bored, so involuntarily he found his hand sliding into his pocket, grasping his Blackberry again until his eyes rested on the grand piano in the corner of the room. Until that moment he had barely remembered he had a piano in this room, in fact he could not remember the last time he was in this room.

He had taken lessons at some point in the past and he thought he would try to see what he remembered. Sitting on the stool he thought to himself that it was probably not in tune, but unknowing to him it was on one of Alfred's many task lists to ensure that the pianos dotted around the mansion were tuned every six months.

After lifting the keyboard cover he tinkled a few notes before remembering a short tune which he hesitantly performed. Stretching his fingers he stood and opened the lid of the stool and lifted out a music book which he placed on the piano and then sat back on the stool and squinted at the music sheet. He frisked himself to see if he had his glasses and after realising he did not he decided he could just about cope without them. With a few practice attempts he managed to play the piece with only a few bad notes, and as he was playing and concentrating he did not hear nor see the door to the room open. It was only as he finished playing did the person speak.

'You'll strain your eyes dad.'

Mr. Gallagher jumped a mile. 'Bloody hell Sally! I would have thought I gave you enough money without you trying to get my life insurance by giving me a bloody heart attack!'

'Sorry.'

'It's okay, it's okay. Crikey though! I thought you'd be asleep?'

'No, not really. I was trying, but I heard the piano. My room is directly above this, remember?'

'Oh yes, of course. Sorry. Inconsiderate of me.'

'You haven't played for years.'

'I was just thinking that. I couldn't tell you the last time I was in this room never mind sat at this piano.'

'You only came in here to listen to mum play anyway. I doubt whether it has been played since, well, you know.'

'You're probably right.' He closed the lid over the keys and walked over to where his daughter was stood. 'Shall we talk?' She nodded. 'Would you like some port?'

'I've never tried it.'

'Try it now. Drink with me.'

'Okay.'

They both settled into the chairs in front of the mantelpiece and stared into the soulless fireplace, both of them searching for something to say. Eventually Sally could not take the silence any longer. 'About last week. I'm so sorry. You're right. It was naïve of me to try and trick you like that. If I'd been honest then none of this would have happened. I was just really shocked before when you told me that they, the security, were always there. I mean, I barely remember saying that about the movie yet you have a record of it on your Blackberry.'

'At the start of last winter we hadn't had a kidnap threat for months so I took them off you. Stupid decision because something did happen. The security guards at the gate were openly avoiding holding a conversation with me; Alfred couldn't look me in the eye. I didn't press it because in my heart, if it concerned you and it was bad, I didn't want to know. Foolish of me I know, but all I cared about was that you were safe. So what did happen?'

Sally explained everything that had happened that frightening night when she met David, how she had been attacked, how he'd helped her, how the Mini had been trashed and how he'd fixed it for her without asking for any money or thanks.

After the story was finished, Mr. Gallagher contemplated it for a few moments. 'In that case I'm in full support of your relationship. To help and support you like that shows he is a good, strong character who is obviously kind and caring. But that wouldn't have happened if the security had been following you. I know this was a random attack, but I know for a fact that my security has stopped a handful of well planned attacks on our family over the years, some of these attacks directed at seizing you.'

'I'm sorry dad, I had no idea.'

Leaning forward he lifted his glass and took a sip of the rich liquor. 'No need apologise. Perhaps I should have told you, but I didn't want to worry you. What's the point of worrying you when it can all be done covertly?'

'True. That doesn't excuse the fact that I lied to you. I'll understand if you withdraw my privileges for a long, long time.'

'No, it's fine. I think you've learned your lesson. Anyway, you'll need your privileges to keep that boy of yours accustomed to the life he's going to be entering. I spoke to him about it, after you'd gone. Considering his background, a mechanic from an average family in an average part of town he doesn't seem too overwhelmed, which again is another good sign to me that he's got a strong head on his shoulders, a strong character. I think he'll fit in well here. I presume he knows about your birthday ball?'

'Of course! We both can't wait!'

'Good, good. Right, although I promised myself a full night off I can't cope.'
'Huh? What do you mean?'
'I'm going upstairs to my office.'
'Oh daddy! Give yourself a break!'
'I have. I had a nice evening with you, until, well, you know, and I've had a nice chat with you to clear the air so now I need to check that my subordinates haven't managed to bring my company to its knees!'
'I'm sure it can survive one night!'
'You clearly don't know these subordinates my dear!'

With a laugh Sally stood, kissed her father on his forehead and they wandered together up to the third floor of the mansion and she left him outside his office which he entered. Quickly he sat down behind his desk and picked up the phone and dialled a number.

'I thought you were having the evening off and spending it with Sally and her boyfriend? The big first meeting?'

'We met. That's why I'm calling James. It's still early days, but I think I've found my successor.'

'Has Sally come round at last after your years of gentle persuasion?'

'No, she'll never come round. She doesn't want it, but someone close to her might be persuaded to become a very good apprentice…'

Chapter 39

Sally was stressed. It was the morning of her birthday ball and she had popped in to speak to her father about a small matter. Now, on top of ensuring everything was perfect for the evening, she now had the added stress of listening to the reason why her father had told her boyfriend to quit his job. 'Why didn't you tell me, us, you had this in plan? Why have you decided to drop this bombshell today of all days?!' She was stood in his office in the mansion, leaning on his desk towering over him with her fists clenched.

'I thought it would be a nice surprise for you, give a good finishing touch to your day.'

'Daddy, I love him to bits, but he has no, none, zero academic qualifications. He's got good common sense though, but he's not a Cambridge or Oxford business school graduate that you usually employ! He'll be totally out of his depth!'

'Neither have I.'

'Neither have you what?'

'I don't have any academic qualifications. Neither does James. What we do have, as you've said, is plenty of common sense. Look at, Bill Gates.'

'What about him?'

'Dropped out of Harvard, self made billionaire. Warren Buffet. Nothing special, standard degree, a Masters too, but self made billionaire. Carlos Slim Helu…'

'Who the hell is he?'

'Watch your tongue and show him some respect!'

'Sorry.'

'You've met him. A few years ago now mind. Mexican, started as a taxi driver and is at the moment second richest man in the world. Limited academic qualifications too. Self made billionaire.'

'Right. What's your point?'

'My point is that the top three richest people in the world have limited academic qualifications and are all self-made!'

'Right. So how does David fit into this?'

'I've not worked my arse for the last few decades only to see my company handed over to a group of business school graduates who couldn't make a correct decision between the lot of them! I want and the company needs a successor. You're not interested; the only other people I meet are these business school graduates who try numerous different ways to impress me and fail miserably!' He stopped for a moment and looked at Sally intensely. 'I need someone fresh, someone with no pre-conceived ideas about how a company should be run that others think they know. I need someone I can groom, someone I can train to fit into the shoes that I'll be leaving empty one day.'

'You need an apprentice.'

'Yes! Exactly that. And he's perfect. He's got good common sense and I can tell he's got a good character. And what better barometer do I need apart from the fact that you're dating him?!'

'And if we break up?'

'Is that likely?'

'Right now, no. But you never know do you?'

'You're right, you don't. But we can cross that bridge if we come to it.'

'That will be a little awkward if I catch him sleeping with someone behind my back and then he's taking over my father's company.'

'True and if you do break up for some reason like him sleeping with someone else then I'll fire him, but this is my decision. Starting from Monday he's working for me.'

'That's it?! You're not even going to ask for my opinion?!'

'I know what your opinion is.'

'Oh yeah?! What?'

'You think I'm crazy.'

'You've got that right in one.'

'Look,' he stood and walked round the desk to take one of her hands and place the other on her shoulder, 'I'm going to be paying him a salary which is double what he earns now. I'm going to lay out the ground rules to him that if this does not work out he's back fixing cars. He presumed that anyway.'

'Hang on. He's already accepted?!'

'Erm yes, although I didn't tell you that.'

'Well this gets better and better and better!' She pushed away from him and walked towards the door.

'I'm sure he's got it in plan to tell you…'

She did not reply. Instead she stormed out of his office slamming the door behind her and made her way in furious anger through the mansion. One of the maids saw her coming who was well used to her mistress's moods and with one glance at her face the maid scuttled out of her way. When she reached the door to her bedroom she flung it open and David jumped as he was stood there naked having just got out of the shower.

'And when the hell did you plan on telling me about my dad's offer?'

'Huh?'

'Don't huh me!'

'Can I get dressed?'

'No, you can't.' She grabbed his Calvin Klein underwear, a present from her to him, and threw them to the other side of the room. 'Well?!'

'Sally, calm down. I was…'

'Don't… tell… me… to calm down!' She grabbed one of his shoes and threw it at him.

'Ouch! Okay, sorry. I was going to tell you now. I was going to tell you directly after I'd spoken to him but I couldn't find you!'

'You're as bad as him!' Her voice screeched as she threw another shoe at him which this time he managed to dodge. 'Scheming together behind my back!'

This time the thrown hairbrush did connect with his lifted arm that was protecting his face from inbound missiles. 'Ouch! Jesus! Look, let's sit down and we can talk about this…'

'We're talking now!'

'Right, okay, okay. He called me up to this office about an hour ago. He spoke to me about his plan. He told me to think about it, discuss it with you. I came down here to talk to you but you weren't here. I then realised there was nothing to think about and went back up to accept his offer.'

'Without speaking to me?! How dare you!'

'Owww! Stop throwing things at me!'

'No!'

'Owww!'

'And what happens if we break up?! Have you thought of that?!'

'Is that likely?'

'Right now, yes it bloody is!'

'Great. I'll get my things.'

'Don't be stupid.' Sally sighed and dropped her hand to her side which was holding a perfume bottle. 'Just talk to me about things like this!'

'I tried, but you weren't here. I guessed you would have said yes anyway?'

'I might have done, but you never know. And what if I said no now?'

'Then I'd go straight upstairs and revoke my acceptance and find another job.'

'Find another job?'

'Yes. I've already quit the garage.'

'What?!'

'Ouch!'

'Another thing you should have spoken to me about!'

'Okay, okay. No matter what and how obvious it is I'll always speak to you first. Okay?'

'Good. He'll be an arse to work for you know?'

'I can imagine.'

'I only worked for him as an admin assistant and he had me run ragged.'

'I can imagine.'

'You shouldn't imagine, you should know. You'll be working long, long hours.'

'I do that anyway.'

'You'll never be home.'

'I'm always here now.'

'Well you'll never be home or here.'

'That's fine. But to work with your dad, surely that is too much of an opportunity to miss?'

'It is. But it is going to have a bad impact on our relationship. Oh my, it will be like being married to my dad! I'm not sure I like this. I've seen the hours he works. He's never home. I'll never see you.'

'You will. I've negotiated with him.'

'You've negotiated with him?! I would have loved to have seen that! And did your negotiation work?'

'Yes. He talked about the impact it will have on my life and our relationship. But he's also said that it won't be as bad for me as it was for him because the company is already set up. He's said that unless I really have to he'll never expect me to work past six, and never on Sundays, but to expect occasional Saturdays. Of course there will be long nights and some days I won't make it home, but thousands of couples do that and survive.'

'I suppose we can see how it goes.'

'Of course we can. And if it doesn't work then I can quit and go back to fixing cars. Sound like a plan?'

'I suppose.'

'Cool. Can I get dressed now?'

'Yes, sorry.'

While David was getting dressed Sally flopped on her bed and stared at the ceiling. She was not sure about this new development because she had seen over the years how hard her father had worked, but she did not want to block this astonishing development and opportunity in David's life. As she propped herself up on her elbow, she looked at him as he got ready and she could already see that something in the young man who she had grown to know a lot and love a lot had changed.

Even now, only a few hours after finding out her father's plan, he seemed to be holding himself differently or was it just the tuxedo he was not used to? Either way, what definitely could not be denied was that there was a glint in his eye that had not been there before, a feeling and an aura of confidence about him.

For a few moments she watched him as he struggled with the bow tie until she called his name and patted the bed beside her. Muttering and cursing under his breath he waved away her offer of assistance so instead she started to count down from ten in her head. Exactly as she reached one, for the final time he muttered and walked over to sit next to her.

'How do you know how to do this?' he growled at her. 'Done it for other boyfriends?'

'No my jealous boyfriend. I've done it for my father loads of times. He's rubbish at it too!'

'Pardon me?! How dare you!'

Quick as a flash he turned round and leapt onto her, forcing her flat onto the bed, pinning her arms while straddling her across her stomach. For a few moments she wriggled and kicked under him but he was far too strong for her. She stopped and stared into his blue eyes with a look of anger at being manhandled in this manner and as they stared into each others' eyes he leaned forward to kiss her. She flung her head to the side so his kissed missed and as he readjusted his aim she flung her head the other way.

Changing tack, he pulled her wrists together so he could hold them in one hand and with his other hand gently grabbed her jaw to keep her head still. He kissed her, running his tongue over her lips, not feeling any response at first, but then her lips parted slightly and he felt her relax under him. Her tongue met his and soon each of their tongues were in and out of each of their mouths, running around and along lips.

Sally was only wearing a thin cotton t-shirt and David glanced down as he moved his lips to her neck and noticed how her nipples were pressing firmly against the cotton top. David's lips gently kissed her neck, flicking out his tongue against her warm flesh and as he did this he stroked her right nipple with his thumb. She gasped and was reaching for his belt before her hands stopped and pressed against his chest.

'Stop David, please stop. I need to get ready.' She could not help notice the flash of emotion across his face. 'Tonight we can carry on from exactly this spot. I promise.'

Smiling he rolled off her and cradled her head in his arms, stroking her hair for a few moments. 'I love you very much Sally.'

'Me too David, very, very much.'

They cuddled for a little longer until there was a knock on the bedroom door.

'Miss Gallagher. The beautician is here. She is waiting for you in the dressing room.'

'I'll be there in a minute. Are you going to take the tuxedo off?'

'Yeah, of course. The party is not for hours. I only put it on to see what it was like. Never worn one before. What colour are you going to have your hair tonight?'

'What colour do you want me to have it? I've got a selection of gowns that I can pick to match.'

'I love it when it's copper red. You know that.'

'Then copper red it shall be.'

'Perfect.'

'I'd better go.'

'No worries. See you later.'

With a kiss Sally left David in the room and walked the short distance to the dressing room. The room was wall to wall mirrors with a seat in front of an ornate dressing table with another mirror on it. Here Sally's beautician waited for her and when she entered the room she was told to sit at the table.

For the next hour or so Sally had a full makeover. She was manicured and pedicured; she was plucked and waxed in all places including her most intimate areas. Attached to the room was another smaller room with sinks and this was where her hairdresser waited. Her hair was washed, deeply conditioned and coloured from black to the copper red that David requested. This took another couple of hours, and while she was waiting, Adrienne, who had been flown in especially so Sally thought, paraded gown after gown in front of Sally, chattering away at her about the pros and cons of each gown.

In the end, after much deliberation, she opted for a beautiful baby-blue coloured gown, with real pearls and diamonds dotted around the gown that gave it a shimmering effect. When her hair was ready and had been lightly curled and her nails painted and polished to match the gown, she returned to the dressing room where Adrienne measured her while she was naked. 'I never forget sizes Sally, and in the last few months since I last measured you you've put on weight.'

'Really? I hadn't noticed.' Sally had noticed and in fact her weight had only been gained in the last couple of weeks since she had started taking the contraceptive pill for the first time in her life in preparation for tonight.

After the measurements had been done, Sally dressed and was dismissed by Adrienne so the necessary adjustments could be made to the gown. When Sally returned to her room David had been chased out by one of the maids as instructed by Sally so she could finish getting ready without the added distraction.

In private she tried on numerous different sets of lingerie and eventually after much deliberation and a frantic call to Michelle as well as some picture messages being sent, she opted for a set of rose lingerie from the Victoria's Secret range.

Once this decision had been made all she had to do was wait for Adrienne to adjust the gown and she was ready for her ball. Anxiously she made a call to the organiser her father had hired and she was informed that everything was proceeding as planned. With her mind slightly more at ease Sally sat and stared out of the window over the lawn to where the large marquee had been erected. Even her mansion was not big enough to hold the number of people that had been invited, but the marquee had been kitted out with wall to wall oak flooring along with ornate tables and chairs. The number of people who were working around the marquee surprised her when viewed like this from her room from a detached point of view. The waiters and waitresses walked quickly between the marquee and the house carrying plates, or glasses or bottles of champagne and other such items.

Eventually there was a knock on her door and Adrienne was told to enter. In her arms was the gown and she told Sally to strip down to her lingerie. She slid into the gown and Adrienne fluttered around her, commenting and muttering as she made some subtle adjustments to the dress. When she was happy she stood behind Sally with a hand on her shoulder, both of them looking into the mirror.

'You look, my dear, astonishing.'

'Thank you.'

'Even in the height of your mother's beauty she could not have competed with you and that is the biggest compliment I can give you.'

'Thank you again. How long have you been seeing my father for?'

The question struck Adrienne like a hammer and for a moment she struggled to compose a suitable reply. 'I've known your father for years as you know. As time has gone by since your mother passed away we've grown closer. I'm sorry you found out in the manner you did.'

'It's okay. I guess my mum would have wanted him to carry on his life, but it was still a surprise.'

'And neither of us would have wanted you to find out like that. I'll be honest with you now Sally, I have no intention of replacing your mother in your father or your affections, but things are growing serious between us. I don't suppose he's told you, but I'm here as your gown designer and I'm also here as his guest.'

'He hasn't told me, but I presumed that. It's okay. I'm not fine with it now; I will be fine with it given a bit more time.'

'You take whatever time you need. Now it's my time to go and get ready. I will see you later.'

'Thank you Adrienne.'

'My pleasure darling.'

Adrienne left her room and Sally glanced across at the clock. It was still an hour before she was due to go down so she walked across to the window and noted that some of the guests had already started to arrive. She perched on the edge of the seat for the next forty-five minutes, noting that Michelle and Simon had arrived being chauffeured in the Rolls-Royce and she watched as they were escorted into the marquee. As Sally's closest friends they would be sat on the top table with her and David, along with Sally's father and now, as Sally has just found out, Adrienne and few more close relations.

Soon there was another knock on her door and Alfred entered who informed her it was time to go. Sally nodded and walked out of her room then through the corridors in the mansion towards the front entrance to the house. There she was met by David who said that she looked stunning, but this did not help ease Sally's nerves. When the last guests had been seated one of the organisers indicated to Sally that it was time to enter the venue.

David linked her arm and she glanced over her shoulder to see that her father had linked arms with Adrienne. This made her surprised again but with a word to herself she concentrated on negotiating the steps down from the entrance to the mansion and along the short path to the marquee. Here, two of Adrienne's assistants made one or two final adjustments to her gown and then Sally and David were beckoned into the marquee by the lead organiser.

Breathing deeply because she was still feeling nervous, Sally entered the marquee with David on her arm. As one the assembled guests turned to look at her and as one they all gasped as they saw how stunningly amazing Sally looked that day. The orchestra played an upbeat song as they walked through the tables, Sally pausing occasionally to speak to people she knew until she reached the table that was raised on a platform. David and she stepped up onto the platform and turned to face the guests and, as one, applause rippled through the guests. Primly Sally curtsied and David bowed and then they took their seats and their place on the platform was taken by Mr. Gallagher and Adrienne. The applause continued while they bowed and curtsied and then they also took their seats.

For a short time the guests chattered amongst themselves and Sally and David talked to Michelle and Simon. Then the first of many courses arrived and the guests enjoyed the sumptuous banquet with a seemingly endless amount of food and drink being brought to them.

As planned, after the meal Sally made a short speech where she thanked the guests for coming and also her father for making such a great party possible. Mr. Gallagher then also made a speech which of course concentrated on Sally, her early days including embarrassing incidents which had her cringing and slumping down in her seat, but which had David and everyone else present chuckling merrily as the champagne started to have an effect on them. His speech concluded by him stating how proud he was of his daughter and how her mother would have been equally proud of her. 'Anyone who knew my wife would know that she was beautiful, and it is clear to see that her beauty has been passed down to my beautiful wonderful daughter. So, may you all be upstanding as I offer a toast to Sally as we celebrate her eighteenth birthday! To Sally!'

Every one of the guests rose to their feet to toast her and after such an endearing speech Sally was quite emotional and wiped away the tears as she stood to hug and thank her father. For a few moments she composed herself and then she took David's hand and led him onto the dance area.

The orchestra played the first few opening beats to Shania Twain's You're Still the One and with a round of applause Leona Lewis took to the stage to sing the song as Sally and David danced together, with Sally's head resting on his chest.

By the end of the song Sally was even more emotional and she buried her head in David's chest to hide her tears from the audience. At the start of the second song her father and Adrienne made their way to the dance floor as did Michelle and Simon. This was also another slow love song, but then the orchestra and Leona upped the tempo and the dance floor filled up with couples. Leona performed for an hour and after she had finished there was demand for an encore to which she obliged and when she left the stage Sally and Mr. Gallagher went and personally thanked her for performing.

The night rolled on, with Sally and David dancing together or sometimes just Sally and Michelle when their boyfriends could not be persuaded to leave their seats. Apart from a minor scuffle involving two very drunk revellers which the security quickly sorted out by escorting them both off the estate, the night went without a hitch and Sally loved every moment of it. When she noticed that the guests had started to dwindle she took David's hand and led him out of the back of the marquee towards the mansion.

'Shouldn't we say goodbye to people?'

'It's okay. No-one will notice we're gone.'

'I'm sure they bloody will. You look amazing, a glowing beacon of beauty, believe me they'll notice!'

'Oh David, you do say the nicest things.' Flinging her arms around his shoulders she kissed him passionately and longingly, shuddering against him as he ran his fingers up and down her spine. 'Let's go in.'

Without waiting for a reply, Sally led David back into the mansion and up to her room. A maid had lit candles in the room as Sally had instructed.

'Very nice. Very romantic,' was David's comment.

She closed the door behind him, locking it too, and then turned to him and kissed him passionately again. This time she did not stop him as his fingers traced a path up and down her spine and she did not stop him when they slid round to the side and he gently slid the zip of her gown down. Gently she pushed him away and took a couple of steps backwards away from him. She slid the gown off her body and stood in front of him in her sexy lingerie.

David admired her figure for a few moments, admired her large breasts that were being pushed up in the bra, her flat stomach, her long slender thighs and the point where her thighs met that he knew no other man had touched. He had shown a lot of patience over the months knowing that she was a virgin and he did not want to rush her. But now as he admired her body and her stunning face he decided he must have her tonight. He was desperate for her.

He took a step towards her and with a show of strength he picked her up in his arms and carried her to the bed where he laid her down. Standing over her he quickly stripped down until he was naked and Sally was pleased to see that he was already fully erect. She had seen his penis before, she had placed it in her mouth until he had an orgasm, but she could not remember ever seeing it looking so large, so hard and so big.

After kneeling onto the bed he lay gently on top of her, kissing her, and she could feel his penis pressing into her belly so she took it gently in her hand and stroked it, feeling it throb and as she peeled back his foreskin she ran her thumb into his glands. Her thumb came away feeling slick with his pre-cum and this feeling that he was so turned on by her, that he found her so desirable, stirred an instinct inside her. She felt a rush of blood to her intimate areas and then she felt her fresh, virgin juices start to flow out of the entrance to her vagina. She had felt turned on by him before, and had only just managed to resist full intercourse with him, but she had never felt this aroused before.

The feeling was enhanced as he reached round to her back and undid her bra, pushing it off her breasts, releasing them and her nipples grew hard and erect. David took one and then the other in his mouth, running his tongue along their tips, sucking delicately on them, causing her to gasp and causing more juices to flow out of her.

With an eagerness she had never felt in him before, her now wet knickers were pulled down her body and flung away. Sally squeezed her legs together, shy and unsure about showing herself to him, but after a few well placed kisses she found her legs involuntarily opening to give David a view of her shaved pubic mound. There was a thin strip of hair leading from her clitoris up her belly for a couple of inches and David noticed that this was a deep black so he now knew her real hair colour. He looked at her vagina and admired it for its perfection. 'My God Sally. Is there any part of you that isn't perfect?!' And he buried his head into her mound, his tongue tracing up and down her vaginal lips, flicking against her clitoris for glorious moments.

This was all new for Sally. She had received hand pleasure before from David, but never oral. This was the first time her vagina had ever been touched like this and after the first shock of the intensity of the feelings she relaxed and it was not long before she was bucking and writhing, pressing her pubic area against his face forcing him to lick harder and faster. He took her to the brink, leaving her feeling pleasured yet frustrated at him stopping when she was just about to climax. He pushed himself along her body, discreetly wiping his soaking face on the duvet, until his hips where lined up with hers. Staring down into her eyes, he kissed her while he took the base of his penis in his hand and lined up the bulbous head with the entrance to her now waterfall wet vagina.

Her breathing increased as she realised she was about to be penetrated for the first time and she tensed as she felt his penis rest gently against her outer lips. He left it there for a moment, until gently he pushed with his hips opening her outer lips with the engorged head of his penis. Again he paused, letting her get used to the feeling, and then with great care he pushed again opening up her virgin vagina which the huge head of his penis filled.

Sally let out a groan as she felt like her vagina was being ripped in two. As the first couple of inches of his engorged organ entered her the pain was intense so she placed a hand on one of his hips pushing gently so he waited until her body got used to the feeling before he entered her further.

When he first entered her he stopped for two reasons. First, her comfort, secondly he almost ejaculated straight away. He had never felt anything so tight in all his life. He could not think of an adequate description apart from a hot, soft incredibly wet tube of flesh that was gripping his penis like it was being squeezed in a vice. The physical pleasure was intense, but the mental pleasure of taking this beautiful young woman's virginity, knowing that no man had entered her before, took him to the edge. But with a great effort he managed to control himself and not orgasm inside her yet.

After a few moments she dropped her hand and nodded so he pushed, literally forcing his penis along her tight vagina for a few more inches. She groaned again as the pain of having her vagina stretched and torn ripped through her body so she placed a hand on his hip again. A part of her wanted him to leave, but she had read that this was the worst action to take. She knew her body would get used to it, but she hoped it would get used it to soon. And it did.

Her vagina quickly stretched around his penis like it was designed to do, so again she dropped her hand and nodded, and again he pushed into her the final few inches until his pubic area was pressing against her with his penis fully penetrating her.

The pain was still quite intense, but was subsiding and Sally could definitely start to feel some pleasure as he paused again with his penis deep inside her body. The pleasure though was intense for David. How he was holding on he did not know but he was desperate not to ruin Sally's first sexual intercourse experience so he was thinking of the most boring politicians he could think of and trying not to think of incredibly wet, hot, tight vagina that was wrapped around his penis which was buried inside the sensationally stunning woman underneath him.

She dropped her hand from his hip again and David took this as the cue to start making love to her. Very gently he pulled half of his penis out of her, which made it feel like it was being ripped from his body at its root as it was being gripped so firmly by her vagina, and then he slid it gently back in. This time he noted that Sally's groan was definitely one of pleasure.

For the next five minutes he slowly, gently made love to her, slowly and gently increasing the tempo until Sally was moaning and groaning under him. Too eagerly though he slammed his penis into her and she screamed making him jump.

'Shit, sorry. Did I hurt you?'

'No! Carry on! That was a scream of pleasure! Please carry on. I'm used to it now. Hard like that!'

So David obliged. He took the full length of this penis out of her so just the head was being gripped by her, and then in one movement he slammed his penis into her hard which caused Sally to buck underneath him and scream loudly.

'Again! Like that! Faster!'

David obliged again. He forcefully rammed his penis in and out of her, enjoying the feeling himself, but also the pleasure he was giving to Sally. This continued for a few more moments, and while he was doing this David sucked on her nipples which caused Sally to buck and writhe under him more, to moan and groan and scream even louder.

The feeling of having him deep inside her, the sensations that were ripping through her body, quickly reached a crescendo and then Sally had the most intense orgasm she had ever experienced. Her whole body tensed and she let out one more almighty scream and then she just moaned and groaned underneath him as the orgasm made her whole body shake and quake under him.

At the start of her orgasm, David had felt her vagina clench even harder, squeezing his penis so tightly it took him over the edge into ecstasy. David slid his penis inside her to its hilt and then for the first time in her life Sally had a man orgasm inside her body. As he did, her own orgasm was subsiding and she felt him tense above her and then moan. Deep inside her body she felt his penis grow harder for a moment and then she felt his ejaculate spray into her, touching the deepest parts of her body.

As she looked up at him, as he gently rotated his hips with his penis still inside her, his eyes closed lost in the pleasure of the moment, she knew at that moment that they would spend the rest of their days together. Seeing how much pleasure she had given him, and how much pleasure he had given her, she knew that she did not want to be with anyone else ever again.

Chapter 40

For the rest of her eighteenth birthday night Sally made love with David until the early hours of the morning until they collapsed in a heap of exhausted intertwined limbs. They slept together for the rest of that night until Sally was woken by a knock on her door. One of the maids informed her through the door that breakfast would be served in half an hour.

She woke David and they showered together, lathering each other's bodies until they had to leave the shower and get dressed for breakfast. When they entered the breakfast room Mr. Gallagher was already present as where Simon and Michelle who had stayed over in one of the many bedrooms.

'Morning daddy.' Sally walked over to him and kissed him firmly on his cheek. 'Thank you so much for last night. It was amazing! I felt like a princess all night!'

'My pleasure. I'm glad you enjoyed it. You deserve it.'

'Did everyone else have a good time? Michelle? Did you sleep okay?'

'Yeah, we had a great time as did everyone. And we slept fine. You left early?' Michelle left the question hanging there but Sally handled it well.

'Yeah, David was too drunk!'

They all tucked into the breakfast, enjoying the conversation and the company until Mr. Gallagher announced that he had to leave for a flight to New York.

'On a Sunday daddy?'

'Unfortunately so dear. Ready David?'

'Pardon me?' asked a surprised Sally.

'Erm, your dad wants me to go to New York with him.'

'Excuse me? You only decided to start to work for him yesterday!'

Simon and Michelle exchanged a look, surprised at the way this conversation was going.

Her father intervened. 'It will be one of the rare opportunities in the next couple of weeks I'll have to speak to him about it. My schedule is totally crammed. An eight hour flight with no interruptions is a perfect opportunity for me to speak to him in private.'

'But, but…'

'I'll be back on Tuesday Sally. Sorry to dump this on you after your birthday celebrations,' stated David.

'We'll be meeting important clients. All David has to do is sit there to watch and learn which is all he's going to be doing for the next few years.'

'Right, fine. Michelle? Shall we go shopping?'

'Yeah, of course. Simon is playing football anyway today.'

'Fine. So you're going now?' Sally asked her boyfriend.

'Yes. Someone should have packed my bag.'

'We need to go,' stated Mr. Gallagher.

He stood from the table and left the room after which David stood to follow him. Reluctantly Sally stood too. 'I'll come and see you off.'

David offered his hand and again reluctantly Sally accepted it and they walked to the entrance to the mansion and watched as their bags were loaded into the back of the Rolls-Royce. 'Sorry about this. I had a fantastic time with you last night. I'll miss you while I'm away.'

'I'll miss you too. Be careful in New York.'

'I will be. Sorry I didn't tell you last night but I knew it would ruin your night.'

'It's okay. I understand and I know that this will be a one off, hopefully.'

'I'm sure it will be. I'll miss you because I love you.'

'Me too David, me too.'

With a kiss they parted and David got into the Rolls-Royce next to Mr. Gallagher and she watched them until the car went out of view in a fold of the land along the driveway. When she returned to the breakfast room she was surprised to see Michelle sat on her own.

'Where's Simon gone?'

'He had to dash. I asked Alfred to sort him out a ride home. He's got to get to his match. He said sorry he didn't see you but that he had a great time last night.'

'Oh right. No worries. Well that was a shock.'

'What's going on with David and your father?'

So Sally explained the situation and she could not help notice Michelle's surprise. 'Yeah, I know. Crazy isn't it? David my dad's, well, apprentice I suppose.'

'But why David? He has no business experience whatsoever?'

'That's the point. He wants someone fresh, clean, unsullied. To tell you the truth Michelle, I'm as baffled as you. I have no idea what my dad is playing at but I can see David ending up getting badly burned. But what can I do? How can I refuse him this opportunity no matter how crazy it seems at the moment?'

'You can't, but it does seem to be moving very quickly with trips to New York.'

'No, that part I understand. It will give them chance to talk about it. Getting my dad available for last night was a nightmare. He's so busy. He had to move so much stuff. I think his secretaries were all on valium by the time they'd finished!'

For a few moments they both laughed together until there was a silence between them. Sally stared at the table thinking about all that happened in the last twenty-four hours, and her eyes rested on Michelle's left hand. It did not register with Sally straight away but there was something not right about what she was looking at, something not right at all. And then it clicked into place. 'What is that on your left hand?!' Before Michelle could react Sally had grabbed Michelle's hand and was scrutinising her ring finger. 'Is that what I think it is?! He didn't?!' With a glance at Michelle's face she knew that he did. 'Oh my! Why on Earth didn't you tell me?!'

'Believe me when I say I was at least a thousand times more surprised than you are!'

'He proposed to you and you said..?'

'Well I'm wearing the ring silly!'

'Good point! I can't believe it! Where did he do it?'

'Well, he wanted to do it in the marquee but he rightfully thought that that would have been inappropriate because it would have taken the spotlight away from you. I would have killed him if he'd done that.'

'I wouldn't have minded.'

'Maybe not, but I would have. I thought there was something wrong with him all night. He seemed tense and a bit moody but I just put it down to the fact his team got beat so I ignored him. Turns out I was a little bit wrong!'

'Just a little bit!'

'So he proposed in the bedroom. It was really romantic, with the four-poster bed and the candles flickering in the wind because the balcony doors were open. He made me close my eyes and he got down on one knee with the box open and asked me!'

'Did you answer straight away?'

'Well I burst into tears and said yes!'

'I can't believe it! I'm so happy for you both!'

'Thank you Sally. That means a lot to me.'

'Right, shopping to celebrate! My treat and no limit to what we spend!'

'Sounds good!'

'Let's go!'

With that Sally ran out of the room waving her arms and whooping in delight. She found Alfred and ordered a car to take them into the city to celebrate her friend's love and new engagement.

*

After the trip to New York David's life was never the same. His work varied from being his new boss's administration assistant to attending high level business meetings, all the while he watched and learned from Mr. Gallagher.

Sally and Michelle both studied at Oxford, Michelle reading Law, Sally studying Physics. Both of them kept their respective relationships strong through hard work from all parties. When Michelle was not studying, she was planning her wedding which was due to take place in the summer of their graduation year, and when they both graduated with Firsts their excitement built. Sally had obtained a position with an airline on a pilot scheme and Michelle had gained a position at a top law firm. Both were due to start in the autumn of that year so that meant they had a full summer to relax and enjoy their time together.

Sally was now twenty-one and her beauty was at its zenith. That summer she looked radiant. Her life was perfect. She had a handsome boyfriend, her best friend was due to be married in the summer and she had landed a modelling contract with one of the best agencies in the country.

At first her modelling jobs were mainly adverts in the body of some of the magazines, but then she started to get cover work. It was not too long before her natural beauty was recognised and she was soon on the front cover of Cosmopolitan and Vogue. And the offers of work kept flowing in. She was offered large amounts of money to do catwalk modelling, television commercials and even a few movie offers, but she did not want the hassle or the fame.

Instead she did the occasional shoot for the magazines just to give herself a small feeling of independence from her father. Any money she did earn she invested so she could contribute to her own wedding and university fees for her children. David had not yet asked her to marry him but her twenty-first birthday ball was approaching and she thought something would happen then. If it did not, she would have to start dropping more unsubtle hints.

Life had rolled on perfectly for all of them, until the summer of Sally's twenty-first birthday.

Chapter 41

It was a beautifully perfect day that summer when the four of them met in the city centre for the final fitting of their outfits for the wedding. Sally and David were maid of honour and best man respectively and they were fitted out for the last time in one of the top wedding shops in the city. Michelle and Simon had to attend separately of course so Simon did not see the dress. After he had visited the exclusive wedding shop he waited in a bar with David while Sally attended with Michelle.

'Do you know who that druggie is who keeps staring at us?' David asked of Simon.

'Nope mate. Never seen her before in my life.'

Simon had though, but her drug ravaged body and face had changed so much since the day he last saw her when she was being escorted out of a department store.

'Well I think she knows us. She hasn't taken her eyes off us since we sat down.'

'Ignore her mate. I'm sure she'll crawl back to whatever sewer she crawled out of.'

'How do they get the money to come and sit in a bar and drink?' David queried.

'I have no idea.'

Sarah was not there to drink though. She had been walking out of an alley when she saw Michelle walk past with another woman by her side and then they were greeted by two handsome men who had stepped out of a wedding shop. She darted back into the alley, peering around the wall, and saw the two women walk into the wedding shop and the two men walk into a bar. Thinking that this was too much of an opportunity to miss, she knew she would not be welcome in the shop though, so she followed the men into the bar, guessing correctly that the women would follow shortly.

'Here they are! My beautiful bride to be and her maid of honour!' After curtseying Michelle sat down next to Simon, taking his hand in hers, and Sally sat next to David giving him a kiss in welcome.

'How's the dress?' Simon asked.

'It's perfect! It fits like a dream!' Sally replied eagerly.

'It doesn't! I look fat!'

'You don't look fat, you look amazing!'

'I can't wait to see you. I can't believe it is only one week away now.' Simon shook his head in seeming bewilderment. 'The time has gone by so quickly...'

'You getting married then Michelle?'

Everyone jumped and turned to look at the woman that stood next to their table.

'Do you know her Michelle?' asked Simon to which she shook her head firmly in the negative. 'I'm sorry, do we know you?'

'You don't recognise me Michelle, your so called friend?'

'No sorry, I don't.'

'How about if I said, Michelle, you are a fat little porker who used to waddle around school. Bring back any memories?'

'Now I don't know who the hell you think you are...'

'It's okay Simon. I'll handle this.'

For a few more moments she studied the face in front of her. She looked about forty, at least. Her face was wrinkled, like old tree bark. When she spoke, Michelle had noticed that she had barely any teeth, and those that were still present were black and rotting. It was the eyes that got Michelle though, those haunted drug taker's eyes, with bags and black circles underneath them and it was the eyes that finally triggered a memory in her mind. It had been years since she had seen her last, and the woman who stood before her now was a shell of the woman she had known then. 'Sarah, is that you?'

'Bingo! We have a winner! And here's your prize, a bacon sandwich and a lump of lard to add to the lard you carry around in your knickers everyday!'

'My God Sarah, what happened to you?'

'Why? What's up? Do you not think I'm pretty?'

'You're pretty sick,' muttered Simon.

'So who's the lucky guy who's going to be sticking his cock into this lump of fat for the rest of his life?'

'Right, that's it...'

Simon made to stand but Michelle lightly placed a hand on his arm to stop him. 'Simon, please. We don't need to lower ourselves to her level. That's what she wants. Sarah, what do you want? Do you want some cash? I'm sure we could scrape together the cost of a few hits of heroin for you if you like?'

'Oh no Michelle. H is old school. Crystal meth is the new black now Michelle. I'm a meth addict and look what it's done to me. Do you not think it has made me pretty?'

'No, not really Sarah. I think it has made you evil. I think you need help. Why don't you come with me now and I'll get you booked into a rehabilitation clinic...'

'You will do nothing of the sort!'

'Simon, please be quiet. What do you think Sarah? I'll help you to help yourself.'

'I'd prefer to be taken into the toilets and given a good hard fucking by your friend there. Who is he? He's gorgeous!'

Sarah made to sit down next to David but with a firm hand Simon pushed her away. 'Go away before something happens that you will regret.'

But Sarah was not listening. Her eyes had fallen onto Sally who had remained motionless and silent in the corner of the seats, mentally restraining herself from intervening, knowing too well that Michelle could handle whatever this vile creature threw at her. 'I know you. I've seen your face, recently too. I know I'm gorgeous, but you make even me look like a hippo! Fuck me. That's it! Front cover of Vogue last week! Well look at me! Little Sarah is in the presence of modelling royalty! Can you get me some work there? I could easily go on the front cover. Get me some work, pleeeaaassseee!'

'The only work you'd get is licking the sewers clean,' retorted Sally.

'Fuck you slag. Can I shag your gorgeous boyfriend, fiancé perhaps? He hasn't been able to keep his eyes off me since I walked in. He wants his cock to slide into my tight vagina don't you honey?'

'Right, that really is IT!'

With speed Simon was up from his seat and he grabbed Sarah by one of her arms and twisted it up her back. Sarah though had lived on the street quite long enough now to deal with such an assault, so as quick and as lithe as a snake she had twisted out of Simon's grip and launched her own attack.

Her hands rained down towards Simon's face, trying to get her nails to scrape at his flesh. One or two of the blows landed, but they had no power, and after a few moments David had grabbed hold of both her arms. The women had also got up to help but for a split second Sarah got one hand free, and without anyone noticing slipped a translucent substance into David's drink.

Quickly she was brought back under control by the two men and they dragged her kicking and screaming to the door of the bar. Unceremoniously between them they swung her up in the air and dumped her in the gutter.

With a scream she leapt to her feet and ran at them with arms swinging and legs kicking but with ease the two men pushed her away. She lost her footing and with a hard fall she crashed back into the gutter but this time she did not get up because the wind had been knocked out of her.

For the first and last time in his life Simon spat at another human being as she lay on the floor, wheezing and gasping, and then they both turned to re-enter the bar.

'I think we'd better go,' stated Simon to the women. 'She's out of it now but I don't think she will be for long. Let's go out the back way.'

They all nodded their agreement and quickly finished their drinks. By the time David had got back to his drink the substance had totally dissolved. None the wiser he knocked his cola back in one.

*

They went for another drink in another bar to calm their nerves and they stayed there for a while, Michelle explaining to them what she knew about how Sarah's life had gone so badly wrong. With a sigh she said she'd had enough for today and wanted to go home but instead Sally invited them to her house for a meal and more drinks.

'You can stay over if you like? Let's not let that wicked woman ruin our day!'

'We'll come for the meal, but we'll see about staying over. Right now, I don't really feel in the mood. What happened to her?!'

'Michelle,' Simon took her hand and stroked it, 'don't worry about it. There is nothing you can do now, and there is nothing you could have done then. I remember her now and she was nothing but trouble back then. I remember she disappeared from college but I didn't give it much thought at the time. I thought good riddance and you should think that too. You've worked so hard; we all have, to have what we have now, to be so happy. If she'd done the same then who knows what she could have made of her life. Instead, she'll be dead in a couple of years whereas we have our lives stretching in front of us. Forget about her, and forget about her forever.'

'I suppose you're right. Thank you, Simon. Everything you say makes sense all the time, that's why I love you!' She kissed him, passionately. 'Shall we go then?'

'Come with me Simon. I'll show you what my new car can do!'

'Okay David. See you there then ladies!'

'Yeah, be careful.'

They walked to the cars and the women got in Sally's while the men got in David's new Audi. Through the city Sally followed David along the crowded streets, but once they reached the country roads that led to Sally's mansion, David pulled away quickly.

'Crikey. He's gone off quickly.'

'Don't worry.' replied Sally. 'He knows this road and he always drives quickly.'

'Yeah, but, he's out of sight already.'

'They'll be fine.'

'I hope so. He was going bloody quickly'

David indeed did know the road and he wanted to impress Simon with his new car. Simon was used to David driving fast, but today he seemed to be taking it to the extreme. Not once did he change gear below the red line and the Audi was literally screaming along the road. About a mile before a pair of s-bends that David intended to take at speed he suddenly started to feel very strange. As quick as a flash a cold sweat broke out of his forehead and his hands started shaking.

The drug that Sarah had slipped into his coke had taken its time to start to affect his body because he had orally ingested it, but when it did start to affect him the chemicals rushed through his body to his brain and took their hold before he was able to react.

His eyes rolled back in their sockets and he slumped over the steering wheel. Before Simon could grab the wheel they were off the road at the first right corner of the first s-bend. They bounced over a small grass verge and down the other side. Simon made a frantic grasp at the wheel but missed, and by then it was too late. With David unable to press the brakes the car hit a large, old oak tree at a tremendous speed.

*

'Sally, what's that up ahead?' Sally was taking her time with the drive and she was fiddling with the radio while Michelle was speaking. 'It looks like there's debris in the road.'

Sally grunted in acknowledgement and started to pay more attention expecting to find that something had fallen off one of the many farm tractors that used these roads. As they got closer though it was clear that it was debris off a car. Slowing down to a stop they both got out of the vehicle and saw the fresh tyre tracks going over the verge. Without saying anything, they both took a few steps up t he verge and looked down the other side.

'Oh my God Michelle, oh my fucking GOD!'

Screaming, Sally ran down the verge to the car but Michelle did not follow. It looked like it was not too badly damaged from the angle she was looking at it from. She was viewing it from the right hand side and the main shell of the car looked like it was intact and the numerous airbags had deployed which obscured her view through the car. She could see David though, and as she approached she heard him moan. 'David! David don't move, please don't move!'

She stuck her head through the side window that was down when they crashed, and moved the airbags off David. It was then that she realised all was not right with the car. 'Oh my God, where's the other half of the car!'

Length ways the car had been ripped in two straight down the middle. Frantically she looked around unable to see where the other half of the car was, and then she looked back up the hill to where Michelle had not moved. For some reason she seemed to be staring at a tree. 'Michelle? Michelle?! David, please don't move!'

At a fast run Sally moved back up to Michelle, stood next to her and followed her eyes. At the base of the large oak tree was a twisted, crumpled, crushed lump of metal that could not be described as resembling anything like a car.

'Sally, oh my God Sally...' whispered Michelle, her voice shaking.

'It's okay Michelle, it's okay! He would have been thrown clear!'

Ripping her eyes from the base of the tree she looked at Michelle who was shaking from head to toe and shaking her head from side to side. Slowly she raised her shaking hand and pointed. Sally quickly saw what Michelle was pointing at.

A solitary arm was lying on the ground and glinting in the sun, clearly visible around the wrist, was the watch Michelle had got Simon for his twenty-first birthday.

Without saying another word Michelle collapsed next to Sally in a dead faint.

Chapter 42

Simon's funeral took place on a Saturday, two weeks to the day after his wedding to Michelle should have occurred. For the first week Michelle had been in hospital on a strong sedative to calm her because every time she woke she was hysterical. After the week the doctors slowly brought her off the sedative and Sally was by her bedside to offer her support whenever she could be away from David's bedside.

He had got through the accident relatively unscathed considering the force of the impact. With cuts and bruises his most serious injury was a broken leg and a fractured wrist. The airbags and the fact that Simon's half of the car had taken all the impact spared him from more serious injury. For him though, like Michelle, the most serious injury was psychological.

The toxicology report had shown a high concentration of chemicals usually associated with the drug crystal meth in David's blood. Everybody of course remembered the encounter with Sarah and the blame for the crash was laid firmly at her feet, but the police had been unable to trace her.

David though was still taking full blame for the crash because he knew he was driving too fast. He had screamed at Sally one day that if he had been driving slower when the drug took its hold Simon would not have died. She stated once again it was not his fault but David became hysterical so the doctors had to sedate him again.

Later, the police spoke to David about the incident as he lay in hospital and when the questions turned to drugs one of Mr. Gallagher's top lawyers swiftly intervened stating that David had never shown any evidence of drug taking, not even a cigarette never mind such a vile substance as crystal meth and that the police had a name to follow up. Confronted by one of the best lawyers in the country whose reputation went before her, the police did not press the matter and David was formally exonerated of all blame for the crash.

This did not help him though. He stayed away from the funeral hiding behind the excuse that it would not be appropriate and it would upset Michelle and Simon's family. Michelle was relieved when Sally told her that he would not be coming, but she would of course be there to support her.

Michelle was relieved because she knew that if he saw him she would end up trying to kill him. In her heart and in her head the blame for her fiancé's death lay firmly with David for driving too fast and she knew that she would never be able to forgive him. Her opinions were never voiced to Sally but they were voiced openly to Simon's family.

But they were not concerned with attributing blame. All they cared about was the fact they had lost a loving son and that the driver had been illegally drugged by a crazed drug addict. That fact was enough for them; they did not want to ruin another young man's life by openly blaming him.

*

For the next few months David's physical wounds healed but his mental scarring did not. He slumped into a severe depression and nothing that Sally could do or say could bring him out of it. Despite numerous vacations to luxurious hotels and appointments with psychologists, David's depression seemed to deepen. Mr. Gallagher noticed it at work but did not do anything about it, deciding to give David whatever time he needed.

Sally did see a slight improvement but one day she walked in on him unannounced at work and caught him drinking from a bottle of whiskey at his desk. Furious she ripped it from his hand and smashed it against a wall where it left an inkblot pattern that a psychologist might have liked to analyse.

The argument raged for over an hour, which included David missing an important meeting, and he pleaded with her not to tell her father. When she had slowly calmed down she reluctantly agreed, knowing that if he lost the job he loved it could finish him off. She did clearly state that if she saw anymore evidence of him drinking that it would be the end of not only his job but also their relationship. So David invested in the strongest mouthwash he could find and carried on drinking.

The numerous private investigators they had hired to try and track down Sarah had so far turned up nothing. All the investigators came back with the same story, that the streets were awash with drugs and trying to find one drug addict out of so many was, well, it was needle in a haystack time.

Without this closure of justice that everybody craved for, David slumped even more into a severe depression. His drinking picked up and Sally suspected this, but in her heart she still loved him and supported him as best she could.

One day though, for the first time David came to work drunk. And not a little drunk either, a lot drunk. The first action he took that day was to swear at his secretary and make a lewd comment about the size of her breasts. The next action he took was to consult his calendar on his computer which showed him that he had a meeting with an important South Korean company about a huge contract that his boss had been negotiating for months. With a loud belch he reached into the bottom drawer of his desk and took a swig from a bottle of vodka. Wiping his hand across his mouth, he farted and then chuckled his way out of his office up to the boardroom.

As soon as he entered the room Mr. Gallagher knew there was something seriously wrong but the South Korean representatives were already present. Desperately he tried to make eye contact with James but he was deep in discussion with one of the Korean directors and before anyone could react David was introducing himself to the Chairman of the massive South Korean conglomerate that could have bought Mr. Gallagher's company at breakfast, Microsoft at lunch, Apple at dinner and Shell at coffee and mints.

'Pleased to meet you. And your name is?'

'Chairman Kim.'

'Chairman Kim. Well at least that's going to be easy to remember. Why are you all called Kim? It's like those fucking Indians; they're all called fucking Patel. Why is that? Well hello legs! And who do we have here?' Brushing past the Chairman who looked at Mr. Gallagher in total surprise, David sat next to a beautiful Korean woman. 'And what is your name? Hang on, let me fucking guess. Kim, right?'

'I'm sorry, but I find you very rude. Please apologise to Chairman Kim or this meeting will go no further.'

Without even bothering to turn round David lifted his hand and waved it in an arrogant fashion. 'Sorry Chairman. Didn't mean to be rude. Hey,' he then said, turning his attention back to the female executive, 'I'm not too keen on being here today. I know the manager of the Hilton who can get us the Presidential Suite right now. We could have a day and night there of some serious fun!'

With a look of total surprise she turned to look at the Chairman and then her eyes met Mr. Gallagher's. He had a look of horror on his face and they all heard him say, 'James, in the name of all that is holy get him out of here!'

James though had not needed any prompting. He was already at David's shoulder by the time Mr. Gallagher spoke and he gently laid a hand on his shoulder. 'David, why don't we go up to your office and we can talk about this?'

'Fuck you old man,' and he shook his hand off. 'I'm talking to this lovely lady. We're bonding, getting to know each other.' Now in a stage whisper from behind his hand he said, 'I think she kind of likes me.'

'David, please. Let's go and talk about this outside.' Again, very gently, he laid his hand on David's shoulder.

Quick as a flash David was up out of his seat and he pushed James hard and shouted, 'Stop fucking touching me!'

James went flying and crashed into the solid oak boardroom table and there was a crackling noise as five of his ribs cracked and snapped with one being pushed firmly inwards puncturing the delicate tissue of one of his lungs. Everyone let out a cry of astonishment and without saying another word David straightened his jacket and walked out of the room.

For a moment nobody moved, but then the Korean female executive leapt out of her seat and rushed over to James. 'I think you'd better call an ambulance, and quickly! He's hardly breathing and his pulse is faint. Quick, call an ambulance!'

Another member of the board called for an ambulance while Mr. Gallagher tended to James and made him as comfortable as he could. Soon the paramedics arrived and after they had stabilised him they carefully placed him on a stretcher, wheeling him out and down the elevator to the waiting ambulance.

Mr. Gallagher saw him down and then had an argument with himself about going to the hospital with James or going back upstairs and trying to calm the Koreans. Thinking about what James would have wanted him to do, he returned back to the boardroom only to be greeted with empty seats where the Koreans had been sitting and flustered members of his own board.

'I'm sorry Mr. Gallagher,' apologised one of his directors. 'I tried to stop them but they stormed out without saying a word.'

Also without saying a word Mr. Gallagher sat in his chair at the top of the table and discreetly snapped a pencil in two. He was beyond angry.

*

'James is lying in hospital with a collapsed lung which the ribs that David broke punctured. This is it Sally. I've supported him for as long as I can. He is no longer part of the family.'

Mr Gallagher had returned home not too soon after the Koreans had left and had called Sally up to his office in the mansion.

'What?! You can't possibly mean that, surely you can't?'

'I've paid for him to have the best psychologists money can buy and they have had no effect. He is not going to snap out of it!'

'So that's it. You're just going to abandon him?!'

'Yes, and so are you. I want you to break up with him.'

'You want me to do what?' Sally's voiced screeched. 'I don't think that is a decision you have the right to make!'

'As long as you live in my house with my ongoing support you will have nothing more to do with that man! If he had not been driving like a lunatic none of this would have happened!'

Before he could stop himself the words were out. Straight away he cursed himself but rallied instantly preparing for the onslaught that he knew was about to happen. But it did not come. Instead, across the face of the daughter he loved more than life itself, was a look of so much hurt he thought his heart would break. But he needed to snap her out of it, to get rid of this man who was like an anchor around the family and the company, dragging them down.

'I cannot believe you just said that.' Tears were now welling up in Sally's eyes.

'Oh wake up and smell the coffee Sally! Everyone blames him for Simon's death, everyone. Michelle does. Simon's family does.'

'They don't. It was Sarah's fault, everyone knows that.'

'No, what everyone knows is what everyone read in the police report which stated that to have such a catastrophic collision that actually ripped a car in two length ways, the car would have had to be travelling at over seventy miles per hour, maybe even over eighty. Eighty miles per hour on that narrow, twisty stretch of road. Eighty Sally, eighty. The police only let him off with my intervention. I only intervened because I thought he and you had suffered enough! If he'd just been driving at thirty or forty… Now you tell me who is to blame?'

'Sarah. He's a good driver it wouldn't have happened if she hadn't spiked his drink.'

'I don't care if he's Michael fucking Schumacher! He should not, should not,' he hammered his fist into the desk for emphasis, 'have been going at that crazy speed!'

'So you blame him?'

'Yes, as does everyone else. And now he's drunk in meetings and he's assaulted my best friend, a sixty year old man, putting him in hospital with fractured ribs and a punctured lung. He'll pull through, but the doctors say he's been lucky. Unsurprisingly that is not the kind of man I want my daughter to be associated with so you *will* break up from him.'

'No, I won't. He needs me.'

'No, he doesn't. He needs a five year one on one session with a psychologist in a padded room! Where are you going?'

'To see David.'

'At last you see sense!'

Sally had one hand on the door out of his office and she turned to look at him. The tears could not hide the fierce look of determination in her eyes. 'No, you misunderstand me. I'm going to see David to tell him that I'll be there for him, forever, and that we are going to get through this, together.'

She opened the door and made to exit the room but her father's voice stopped her. 'You step out of this room now in this manner and you can expect no more support from me. You'll no longer be allowed to live in my house. Your bank accounts that I am trustee of will be frozen which will leave you penniless. You need to realise the mistake you are making and the actions I take will make your life unbearable until the day he has nothing more to do with your life. Do you hear me?'

Without responding Sally stepped out of the room and gently closed the door behind her.

Chapter 43

She stepped across the threshold of the small flat and managed to avoid stepping on the mail that had been sitting there all day. With one hand full of bags of shopping and her heavily pregnant body hindering her even more, she managed to stoop and pick up the letters. Walking a few more steps she turned right and entered the kitchen which consisted of second hand appliances and battered old work surfaces.

Dumping the shopping on one of them she opened the letters and was not surprised that they were rejection of employment letters along with a couple of red utility bills. Without giving them another thought she dumped them all in the bin and took the few paces into the small living room where she lowered herself onto the settee with the faded upholstery and broken springs.

For a moment she contemplated the unshaven man sat in a scruffy old armchair staring at the television. His once slim body now had a beer belly and his once olive coloured skin was pale. He looked sad and scruffy and the beard on his face did nothing to detract from this look.

'Did you make it out to the job centre?'

'No.'

'Oh well, never mind. Maybe you can make it out tomorrow. I managed to get us some food with the last of the benefit money but that's it now until next week so we'll have to make it last as long as we can. I had a small modelling job today. Of course given my current condition it was for a facial product.'

'Yeah, I know. I'm trying to watch this.'

'But as I was leaving they received a call and said that tomorrow's shoot had been cancelled.'

'That's a shame. We can talk about it later. I'm watching this.'

But Sally knew they never would talk about it later. The stack of rejection letters was from modelling agencies refusing to represent her. Sally could not even get work at a supermarket stacking shelves. Everywhere she turned she saw the hand of her father hovering over her like a phantom. As promised he had thrown her out, frozen her bank accounts seemingly in the attempt to leave her destitute so she would come crawling back to him and beg for his forgiveness. But what her father did not know was that she still had the money she put away from modelling work but this had not lasted them long.

David was no help. Again her father's hand hovered over his life, but eventually David managed to get some labouring work for cash on a building site until he lost his temper with the foreman and hit him with a spade. Since that day David had rarely left the tiny flat that they were renting.

Over the following months their relationship had hit rock bottom. They had not made love since the day that David had got the job and was for once full of life. Unfortunately in their short lived happiness they had forgot to use birth control so Sally was now heavily pregnant with twins. Despite Sally's best attempts they had not made love for eight months since that night the twins were conceived and now David barely looked at her and rarely slept in their bed with her.

Now conversation was practically non-existent between them as he slumped further and further into a depression that he had not been able to get out of since Simon's death. And Sally was close to breaking point. She was at a loss as to how she could support him through this time in his life when he was not willing to support or help himself. Her last hope was the twins. If they did not snap him out of it nothing would and she might as well give up.

For the next month she tried everything to try and bond with David. She suggested going to the movies, walks in the park or even a trip to the seaside, but all suggestions were greeted with negative words or not even words, sometimes just negative grunts. Then one day as she was getting up out of bed her waters broke a week early.

Calmly she walked into the living room and asked David to take her to the hospital. In a moment that she thought she would never be able to forgive him for, he shook his head and pointed at the television. Instead Sally picked up the telephone and called the one person who had never let her down in the past, Michelle.

They had not spoken in a few months, and certainly neither of them had called each other. The last time they met was by accident on the high street in the town. The proceeding few months after Simon's death, Sally knew that Michelle was avoiding her, not answering her phone and not seeing her when Sally went around to her house.

That day on the high street Sally could not believe how much weight her friend had lost, how skinny and ill she looked. But even now, after so many months of not speaking to her Sally knew she had no option. David was no in fit state to help with anything never mind a woman entering labour so that left her only one option. Before she dialled Sally withheld her number and was relieved when Michelle answered.

'Hello?'

'Michelle, it's Sally.'

For a moment Sally thought Michelle had hung up straight away, but then in a reluctant voice like she was forcing herself Michelle said, 'Hi. You withheld your number.'

'I know. I needed to speak to you urgently.'

'What about?'

'My waters have broken.'

'Oh.'

'Can you give me a ride to the hospital?'

'Can David not take you? At least you've still got a partner who can run you around to places.'

The words struck Sally like a dagger. 'Please Michelle, I really need you.'

Over the phone Michelle then heard the words, 'I'm trying to watch the fucking television! Will you shut the fuck up whining at her?!' being shouted at Sally. Michelle then said, 'Can you not get a taxi?'

'I can't. I've got no money.'

Michelle could not stop the smile spreading across her face. 'You've got no money? Nothing? Even for a taxi journey?'

'They're coming a week early! I was going to take some money out of next week's benefits to take care of the taxi. I've just spent all my money on food and stuff for the babies in preparation for next week.'

'Benefits?' Another smile grew on Michelle's face.

'Please Michelle, I really need you now. I'm scared. I don't want to do this on my own.'

'Where are you?'

'At home.'

'I guessed that. Where is home now?'

Sally told her the address and Michelle told her she would be there in fifteen minutes. Quickly Sally went into her bedroom and threw some basic essentials into a bag and then perched on the edge of the bed.

After twenty minutes she heard the apartment buzzer and she took the bag and walked to the apartment door. On passing the lounge she looked in and David was still sat in his chair, sipping from a can of beer, staring at the television. With a tear in her eye Sally went down to Michelle to face her gloating looks.

*

'Come on Sally, you can do it! One more big push! Go on!'

With her face bright red and a thick sweat on her brow, Sally took the deepest breath of her life and pushed and pushed as hard as her exhausted body could manage.

'That's it! Well done! The head is out!'

Michelle hovered in the room in the background, now dressed in an appropriate hospital gown and cap, but even the gown could not hide how skinny and gaunt she had become.

Since her fiancé's death she had started her new job with a law firm but after numerous sick days off that culminated in two weeks absence she did not pass her probation period and was released by the company after only six months. When she received the news from her manager the psychological strain on her was too much and her anorexia got worse.

The depression she had entered after Simon's death and her low self-esteem of being slightly overweight contributed to her decline. After losing her job it got worse. Now she rarely ate, and when she did it was quickly followed by a trip to the toilet where she forced herself to vomit. So far she had managed to hide the condition from her parents who just put her weight loss down to the grieving process and that Michelle would recover given time, but she did not. Instead she got worse. Her withdrawal from previous friendships, including her close friendship with Sally, was another sign of this, but again her parents again put this down to grieving.

Now, as Michelle watched Sally give birth to new life, she started to feel sick. Her already pallid complexion was even paler and her sunken eyes watched as the midwife lifted the newborn baby girl, cleaned it with a towel and then slapped its bottom which caused it to start crying. Quickly the midwife studied the baby and when satisfied passed the baby girl to a nurse who placed her in a small crib. Then the midwife returned her attentions to Sally.

For a moment or two Sally was relieved and then the second baby started on its journey out of her body, but the passing of this second child was much easier for her. With another almighty effort she pushed the baby boy out of her and the midwife gave a whoop of delight and repeated the same process she had done with the baby girl.

Once the afterbirth had been passed and Sally was cleaned, the midwife lifted up the baby girl from her crib and passed her to Sally who cradled her in her left arm, and then received the boy in her right arm.

With a beaming smile the midwife said, 'And do we have any names yet?'

Sally's eyes were brimming with tears. 'Yes. The girl will be called Sophia after my mother, and the boy will be named after my father, Jacob.'

'Two beautiful names. Now I presume your family will be outside so I will call them in.'

'No, no-one will be there. It's just me and…' But as Sally looked up to find Michelle she realised she was no longer in the room.

After the birth of Jacob, Michelle had run from the room un-noticed, threw up in a toilet and was now making her way home trying to erase the vision of the two new additions to Sally's life and the vision that would haunt her for the rest of her life, the vision of Simon's arm lying in the grass.

*

Sally stayed in hospital for a week, enjoying tending to Sophia and Jacob, feeding and caring for them. By the time she was ready to leave her benefit payments had gone into her account so she was able to take a taxi home carrying the babies in each arm.

As she entered her apartment she dumped her bag in the hallway and entered the lounge and as expected David was sat there watching television. Sally stepped between him and the media device and showed him his children. 'The girl is Sophia, the boy is Jacob. Sophia, Jacob, this is your dad, David.'

'Get those two horrible little creatures out of my sight! Ugly little things.'

'You're going to have to help me! I can't bring them up on my own!'

'I'm watching television! Get them away!'

Unbelievably hurt, Sally walked out of the lounge and placed them gently in their cots. Sophia kicked her legs a little but Jacob did not wake from his slumber. Carefully Sally covered them both in a small blanket. Exhausted she collapsed in a chair next to the cots and it was not too long before she joined them in a deep sleep only to waken an hour or so later by their cries of hunger.

*

In the last month since Sally had brought his children home David had barely looked at them. He had never once fed them, and he had never once even touched them. They reminded him of better, happier times and he hated to even look at them.

One night though Sally was exhausted. She had been up all the previous night t as they would not settle at all and now, deep in the heart of the night, Sophia was crying but Sally did not wake up even when David shook her. Cursing, David wrapped the pillow around his head but could not get back to sleep while she cried and cried.

With another loud curse he got up and walked over to the cot where she was lying, kicking her tiny legs. As David leaned over the cot he made eye contact with her for the first time and with a few more kicks and cries she stopped crying. 'Thank fuck for that. Go to sleep now!'

He turned to return to his bed, but as soon as Sophia could not see David she started to cry again. With another curse he turned back and looked down on her, staring into her green eyes. With a gurgle and another kick, David was sure that she chuckled and smiled at him. Relieved again that she had stopped crying, he returned to bed. As soon as he had pulled the duvet back over him and closed his eyes the crying started again.

Now continually cursing David got up again and stormed over to the side of her cot. 'What? What do you want?!' Again, as soon as Sophia saw David she stopped crying. 'Right, what is wrong with you? I'm trying to sleep!'

Gurgling and kicking some more David looked down into those green eyes and his heart skipped a beat. 'Right, well, maybe you want some attention? If I give you some attention will you let me go to sleep? You're going to be a right one in eighteen years. How the hell do you pick up a baby?'

Placing a tentative arm under her legs and one under her head, he carefully lifted her up and placed her against his chest. Her big green eyes looked into his blue and again he was sure she smiled at him. Gently he rocked her in his arms and he walked over to the chair carefully lowering himself into it, reclining backwards. David rested her again against his chest, holding her firmly.

She was warm and he studied her tiny fingers and toes. As he lifted her hand with his index finger her own fingers wrapped round his finger with surprising strength and her eyes met his again. 'Has your mother been training you to break my heart?'

Looking into her emerald green eyes he saw them close briefly, and then with a struggle she opened them again to look into his eyes. They closed again, half opened and then closed as she fell quickly asleep. Rocking gently in the chair, her warmth and the feel of her body was comforting to David and it was not too long before his eyes started to droop and soon he was asleep with Sophia wrapped securely and firmly in his arms.

*

A ray of sunshine through the thin curtains struck Sally's face waking her from her sleep. When she opened her emerald eyes she was surprised to see David's side of the bed was empty. Rolling over to get out of bed her eyes saw David asleep in the chair with Sophia being cradled in his arms also fast asleep.

Rays of early morning sunshine were lighting them with an ethereal quality. As soon as she saw this sight before her, tears welled up in her eyes and she grabbed her cheap mobile phone off the bedside table. Even though it was cheap, the phone still had a camera function and she took a picture of David and Sophia, a picture that she would grow to treasure.

For an hour she lay in bed looking at the man she still loved with all her heart, cradling her beloved daughter. She noted how David's finger was being grasped by one of Sophia's hands and using the zoom function she took a photograph of this image. Unfortunately the perfect scene before her of father with child was broken shortly after by Jacob waking and starting to cry. His cries woke Sophia straight away and showing her indignation at being woken from such a deep slumber, she also burst into tears.

This woke David and his eyes met Sally's. She smiled at him, and for the first time in as long as Sally could remember, he smiled back at her. 'I think she got me at a moment of weakness.'

'So she's already a minx who can manipulate men however she wants to?'

'Looks like it.'

'Want to help me feed them?'

'I'll feed…' David stopped, unable to complete the sentence.

'The name of your daughter is Sophia. The name of your son is Jacob. Come through to the kitchen and you can make Sophia's bottle. You're holding her properly which is a good start I suppose.'

'I guessed.'

'Come on.'

Sally got out of bed and took the few steps to pick up Jacob who was now giving full voice and taking David's hand she led him through to the kitchen. Giving him precise instructions she helped him make Sophia's bottle while she made Jacob's and then they all returned to the bedroom where David sat back in the chair to feed Sophia and Sally perched on the bed feeding Jacob. All that day Sophia did not leave David's arms. He fed her again and changed her nappy a couple of times, cuddling her in his arms and not even turning on the television throughout the whole day.

At night, David wanted to sleep with Sophia in his arms again but Sally did not let him. 'No, I'm sorry David; she needs to sleep in the cot. She can't sleep in your arms every night because she'll get used to it and never be able to sleep on her own. If she wakes in the night feel free to tend to her and you can look after her tomorrow again.'

'I'll look forward to it.'

With a care that she had not seen in him for months, David lay his daughter in the cot and tucked the blankets around her. Standing over her he only left her side when she was sound asleep and then he got into bed with Sally. He was surprised when Sally draped an arm over him. It was the first show of affection either of them had shown to each other for months and months. 'Did you enjoy looking after your daughter?'

'She's got your eyes.'

'And Jacob has got your eyes.'

'Has he?'

'Yes. It would be good if you spent some time with him too.'

'I might. Sophia has got me wrapped round her little finger at the moment.'

'I can't tell you how happy I am to see you as happy as you've been today.'

'I've enjoyed it. I'll look forward to caring for her more.'

'Good. Night honey.' Sally gave him a light kiss on his cheek and then rolled over and switched off the bedside lamp.

David did not sleep much that night. Instead he did a lot of thinking.

The first subject he could not help thinking about as he saw the duvet bulging over his belly was how much weight he had put on. Then his thoughts turned to Sophia, and now also Jacob slipped into them.

The last year since the accident had been the hardest of his life. Knowing and living with the fact that his driving had killed his best friend and ruined Michelle's and Sally's lives had been eating him from the inside. The only way he could cope was to ignore everyone and drink until drunk every day, staring at the television. He had not thought until now about how Sally had supported him, how much love and effort she had given him in his time of need and how horribly he had treated her. And now he had two children that needed caring for.

Even now, even though he had rejected the babies outright, Sally had still stood by him. What kind of person did she have to be in order to do that? How could she still love him so much despite the way he had been acting? These thoughts raced and crashed through his head all night, and even when he tended to Sophia when she woke he carried on thinking about the mess he was in.

As he stood over her cot, he glanced over at his son, and his heart missed a beat as tears started to brim in his eyes. It was then that he made his decision to straighten out his life and the lives of his family once and for all.

*

When Sally woke because the babies were crying she was again surprised to see that David was not in bed. Glancing at the clock she saw it was eight in the morning and she stood up out of bed to tend to the children. When they had settled she quickly looked through the apartment for David and was concerned when all the rooms were empty.

For the rest of the morning she anxiously looked after the babies and it was only in the early afternoon that she heard the door to the apartment open and David walked into the lounge. He ignored Sally at first and walked over to where Sophia was lying in her cot. He bent over and kissed her forehead and then he touched Jacob's cheek as he turned to look at Sally.

'Where have you been? I've been worried.'

'Sorry, but I didn't want to wake you when I left. I've been to the job centre and then to a job interview.'

'A job interview?' Sally's surprise clearly showed on her face.

'Yeah, a job interview. I'm not completely useless you know.'

'I didn't say you were. And?'

'Well, I got it!'

'You got it?! Wow! Fantastic!' She ran across the room and threw her arms around him, giving him a big hug.

'Well don't get too excited. It's only labouring on a site, minimum wage.'

'I don't care! It's a start! I'm so happy for you!'
'I gave a different name.'
'Oh. Why?'
'Your dad. Hopefully he won't find out about it.'
'Yeah, of course. Sorry you have to do that.'
'It's okay. They pay cash so it's not like I'm going to be getting cheques made out in this other name.'
'Sounds perfect. I'm so happy for you!' She hugged him tighter and Sophia did not like this at all. While they were hugging she screwed up her eyes and burst into tears, crying as loud as they had ever heard her cry. 'Oh my! She's jealous of me!'

Quickly David bent down and scooped her into his arms and almost instantly she stopped crying and snuggled her head against his chest. 'You know something, I think she is!'

'Looks like I've got some pretty serious competition!' Sally exclaimed.
'Very serious.'

Sally picked up Jacob and cuddled him against her bosom and then she said, 'You've never held him before. Do you want to?'

'Yeah, I suppose, if our little princess will let me!'
'Well, we'll try.'

Carefully they exchanged children and David held his son for the first time. 'He has got my eyes.'

'Told you.'

'He's got your nose though, and Sophia has got your everything!'

Sally laughed and they both sat down on the battered old sofa and cuddled the children, swapping them occasionally. They stayed like this for hours with David, after all his trauma and mental anguish, at last getting to know his children. At last, they were a family.

Chapter 44

'Why?! Why did you do this?! Why can't you just leave us alone and let us get on with our lives in peace?!'

For the first time in five years Sally was in her father's office at the mansion. The years had aged him greatly Sally noticed, and from the brief word she had managed with James before she entered his office, he mourned greatly for the daughter he had lost. James informed her that he would do anything to have her back in his life, but he was also stubborn, a stubborn bitter man who refused to back down on the promise he had made to Sally.

For three years since obtaining the labouring job David had worked solidly, never taking a sick day off and only taking a day off when the sites he worked on closed for bank holidays. His managers noticed his work ethic and realised that he also had a good head on his shoulders. It was not long before he was promoted to foreman and excelling in this position he was moved up the ladder to become Site Manager.

Even though Mr. Gallagher did not want his daughter back in his life with David, his network of informants made sure he was aware of every move either of them made. After discovering that David was now Site Manager, Mr. Gallagher made some phone calls despite the pleas of James to stop him ruining his daughter's life again.

Once the phone calls had been made, he opened his safe in the office and took out a file which had the name Simon scrawled across it. He opened the file and removed two photographs from the stack of photographs within it. One was a picture of the full crash site, and another was a close-up of Simon's severed arm lying in the grass.

On an envelope he wrote David's name and address and then placed the two photographs in the envelope. His secretary was informed to post the letter first class and David received the envelope containing the pictures on the morning he returned home from work after finding out he had lost his job.

'I did this because I want my daughter back.'

'You could have me back if you just accepted David's mistake, forgave him and welcomed us both back into your life!'

'As I told you those years ago, I do not want that man in my family and until you see sense I will continue to make your lives a misery!'

'You know something daddy, I nearly called you a couple of months ago. Our lives were going well. Our twins are now four and about to start school…'

'I know.'

'Yeah, you would. David had a good job. Thanks to you continually watching over me with your spies I still couldn't get a job but we were getting by. And now I'm glad I didn't call because you have just become a bitter, evil, twisted old man!'

'And it is your fault that I have become this.'

'No, it's your fault daddy. If you'd just forgiven him.'

'Never.'

'And why did you wait so long before getting David sacked? Why not get him sacked after his first day like you usually did? Did you want to give him hope that you'd forgotten about us so you could bring our lives crashing down again at your convenience?'

'My grandchildren.'

'Your what?!' Sally's voice screeched. 'Your WHAT?! Believe me when I say that they will never, ever be your grandchildren!'

'I did not want my grandchildren to suffer during their critical early years. It is still my hope that one day you will see sense and come back to me and when you do I want my heirs to be fit and healthy.'

'Now they are your heirs?! Not only have you become a bitter, evil, twisted old man you've also become delusional!'

'Have you seen Michelle recently?'

For a moment Sally was surprised but she managed to compose a reply. 'Not for years. How does she fit into this?'

'She's dying.'

'Pardon me?'

'She's dying. She never recovered from losing Simon, never recovered from losing him in that way. Seeing your fiancé's severed arm lying in the grass can really destroy someone's life. She became severely anorexic and now the doctors have said there is nothing they can do. I've heard from my sources she has only days to live, if that.'

Sally slumped into a chair in front of his desk. 'I had no idea.'

'Yes, I know you don't. If you'd only supported her as much as you did David perhaps she would have pulled through.'

'Don't you dare try to blame me for this. Don't you dare! I tried my hardest to support her but she cut me off...'

'Do you blame her? After all, you still insisted on being with the man who had killed her fiancé. Not exactly the greatest foundation for a friendship is it?'

'Are you done? Anything else you'd like to blame David or me for?'

'I think I'm done, but depending on how long you're planning on staying for I'm sure I could think of something else.'

'For the last and final time it wasn't his fault!'

'Oh yes, it was this mystical Sarah's fault. For the last few years I've had private investigators combing the country trying to find her. Ex-police detectives and a couple of ex-members of MI5 and nothing. I've had people camped outside any address that I could find a record of her living at and she has never once returned to those addresses. It's like she never existed. Funny that.'

'So now you're saying that Sarah doesn't exist? I think you need to speak to Michelle again about that.'

'Yes, Michelle's testimony certainly helped save David. How much did you pay her to go along with that story?'

'My God. How can you say that? What's happened to you?'

'No Sally. The question you should be asking is what happened to you? You abandoned your best and closest friend in her darkest hour, and you abandoned me, the loving father who gave you everything you ever needed or wanted, who raised you as a father and a mother.' His voice broke as he finished the sentence.

Sally looked up at him and noticed the tears rolling down his face. 'You broke my heart the day you left, you broke my heart and I'll never, ever be able to forgive you for that, and I'll never, ever be able to forgive David for the pain he has caused. Please, leave now.'

'And I'll never, ever be able to forgive you for the pain you've caused me. With one phone call and one letter you've ruined our lives again, your only daughter. David is slumped in his armchair drinking again; I can't work because every time I apply for something you stop it. There is no point even attempting to change my identity because you'd find me. Our lives were back together. We were a family. We were happy.'

'I think you need to speak to your dying friend about ruined lives and happiness. She's in a room off ward six at St. Katherine's. Go and see her. I have. Then you'll know about ruined lives! Now get out, get out, get out and never, ever return to this house! Get OUT!'

Sally burst into tears and ran out of the room, past James who tried to speak to her, and down to her old car that she had managed to save up and buy. Quickly she drove down the long driveway, past the lake and the island where her mother was buried and out through the gates.

*

Sally walked along the corridor off ward six at St. Katherine's until she found the room with Michelle's name scrawled on a whiteboard attached to the door. Hesitantly she stepped away from the door and then with a deep breath she approached it and looked through the window.

Through the gloomy light Sally saw a human form with a single sheet thrown over. The form was skeletal and could hardly be recognised as a woman. From this distance the person in the bed looked like they were asleep so careful to not make a noise she opened the door and entered the room.

The first thing that struck her as she entered was the amount of machines in the room, all of them whirring and clicking, doing whatever they needed to do. Sally did not need to be a doctor to know that these machines were keeping Michelle alive. As she approached the bed she stopped and studied her friend.

Her eyes were drawn first to Michelle's hair. Her hair was not just thin; she was practically bald with a few wispy strands of hair covering her scalp. The skin of her face looked dry and pallid; her eyes looked like they had collapsed into her head. It was clear that her lips were also dry, they were cracked and broken. One arm was out from under the sheet and Sally noticed bruises, a lot of bruises, dotted up and down her lower and upper arm. Then Sally's eyes looked at Michelle's body.

There was no trace of breasts bulging the sheet, instead what bulged the sheet were Michelle's ribs, Sally could see each individual one, and her sharp hips were also protruding into the sheet. Her once voluptuous body did not have flesh on it, she was purely skin and bones and nothing else.

Not wanting to wake her, Sally was about to leave when suddenly, but slowly, Michelle turned her head. For the rest of her life Sally did not forget the sounds of Michelle's joints creaking and cracking as she moved so very slowly and gently. Sally would also never forget the look in her once sparkling eyes as she opened them and looked into Sally's sparkling green eyes.

Michelle seemed to try to take a breath which she struggled to do, and when she did the sound made Sally want to run screaming out of the room. The single breath rasped and rattled around the room as Michelle made a desperate attempt to suck oxygen into her frail body. When she spoke her voice was faint and crackly so Sally had to take a step closer to hear her. She wished she had not. As Michelle said the first words to her in years Sally smelled her breath and it smelled of death.

'Why… are… you… here?' Michelle spoke the sentence hesitantly, pausing over every word.

'I came to see you.'

If she had physically been able to Michelle would have laughed but instead she stared at Sally with venom of pure hate in her eyes. 'I… don't… want to see… you.'

'I came, I came…' And for a moment Sally could not think of why she had come to see her dying friend. 'I came to see if there was anything I could do for you…' The words she spoke trailed off as she realised the emptiness of them even as she spoke them.

Now Michelle did laugh; a bitter, hollow, rasping, coughing, spluttering laugh that had Sally reaching for the emergency button to call a nurse. But Michelle managed to bring herself back under control and took a few more deep breaths that caused Sally to think of graves when Michelle's expelled air was sucked into Sally's nose.

'You came here to see… And what the… hell can you do for… me? A bit late don't you think?' Michelle started to cough as she finished speaking, and with a great effort she reached for a tissue by her side and spat a blood stained glob into it.

'I'm so sorry Michelle. I had no idea you were so sick.'

'And why is that?'

'Why is what?'

'Don't be… thick Sally. You had no idea I was sick because you… have not spoken to me… or my family… for years. You abandoned me for that murdering bastard!' Michelle coughed again, her body now curling up being racked with pain. Eventually she stopped and her eyes bore into Sally's again.

'He, David, didn't murder anyone. It was a tragic accident.'

'It was no accident!' She shook her head from side to side causing Sally's stomach to flop over again as she listened to her joints groaning and creaking. 'He was driving like a… lunatic! If he'd been driving at thirty instead of eighty… Simon would still be alive!'

Now at a whisper Michelle said the words that would haunt Sally for the rest of her life, her breath rasping the words out, and the stench of the words would also stay with her forever. In a haunting, crackling, rasping whisper Michelle said, 'Why… why did you not drive with David that day? Why was it Simon's arm lying in the grass when it should have been yours?' Michelle saw the look of intense pain in Sally's eyes and she enjoyed the pain she was causing her.

'You can't, you can't mean that?' Tears now brimming in her emerald eyes.

'My life was ruined that day… and now… and now I hope that yours is ruined too. The girl who had everything…, now I hope you forever have nothing. I curse you Sally with all the soul that is still left in my body! I curse you to a life of misery…, a life full of pain, suffering and misery so then you'll have a small idea of what my life has been like since you chose him over me, since you abandoned me. I curse you Sally, and your children, with all my broken heart and broken soul I curse you for eternity!' The last word was a rattle of death as Michelle forced it out of body. For the second time that day Sally burst into tears and ran from a room.

Michelle though simply closed her eyes; at last at peace now that she had said to Sally what she had wanted to say to her for years. As she closed her eyes a warning buzzer went off on the blood pressure machine as her pressure sank to a dangerously low level. This buzzer caused a warning light to go off on the nurse's station in ward six but by the time the nurses got there it was too late.

As Michelle closed her eyes she saw Simon stood in front of her, a heavenly glow radiating around him. He was dressed how she remembered him best, the night he proposed to her. Smiling at her, with a single finger he beckoned her towards him. With a smile of her own she took a couple of steps towards him as he started to walk away. So she followed him, catching him up, taking his hand as they entered what was waiting for them through a bright circle of light.

*

Nobody ever knew about Sally's visit to Michelle that day. Sally never told anybody and she did not believe that anybody could truly curse another person. But through the dark days that were rapidly approaching the words would haunt Sally, and they would haunt her for the rest of her life.

Chapter 45

He noticed her for the first time as she was walking along the high street in t own. Her long black hair cascaded down her back and he nearly crashed his Ferrari as he watch her tight bum in the tight jeans wiggle along in front of him. Slowing right down he passed her and looked in his rear view mirror. Her face was unbelievably beautiful and considering she was holding hands with two children her figure was still amazing.

Quickly he floored the Ferrari, racing down the high street until he came to a roundabout which he quickly negotiated and then raced back up the high street f rantically looking for a car park space. Giving up he left the car in a disabled space and dashed back along the street to find the woman. Cursing he realised he had lost her so he frantically backtracked and started to look through the windows of shops near where he had seen her. Cursing even more he looked into a bank and found her stood in the queue.

In a flash he had entered the bank and barged an elderly lady out of the way so he could be next to her in the queue. As he stood behind her he admired her bum, her long slim legs and the shine of her black hair. He listened as she chatted to the two young children, both of them about seven years old, and he realised that they were twins. With a shout of glee in his head he did not see a wedding or engagement ring but that would not have stopped him anyway. They reached the end of the queue and she went to a cashier and he went to the one next to her.

He did not bank there so he asked for an interest rate leaflet and chatted to the cashier about the accounts. But he was not really listening to his replies. All his attention was on listening to the mother next to him as she discussed the accounts with the young children.

Apparently the young boy was not impressed that his sister had more money but the mother delicately reminded him that he had taken some money out to buy a toy the previous month. The boy shrugged his shoulders as he accepted this explanation and then the girl commented that in a few more months she would have a hundred pounds. She announced proudly to the cashier, hesitating as she worked out that she now had ninety-five pounds in her account. This was too much of an opportunity for him to miss.

'So, that means you're how much short of one hundred?'

The mother jumped as the man started to speak to her daughter and she laid a protective hand on her shoulder. But the man looked harmless enough, in fact he look more than harmless, he was in fact good looking with a deep tan and he was dressed immaculately.

The man was very impressed when almost straight away the young girl replied, 'Five pounds.'

'Yes, well done! And I'll tell you what I'll do. Considering you're so good at maths and you obviously work hard at school I'll give you five pounds.'

Excited the girl nodded eagerly and the man offered her a five pound note.

'No, honestly, it's okay, you don't need to do that.'

For the first time he made eye contact with the mother and his heart skipped a beat as he looked into her green eyes that were shining like emeralds. 'Really,

I insist. I don't know much about kids, but she seems very intelligent?'

'Thank you, but it's okay.'

'I want the five pounds mummy!'

'She's going to be a right one in a few years!'

'She a right one now. Okay then, but keep in mind you need to be careful approaching children and offering them money. Doing stuff like that can get a man a reputation.'

'I didn't really think of it like that. Right then my little darling,' he said, turning his attention back to the girl, 'here you go. Pass it to the cashier.'

Eagerly she snatched the money from the man's eyes and he thought his heart would melt as he watched the mother roll her eyes and snatch the money back from her daughter and gave it back to the man. 'You know better than that young lady! Don't snatch and say thank you!'

'Sorry mummy. Thank you sir. This is very kind of you.'

Gently this time she took the note and offered it to the cashier, stretching up on her tip-toes. The mother smiled at the man as her daughter took the savings book back from the cashier, who smiled back at her and he walked with her out of the bank, the woman calling her son to her side as they exited.

The two children scampered off a short distance ahead, the mother keeping a sharp eye on them as they walked. 'That was a really nice thing you did back there. I think you've got a friend for life now.'

'Thank you. I was hoping you wouldn't mind.'

'Well, usually I would. You have to be careful these days, but you seem harmless enough.'

'Thank you again.'

They approached his Ferrari and as they did the children ran back to their mother and took a hand each. 'Erm, this is me.' He could not help noticing the flash across her eyes as she realised that the man she had been speaking to was clearly rich.

'It was nice to meet you,' said the woman.

'You too.'

'What do you say to the nice man?'

'Thank you.'

'Hey, erm, would you like to go for a coffee sometime?' the man asked. 'I mean, I know you don't know me but it would give us chance to get to know each other if you like?'

'Erm, sure.'

'Well, here's my card. Give me a call when you would like to meet.'

'I will.'

'What's your name so I know it's you when you call?'

'My name is Sally.'

'Well, nice to meet you Sally. My name is Peter, Peter Johnson. Please, give me a call sometime.'

'I will, definitely.'

'Bye then.'

'Bye.'

He offered his hand to shake which she accepted, liking the feel of his firm handshake, he liking the feel of her soft, gentle hand, and then he got into the Ferrari and with a wave he raced off with a roar down the high street.

*

Sally lay in bed alone, rotating the business card through her fingers, studying the gold embossed writing. Peter Johnson the card said, just that, with a mobile number written under his name. Nothing else. No company name, no address, no title.

It was the morning after she had met him. The twins had already been taken to school and now she lay alone in bed thinking about how handsome he was, how nice he had been to her children, how smartly dressed he was and how he was clearly wealthy with his brand new Ferrari.

Sally ran the card through her fingers some more, and thought about the man in the lounge who was no doubt sipping from a can of beer watching some rubbish on television, resting the beer on his huge belly as he ate crisps or ordered some takeaway pizza.

All she wanted, all she truly wanted was her partner back, her true partner though, not the fat, horrible slob in the living room who showed no love or affection to her or his children. She knew that hidden inside that horrible body was the David she had fallen in love with but he seemed now to be forever lost to her. He had never recovered from the setback her father created and she knew that he blamed her for it. Even the children could not bring him round.

For months the children, especially Sophia, were confused about the swift change that had overcome their father and for months she tried to coax them into David's life. She gave up though one day after David had pushed Sophia over when she walked in front of the television and David missed a goal being scored. From that day, as much as possible she kept the children away from him, enrolling them in as many free afterschool activities that she could find to keep them away from home.

Now as she lay on the bed she longed for a real man to enter her life, someone who could support her and the children, someone who cared for and loved them. In her heart she knew that she should have left him ages ago, but for the sake of the children she forever hoped that eventually he would get better and out of the self-destructive cycle he was in.

She had no friends, no social life and could not get a job so she never met anyone, but this chance encounter had occurred with the good looking wealthy man and a strong part of her told her she would be crazy to pass up on this opportunity.

From the living room she heard David call her name but she ignored him at first and only responded to his shouts when he started to swear. Fearing the neighbours would hear him, she walked quickly into the room where he sat in the arm chair munching last night's left over chicken.

'Get me a beer.'

'David, it's barely past eight in the morning. Do you not think it's a little earl y...'

'Shut up nagging me and get me a beer!'

'Get it yourself!'

Sally tried to walk away but he grabbed her wrist and started to squeeze and twist it. 'Get me a fucking beer or I'll snap you arm off, shred it and feed it to your precious kids!'

'You're sick and they're your kids too!'

'No, they're not. Get me a beer NOW!'

For some peace and quiet Sally nodded and David released her wrist. She got him the requested beer and then returned to her bedroom and cried silently into her pillow. Slowly she managed to get control of herself and as she sat up her eyes landed on the business card which she had thrown onto the bed when she went in to see David. Quickly she picked it up, grabbed her mobile and dialled the number.

'Yes?'

'Hello? Is that Peter?'

'Yes. Who is this?'

'Erm, it's Sally. I don't suppose you remember me from…'

'Ah Sally!' His voice noticeably brightened. 'Of course I remember you. How are you?'

'Fine thanks. Erm, I was wondering if you'd like to meet for that coffee?'

'Yes, of course I would. I'm a bit busy this morning. How about this afternoon?'

'Sounds perfect, but it would have to be before three though.'

'Not a problem. Shall we say one at Starbucks on Church Street?'

'I know it. I'll be there.'

'Perfect. See you then. Bye.'

'Bye Peter.'

With a sigh Sally lay the phone and the card on the bed next to her and contemplated what she was about to do. The one thing she always said she would never do she was contemplating doing. She had decided long ago to support and show her love to David no matter what, but he had changed, he had changed beyond all recognition and he was no longer the David she had fallen in love with. And now this man, this Peter, had entered her life seemingly by chance, and she had to think of the children. She could not continue to bring them up with this aggressive drunk in their lives, something had to change.

For the next couple of hours she stayed in the bedroom only leaving the room to fetch David a couple more beers. At eleven thirty she started to get ready. She searched through her wardrobe of supermarket clothes looking for anything even remotely sexy. Eventually she found a short pink skirt that she put on only to find that it barely covered her knickers and she decided that she looked like a prostitute, a cheap prostitute at that. As she removed the skirt she caught a glance of herself in the mirror and she stood to look at her body.

Considering she had given birth to two children and was now closer to thirty than twenty being that she was now twenty-eight, she still looked astonishingly beautiful. Unable to afford the best moisturisers or beauty products a few lines w ere starting to appear on her face and at the corner of her eyes, yet her eyes still sparkled like emeralds.

Sally's eyes made their way down her body she grabbed hold of one of her breasts and pushed it up. When she released it barely moved down at all, still firm and full. Turning she looked at her round tight bottom, which she thought was starting to droop a little, but Peter was not the only man to have nearly crashed their car when they saw her behind wiggling down the street in town wrapped in tight denim. Over the years her legs had filled out as had her hips and waist, but she still had a slim and slender figure. With ease she could have still made it onto the front cover of Vogue, but her father still put a stop to any attempt she made at obtaining any kind of work.

Making a decision she decided to dress like who she now was, a mummy going for a coffee with an acquaintance. So she opted for a simple white t-shirt, over which she placed a small cardigan, and a simple pair of jeans. Quietly she walked into the bathroom and applied a little makeup, a touch of rouge to the lips and squirt of perfume to her neck. She knew that she could have dressed better with a thousand pounds to spend, but she decided that what she was wearing now would have to do.

When she opened the bathroom door she jumped because David was directly outside the door leaning on the wall. 'Where are you going?'

This surprised Sally. For as long as she could remember he had not shown any interest in where she was going or who she was seeing. Why was he asking today of all days? 'Out. Why are you bothered?'

'I'm not. Do you usually put makeup and perfume on if you're just going out? Got a date?'

'No. Even if you don't love me anymore I still love you.'

'Whatever. Can I use the bathroom now?'

'Of course. I'll be gone by the time you come out.'

'Good.'

David brushed past her and closed the bathroom door behind him. Now happy that he was just waiting outside the bathroom to use it not to see her, she left the apartment and started to walk into the town. The old car she had managed to buy had long since been scrapped so now the only means of transport she had was the bus or to walk. She wanted to put a little extra into the children's savings account this week if possible and as the weather was nice she was trying to walk as much as possible.

For the first time in as long as she could remember, as she walked through the streets she listened to the birds singing and she breathed in the early autumn air deeply. Occasionally in quiet moments like this she reflected on how her life had changed since that fateful day seven years ago. Although a part of her wanted her old life back, the money, the riches, the privileges, another part of her was quite content. The last few years had made her stronger, they had made her fight for survival and now that she had set herself on a course of action to rid herself of the one last thing from that old life there was almost a skip to her step.

It took her half an hour to walk into the town and she arrived at the coffee shop fifteen minutes before he was due but she still went in. Before she sat down s he went to the toilet to run a comb through her black hair and make sure she looked as attractive as possible. She succeeded, and although she did not notice, as she made her way to a seat near the window, every man in the shop turned to look at her, a couple of them being spotted by their partners to which they received a telling off.

At nearly one Sally heard before she saw the Ferrari as it roared up the street and parked quickly in a space a little down the road from where Sally waited. Nervously she waited and watched the doors looking for him to enter then she spotted him. He stood in the doorway to the shop and removed his sunglasses then adjusted the jumper that been draped casually over his shoulders. The top buttons of his shirt were undone showing a muscular, firm chest and Sally could not help herself as she dropped her eyes down his slim body to the area of his crotch. She ran her hand through her hair, wriggled in her seat and crossed her legs even tighter as he spotted her, smiled, and weaved his way through the tables. As he approached her heart skipped a beat as she realised that he was actually more handsome than she remembered and he smiled again showing perfect white teeth as he arrived next to the table.

'Hi. Nice to see you again.' He offered his hand which Sally lightly accepted and he sat down in the chair opposite her. 'How are you?'

'I'm fine Peter, thank you. And you?'

'Yep, I'm good. Damn it's good to see you again. I didn't expect you to call at all, but I was happy, very happy when you did.'

'Well it's not very often I receive a guy's number nowadays.'

'Now I find that very hard to believe. Have you ordered anything?'

'No, I was waiting for you.'

'What would you like then?'

'A latte please.' Sally made to get her purse out of her small handbag but Peter shook his head.

'No, honestly, I insist. My treat.'

Reluctantly Sally nodded and he wandered over to the counter and as he walked she could not help watch his tight rear end in the expensive looking jeans. He was quickly served and for the rest of the afternoon they made small talk with each other, getting to know one another. Sally told him her partner had left her about six months ago and she was now coming to terms with it. 'I mean, I'm over him now, but, you know, I don't want to bring my children up without a strong male role model in their lives, but I don't know who is going to be interested in me now that I'm damaged goods.'

'Damaged goods?! That's a laugh!'

'What do you mean?'

'Believe me, I know many men, me included, who would love to get to know you better.'

'Well thank you for saying that, but I don't believe you. How about you? Are you seeing anyone?'

'Funny you should say that. My girlfriend of five years left me about eight months ago.' Peter could still lie effortlessly.

'Oh, right. So are you over her?'

'I mean, I was pretty shook up at the time, but now if she walked in here now I wouldn't give her a second glance.'

'Did you like my children?'

'They seemed very nice, very bright. The girl looks like a tiny version of you, very beautiful.'

'That's a very nice thing to say.'

'I wouldn't mind getting to know them better and you of course.' Peter lied again. One night was all he wanted with his head buried in those breasts and buttocks, one night that was all.

For a moment or two Sally contemplated the man across the table from her. He was good looking, easy to talk to, charming and rich. Thinking about her life now and what she used to have, she knew that she did not want or need the riches she had, but some stability in her life, in her children's lives, was what she craved for. A man that went out to work, made an honest living and cared for her and the children was all she wanted. It was then as these thoughts flew through her head that she made her decision. 'Would you like to go to dinner with me?'

The question came as a shock to him. He would have thought he would have had to do a lot more work before dinner dates were offered and accepted, but he was not shocked for long. 'Sure. Why not? What have we got to lose?'

'Exactly. Shall we say tomorrow night, at eight? We can meet at whichever restaurant you choose?'

'Sounds perfect. Will you be able to get a babysitter at such short notice?'

'Yeah, I have a friend, another single mum. I've looked after her kid a few times when she's gone out. She owes me a favour or two.'

'It sounds like we have a plan. Let's meet at Giordano's, the Italian over on King Street in the city. Do you know it?'

'Yes, I do. It looks like a nice place.'

'It is. Hey, it's gone three. Didn't you say you had to be somewhere at three?'

'Yeah, the school gates!'

'Oh right, of course. Come, I'll give you a lift.'

'No, it's okay. Honestly, it's not far.'

'Okay, no problem. Well I see you tomorrow at eight. Let me know if you have any problems.'

'I will do. Thanks for a lovely afternoon.'

'And thank you,' replied Peter, after which he hesitantly leaned forward and gave her a light kiss on her cheek. 'See you tomorrow.'

'Definitely.'

Peter left the shop and Sally spent a couple of moments to gather her thoughts. With a sigh as she contemplated what she was planning to do, she also left the shop and walked to the school where she spoke to her friend who agreed to look after Sophia and Jacob all night and bring them to school the next day.

*

The morning after meeting Peter at the coffee shop Sally grabbed her childre n's savings books and without saying a word to David she walked back into town. Asking for her children's forgiveness, but also stating to herself that her actions would hopefully eventually lead to a better life for them, she withdrew fifty pounds from each of them and then spent the rest of the morning strolling through the shops trying to find a perfect dress for the night, a dress that said sexy yet was quite reserved too. Eventually she found a perfect red dress within her budget that was sexy yet classy too. It was just short of knee length and it showed some cleavage but not too much.

After buying the dress she walked home and sneaked into the bedroom hiding the new dress in the depths of her wardrobe. She spent the rest of the day getting ready. She shaved and plucked all the hair from her legs and armpits, ensuring that they were all smooth and silky to the touch. With the use of a mirror she carefully tidied up her pubic region, a region that had not been touched by another person for many years.

When she would have usually left the apartment to pick up the children she did not, but she was not surprised that David did not notice. By that time in the afternoon he would be drunk beyond thinking so she was able to continue to get ready without him knowing. She washed and lightly curled her long, black hair, leaving it to fall naturally over her shoulders and down her back. Carefully she applied makeup, using more than she had when she went for a coffee, and by the time she had finished Sally could have walked straight onto a photo shoot for any of the leading fashion houses.

Quietly returning to the bedroom she took the red dress out of its bag and slid it onto her body over the black lingerie she was wearing. Finally, she slipped on black sandals and studied herself in the mirror. She decided that with a bit more money she could have made herself look even better, but after contemplating her image she gave a satisfied nod and left the bedroom this time sneaking out of the apartment.

*

Nervously Sally entered the restaurant and glanced over to the bar area hoping to see Peter already sat there, but she was disappointed. In fact, Peter was going to be late as there had been an accident in one of his meth warehouses. Usually he did not go near the places, but tonight he had to.

Over the years Peter had taken more and more responsibility for Reg's business, until Reg was nothing more than a figure head with Peter making all the key decisions. By keeping himself clear of the police he was now slowly legitimizing his businesses with the plan to make all his activities perfectly legal. But this was still some time away, and for now the drugs were still the core of his income.

Recently one of his warehouses had employed a few new men to prepare the meth and unfortunately tonight one of them had used slightly too much of a volatile chemical causing the whole caustic substance to explode. The worker who was closest was killed instantly and the rest of the men were covered in burns. One of them had somehow managed to ingest some of the substance and he had me lted from the inside out, his digestive organs burning causing him to die in agonising pain.

By the time Peter arrived it was total chaos with men lying on the ground, rolling around in agony as their skin was burned from their bones. Making a quick decision Peter told his uninjured workers to help the people who could be saved into the vans and shouted, 'Get them the hell out of here! You two, with me!'

He waited until the men were clear of the building, and then ordered the two men to open up the barrels of acid that they used in the production of the drug. 'Right, get them two and dump them in the barrels!'

'But, but one of them is still alive?'

'He won't be for long. Do it!' Peter pulled out a gun that had been tucked in his waistband and pointed it at the men. 'Now!'

Quickly they walked across and lifted each of the men between them and dumped them into the barrels both of them jumping back as displacement occurred and the acid overflowed from their containers.

'Right, you, dump the remains of that stupid fucking idiot,' Peter indicated the melted remains of the worker who had blown himself up, 'into another barrel and you, pour some from another barrel over where the worst of his blood and guts are. Wash it all away! Do it quick!'

Peter's idea was to leave no trace of what had occurred here so he spent some time pouring petrol over the walls of the warehouse, throwing some up onto the ceiling too. His thoughts were by the time the fire department put the fire out and were able to investigate the cause; the men in the barrels would be unrecognisable therefore eliminating the trouble of getting rid of their bodies.

When they were ready Peter told the two men to leave and he screamed into the empty warehouse in frustration and anger. 'For fuck's sake! Useless mother fucking bastards! Follow the simple fucking instructions!'

With a rage he pulled out his gun again and started firing to the far side of the warehouse, causing sparks to fly. After a few shots one of the sparks ignited some of the petrol and Peter watched as flames whooshed up and took hold, burning the structure of the warehouse. For a few minutes he watched as the building burned, and when he could feel the heat of the flames on his face he turned and left. The two men had taken their car so with another curse Peter got into one of his other cars, a Porsche, and drove quickly home to get changed for his date.

*

Swearing Peter turned his Ferrari into the car park of the restaurant and quickly parked it. As he ran towards the entrance he sniffed himself making doubly sure that he no longer smelled like he had spent the last day swimming in a pool full of petrol. Satisfied he burst through the doors and saw Sally sat on her own at the bar nursing a small glass of wine. He muttered a swear word and walked quickly over to her. 'Sally! I'm so, so sorry! I tried to call but all I got was your answer phone?'

'It's okay. I'm just glad you came. You're only a bit late anyway.'

'Fifteen minutes isn't a bit late, it's rude late.'

'No, honestly, it's fine. Don't worry about it. What was the problem?'

'Oh, a nightmare at work. Some junior made a mistake, a big one. I had to sort it out. Imbecile, but I suppose we all have to start somewhere.'

'Yeah, we do. Would you like a drink?'

'Usually when I drive I don't at all, but I really want a beer now so I'll have a bottle of,' he paused while he looked in the refrigerators behind the bar, 'Corona.' As Sally reached into her handbag to get some money Peter touched her arm lightly and said, 'No, tonight is on me.'

'I can pay my own way.'

'No, I insist and it is not negotiable! Barman, a Corona and some more wine please, make it a bottle actually.'

After their drinks were brought and he had topped up Sally's wine he asked whether she was ready to go through to the table. She replied with a nod and a waiter led Sally to their table. As he walked Peter could not help admire Sally, her toned muscular back that led down to her tight bottom and her long, slender legs. Peter was surprised at the rudeness of the waiter and tutted as the waiter brushed past him. 'Here, allow me.' He quickly walked round to her side of the table and pulled the chair out for her. With a smile at him she sat down and so did he in his seat. 'Terrible service, good food though. Sorry about that.'

'It's okay. Can't remember the last time I was in a restaurant to be honest.'

'I don't understand why a woman like you would have not been in a restaurant for a long time.'

'What do you mean a woman like me?'

'Well just in case you haven't looked in the mirror recently, you're beyond gorgeous.'

He watched as Sally flushed. 'I can't remember the last time I received such a lovely compliment either.'

'Well, you are. So why have you not been on a date for so long?'

'I don't get out much. I have children to look after so I don't get to meet many men, and any men I do meet usually run a mile when they find out I have children.'

'Those men should be locked in an asylum because they are clearly nuts!'

'Thank you, again.'

'No worries, but it is only the truth. Here,' and he passed her a menu, 'I highly recommend the Cannelloni but order whatever you like. And don't you dare go for the cheapest thing on the menu!'

Sally nodded and they both spent some time consulting the menu, Sally picking out a starter and a not too cheap, not too expensive main course. While she was looking, Peter's mobile rang.

'Shit, sorry. I forgot to turn it off.' He looked at the screen. 'Ah, bugger. It's my boss. I need to answer. Sorry.'

'It's fine. Go for it.'

'Thank you.' Peter touched her hand lightly as he walked away from the table and stepped out of the restaurant. Hesitantly he answered the phone.

'And what the hell happened tonight?!'

'I don't exactly know yet Reg. There was an explosion. One of the new guys

got the ingredients mixed up.'
'I didn't think it was that difficult to make?'
'You know it's not. Bar that spillage a few years ago this is the first accident we've ever had which, when you consider the chemicals we're dealing with, is pretty good going in my eyes.'
'I suppose. You destroyed the place?'
'Should be burned to a cinder by now.'
'Good. Come by my house tomorrow. I want more information about it.'
'I will.'
'Where are you now?'
'On a date.'
'On a date?! A few of our men have just been melted and you're on a date? Fuck me Peter, that's what I like about you; you just don't give a shit do you?! See you tomorrow.' As Reg rang off Peter shrugged his shoulders and went back into the restaurant.
'Sorry about that. He wanted more info about what had happened. It's off now. Very rude of me again.'
'That's fine, don't worry about it.'
'You okay. You're not saying much?'
'Just a little nervous. Can't remember the last time I was on a date with someone new.'
'Ah well, have some more wine, relax and I'm sure we can get through the night together. First dates are always a bit awkward. So are you working at the moment?

So Sally made up some story about having to look after children and she did not mention anything about her father, how she had always relied on her partner to work and how she did not have many skills to offer companies. That was how the rest of the night went, both of them making small talk, getting to know each other.

By the time the coffees arrived Sally was feeling quite tipsy. She had drunk a full bottle of wine, alcohol that she was not used to, and Peter could tell this.
'This coffee is abysmal. Tastes like wet cardboard...'
'Whatever wet cardboard tastes like!'
'Indeed! Come back to my place and I'll make you a proper cup.'
'I don't know Peter, I hardly know you...'
'Come on! Live life! It's only a five minute drive from here and afterwards I'll take you home.'

Sally pretended to think about it for a few moments, but she had already decided what her answer would be if a situation like this developed before she had even entered the restaurant. 'Okay then. One coffee is not going to hurt and then I'll go home.'
'Perfect. Garcon! The bill!'
Their waitress walked over with the bill in her hand, threw it on the table and muttered, 'Garcon means boy.'
With a slight look of surprise on his face at the cheek of the waitress, Peter shook his head, pulled a wad of cash out of his pocket, placed the appropriate am

ount on top of the bill along with the smallest of small tips. Quickly he stood and took Sally's hand, leading her out of the restaurant to his Ferrari.

Sally sunk into the luxurious leather seats of his supercar and let out a sigh of contentment as Peter fired up the engine and then left the car park. 'I love the feel of leather seats. Can't remember the last time I sat in such a lovely car.'

'So you've been in a Ferrari before?'

'Yeah, but that was another life, another time.'

'Comfy?'

'Very.'

Peter looked across at her and she had her eyes closed. She looked totally relaxed, breathing deeply.

'I love the smell of the leather too,' Sally mumbled, 'and I think this car is quite new.'

'It is. Hey, my apartment is just down the road but you seem to be enjoying yourself where you are. Want to go for a little drive?'

'Definitely.'

Peter drove them out of the city into the surrounding countryside and for the first time in as long as she could remember Sally felt relaxed. She was being chauffeured in a luxury car with a handsome man next to her and she felt quite contented. While they drove, Sally thought that if she could not get her exact life back she could at least find a man who can look after her and the children too. She had devoted enough of her life to David and now he had gone beyond depressed. Now he was bitter and evil, unable to forgive her for what her father had done to them. It was time to change.

Slowly she partly opened her eyes to see where his hand was and it was resting on the centre console. Casually she lifted her own hand and placed it gently on his. Sally felt the car jerk slightly as this simple gesture caught him off guard, and inwardly she smiled, remembering how easy it was to manipulate men.

All too soon for her the drive in the supercar that reminded her so much of her previous life was over and Peter pulled into his space under the apartment block. It was only when they entered the lobby did she realise where they were. He led them over to the elevator and pressed his card against the scanner and then pressed the button labelled PH which made Sally cringe as she realised she was about to be taken into the apartment that she used to own.

When they entered the apartment it was dark and Peter said, 'You'll like this! Lights! Four!'

For a moment Sally could not believe she was back in her apartment but she had to feign surprise and with obvious excitement she voice controlled the lights, smiling at Peter as she did so. 'Nice place.'

'Yeah, this apartment came on the market a couple of years ago. As soon as I saw it I had to have it. Never did meet the owner. It was all done very quickly and quite mysteriously through an agent.'

'Wow! It is an amazing place!' Sally wandered over to the balcony doors and looked out at the river and over the city.

'Thank you.' He walked over to where she was stood and hovered behind her. 'Would you like that coffee?'

'No, not really.'

A look of surprise flashed across his face and one of even bigger surprise as she took a step towards him, placed her arms around his neck and kissed him, passionately. Sally longed for some affection and the wine had made her bold. It was not just the sex she longed for, although after not making love for a long time her body was raging for sex. She also longed for the feel of a man in her arms, to be kissed and cuddled, to have a firm man between her legs as he made love to her all night.

As these thoughts crashed through her mind she increased the passion of her kiss and instantly she felt his body respond, pressing himself hard against her, rubbing his body against her. Slowly he moved his lips away, finishing the kiss, and then took her hand and led her up the stairs to his bedroom.

Before he had even closed the door Sally had unzipped and lowered her dress, standing in front of him in her sexy black lingerie. Peter flung the door closed and approached her to continue the kiss while leading her to his bed.

Chapter 46

They continued to date for the next couple of months, mostly meeting during the day when her children were at school, but when she could offload them to her friend sometimes they met at night. For Peter his initial intentions were to have a one night stand with Sally, but once he had seen her naked, laid between her legs, placed her body into all the positions he could think of and made love to her over and over again, he wanted more of her luscious body, he wanted more of watching her beautiful face orgasm again and again.

During these months Sally was in a daze of fresh love. From being unloved and having no affection shown to her to having such a wonderful man loving and caring for her after all she been through in the last seven years was amazing for her. He was eager to get to know her children some more, even agreeing with her to meet them after school or during school holidays. Those wonderful days spent in the park or having trips out to the zoo with her wonderful new man meant the world to her, but for Peter it was all an act, an act to ensure that he could continue to enjoy her body. He did not care about her and certainly did not care about another man's children.

All this time Sally managed to keep her new relationship hidden from David and he did not question why all of a sudden she was spending so much time out of the apartment, including sometimes spending nights away. If he had been sober he may have realised the truth sooner, but it was only when he came to bed very late one drunken night and lay down in the bed next to her did he it finally sink in that something was not quite right. The trigger for this thought was the fact that Sally smelled of aftershave, and not a cheap aftershave either, an expensive smelling brand.

Sally had gotten careless and complacent. Usually after spending time with Peter she would shower and shampoo ensuring that no traces of him could be found on her body. Although it was her plan to leave David she wanted to do it on her terms, with her in control of it so she could ensure the safety of Sophia and Jacob.

That night she had been exhausted after a day of frantic sex with Peter and she had collapsed onto the bed after returning home meaning to have a little rest before showering. Unfortunately she fell asleep. Now, as David lay sniffing her sleeping body the thought that she was cheating on him entered his alcohol addled mind. Far too drunk to do anything about it at that moment, he collapsed into a dreamless sleep, but in the morning the thought occurred to him again when he woke and he sniffed her pillow. The scent still lingered and it was unmistakable.

David stormed around the apartment looking for her but she was out, so he stormed into the kitchen and cracked open a can of beer, swigging a big mouthful and then let go a large burp. He looked at his watch and noted it had just gone noon so he settled down in front of the television with the intention of heading out to his children's school later that afternoon.

At three he stood up and threw some scruffy clothes on and stepped out of the apartment for the first time in six months. He was surprised as he walked along that he was out of breath after only a few hundred meters, but he looked down at his beer belly and realised it was no wonder. He had to slow down his pace but he did not have to rush as he had plenty of time before the school finished.

When he reached the road where the school was he approached it carefully, not wanting Sally to see him. At first he could not see her and he was surprised when the children started to come out of the school and he was even more surprised when he saw Sophia and Jacob holding hands, with Jacob holding the hand of another woman who was also holding hands with another child.

For a moment David was going to intervene thinking his children were being abducted, but when they passed where he was standing David turned his back and he heard Jacob speak to the woman and it was quite clear when he asked her what was for dinner that he knew her. Now puzzled David followed the woman and the children as they walked slowly through the streets until they arrived at a small terraced house. The woman opened the door and David watched as his children disappeared into the house.

He waited outside that house for hours, not moving from the darkness of an alley opposite until he heard a powerful sounding car pull up at the end of the street. Quickly he looked around the corner of the alley, up the street where he saw a brand new Porsche had pulled up and in the passenger seat of the car was his partner of so many years, his Sally.

The shock and hurt that flowed through is body when he saw her lean across and kiss this man passionately was astounding in his power. He did not think he had any feelings left in him for Sally, but when he saw her openly kissing another man he thought his heart would break.

With a wave she started to walk down the street towards him and he was about to confront her when he decided he desperately wanted to know who this man was so instead he quickly ran down the alley, away from the house and Sally, picking up a small wire as he ran.

Frantically he searched the street at the other end of the alley for an old car and when he found one it only took him a moment to pick the lock of the car and using his mechanical skills he quickly hotwired the car and sped away in search of the man in the Porsche. Guessing correctly, David headed out of the suburb towards the city centre. It did not take him long to find the Porsche driving sedately along one of the main routes into the city. David maintained a gap of a few hundred yards and followed the car as it turned off the main road and entered a side street that led to a large industrial park. As he entered the park, David maintained the distance and he also turned off his headlights and followed the Porsche until it stopped outside a warehouse that had no indications on the outside of what went on inside.

For a few hours David watched the outside of the warehouse and it was late in the evening when at last a door to the building opened and he watched the man and other men leave it. One of the men locked the door and while David watched the men mingled for a few minutes talking amongst themselves before they all got into their cars and went their separate ways.

At first it was David's intention to follow the man who had clearly been sleeping with Sally, find out where he lived and beat the living daylights out of him. But on second thoughts David decided that the warehouse probably belonged to him and he could do more damage by having a little fun in the building.

He waited half an hour before he approached the warehouse to ensure no-one returned and then David left the car taking the wire from his pocket. Again, with his knowledge of locks that he learned while he was a mechanic, it did not take him long to pick the lock and open the door. Carefully he closed it behind him, locking it behind him, and then he flicked on a light switch. He was expecting one light to come on after he flicked this switch but the whole place lit up like a floodlit football pitch which made David jump. Without hesitating he flicked the switch off deciding that there was enough ambient light coming through the windows high up in the walls for him to see what he was doing.

Slowly he walked around the large room, looking at the piles of chemicals laid all around the walls, curiously looking at the barrels of substances stacked in the room. On benches towards the middle of the room looked like some kind of production line. Here the chemicals had been placed into smaller containers and there were bottles of distilled water. Next to these were labelled glass beakers and David peered at them and read the labels. On one was written acetone, on another acid and he noticed that the labels were different colours that matched the colour of the containers. In a pot that he peered into was a powdery substance, red in colour and for the life of him David could not think what these ingredients could be used for.

Whatever it was used for it was clearly making the man with Sally very wealthy given his brand new Porsche and he was not dressed too shabbily either. As his thoughts returned to the man his stomach flopped over. She had been cheating on him and David in his drunken depressed state had not realised or noticed anything. Then his thoughts turned upon himself.

When was the last time he had shown any love towards her? One, two, three years ago? And this fact stung him because he knew the fact existed that she had stood by him for so long and he had treated her and the children like something he had found on the sole of his shoe.

With anguish etched on his face, through the tears that had welled up in his eyes he stumbled and slumped down a wall of the warehouse, crying, mumbling and muttering to himself. When was the last time he had made love to her? When was the last time he had held her in his arms and told her he loved her? Why would she want to be held in his fat, drunken arms? All these thoughts crashed through his head. The last one being is it any wonder that she has looked elsewhere for the love that he should have been giving her?

And then something happened to David that had taken too long to happen, and all the pent up frustration, grief and sadness that he had lived with for all these years collapsed his mind and he had a full mental breakdown. He had managed to avoid this happening to him by hiding away, drowning his sorrows with alcohol, but seeing the long, lingering, passionate kiss that Sally had given to that man was the final trigger.

For hours he lay slumped against the wall, his knees tucked under his chin, mumbling and muttering, tears, endless tears cascading down his face dripping on his curled up body. Slowly he rocked, rocking back and to with all these thoughts, all the misery that he had blocked out for so long overwhelming him.

To say he was not in his right mind when he stood up hours later and started to pour the acetone over the building would be a monumental understatement. He splashed and threw it everywhere he could, laughing occasionally as he watched it drip of the ceiling onto the barrels of chemicals. As he walked past the benches, almost unknowingly he grasped one of the containers of acid in his hand and then as he looked around the building he found a lighter on a ledge near the door. Shaking more acetone out onto the floor right up to the door, with another giggle that sounded like the laugh of an insane man, he stuffed an old rag he found into the top of the container and then lit it.

After making sure the flames had taken hold he threw the container deep into the depths of the warehouse, watching as it arced prettily over the benches, breaking as it hit the ground causing the acetone to catch light as it seeped out of the broken container. Sparks of the lit chemical sprayed out of the smashed vessel causing the acetone that David had thrown down to catch and the fire quickly took hold. Just as Peter had done, David watched the flames for a few moments as they quickly spread through the building, only fleeing to the safety of the stolen car when he felt the heat of the flames on his face. As he sat down in the driver's seat he carefully laid the container of acid on the seat next to him and he patted it gently thinking about what fun he was going to have with it.

*

The next morning Peter surveyed the melted, molten mess of his warehouse from a safe distance not approaching too close because there were still police and fire officers present. The warehouse was registered to some phantom company that would never be able to be traced back to him so he was safe from any further investigation. What he was not safe from was the loss of income this fire was going to cause him and he swore his vengeance on whoever had done this.

Chapter 47

Sally did not show any concern that David had not returned home the previous night. She was quite relieved actually because for once she could get the children ready without having to keep them quiet and tip-toe around David. Sophia and Jacob felt there was something different about their mummy too. She seemed happier, especially this morning when their daddy was not there. This rubbed off on them and they ran around the apartment, for once being children as their mummy chased after them, laughing at their antics as she tried to get them ready for school. Eventually they were all ready and she left the apartment with her beautiful children holding a hand each, and as she walked along listening to the birds sing and her children natter away to each other, she breathed in the fresh air and sighed a sigh of contentment.

She was due to see Peter tonight and after making love to him, when they were curled up in his apartment, she was going to tentatively broach the subject of her moving in. She knew what his reaction would be at first, one of complete and utter fear, but she would give him time to get used to the idea and she was sure because she now knew him so well that he would say yes in due course.

As she walked to the school she had no idea that David had returned home and was now searching through the wardrobe for the shoebox that contained his passport and a large bundle of cash he had kept stashed there for a long time without Sally knowing about. Stuffing both into his pocket he exited the apartment and ran through the streets quickly finding Sally and he followed her just to make sure she was not doing anything else that day and was indeed taking the children to school. Satisfied as he watched his children run into the school, for the rest of the day he followed her around. A dry smile crossed his face as he watched her buy some sexy lingerie and another one crossed his face as he watched her spend some more of their precious money taken from their joint bank account on a new skirt and top.

When she was done with shopping and blowing more of their money on an expensive coffee and sandwich, he followed her as she walked back to their apartment, but instead of following her in he waited down the street knowing she would pass this way when she went to collect the children. He did not have to wait long and as he watched her walk past the end of the alley were he stood hidden in the shadows, he noted that there was a glow about her, a spring in her step as she walked along in her new skirt and top, the strap of which had slipped a little revealing the strap to the bra of the lingerie he had watched her buy.

Watching her from a discreet distance while she walked along, his thoughts took an ironic twist as he could not help wonder at how she had ruined their lives by cheating on him. Never once that day did the thought enter his head that he had not contributed at all to the success of their relationship with his appalling attitude towards her and the children. This thought never entered his head because his mind was solely set on exacting his revenge for her cheating on him.

*

From where he was stood in the shadows he heard the school bell ring for the final time that day and following that the squeals and shouts of the children as they ran out of numerous doors from the school. He could still see Sally as she held her hand up against the glow of the sunlight looking for Sophia and Jacob and with a wave he saw her beckon them over to her.

When he saw his children approaching their mother he stepped out of the shadows at a quick walk, one of his hands he slipped into one of the pockets of his jacket seemingly fiddling with something in there. As he continued to walk he pulled a container out of his pocket and cursed as some of the liquid spilled out onto his hand burning it. Discreetly he poured some of the liquid on the floor, hearing it sizzle as it burned through a piece of paper that was lying there. Quickly he approached her and when he was nearly at her side she heard footsteps quickly approaching so she turned.

'David? What are you doing…'

But she never finished the sentence. With a movement of his arm David flung the acid into Sally's face, watching with glee as the liquid instantly started to burn the skin off her face.

With a scream that would haunt her children forever, Sally clutched at her face as she slumped to the ground, screaming and screaming as she felt the acid eating away her facial flesh, then screaming even louder as she tried to wipe the acid off her face and in doing so it burned her hands, ripping her skin away.

The other parents heard her screams and they ran over, covering their children's eyes as they saw the woman rolling on the floor in burning agony. One of them acted quicker than the rest and pulled Sally's children away from the sight of their screaming mother and another reached for her mobile phone and called for an ambulance. By the time the emergency call was connected Sally had stopped screaming. She had passed out from the pain, her face badly burned.

*

As he ran away from the school down the alleys to where he had left the stolen car, David approached a figure slumped on the floor of the alley, sitting in the dirt. Totally out of breath now he had to stop running so he approached the person with care, walking quickly on the other side of the alley.

He noticed the needle hanging out of her arm, and when he passed the woman she slowly lifted her head and for a moment their eyes met. A flash of disgust passed across David's face and then their eye contact was broken as he exited the alley and found the car where he had left it, quickly driving to the airport, using the cash to buy a one way ticket on the first available long haul flight, his thoughts never once returning to the figure he had encountered in the alley.

By the time the police at the school had taken the witnesses' accounts of what had happened, David was sat at the back of a plane staring out of the window at the passing clouds, relaxed and contentedly sipping on a beer.

*

The woman in the alley near Sophia and Jacob's school tried to stand but she was too weak. With one almighty effort she tried again only to collapse in a heap into the filth of the alley, the needle still hanging out of her arm.

Unable to move, her head slumped onto her chest and her weakened heart finally broke after all the years of misery and anguish it had witnessed. She suffered a massive heart attack, her whole body going rigid for a few moments before relaxing.

After so many years of heartbreak and desolation, Sarah was finally at peace.

An Acknowledgement

The ending of this book was decided a long time before the author had ever heard of Katie Piper, however, an acknowledgement should be made to the real life horrific burns injuries she, and others, have suffered.

If you wish to make it easier for people to live with burns and scars please donate to The Katie Piper Foundation at www.katiepiperfoundation.org.uk.

As noted at the beginning of this book, all characters in this publication are fictitious and any resemblance to real persons, living or dead, is purely coincidental.

Made in the USA
Charleston, SC
18 January 2012